Little Voices Praise Him

Little Voices Praise Him

REVIEW AND HERALD® PUBLISHING ASSOCIATION
Since 1861 | www.reviewandherald.com

Published by the Review and Herald® Publishing Association in cooperation with the General Conference of Seventh-day Adventists Sabbath School/Personal Ministries Department

General Conference of Seventh-day Adventists

Coordinator, GraceLink Sabbath School Curriculum	Patricia Habada
Director, World Sabbath School	James Zachrison
Adviser, GraceLink Curriculum (Vice President, GC)	Lowell Cooper

Writers, GraceLink Curriculum for Beginner and Kindergarten Lessons

Audrey Boyle Andersson	Vikki Montgomery
Jackie Bishop	Edwina Grice Neely
DeeAnn Bragaw	Becky O'Ffill
May-Ellen Colón	Evelyn Omaña
Helga Eiteneier	Denise Pereyra
René Alexenko Evans	Dawn Reynolds
Martha J. Feldbush	Janet Rieger
Adriana Itin Femopase	Robert J. Robinson
Dorothy Fernandez	Judi Rogers
Renee Garrigues-Goodwin	Denise Ropka-Kasischke
Feryl Harris	Eileen Dahl Vermeer
Donna Meador	

Songbook Manuscript Compiler	Eileen Dahl Vermeer

Review and Herald® Publishing Association

Editor	Patricia Lance Fritz
Art Director	Reger Smith, Jr.
Designer	Madelyn Ruiz
Music Editor	Kenneth D. Logan
Permissions Editor	Raymond H. Woolsey
Copy Editors	Jocelyn Fay
	James Cavil
Photographer	Joel Springer
Electronic Makeup	Shirley M. Bolivar
Sales/Children's Ministries	Judi Rogers

We thank the various copyright owners for granting us permission to include their songs in *Little Voices Praise Him.* Every effort has been made to locate owners and to provide proper credits for each song under copyright. If, however, such copyright notices are missing or incorrect, please contact the publisher, and corrections will appear in future printings.

PRINTED IN U.S.A.

16 15 14 13 12 6 5 4 3 2

R&H Cataloging Service
Little voices praise Him.

1. Sabbath School—Music. I. Seventh-day Adventists. General Conference Sabbath School Department.

782.6

ISBN 978-0-8280-1522-6

Introduction

Little Voices Praise Him contains more than 300 songs for beginner and kindergarten children. This compilation features familiar Sabbath School favorites and brand-new songs that complement the new GraceLink Sabbath School Curriculum beginner and kindergarten lessons.

How to Use This Book

Each song appears in one of the five sections: **Prayer and Praise, Grace, Worship, Community,** and **Service.** The GraceLink curriculum themes of Grace, Worship, Community, and Service reflect the richness of the Christian experience:

Grace—Jesus loves me.
Worship—I love Jesus.
Community—We love one another.
Service—Jesus loves you too.

Songs relating to welcome, offerings, missions, prayer responses, birthdays, closing, promotions, and other transitional segments appear in the Prayer and Praise section.

You can quickly and easily find songs by using the **Index of Titles and First Lines** (p. 259).

Many songs are expressions of more than one theme or aspect of a growing Christian experience. The **Topical Index** (p. 268) cross-references the songs and provides a variety of suggestions for use (family, Jesus, nature, God's love and care, Bible verses, Bible stories, plus more than 50 additional cross-reference possibilities).

Kindergarten children will enjoy singing all of the songs in *Little Voices Praise Him*. The icon B♫ beside the title of some songs identifies simple songs that are especially suitable for younger singers.

We hope that *Little Voices Praise Him* will help you share the grace of God with the children you teach.

—General Conference Sabbath School Department
—Review and Herald® Publishing Association

CONTENTS

Prayer and Praise

- Welcome 1
- Prayer 9
- Prayer Response 18
- Visitor 24
- Memory Verse 27
- Offering 29
- Missions/Offering 35
- Birthday 36
- Transitions 41
- Promotion 43
- Closing 44

Grace

- Angels 47
- Bible 51
- Bible Stories 54
- Creation 66
- Forgiveness 75
- God's Gifts 78
- God's Love and Care 85
- God's Protection 119
- Heaven 127
- Jesus 136
- Jesus' Birth 140
- Jesus' Death and Resurrection 154
- Nature 157
- Praise 176
- Salvation 178
- Second Coming 182

Worship

- Church 185
- Commitment to Jesus 191
- Happiness 198
- Healthy Living 203
- Loving God 205
- Praise 211
- Prayer 228
- Sabbath 234
- Thankfulness 239

Community

- Comfort 246
- Family 247
- Friendship 254
- God's Family 257
- Cooperation 259
- Kindness 260
- Loving Others 262
- Obedience 266
- Sharing 275

Service

- Bible Story—Noah 281
- Care for Animals 282
- Giving 285
- God's Love and Care 286
- Helpfulness 287
- Living for Jesus 302
- Missions 308
- Witnessing 310

Indexes *Pages*

- Index of Titles and First Lines 259
- Topical Index 268

Good Morning 1

JANET SAGE — JANET SAGE

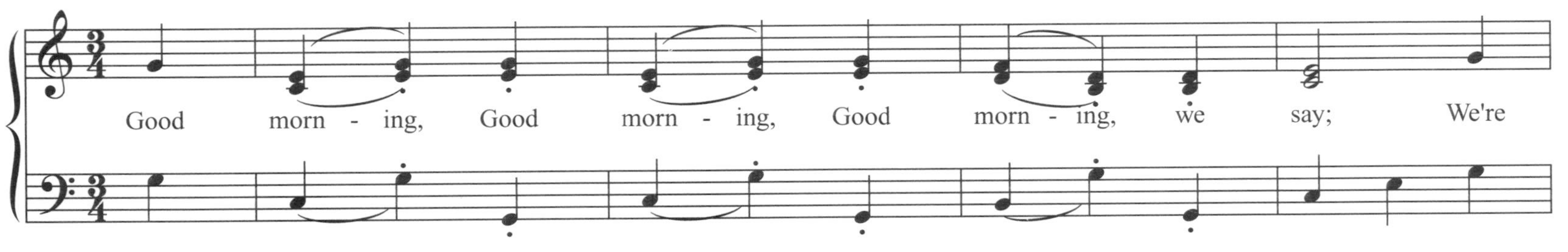
Good morn - ing, Good morn - ing, Good morn - ing, we say; We're

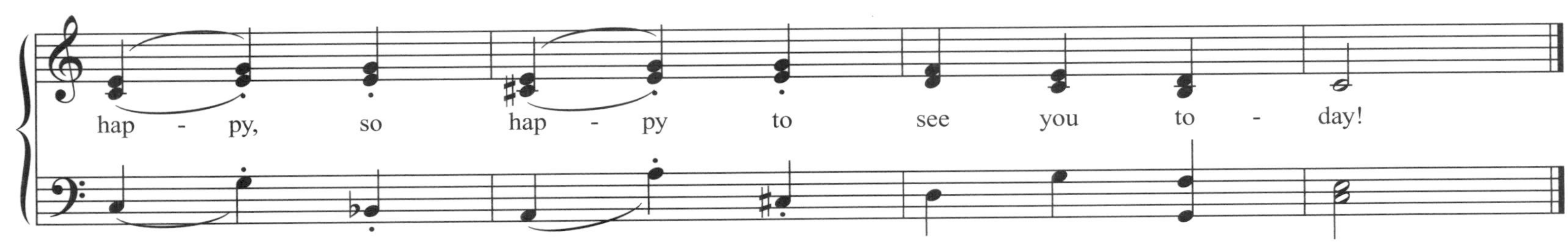
hap - py, so hap - py to see you to - day!

Tick-tock Song 2

CLARA LEE PARKER — CLARA LEE PARKER

This is what the clock says, Tick-tock, tick-tock, This is what the clock says, Tick-tock, tick-tock,

This is what the clock says, Tick-tock, tick-tock, Come to Sab-bath school at half past nine o'-clock.

3 Good Morning to You

Mildred Adair — Mildred Adair

1. Good morning to you, Good morning to you, How are you today? Good morning to you, Good morning to you, This happy Sabbath day.
2. We're glad to see you, We're glad to see you, On this Sabbath day. We're glad to see you, We're glad to see you, This happy Sabbath day.

4 Greeting Song

Mary E. Key McKinley — Mary E. Key McKinley

1. Who's come to Sab-bath school? Ma-ry, Ma-ry!* Who's come to Sab-bath school? Ma - ry.
2. We're glad you came to - day, Ma-ry, Ma-ry; We're glad you came to - day, Ma - ry.

*Insert child's name.

I'm Glad I Came to Sabbath School 5

EDITH SMITH CASEBEER — EDITH SMITH CASEBEER

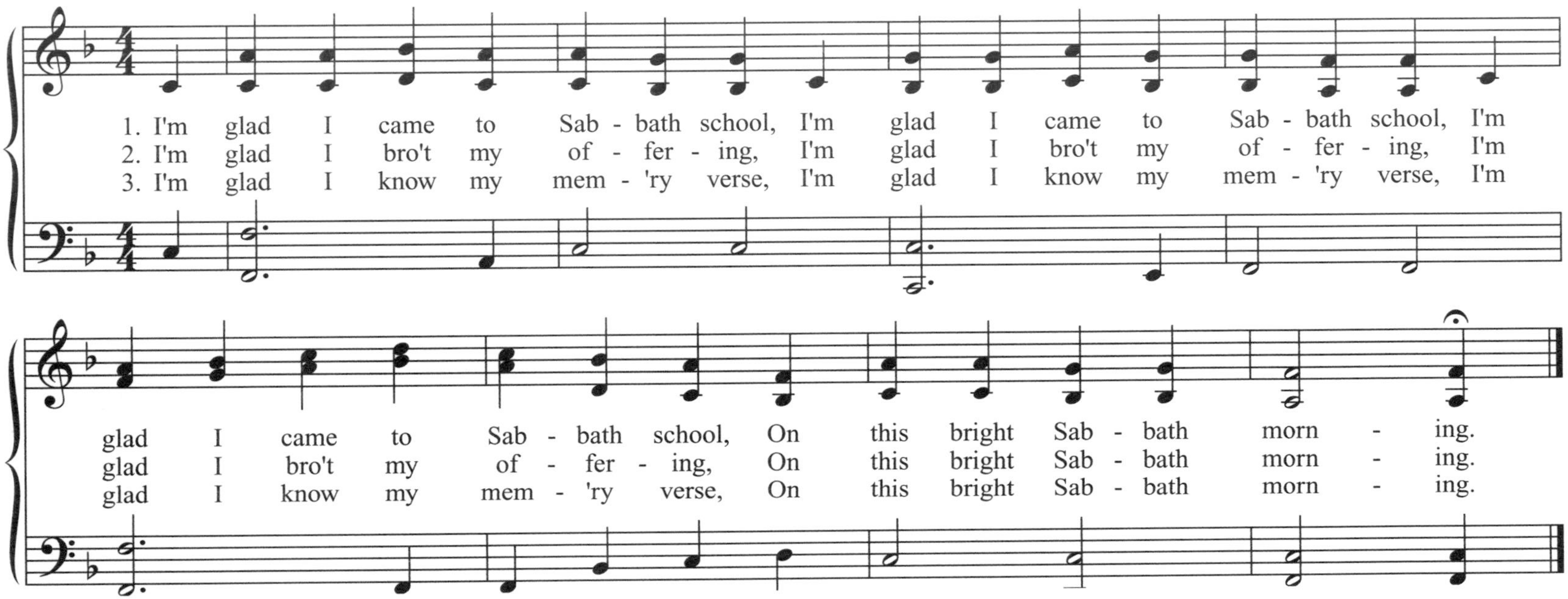

1. I'm glad I came to Sab - bath school, I'm glad I came to Sab - bath school, I'm glad I came to Sab - bath school, On this bright Sab - bath morn - ing.
2. I'm glad I bro't my of - fer - ing, I'm glad I bro't my of - fer - ing, I'm glad I bro't my of - fer - ing, On this bright Sab - bath morn - ing.
3. I'm glad I know my mem - 'ry verse, I'm glad I know my mem - 'ry verse, I'm glad I know my mem - 'ry verse, On this bright Sab - bath morn - ing.

Shake a Little Hand 6

NOELENE JOHNSSON — TRADITIONAL / ARR. BY KENNETH D. LOGAN

Shake a lit - tle hand and say, "Good morn - ing." Shake a lit - tle hand and say, "Good morn - ing." Shake a lit - tle hand and say, "Good morn - ing, We're glad you came to Sab - bath school."

7 We Welcome You

MILDRED ADAIR

MILDRED ADAIR

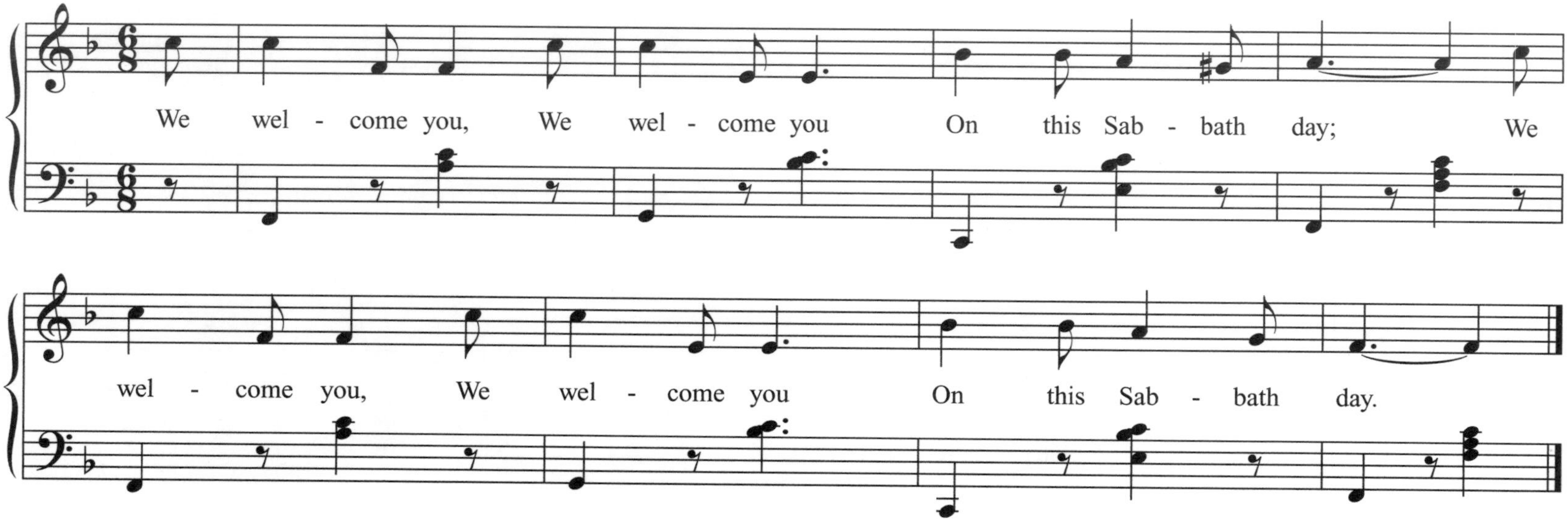

We wel - come you, We wel - come you On this Sab - bath day; We wel - come you, We wel - come you On this Sab - bath day.

8 Get Ready to Pray

NANCY J. STAGL-SCHIPPMANN

NANCY J. STAGL-SCHIPPMANN

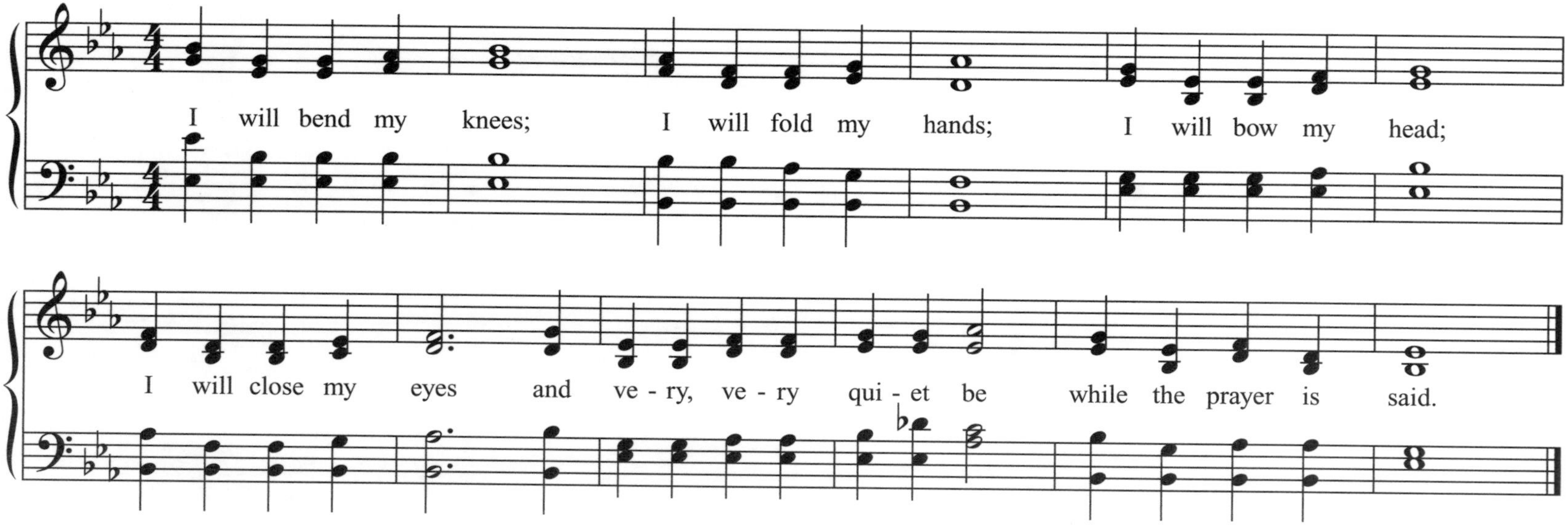

I will bend my knees; I will fold my hands; I will bow my head; I will close my eyes and ve - ry, ve - ry qui - et be while the prayer is said.

Motions: Follow instructions in text.

Dear Jesus

9

JANINE MAX — JANINE MAX

Moderato
Close my eyes,
kneel to pray.
Fold my hands,
now I say,
"Dear Je - sus, Dear Je - sus, I'm
here to talk to You."

10 I Talk to Jesus

DOROTHY ROBISON

DOROTHY ROBISON/ARR. BY HAZEL NIELSON SERNS

1. I talk to Grand - ma on the phone, On the phone, on the phone, I talk to Grand - ma on the phone, And she hears me, I know.
2. I talk to Je - sus when I pray, When I pray, when I pray, I talk to Je - sus when I pray, And He hears me, I know.

11 Let's Have a Talk With Jesus

KATHLEEN MAGUIRE

KATHLEEN MAGUIRE

Let's have a talk with Je - sus, Let's close our eyes and say, "Dear Je - sus, please be with us In Sab - bath school to - day."

I Will Pray Unto the Lord

12

1 SAMUEL 7:5

JANET SAGE

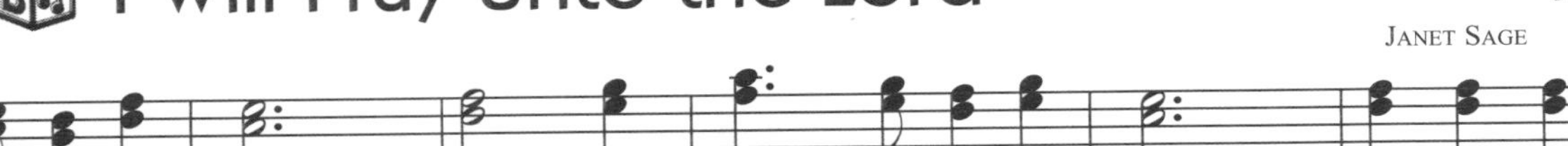

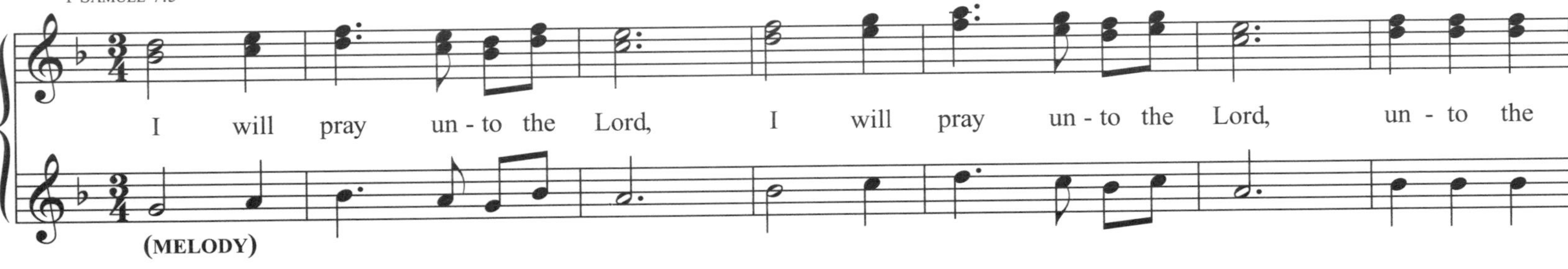
I will pray un - to the Lord, I will pray un - to the Lord, un - to the
(MELODY)

Lord, un - to the Lord, I will pray un - to the Lord.

Musical note: Play the opening melody note clearly before singing to be sure the singers know where to pitch their voices. This song's minor key creates a mood of serenity. The simple harmonies produced by the right-hand notes depict a certain ethereal quality. Be sure to emphasize the melody throughout.

Jesus, Listen Now to Me

13

VIRGINIA CASON

VIRGINIA CASON / ARR. BY J. SPEAR

Je - sus, lis - ten now to me, While I kneel and talk to Thee. A - men.

14 Now We'll Talk to God

Dot Cachiaras

Dot Cachiaras

We'll fold our hands, We'll bow our heads, And now we'll
talk to God; And now we'll talk to God.

Motions: Follow instructions in text.

O God, Listen to My Prayer 15

PSALM 61:1, RSV

JANET SAGE

O God, list - en to my prayer, O God, list - en to my prayer, O
God, lis - ten to my prayer, to my prayer, lis - ten to my prayer.

Musical note: This hymnlike song needs to be sung and played with intensity and solemnity.

16 Talk to God

Martha J. Feldbush

Martha J. Feldbush/Arr. by Kenneth D. Logan

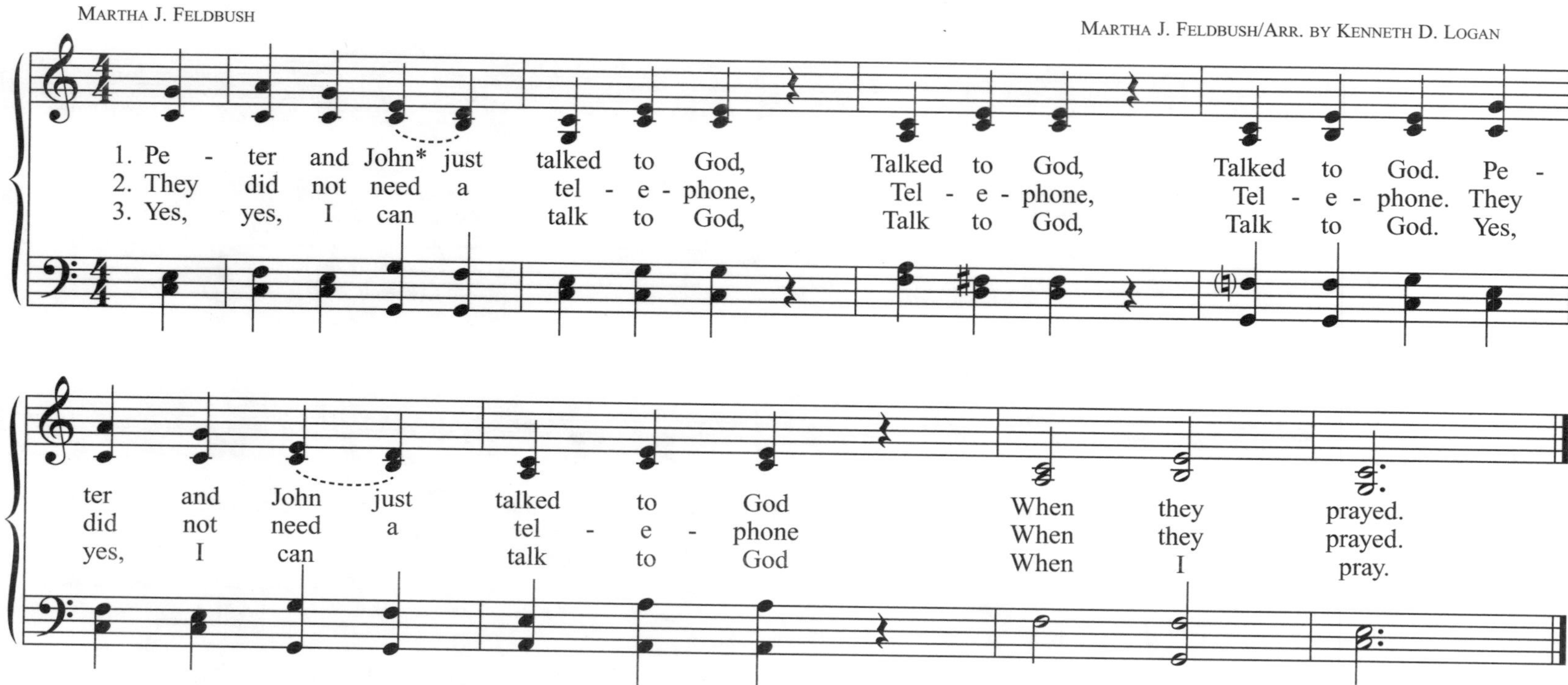
1. Pe - ter and John* just talked to God, Talked to God, Talked to God. Pe - ter and John just talked to God When they prayed.
2. They did not need a tel - e - phone, Tel - e - phone, Tel - e - phone. They did not need a tel - e - phone When they prayed.
3. Yes, yes, I can talk to God, Talk to God, Talk to God. Yes, yes, I can talk to God When I pray.

*Add other Bible characters' names.

17 When It's Time to Pray

JANET SAGE JANET SAGE

1. When it's time to pray I bend my knees, bend my knees, bend my knees;
2. When it's time to pray I fold my hands, fold my hands, fold my hands;
3. When it's time to pray I close my eyes, close my eyes, close my eyes;
When it's time to pray I bend my knees, and then I talk to Je - sus.
When it's time to pray I fold my hands, and then I talk to Je - sus.
When it's time to pray I close my eyes, and then I talk to Je - sus.

Pianist: While the song is to be slow and reverent, it is important not to let it drag. The song gives time enough for the little ones to be helped into their positions.

Leader: If you find your Beginners tiring of their positions before the last stanza is finished, consider having a doll or jointed figure go through the motions as the song is sung, then have the children copy what was done without repeating the whole song again. Little ones respond beautifully to this piece and learn quickly what to do.

18
Prayer Song
NORMA JUNE BELL
NORMA JUNE BELL
Listen, little children, quiet as can be.
Can you kneel, fold your hands, Close your eyes, and pray with me?
© 1976 Sabbath School Productions. Used by permission of AdventSource.
19
Prayer Song
KATHRYN B. MYERS
KATHRYN B. MYERS
Dear Jesus, we thank Thee for Thy loving care. We
thank Thee for list-'ning to our prayer. A - men.
(20)
Copyright © 1980 by Review and Herald® Publishing Association.

20 Thank You for Hearing Our Prayer

JANET SAGE
JANET SAGE

Thank You, God, Thank You, God, Thank You for hear - ing our prayer. A - - - - men.

21 Tiny Tot Response

JOY HICKLIN STEWART — JOY HICKLIN STEWART

Thank You, Je - sus, for ev - 'ry - thing. A - - - men.

22 Thank You, Dear Jesus

JANET SAGE — JANET SAGE

Thank You, dear Je - - - - - sus. A - - - - - men.

Pianist: Make an almost imperceptible pause after "Jesus" to help set off the "Amen" as a separate thought. To help the children know when to begin singing after the prayer, and to establish the right pitch, be sure to play the preparatory chord shown.

23 Response

MARY E. SCHWAB — MARY E. SCHWAB

Thank You, Je - sus, for lov - ing me. A - men.

We Have a Visitor 24

JANET SAGE · JANET SAGE

We have a vis - i - tor here to - day; Hel - lo! Hel - lo! Hel - lo!
We have a vis - i - tor here to - day; Hel - lo! Hel - lo! Hel - lo!

Leader: You might like to try having the children stand for this song and bow slightly at the waist with each "Hello" for the visitors. Let them sing the song at least once, however, without any activity so they will learn it better.

25 We're Glad You Came to Our Sabbath School

Mary E. Schwab | Mary E. Schwab

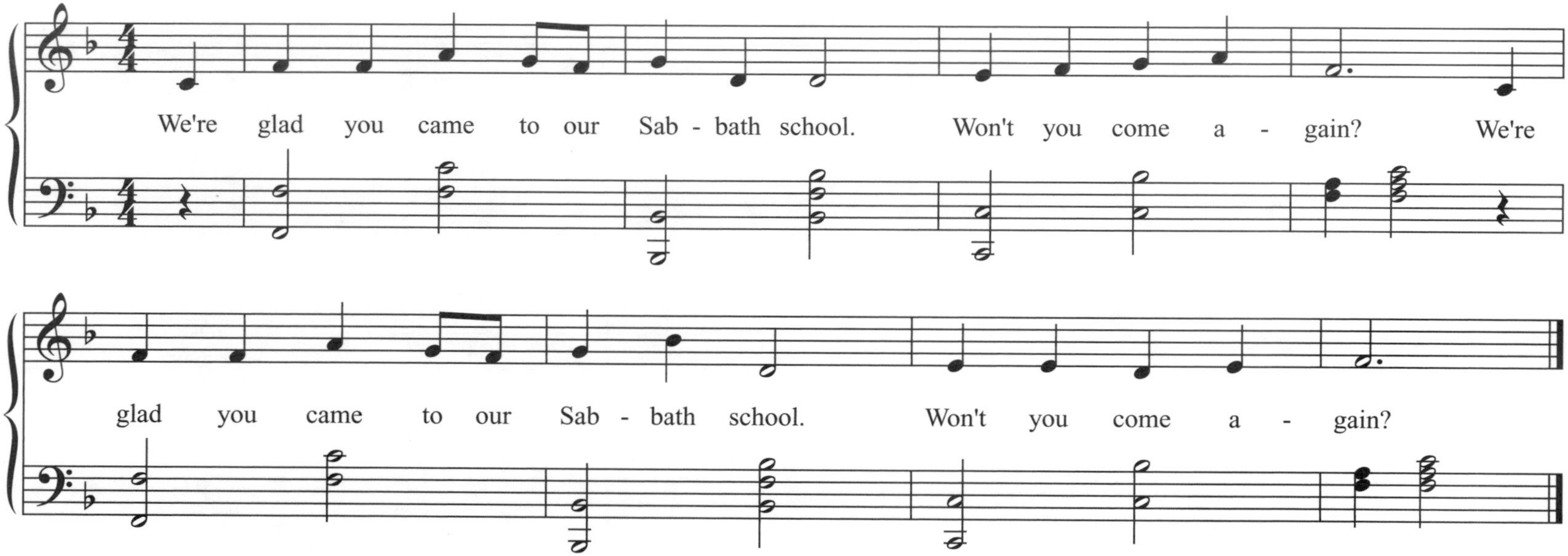

We're glad you came to our Sab - bath school. Won't you come a - gain? We're
glad you came to our Sab - bath school. Won't you come a - gain?

26 I Open My Bible and Read

Pheroba Thomas | Pheroba Thomas

I o - pen my Bi - ble and read: "God loves me."*

*Substitute: "Jesus healed the sick," "Be ye kind," "God made me," etc.

Option: For stronger reinforcement of ideas, sing each verse twice.

I Open My Bible Book and Read 27

JOHNIE B. WOOD JOHNIE B. WOOD

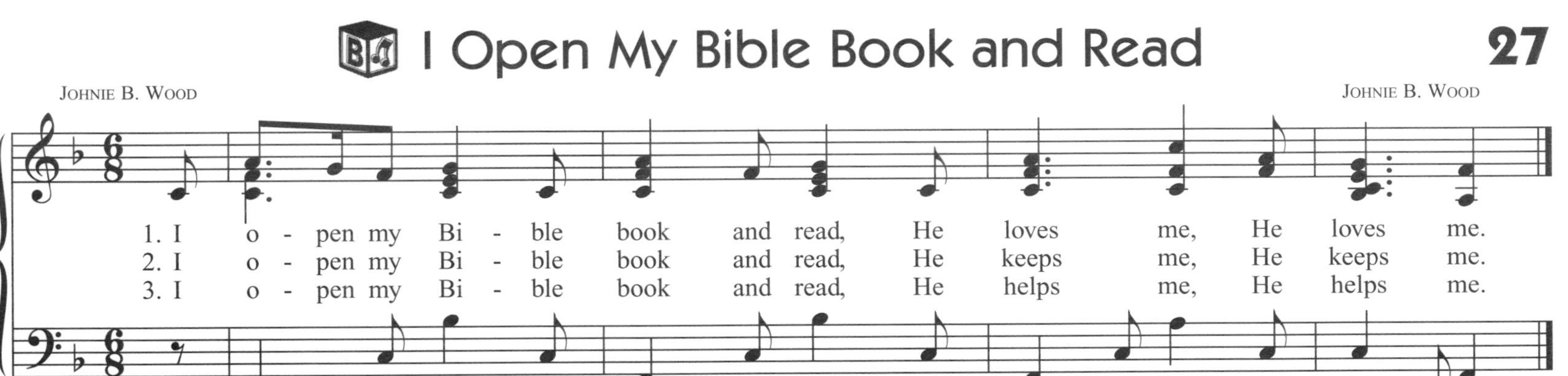
1. I o - pen my Bi - ble book and read, He loves me, He loves me.
2. I o - pen my Bi - ble book and read, He keeps me, He keeps me.
3. I o - pen my Bi - ble book and read, He helps me, He helps me.

I Open My Bible Carefully 28

JANET SAGE JANET SAGE

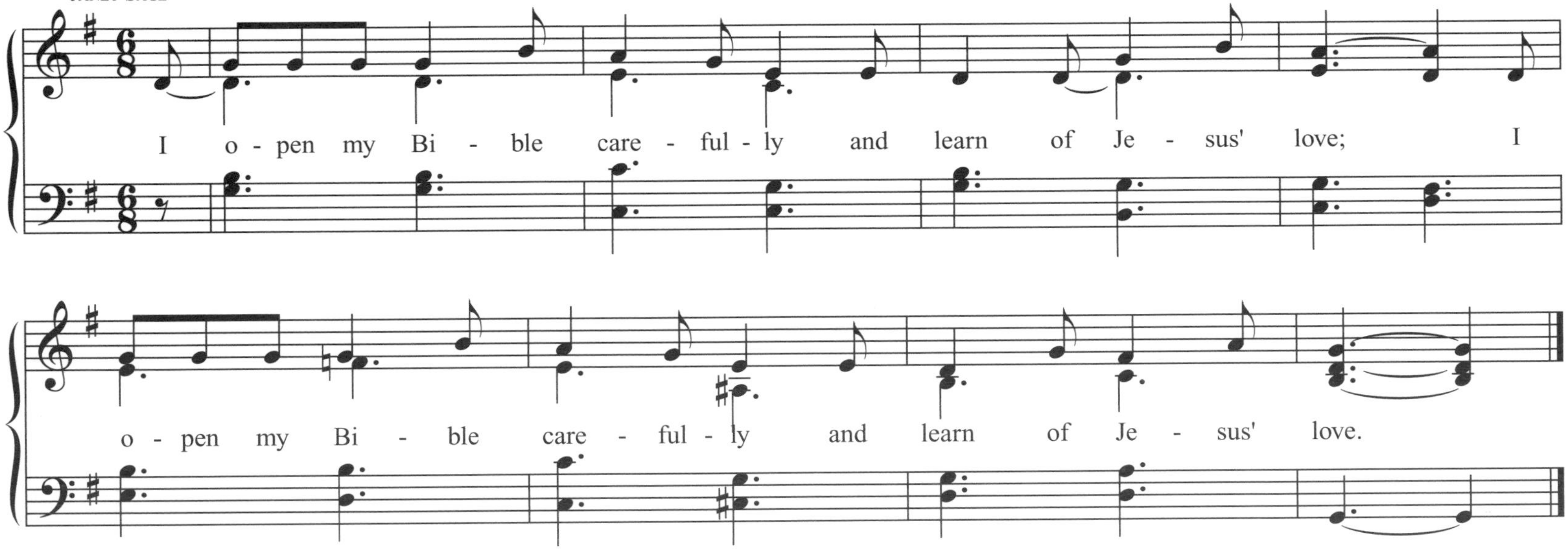

I o - pen my Bi - ble care - ful - ly and learn of Je - sus' love; I

o - pen my Bi - ble care - ful - ly and learn of Je - sus' love.

29 God Loves a Cheerful Giver

Based on 2 Corinthians 9:7, RSV

Janet Sage

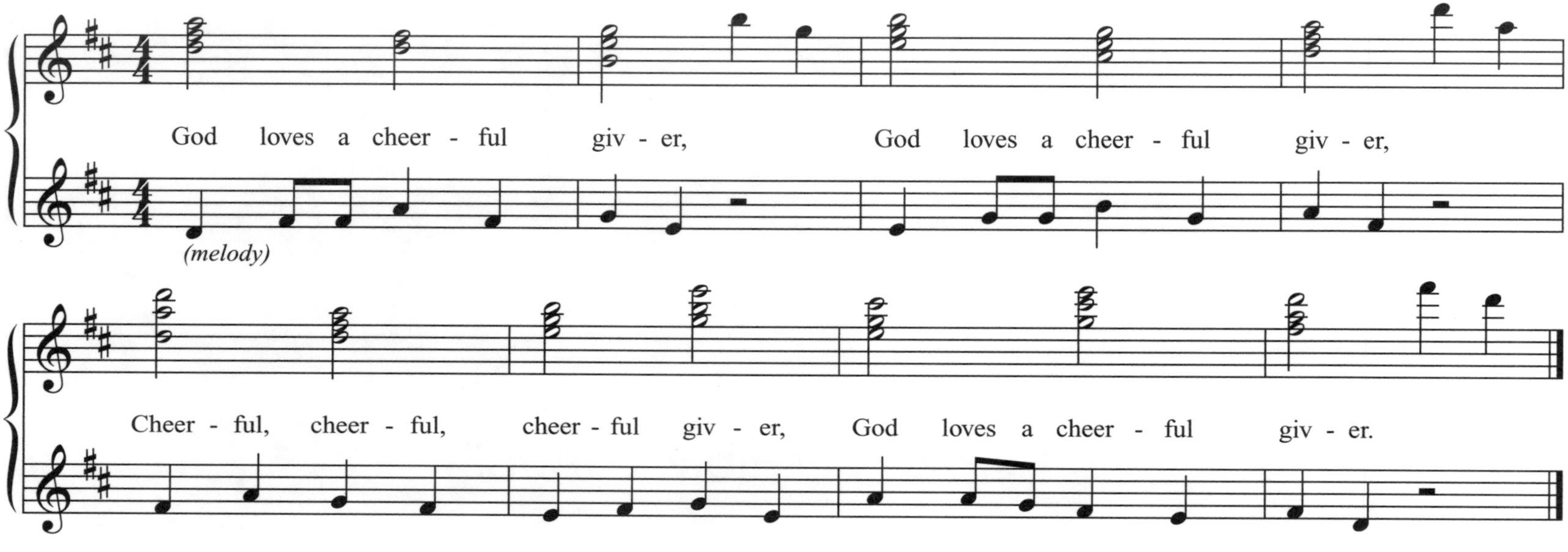

God loves a cheer - ful giv - er, God loves a cheer - ful giv - er,

(melody)

Cheer - ful, cheer - ful, cheer - ful giv - er, God loves a cheer - ful giv - er.

Musical note: Give the starting melody note before beginning the song so the singers will know their pitch. Perform the piece in the light, happy spirit of its message.

30 Offering Response

Nancy J. Stagl-Schippmann

Nancy J. Stagl-Schippmann

Thank You, Je - sus, now we sing, For this off - 'ring that we bring. A - men.

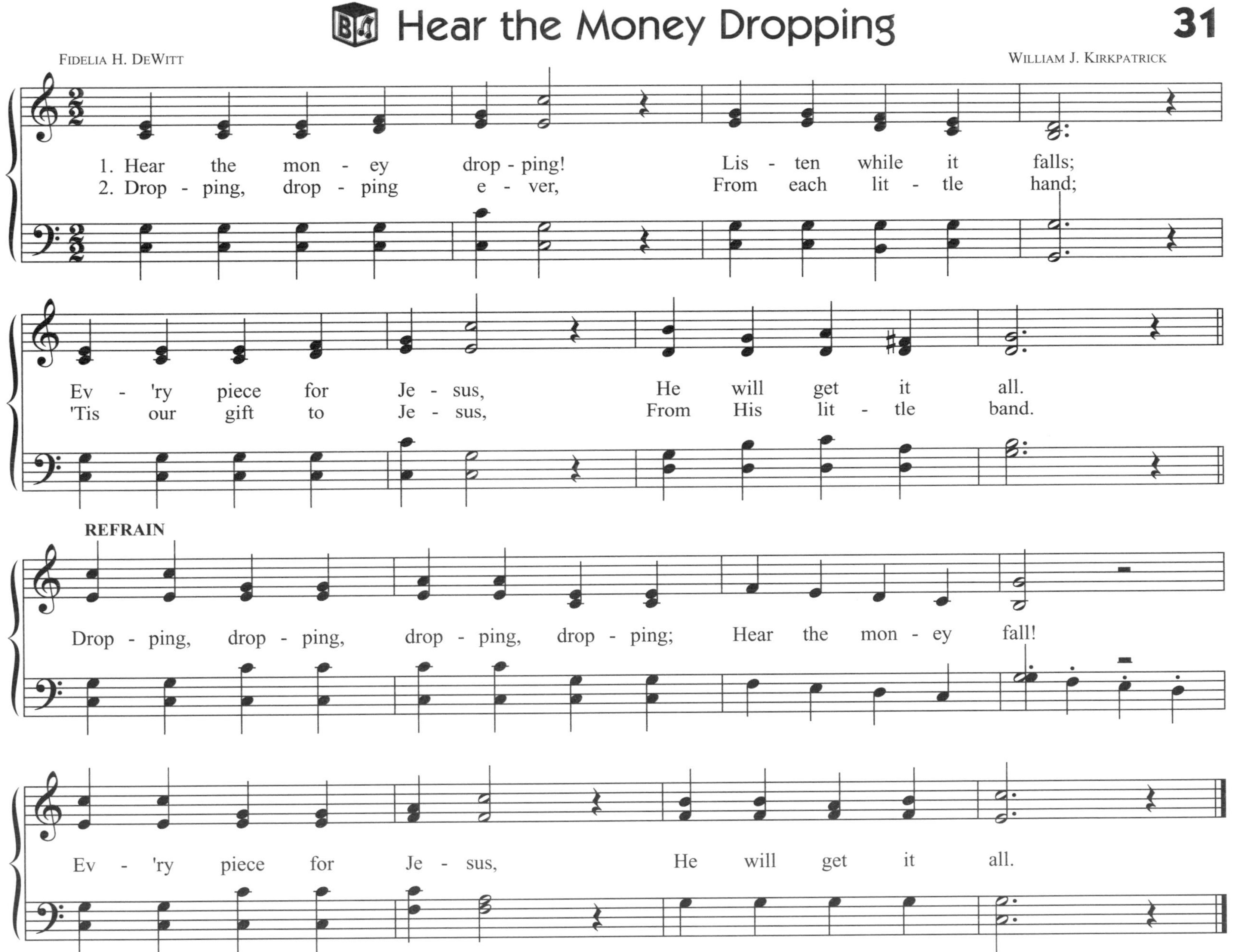
Hear the Money Dropping
31
Fidelia H. DeWitt
William J. Kirkpatrick
1. Hear the mon - ey drop - ping! Lis - ten while it falls;
2. Drop - ping, drop - ping e - ver, From each lit - tle hand;
Ev - 'ry piece for Je - sus, He will get it all.
'Tis our gift to Je - sus, From His lit - tle band.
REFRAIN
Drop - ping, drop - ping, drop - ping, drop - ping; Hear the mon - ey fall!
Ev - 'ry piece for Je - sus, He will get it all.

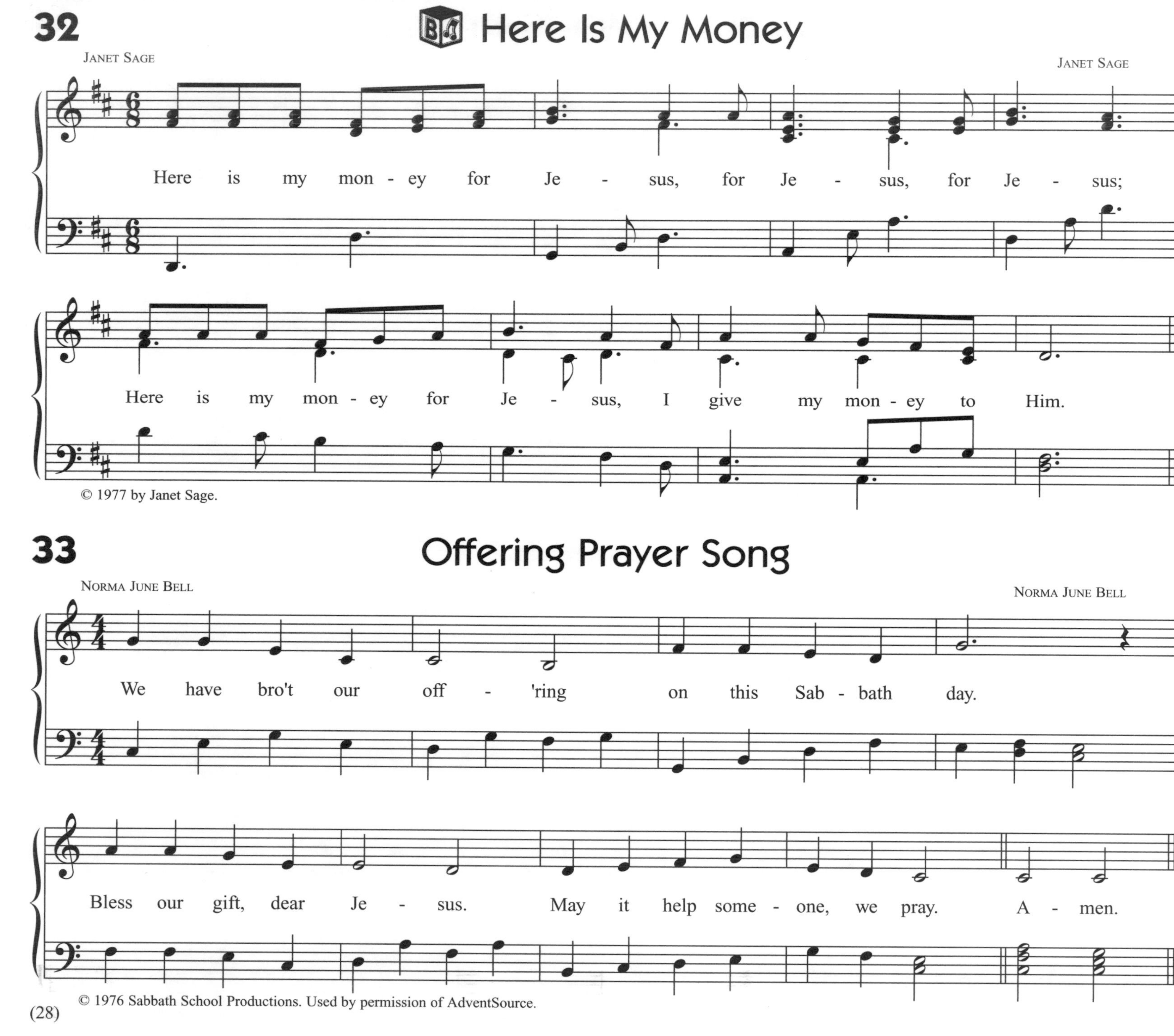
32
Here Is My Money
Janet Sage
Janet Sage
6/8
Here is my mon - ey for Je - sus, for Je - sus, for Je - sus;
Here is my mon - ey for Je - sus, I give my mon - ey to Him.
© 1977 by Janet Sage.
33
Offering Prayer Song
Norma June Bell
Norma June Bell
4/4
We have bro't our off - 'ring on this Sab - bath day.
Bless our gift, dear Je - sus. May it help some - one, we pray. A - men.
© 1976 Sabbath School Productions. Used by permission of AdventSource.
(28)

To God's House

JANINE MAX

JANINE MAX

To God's house I bring an of - fer - ing. I thank Him for all He's giv - en me.
To God's house I bring an of - fer - ing. I bring an of - fer - ing to God's house.

35 A Boat Goes Sailing

A. HAAS

A. HAAS

1. A boat goes sail - ing to the mis - sion land, Sail - ing, sail - ing mis - sion boat. It takes a teach - er to the chil - dren there, Sail - ing mis - sion - ar - y boat.
2. A plane goes fly - ing to the mis - sion land, Fly - ing, fly - ing mis - sion plane. It takes a doc - tor to the chil - dren there, Fly - ing mis - sion - ar - y plane.
3. A train goes chug - ging to the mis - sion land, Chug - ging, chug - ging mis - sion train. It brings a Bi - ble to the chil - dren there, Chug - ging mis - sion - ar - y train.
4. I'll send my of - f'ring to the mis - sion land, Of - f'ring for the chil - dren there, To tell them all that Je - sus loves them too; Je - sus loves our mis - sion land.

A Birthday

36

MILDRED ADAIR | MILDRED ADAIR

A birth - day, a birth - day, O who has had a birth - day? Come sit right here and we will sing, To wish you hap - py birth - day.

Count the Birthday Money

37

JOHNIE B. WOOD | JOHNIE B. WOOD

Ma - ry* has a birth - day, we're so glad. We will see how man - y she* has had. As we count the mon - ey we are told [Count] Yes, the mon - ey says she's* six* years old.

*Insert name, appropriate pronoun, and age of child.

38
Happy Birthday!
C. HAROLD LOWDEN
C. HAROLD LOWDEN
Just five* years old to - day, Just five* years old to - day; Hap - py
birth - day, hap - py birth - day! Ed - na's* five* years old to - day.
Copyright Heidelberg Press.
*Insert child's name and age.
39
Happy Birthday!
JANET SAGE
JANET SAGE
Hap - py birth - day, hap - py birth - day, Hap - py birth - day to
you; Je - sus loves you, dear ______,* Hap - py birth - day to you!
© 1977 by Janet Sage.
*Insert child's name.

Happy, Happy, Happy Birthday

40

CAROL GREENE
CAROL GREENE
Briskly
Hap - py, hap - py, hap - py birth - day And a lot more too.
Hap - py, hap - py birth - day, _______.* May God bless you.

*Insert child's name.

41 Our Parade

Traditional

Traditional / Arr. by Kenneth D. Logan

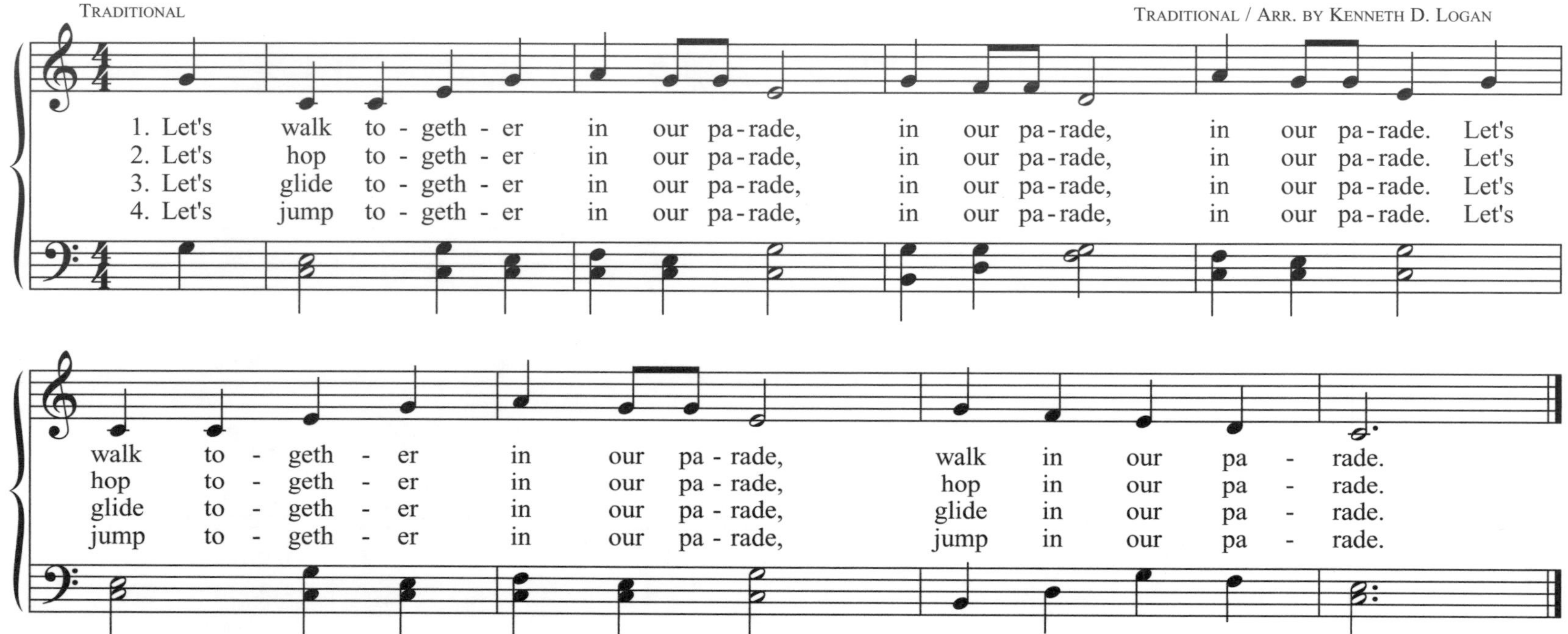
1. Let's walk to - geth - er in our pa-rade, in our pa-rade, in our pa-rade. Let's
2. Let's hop to - geth - er in our pa-rade, in our pa-rade, in our pa-rade. Let's
3. Let's glide to - geth - er in our pa-rade, in our pa-rade, in our pa-rade. Let's
4. Let's jump to - geth - er in our pa-rade, in our pa-rade, in our pa-rade. Let's
walk to - geth - er in our pa - rade, walk in our pa - rade.
hop to - geth - er in our pa - rade, hop in our pa - rade.
glide to - geth - er in our pa - rade, glide in our pa - rade.
jump to - geth - er in our pa - rade, jump in our pa - rade.

5. Let's trot together in our parade,
in our parade, in our parade.
Let's trot together in our parade,
trot in our parade.

6. Let's clap together in our parade,
in our parade, in our parade.
Let's clap together in our parade,
clap in our parade.

Quietly Tiptoe

42

NANCY J. STAGL-SCHIPPMANN NANCY J. STAGL-SCHIPPMANN

1. Qui - et - ly, so qui - et - ly our les - son we will hear; We'll
2. Qui - et - ly, so qui - et - ly our les - son we have heard; We'll
tip - toe soft - ly from our chairs to lis - ten, teach - er dear.
tip - toe soft - ly to our chairs; we love God's Ho - ly Word.

43 Promotion Song

Joy Hicklin Stewart

Joy Hicklin Stewart

You're go - ing to kin - der - gar - ten on this Sab - bath day. You'll learn some more of
Je - sus; you'll sing to Him and pray. You're go - ing to kin - der - gar - ten
on this Sab - bath day. May Je - sus bless and help you. Good - bye, good - bye to - day.

Good-bye Prayer 44

KATHLEEN MAGUIRE — KATHLEEN MAGUIRE

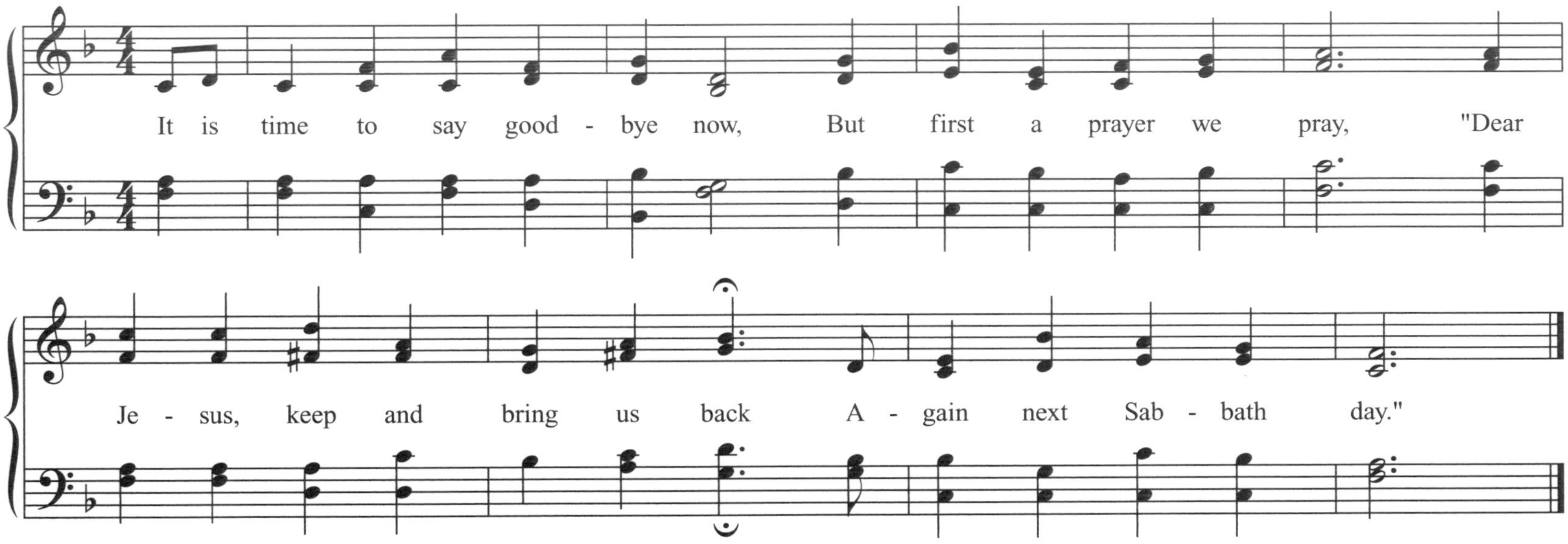

It is time to say good - bye now, But first a prayer we pray, "Dear
Je - sus, keep and bring us back A - gain next Sab - bath day."

Good-bye to You 45

S. VANCE — S. VANCE

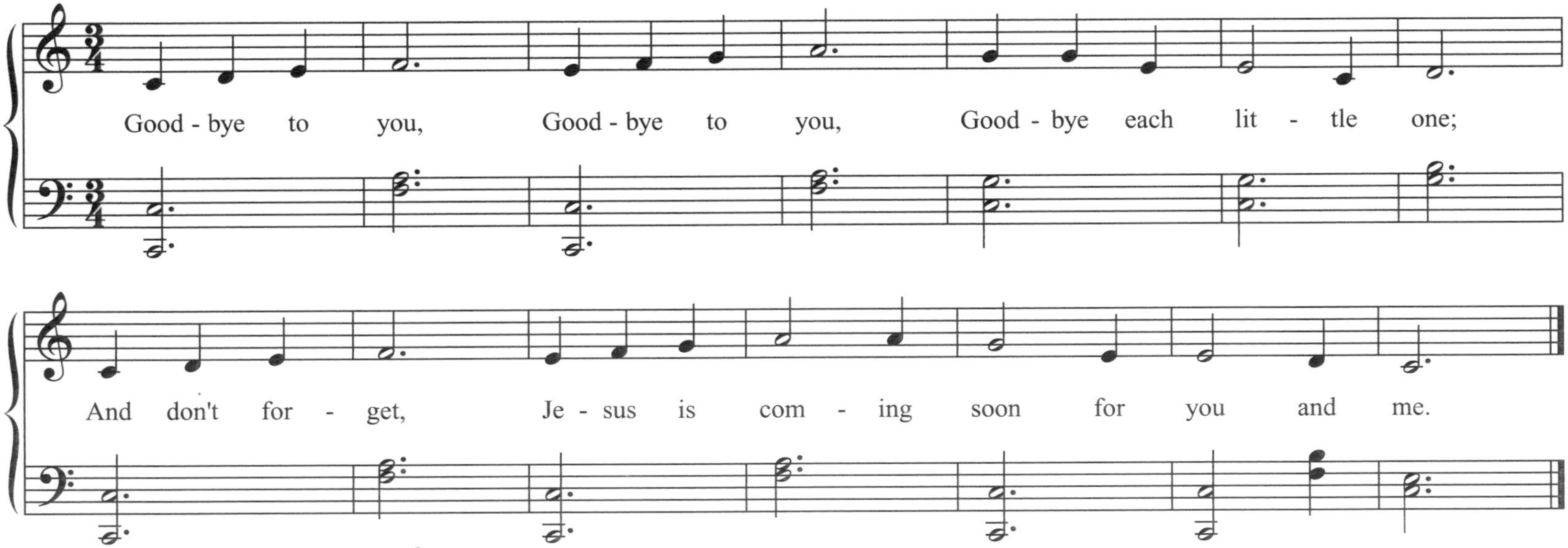

Good - bye to you, Good - bye to you, Good - bye each lit - tle one;
And don't for - get, Je - sus is com - ing soon for you and me.

46 Sabbath School Is Over

(wave)
Our Sab - bath school is o - ver, And we are go - ing now. Good - bye, good - bye, Be
(wave)
al - ways kind and true. Good - bye, good - bye, Be al - ways kind and true.

God Sent His Angels

47

MARY E. SCHWAB — MARY E. SCHWAB

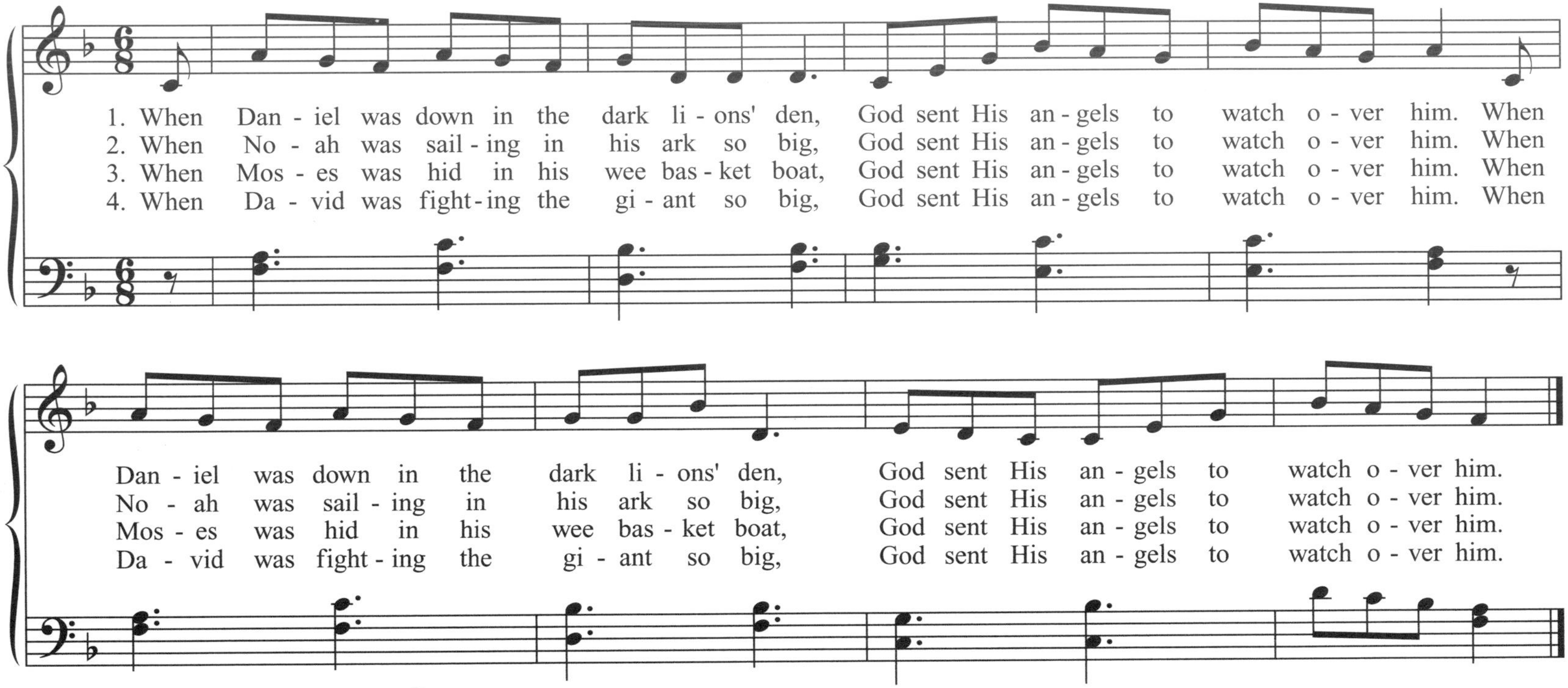

1. When Dan - iel was down in the dark li - ons' den, God sent His an - gels to watch o - ver him. When Dan - iel was down in the dark li - ons' den, God sent His an - gels to watch o - ver him.
2. When No - ah was sail - ing in his ark so big, God sent His an - gels to watch o - ver him. When No - ah was sail - ing in his ark so big, God sent His an - gels to watch o - ver him.
3. When Mos - es was hid in his wee bas - ket boat, God sent His an - gels to watch o - ver him. When Mos - es was hid in his wee bas - ket boat, God sent His an - gels to watch o - ver him.
4. When Da - vid was fight - ing the gi - ant so big, God sent His an - gels to watch o - ver him. When Da - vid was fight - ing the gi - ant so big, God sent His an - gels to watch o - ver him.

Jesus Sends the Angels

48

FLORENCE P. JORGENSEN — FLORENCE P. JORGENSEN

1. Je - sus sends the an - gels, an - gels, an - gels; Je - sus send the an - gels To watch me when I'm play - ing.
2. Je - sus sends the an - gels, an - gels, an - gels; Je - sus send the an - gels To watch me when I'm walk - ing.
3. Je - sus sends the an - gels, an - gels, an - gels; Je - sus send the an - gels To watch me when I'm rid - ing.
4. Je - sus sends the an - gels, an - gels, an - gels; Je - sus send the an - gels To watch me when I'm sleep - ing.

49 Guardian Angel Song

Kathryn B. Myers

Kathryn B. Myers

1. When mo - ther tucks me in at night and I go fast a - sleep, God
2. When morn - ing comes and I a - wake and go a - bout my play, A
sends a love - ly an - gel down His faith - ful watch to keep.
love - ly an - gel still is near to guard me all the day.

Grace

Angels

Thank God for Angels Bright

50

Lauretta Wilcox Jarnes
Lauretta Wilcox Jarnes
1. An - gels are watch - ing ov - er me, I am glad, I am glad.
2. An - gels are see - ing all I do, Good or bad, good or bad.
An - gels are watch - ing ov - er me, Thank God for an - gels bright.
An - gels are see - ing all I do, Thank God for an - gels bright.

51
Jesus Talks to Me

SUSAN DAVIS

SUSAN DAVIS

Bi - ble, Bi - ble, Je - sus talks to me. Bi - ble Book,

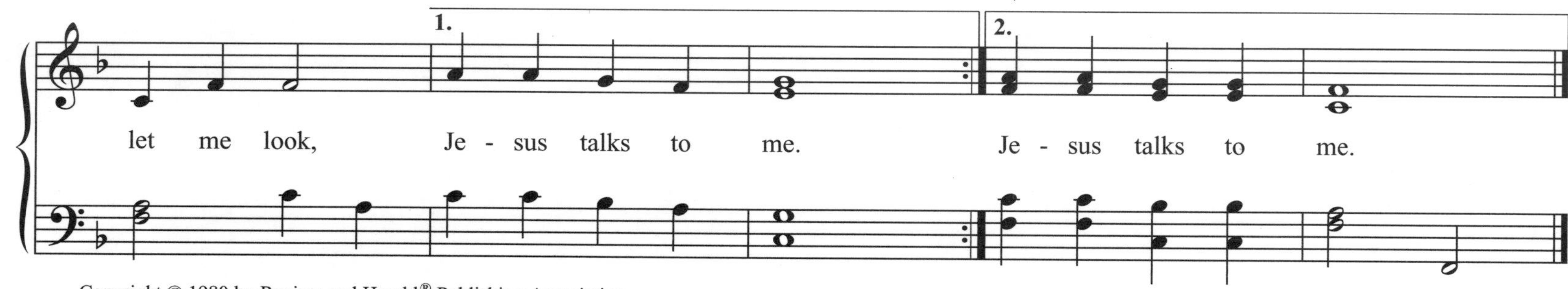
1.
2.
let me look, Je - sus talks to me. Je - sus talks to me.

52
The Bible Is God's Word to Me
ENID G. THORSON
ENID G. THORSON
The Bi - ble is God's Word to me. The Bi - ble says that God loves me.

Suggested uses: Parents and teachers can help find the memory verse in the Bible for the little ones. They can say it a few times together, then when holding their Bibles they can either say or sing the verse with motions. This can be done every Sabbath.

The Bible

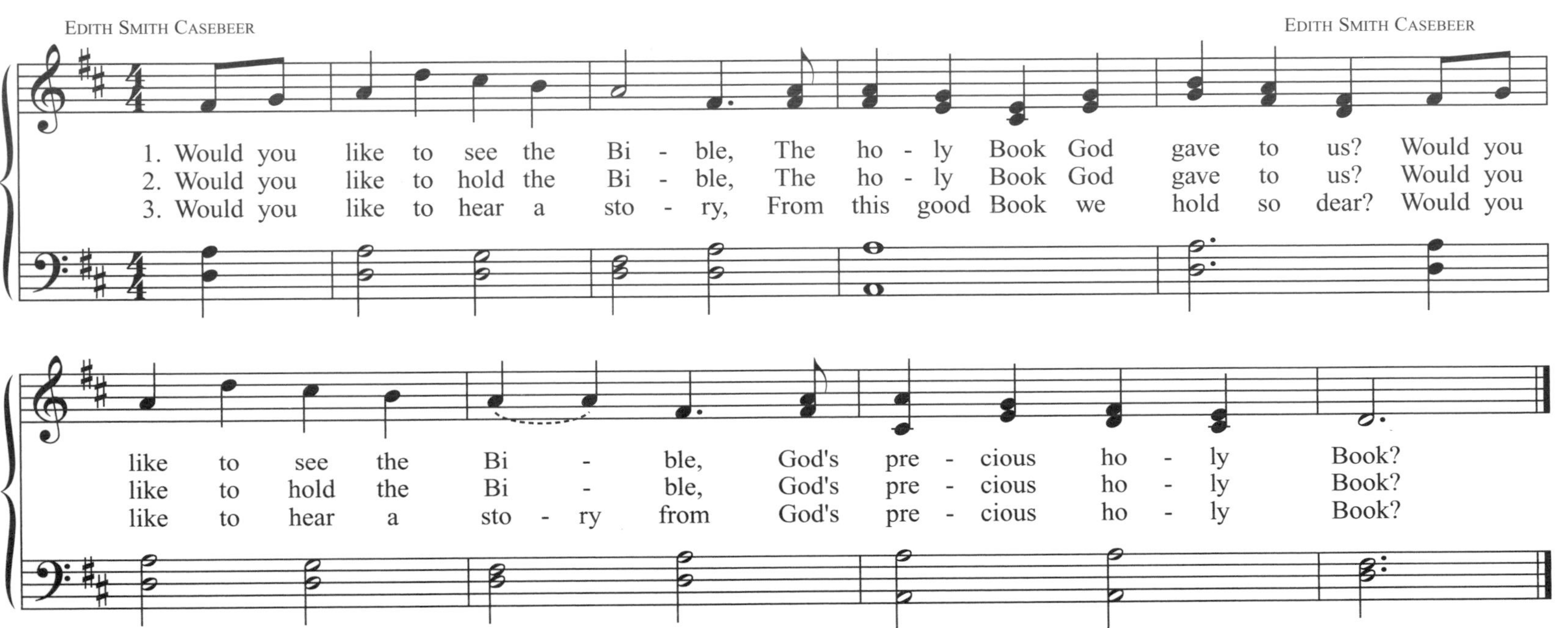
Edith Smith Casebeer
Edith Smith Casebeer
1. Would you like to see the Bi - ble, The ho - ly Book God gave to us? Would you like to see the Bi - ble, God's pre - cious ho - ly Book?
2. Would you like to hold the Bi - ble, The ho - ly Book God gave to us? Would you like to hold the Bi - ble, God's pre - cious ho - ly Book?
3. Would you like to hear a sto - ry, From this good Book we hold so dear? Would you like to hear a sto - ry from God's pre - cious ho - ly Book?

54 The Blackbird Song

Janet Sage
Janet Sage
1. Where are you go - ing, Black-bird, Black-bird, Where are you go - ing, Black-bird?
2. What do you have there, Black-bird, Black-bird, What do you have there, Black-bird?
3. Who sends you to him, Black-bird, Black-bird, Who sends you to him, Black-bird?
4. Why does He send you, Black-bird, Black-bird, Why does He send you, Black-bird?
"I am go - ing to help E - li - jah, Have-n't you heard? Have-n't you heard?"
"I have food to feed E - li - jah, Have-n't you heard? Have-n't you heard?"
"Je - sus sends me to E - li - jah, Have-n't you heard? Have-n't you heard?"
"All be - cause He loves E - li - jah, Have-n't you heard? Have-n't you heard?"

55 The Loaves and the Fishes

JANET SAGE
JANET SAGE
One lit-tle fish, two lit-tle fish, One, two, three, four, five lit-tle loaves of bread,
One lit-tle fish, two lit-tle fish, One, two, three, four, five lit-tle loaves of bread.

56 Dip, Dip, Dip, in the River

JEANNETTE JOHNSON

TRADITIONAL / ARR. BY KENNETH D. LOGAN

"Dip, dip, dip in the riv-er, oh, Dip, dip, dip in the riv-er." E-li-sha told Naa-man to dip in the riv-er, and His lep-ro-sy would be gone.

57 Run to Jesus

JANINE MAX

JANINE MAX

1. When the child-ren came to play His friends said, "Go a-way." But
2. It's a brand-new day to-day, and I know when I get up,

Je-sus loved them and they heard Him say, "Let the child-ren stay. Come on and run, run, run to
Je-sus is here and I'll hear Him say, "Let's go out and play. Come on and run, run, run to

Me. Jump up on My knee. I'll hold you tight, day and night. Run, run, run to Me."
Me. Jump up on My knee. I'll hold you tight, day and night. Run, run, run to Me."

GRACE

BIBLE STORIES

Noah Built a Great Big Boat

MARY E. SCHWAB

MARY E. SCHWAB

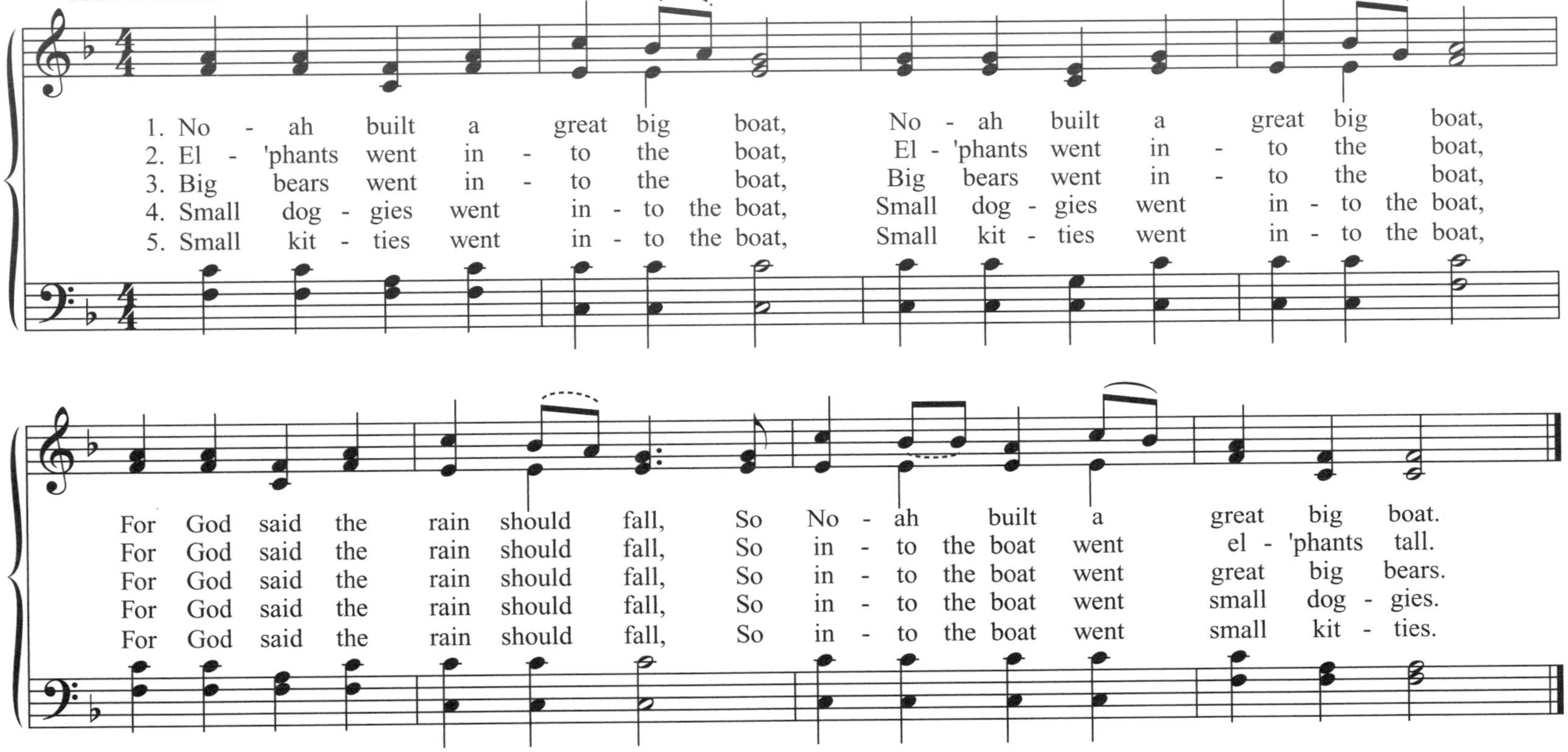

1. Noah built a great big boat, Noah built a great big boat,
For God said the rain should fall, So Noah built a great big boat.

2. El'phants went into the boat, El'phants went into the boat,
For God said the rain should fall, So into the boat went el'phants tall.

3. Big bears went into the boat, Big bears went into the boat,
For God said the rain should fall, So into the boat went great big bears.

4. Small doggies went into the boat, Small doggies went into the boat,
For God said the rain should fall, So into the boat went small doggies.

5. Small kitties went into the boat, Small kitties went into the boat,
For God said the rain should fall, So into the boat went small kitties.

59 The Animals Came a-Walking

VIRGINIA CASON VIRGINIA CASON

The an - i - mals came a - walk - ing, a - walk - ing, a - walk - ing. The an - i - mals came a - walk - ing to the ark that No - ah made.

60 Who Made the Rainbow?

B. B. MCKINNEY B. B. MCKINNEY

1. Who made the beau - ti - ful rain - bow? I know, I know; God made the beau - ti - ful rain - bow, That's why I love it so.

2. God sends the beau - ti - ful rain - bow, So bright, so clear; God sends the beau - ti - ful rain - bow To show us He is near.

Who's in the Ark?

Janet Sage

Janet Sage

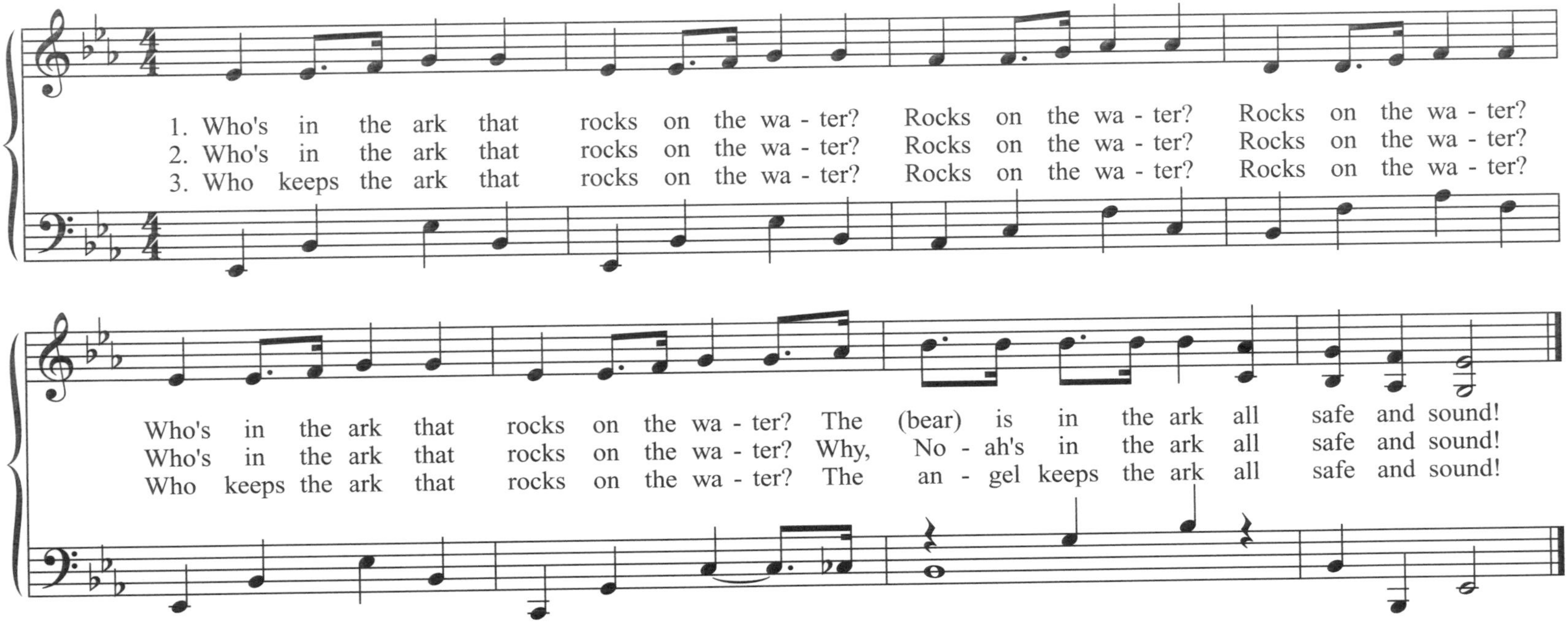

1. Who's in the ark that rocks on the wa - ter? Rocks on the wa - ter? Rocks on the wa - ter?
Who's in the ark that rocks on the wa - ter? The (bear) is in the ark all safe and sound!

2. Who's in the ark that rocks on the wa - ter? Rocks on the wa - ter? Rocks on the wa - ter?
Who's in the ark that rocks on the wa - ter? Why, No - ah's in the ark all safe and sound!

3. Who keeps the ark that rocks on the wa - ter? Rocks on the wa - ter? Rocks on the wa - ter?
Who keeps the ark that rocks on the wa - ter? The an - gel keeps the ark all safe and sound!

62 The Wise Man and the Foolish Man

UNKNOWN
UNKNOWN
1. The wise man built his house up-on the rock, The wise man built his house up-on the rock; The wise man built his house up-on the rock, And the rains came tum-bling down. The rains came down and the floods came up; The rains came down and the floods came up, The rains came down and the floods came up, And the house on the rock stood fast.
2. The fool-ish man built his house up-on the sand, The fool-ish man built his house up-on the sand; The fool-ish man built his house up-on the sand, And the rains came tum-bling down. The rains came down and the floods came up; The rains came down and the floods came up, The rains came down and the floods came up, And the house on the sand went smash.

Zacchaeus

63

UNKNOWN

ARR. BY MRS. N. R. SCHAPER

1Zac - chae - us was a wee lit - tle man, 2A wee lit - tle man was he. 3He
climbed up in a sy - ca - more tree, 4For the Lord he want-ed to see. And
as the Sav - iour passed that way, 5He looked up in the tree,
6Spoken:
And he said: "Zacchaeus, you come down, 7For I'm
go - ing to your house to - day, For I'm go - ing to your house to - day."

Motions: 1. Hands in front, right palm raised above left palm. 2. Bring palms a little closer. 3. Alternate hands in climbing motion. 4. Shade eyes with right hand and look down. 5. Shade eyes with right hand and look up. 6. Words are spoken, while looking up and wagging a finger in admonition. 7. Clap hands on accented beat.

64 Go and Wash

Anita L. Jacobs

Traditional / Arr. by Kenneth D. Logan

1. Naa - man was a man who had lep - ro - sy. (Lep - ro - sy.) He need - ed
2. "Go and wash," said E - li - sha that day. (That day.) "Go and
3. In the wa - ter Naa - man dipped sev - en times. (Sev - en times.) One, two,
help 'cause he was sick as can be! (As can be.) He said, "Can your God heal me? Can He
wash in the riv - er right a - way." (Right a - way.) Naa - man washed in the riv - er, where his
three, four, five, six, sev - en times. (Sev - en times.) On the sev - enth he was well— ev - er
cure lep - ro - sy?" Lit - tle Maid said, "Yes, He can. Wait and see."
life was changed for - ev - er. Ev - en though it was hard to o - bey.
af - ter he would tell Of God's love, and how he dipped sev - en times.

GRACE

BIBLE STORIES

Naaman's Song

Anita L. Jacobs

Traditional / Arr. by Kenneth D. Logan

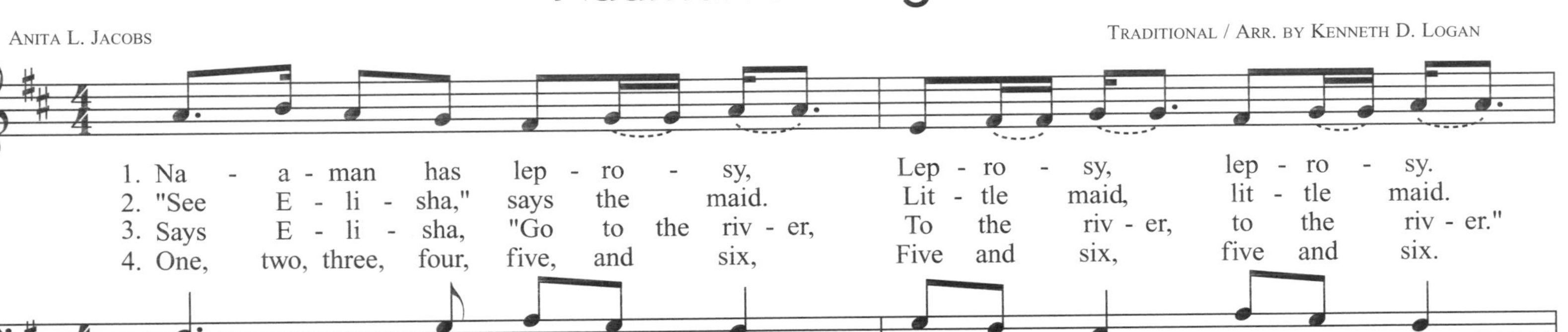
1. Na - a - man has lep - ro - sy, Lep - ro - sy, lep - ro - sy.
2. "See E - li - sha," says the maid. Lit - tle maid, lit - tle maid.
3. Says E - li - sha, "Go to the riv - er, To the riv - er, to the riv - er."
4. One, two, three, four, five, and six, Five and six, five and six.

Na - a - man has lep - ro - sy; He needs help.
"See E - li - sha," says the maid. "He loves God."
Says E - li - sha, "Go to the riv - er, Dip sev - en times."
One, two, three, four, five and six— Still not bet - ter.

5. One more time and he is clean.
He is clean. He is clean.
One more time and he is clean.
God has healed him.

6. Naaman is a happy man.
Happy man, happy man.
Naaman is a happy man.
How God loves him!

Grace

Bible Stories

And God Said

Johnie B. Wood
Johnie B. Wood
1. And God said the sun should shine, The rain should fall, the flow'rs should grow,
2. And God said the grass should grow, The trees bear fruit, the winds should blow,
3. And God said that we should rest; The Sab - bath day, it should be blest;
And God said the birds should sing, And it was so, was so.
And God said the streams should flow, And it was so, was so.
And God said He'd be our guest, And it was so, was so.

Grace

Creation

Animals, Animals

JANET SAGE
JANET SAGE
mf
f
p
An - i-mals, an - i-mals, Je - sus made the an - i - mals— Great big an - i-mals, lit-tle ti - ny an - i - mals—
mf
An - i-mals, an - i-mals, Je - sus made the an - i-mals; Here is an an - i-mal that I know. . .

Leader: Sing animatedly, with a loud, deep voice for the "great big animals," and a soft, small voice for the "little tiny animals." You may add action by spreading your hands wide apart or bringing them close together for big and little animals, but don't have the children do it with you until they know the song well. The song is intended to be sung several times, letting a child hold a toy animal or picture that will be named and discussed at the end of each repetition.

Creation

T. S. Knox

Alan Gray M. Campbell

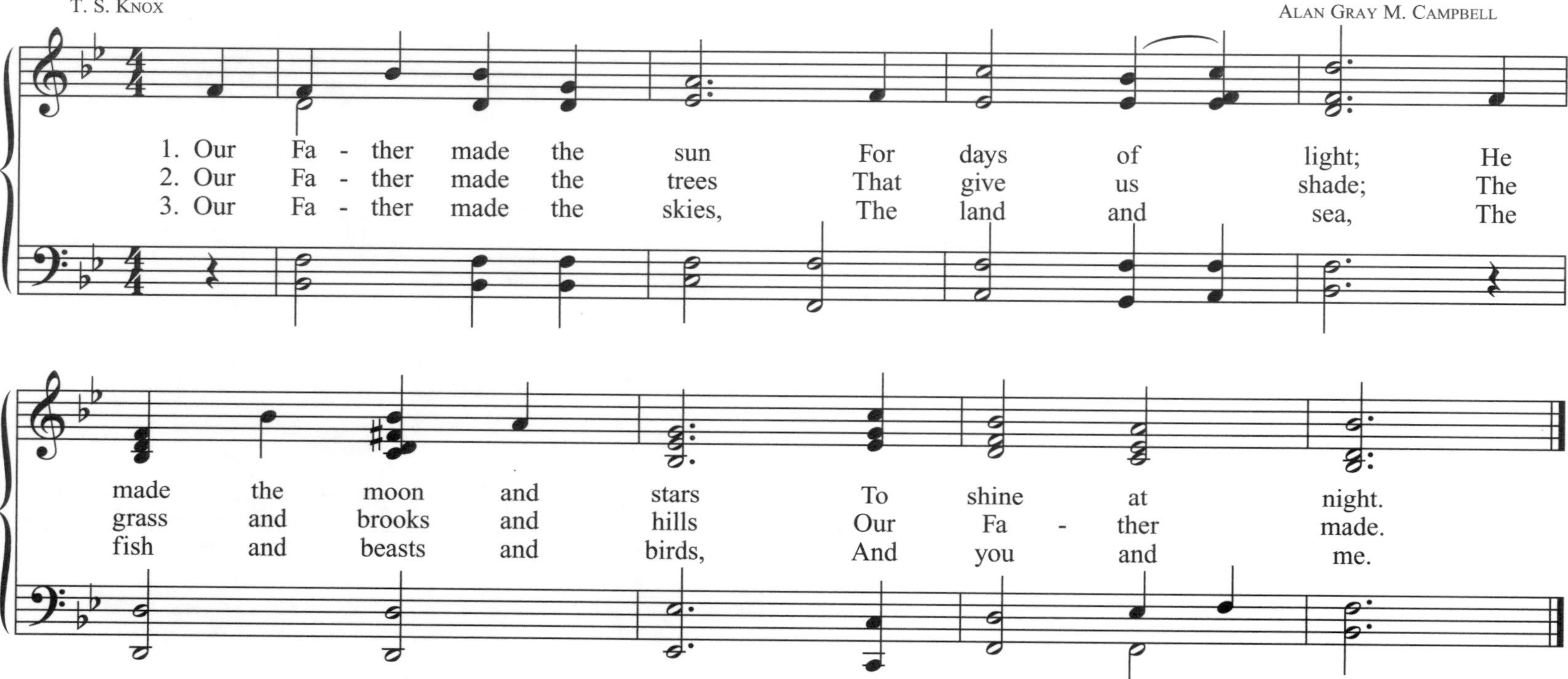
1. Our Fa - ther made the sun For days of light; He made the moon and stars To shine at night.
2. Our Fa - ther made the trees That give us shade; The grass and brooks and hills Our Fa - ther made.
3. Our Fa - ther made the skies, The land and sea, The fish and beasts and birds, And you and me.

Everything He Makes Is Good

69

JANINE MAX

JANINE MAX / ARR. BY KENNETH D. LOGAN

Bouncy

Ev - 'ry thing that God makes is good. Ev - 'ry thing that God makes is good.

I know be - cause He made the sun and moon, Made all the stars you can see. I

know be - cause He made the un - i - verse, And He made me! Ev - 'ry thing that God makes

is good, Ev - 'ry thing that God makes is good, Ev - 'ry thing He makes is good!

70 God Made Me

JANINE MAX JANINE MAX

God made me God made me. I'm made in His im - age, spe-cial, you see. There's
no-bo-dy else like me. Eyes to see, ears to hear, Mouth to eat and talk,
Nose to smell, hands to touch, Feet to run and walk. God made me,
God made me. I'm made in His im - age, spe-cial, you see. There's no-bo-dy else like me.

God Made Our World

Lena S. Lawrence
Lena S. Lawrence
1. God made our won-der-ful world, God made our won-der-ful world. He made the stars bright, He made the day-light. God made our won-der-ful world.
2. God made our won-der-ful world, God made our won-der-ful world. He made all the trees, He made all the flowers. God made our won-der-ful world.
3. God made our won-der-ful world, God made our won-der-ful world. He made all the birds, He made all our pets. God made our won-der-ful world.
4. God made our won-der-ful world, God made our won-der-ful world. He made all the fruit, He made all our food. God made our won-der-ful world.

72 God Made the Kangaroo

JANINE MAX JANINE MAX

Kang - a - roo, kang - a-roo, Kang-a - roo-oo - oo, Can I hop with you? Kang - a-

roo, kang - a-roo, Kang-a - roo-oo - oo, Can I hop with you? God made the

Kang-a-roo, And He made me too. I love my great big God; He makes all things
new. Kang - a - roo, kang - a-roo, Kang-a - roo-oo - oo, Can I hop with you?

God Made Us All

Bertha D. Martin

Dorothy P. Boggs / Harmonized by Audra L. Wood

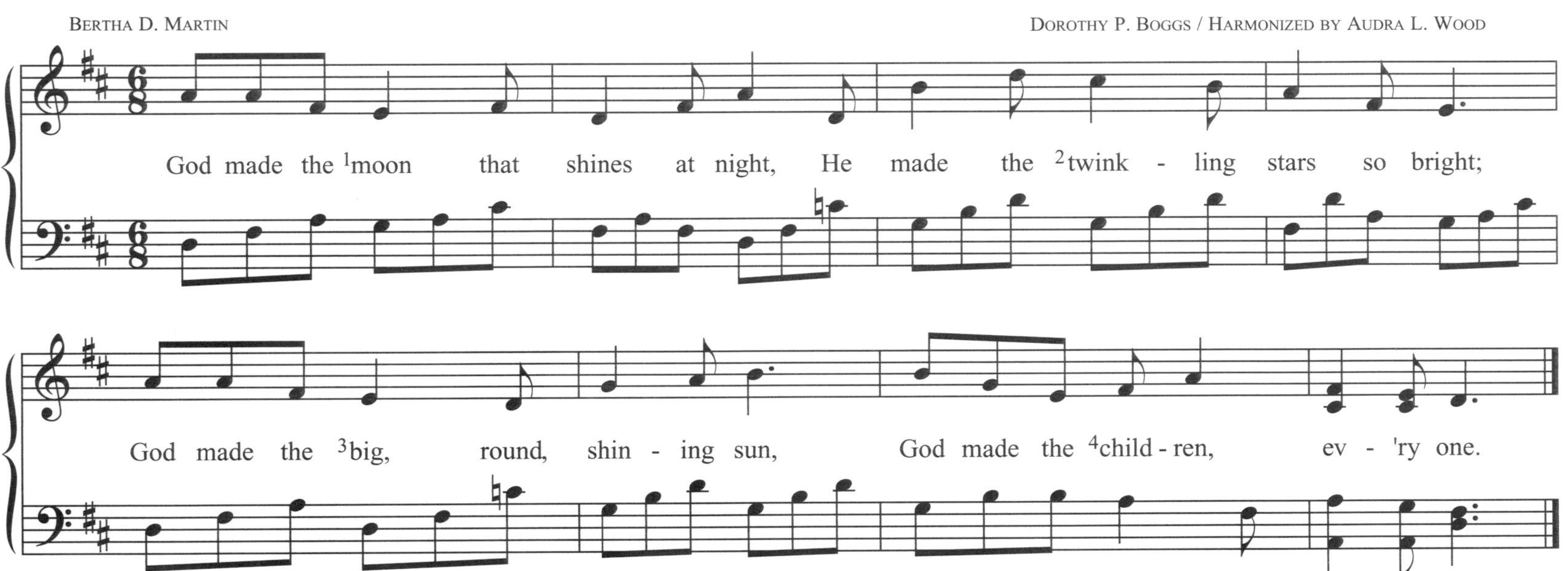
God made the 1moon that shines at night, He made the 2twink - ling stars so bright;
God made the 3big, round, shin - ing sun, God made the 4child - ren, ev - 'ry one.

Motions: 1. Arms above head, make circle with hands. 2. Arms above head, wiggle fingers. 3. Make larger circle with arms above head. 4. Outstretched arms.

74 Wonder Song (Who Can?)

Grace W. Owens

Clara Lee Parker

1. Oh, who can make a flow - er? I'm sure I can't, can you? Oh, who can make a flow - er? No one but God, 'tis true.
2. Oh, who can make the rain - drops? I'm sure I can't, can you? Oh, who can make the rain - drops? No one but God, 'tis true.
3. Oh, who can make the sun - shine? I'm sure I can't, can you? Oh, who can make the sun - shine? No one but God, 'tis true.
4. Oh, who can make the wind blow? I'm sure I can't, can you? Oh, who can make the wind blow? No one but God, 'tis true.

Forgiveness Is a Gift

75 Forgiveness Is a Gift

ANITA REITH STOHS

TRADITIONAL / ARR. BY KENNETH D. LOGAN

(with pedal)

For - give-ness is a gift of the Lord to me, Gift of the Lord to me, Gift of the Lord to me. For - give - ness is a gift of the Lord to me, A gift of grace so free.

76 I'm Forgiven

ANITA REITH STOHS

KENNETH D. LOGAN

I'm for - giv - en, I'm for - giv - en. On the cross Christ died for me. From sin and death, I now have been set free. Christ died for me.

GRACE

FORGIVENESS

77 Jesus Smiles and Forgives

ADRIANA ITIN FEMOPASE

ADRIANA ITIN FEMOPASE / ARR. BY KENNETH D. LOGAN

I did wrong, that's too bad; I'll tell Je - sus I am sad. He will
smile from a - bove And for - give in His love.

GRACE

FORGIVENESS

78 Look, Look, Look at the World

Carol Greene

Carol Greene

Look, look, look at the world.
Look, look, look at the world.
1. Look at the tu - lips, Danc - ing red tu - lips.
2. Look at the tree - tops, Sway - ing green tree - tops.
3. Look at the a - corns, Bounc - ing brown a - corns.
4. Look at the snow - flakes, Swirl - ing white snow - flakes.
Oh, what a gift from God!
Oh, what a gift from God!
Oh, what a gift from God!
Oh, what a gift from God!

GRACE

GOD'S GIFTS

79 My Little Lips Are Smiling

KATHRYN B. MYERS KATHRYN B. MYERS

My lit - tle lips are smil - ing. I'm hap - py you can see, Be -

cause I have a lit - tle dog* that Je - sus made for me.

*little cat, little lamb, little duck, etc.; mother dear, father dear, happy home, etc.

Additional suggestions for last line:

Because I love dear Jesus, who loves and cares for me.
Because I love dear Jesus, who's coming soon for me.
For I can be obedient with Jesus helping me.
For I can tell the truth each day with Jesus helping me.
For I am safe through all the day (night) with angels watching me.

Presents

80

Mary E. Schwab

Mary E. Schwab

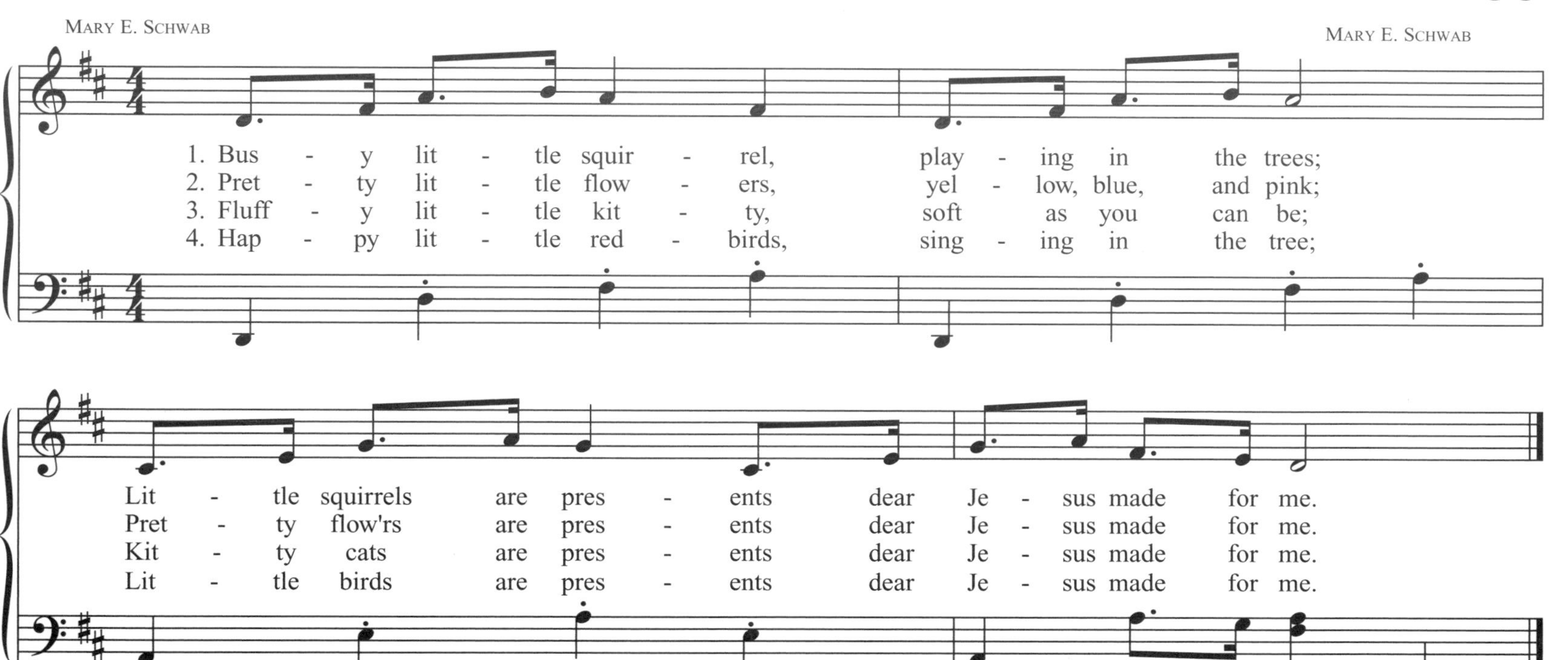
1. Bus - y lit - tle squir - rel, play - ing in the trees;
2. Pret - ty lit - tle flow - ers, yel - low, blue, and pink;
3. Fluff - y lit - tle kit - ty, soft as you can be;
4. Hap - py lit - tle red - birds, sing - ing in the tree;
Lit - tle squirrels are pres - ents dear Je - sus made for me.
Pret - ty flow'rs are pres - ents dear Je - sus made for me.
Kit - ty cats are pres - ents dear Je - sus made for me.
Lit - tle birds are pres - ents dear Je - sus made for me.

5. Red and yellow apples, sweet and good to eat;
Apples sweet are presents dear Jesus made for me.

81 Roses Bloom in My Garden

Mildred Adair Stagg — Mildred Adair Stagg

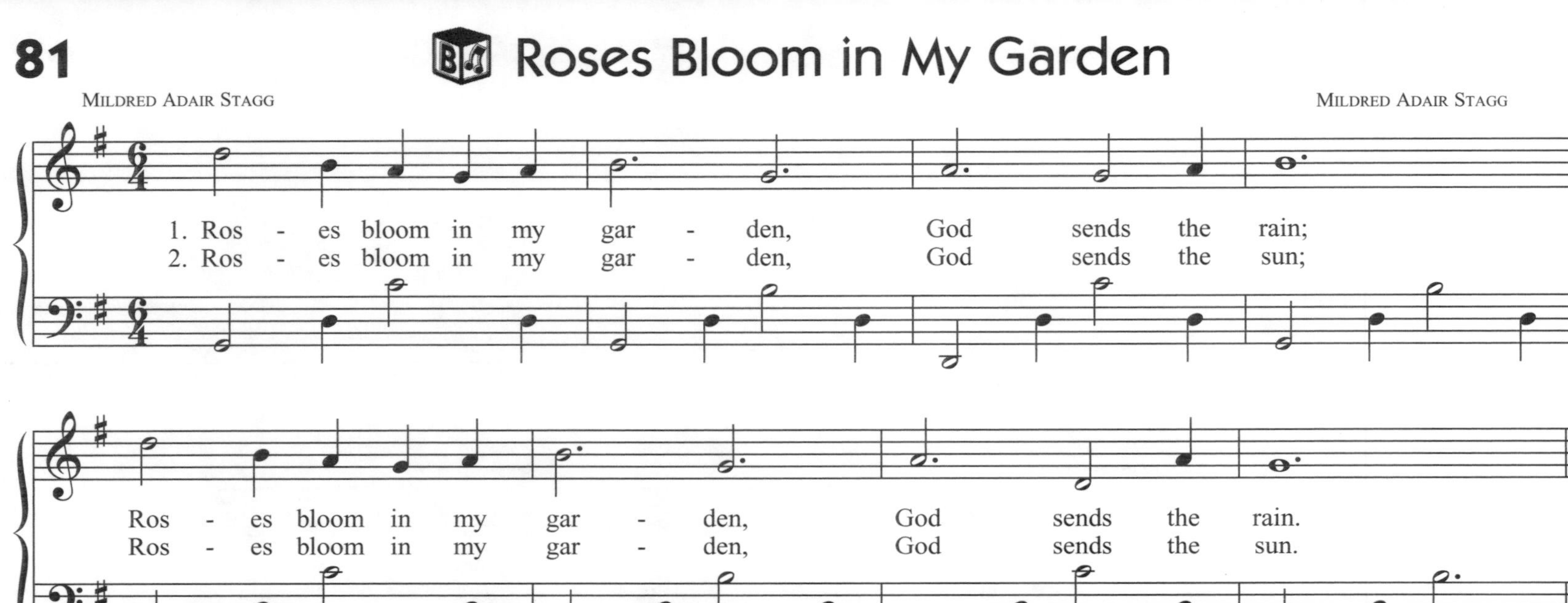
1. Ros - es bloom in my gar - den, God sends the rain;
2. Ros - es bloom in my gar - den, God sends the sun;
Ros - es bloom in my gar - den, God sends the rain.
Ros - es bloom in my gar - den, God sends the sun.

Grace

God's Gifts

Shall We Go for a Walk Today?* 82

Aurora M. Shumate Ida T. Truss

Leader: 1. Shall we go for a walk to - day, a walk to - day, a walk to - day?
Children: 2. Yes, we'll go for a walk to - day, a walk to - day, a walk to - day;
Leader: 3. Shall we smell the flowers to - day, the flowers to - day, the flowers to - day?
Children: 4. Yes, we'll smell the flowers to - day, the flowers to - day, the flowers to - day;
Shall we go for a walk to - day, and see what God has giv - en?
Yes, we'll go for a walk to - day, and see what God has giv - en.
Shall we smell the flowers to - day, the flowers that God has giv - en?
Yes, we'll smell the flowers to - day, the flowers that God has giv - en.

*Dialogue

83 With the Fingers Jesus Gave Me

JANET SAGE JANET SAGE

I can feel things that are soft, soft, so soft;* With the
(with pedal)
fin - gers Je - sus gave me I can feel things that are soft.

*Hard, wet, cold, warm, scratchy, squeezy, etc.

GRACE

GOD'S GIFTS

Wonderful Jesus* 84

KATHRYN B. MYERS KATHRYN B. MYERS

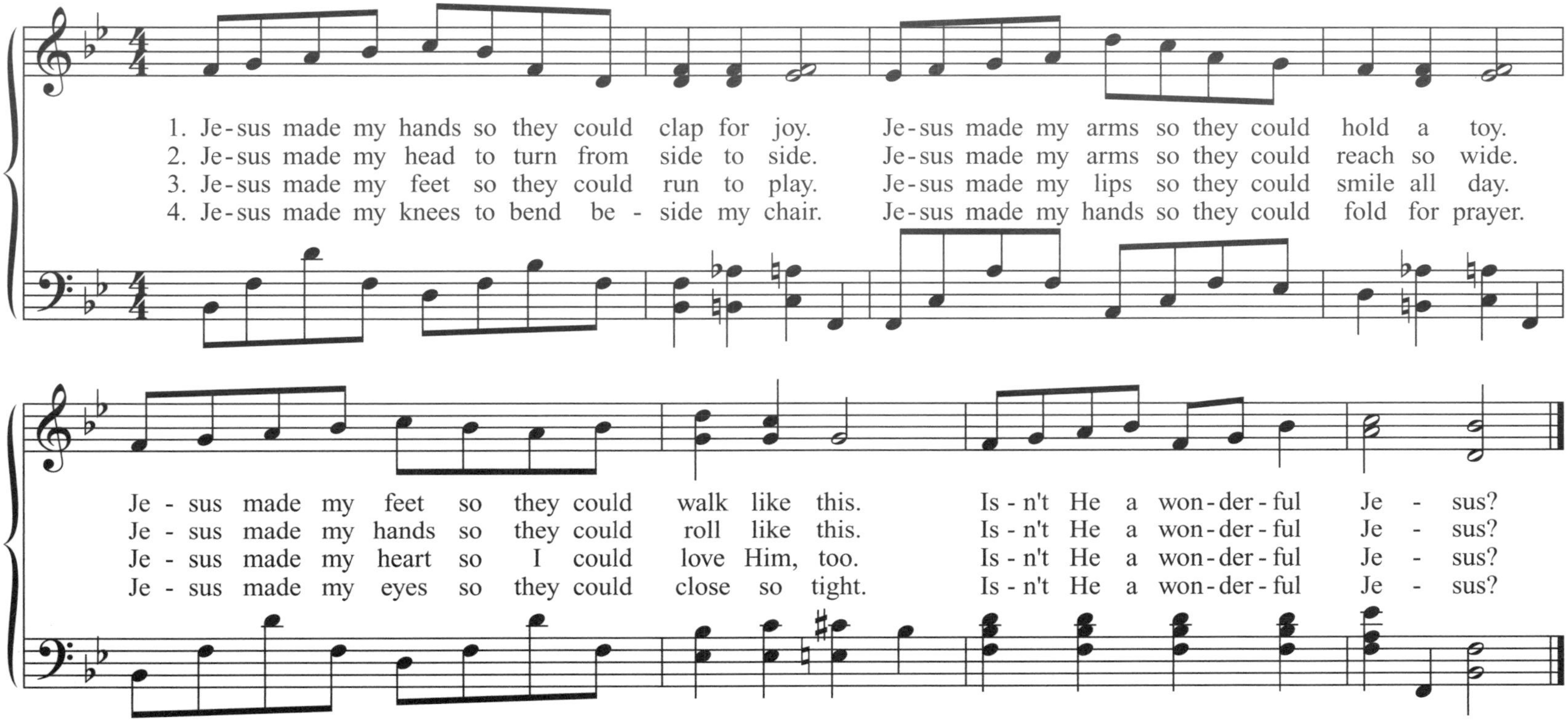

1. Je-sus made my hands so they could clap for joy. Je-sus made my arms so they could hold a toy.
Je - sus made my feet so they could walk like this. Is - n't He a won-der - ful Je - sus?

2. Je-sus made my head to turn from side to side. Je-sus made my arms so they could reach so wide.
Je - sus made my hands so they could roll like this. Is - n't He a won-der - ful Je - sus?

3. Je-sus made my feet so they could run to play. Je-sus made my lips so they could smile all day.
Je - sus made my heart so I could love Him, too. Is - n't He a won-der - ful Je - sus?

4. Je-sus made my knees to bend be - side my chair. Je-sus made my hands so they could fold for prayer.
Je - sus made my eyes so they could close so tight. Is - n't He a won-der - ful Je - sus?

*Motion Song

85 All Our Needs

CAROLYN BERGE

TRADITIONAL / ARR. BY KENNETH D. LOGAN

1. Jesus cares for all our needs, All our needs, all our needs; Jesus cares for all our needs. Thank You, thank You, Lord.

2. I will trust in Jesus' care, Jesus' care, Jesus' care; I will trust in Jesus' care. Won't you, won't you, too?

86 God Cares for Me

AURORA M. SHUMATE

IDA T. TRUSS

God sees me when I am asleep, He sees me when I play; I love to think God cares for me, Yes, ev'ry night and day.

God Cares for Me

Eleanor L. Doan   Eleanor L. Doan

1. Little birds are singing, merrily, merrily;
2. Pretty flowers are blooming, look and see, look and see;
3. God loves little children; He loves me, He loves me.
I think they are singing, "God cares for me."
I think they are saying, "God cares for me."
That's why I am singing, "God cares for me."

GRACE

GOD'S LOVE AND CARE

LVPH-10

God Is So Good

African Christian Folk Song

1. God is so good, God is so good,
God is so good, He's so good to me.

2. He died for me, He died for me,
He died for me, He's so good to me.

3. I love Him so, I love Him so,
I love Him so, He's so good to me.

4. He's com - ing soon, He's com - ing soon,
He's com - ing soon, He's so good to me.

5. God loves me so,
God loves me so,
God loves me so,
He's so good to me.

6. God answers prayer,
God answers prayer,
God answers prayer,
He's so good to me.

God Sees Me

Rebecca Edwards-Lesser — Rebecca Edwards-Lesser

1. God sees me when I work, God sees me when I play; God sees me when I sing a song, God sees me when I pray.

2. God sees me when I walk, God sees me when I run; God sees me when I am so sad, God sees when I have fun.

90 God Takes Care of Me

REBECCA EDWARDS-LESSER REBECCA EDWARDS-LESSER

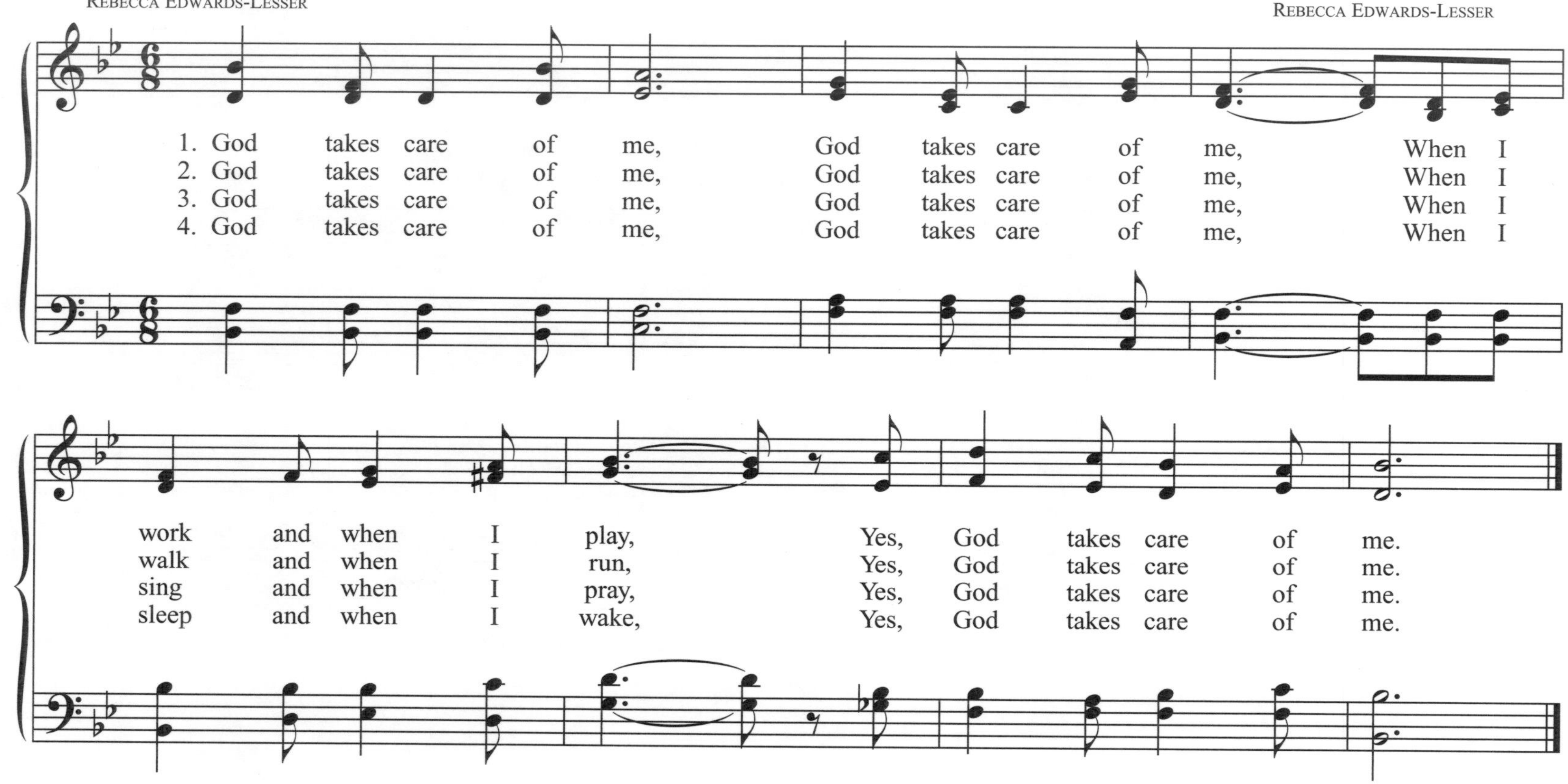

1. God takes care of me, God takes care of me, When I work and when I play, Yes, God takes care of me.
2. God takes care of me, God takes care of me, When I walk and when I run, Yes, God takes care of me.
3. God takes care of me, God takes care of me, When I sing and when I pray, Yes, God takes care of me.
4. God takes care of me, God takes care of me, When I sleep and when I wake, Yes, God takes care of me.

5. God takes care of me,
God takes care of me,
When I'm riding in a car,*
Yes, God takes care of me.

*bus

GRACE

GOD'S LOVE AND CARE

He Cares About You 91

BASED ON 1 PETER 5:7, RSV

JANET SAGE

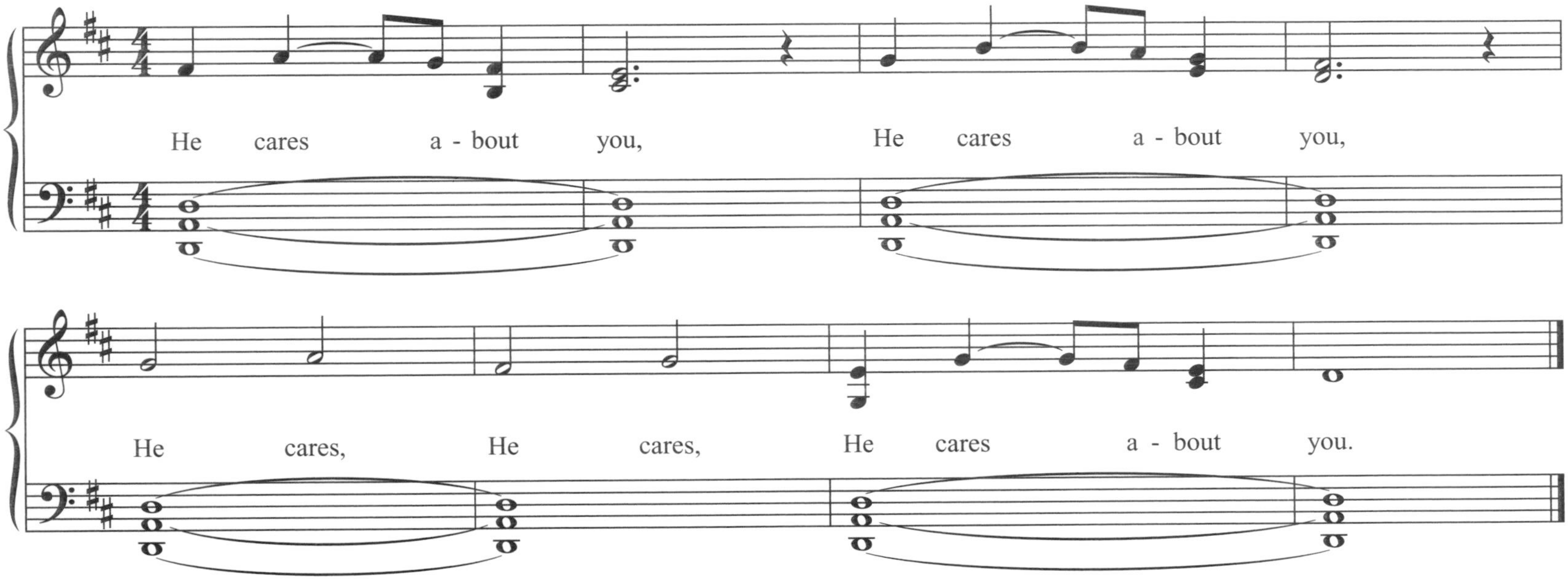

He cares a - bout you, He cares a - bout you,

He cares, He cares, He cares a - bout you.

Musical note: The drone of the left-hand accompaniment should help produce a peaceful feeling, portraying the reassurance we may find in the changeless care of Jesus.

Jesus Cares for You 92

1 PETER 5:7, ICB

BEGINNERS WRITERS GROUP / ARR. BY KENNETH D. LOGAN

Je - sus cares for you, Je - sus cares for you. He cares for you.

He's Able

Paul E. Paino Paul E. Paino

Fine
He's a - ble, He's a - ble, I know He's a - ble, I
know my Lord is a - ble to car - ry me through.
He's a - ble, He's a - ble, I know He's a - ble, I
know my Lord is a - ble to car - ry me through; He

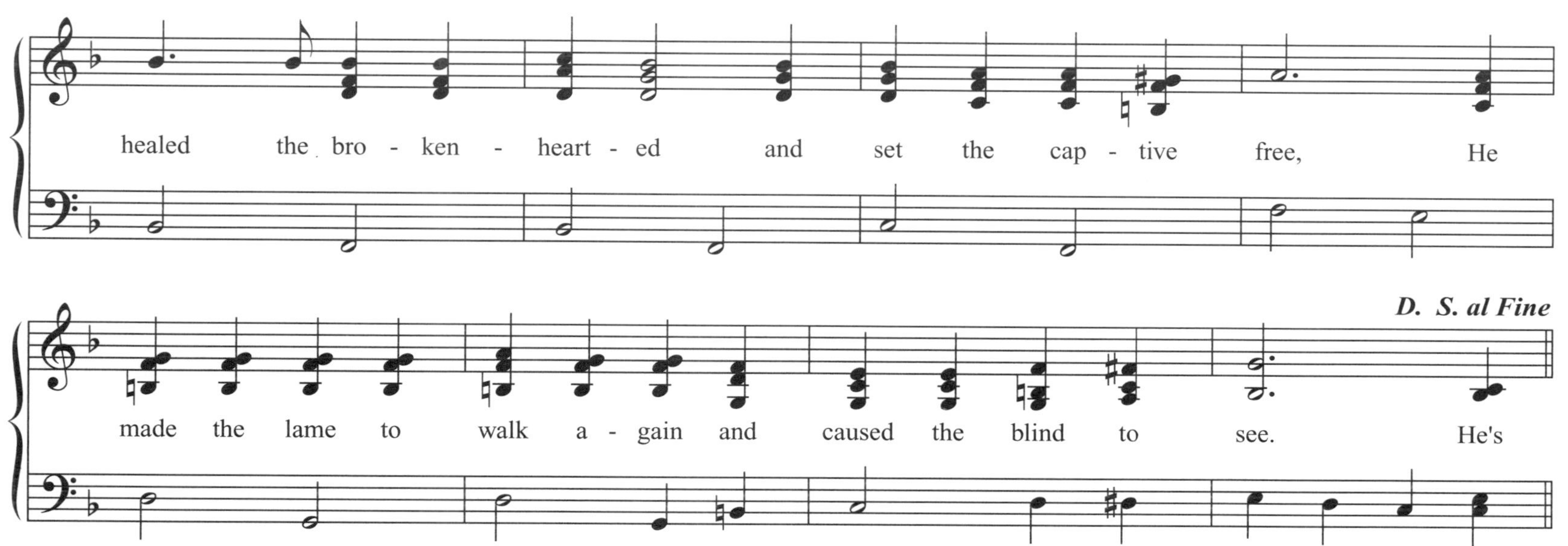
healed the bro - ken - heart - ed and set the cap - tive free, He
D. S. al Fine
made the lame to walk a - gain and caused the blind to see. He's

The Raindrops Fall 94

Mildred Adair — Mildred Adair

The rain-drops fall with a pit-ter, pat-ter, pit, Pit-ter, pat-ter, pit, pit-ter, pat-ter, pit, The rain - drops fall with a pit - ter, pat - ter, pit, Show - ing God's great love.

95 I Know That Jesus Loves Me

ADAPT. BY NOELENE JOHNSSON

TRADITIONAL / ARR. BY KENNETH D. LOGAN

I know that Je - sus loves me; The Bi - ble tells me so. And
so He gave me mo - ther* To help my love to grow.†

*father, brother, sister, sunshine, raisins, rainbows, squirrels (any soft toy)

† Variations for second verse:

He always watches o'er me
to keep me safe I know.

He always watches o'er me
to help my love to grow.

GRACE

GOD'S LOVE AND CARE

96

I'm So Small

Yvonne Scott — Yvonne Scott

1. Fa - ther God, I know You love me so, Fa - ther God, I know You care for me.
2. Fa - ther God, I'm small, but I love You so, Fa - ther God, I'm small, but I'll fol - low You.

Fa - ther God, I know You love me so, Fa - ther God, I'm small, but You care for me.
Fa - ther God, I'm small, but I love You so, Fa - ther God, I'm small, but I'll fol - low You.

97 I'm Special

Edwina Grice Neely — Edwina Grice Neely / Arr. by Kenneth D. Logan

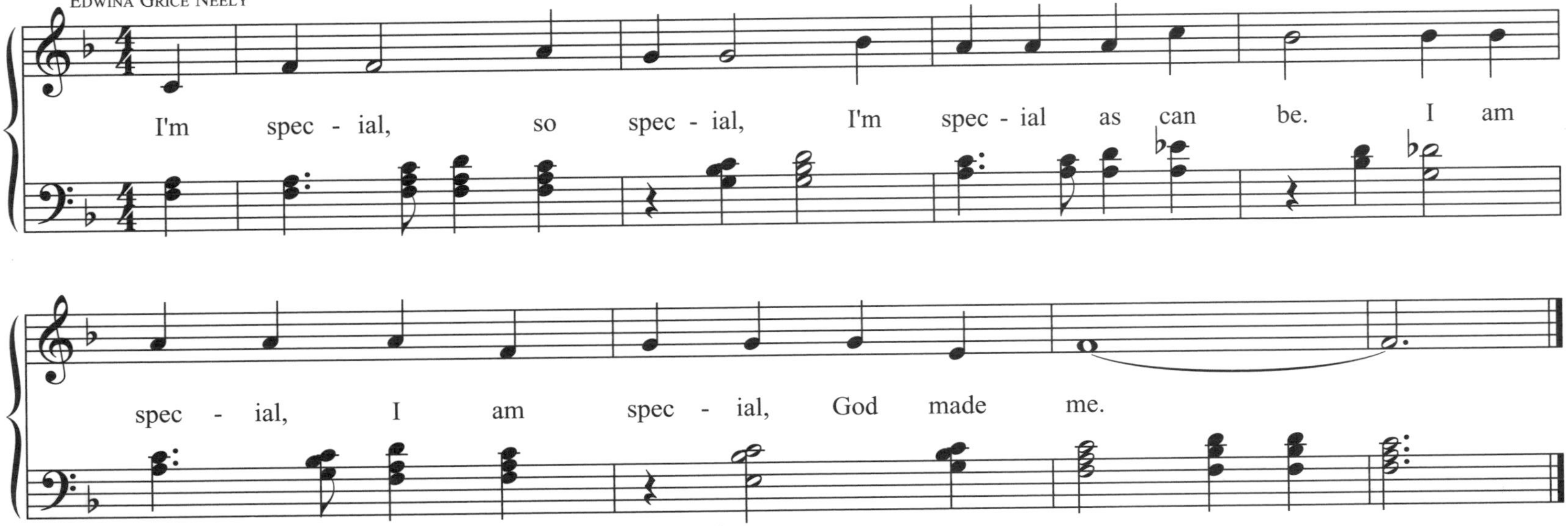

I'm spec - ial, so spec - ial, I'm spec - ial as can be. I am

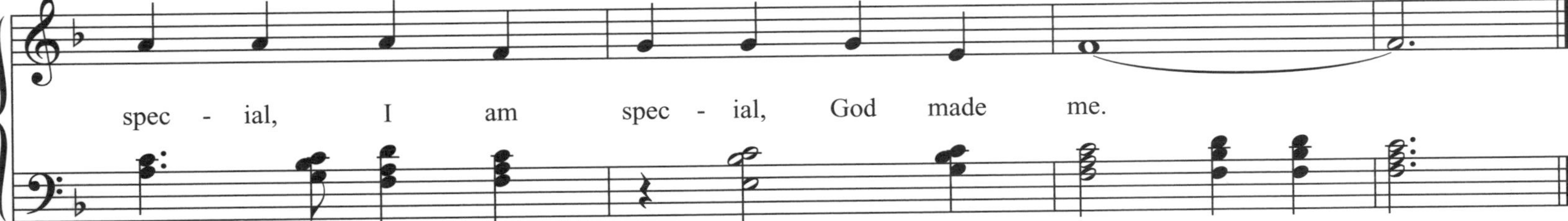
spec - ial, I am spec - ial, God made me.

It's About Grace

J. M. Herrington

J. M. Herrington

It's a-bout grace, grace, Je - sus took my place; It's a-bout love, love, He came down from a - bove.
Jus - tice, sin, and mer - cy meet at Cal - va-ry's tree. Je - sus shed His blood to save a sin - ner like me.
Be - cause of Je - sus' love, I am for - giv - en and free. Thank God for His a -
2nd time to Coda

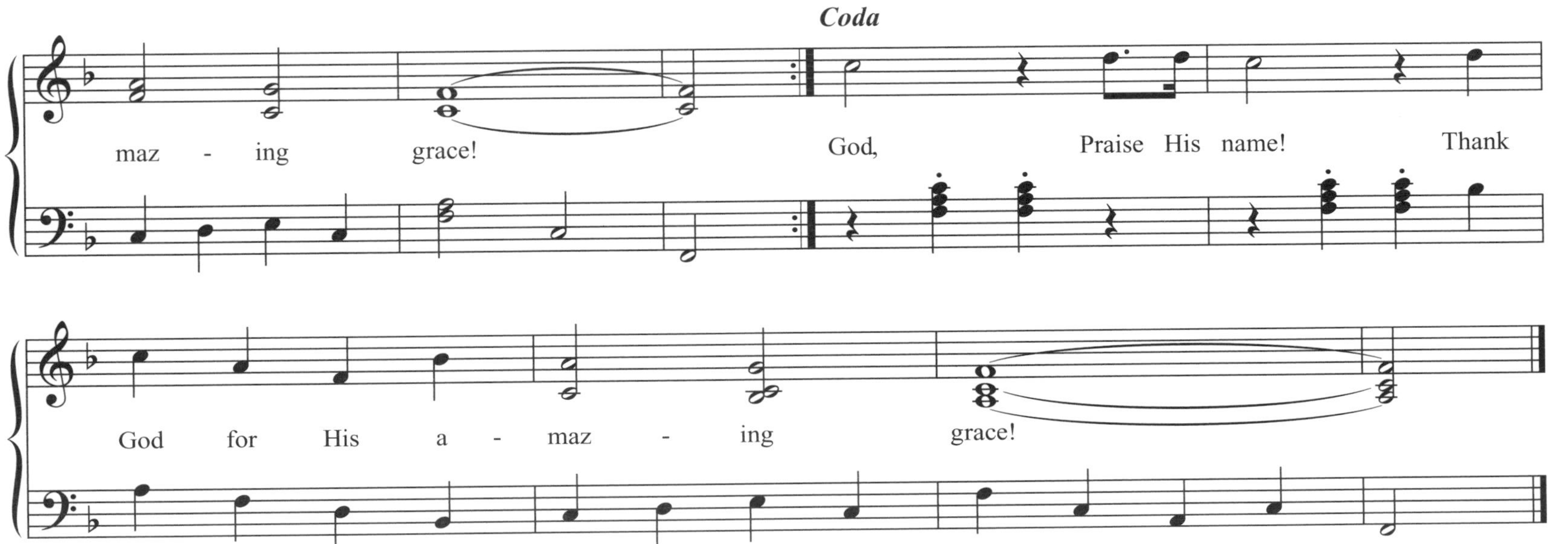
Coda
maz - ing grace!
God, Praise His name! Thank
God for His a - maz - ing grace!

Jesus Is Love 99

SUSAN DAVIS

SUSAN DAVIS

Love, Je - sus is love. Love, Je - sus is love. Je - sus loves
Bob - by* and Da - vid* and Su - sie* be - cause Je - sus is love.

*Other names may be used.

100 Jesus Cares for Me

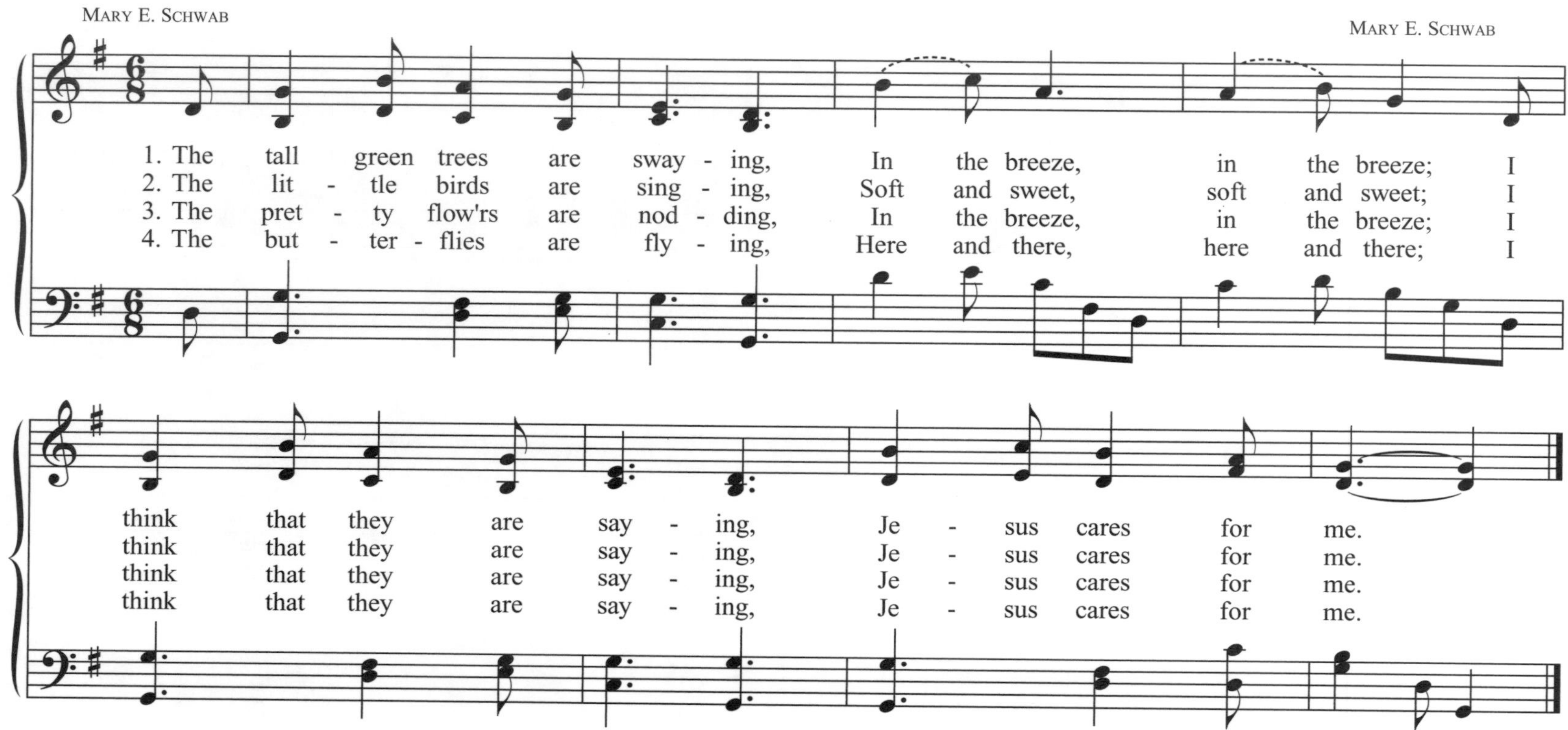
MARY E. SCHWAB
MARY E. SCHWAB
1. The tall green trees are sway - ing, In the breeze, in the breeze; I
2. The lit - tle birds are sing - ing, Soft and sweet, soft and sweet; I
3. The pret - ty flow'rs are nod - ding, In the breeze, in the breeze; I
4. The but - ter - flies are fly - ing, Here and there, here and there; I
think that they are say - ing, Je - sus cares for me.
think that they are say - ing, Je - sus cares for me.
think that they are say - ing, Je - sus cares for me.
think that they are say - ing, Je - sus cares for me.

5. The little cats are purring,
   Softly, softly,
   I think that they are saying,
   Jesus cares for me.

6. The little dogs are playing,
   'Neath the trees, 'neath the trees;
   I think that they are saying,
   Jesus cares for me.

Jesus Loves Even Me

Pamela Conn Beall / Susan Hagen Nipp

Pamela Conn Beall / Susan Hagen Nipp / Arr. by Kenneth D. Logan

8va
(bell-like)
I am so glad that Je - sus loves me, Je - sus loves me, Je - sus loves me,
(melody)
(8va)
I am so glad that Je - sus loves me, Je - sus loves e - ven me.

102 Jesus Loves Me

Anna Warner — William B. Bradbury

1. Je - sus loves me! this I know, For the Bi - ble tells me so;
2. Je - sus loves me; He will stay, Close be - side me all the way,
Lit - tle ones to Him be - long, They are weak, but He is strong.
If I love Him, by and by He will take me home on high.
REFRAIN
Yes, Je - sus loves me! Yes, Je - sus loves me!
Yes, Je - sus loves me! The Bi - ble tells me so.

Alternate ending, by Margaret Spivey, for second verse:
Whether I am big or small,
I know Jesus loves us all.

Jesus Loves Me

103

GENERAL CONFERENCE SABBATH SCHOOL DEPARTMENT

TRADITIONAL / ARR. BY KENNETH D. LOGAN

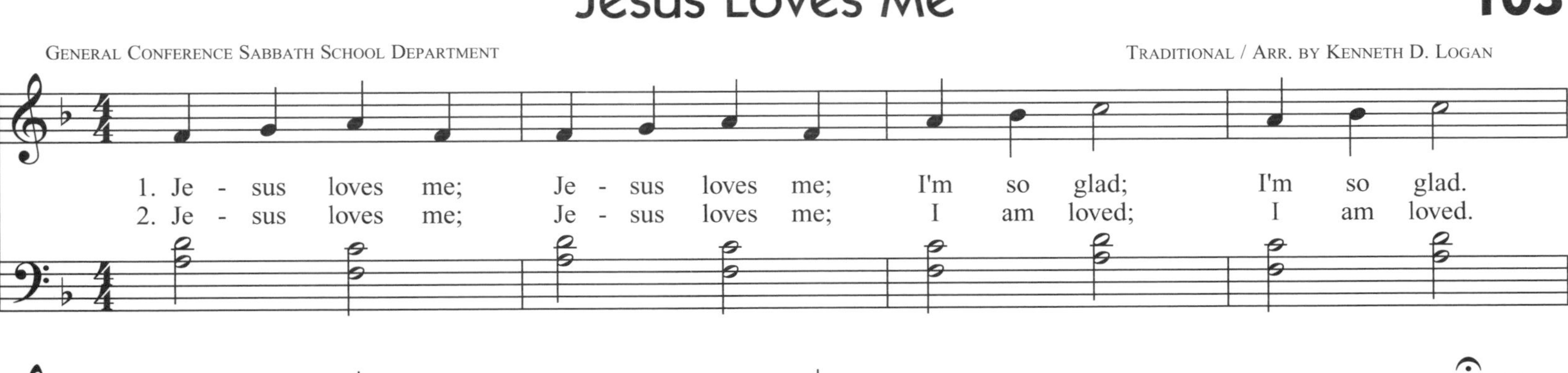
1. Je - sus loves me; Je - sus loves me; I'm so glad; I'm so glad.
2. Je - sus loves me; Je - sus loves me; I am loved; I am loved.

He will nev - er leave me; He will nev - er leave me. I feel safe, I feel safe.
He will nev - er leave me; He will nev - er leave me. I am loved; I am loved.

Jesus Loves Me More

104

JANET SAGE

JANET SAGE

1. I know my mom - my loves me, She loves me, she loves me; I know my mom - my loves me, But Je - sus loves me more.
2. I know my dad - dy loves me, He loves me, he loves me; I know my dad - dy loves me, But Je - sus loves me more.

105
Jesus Loves Me Much, Much More
Enid G. Thorson
Enid G. Thorson
Dad - dy loves me; Mo - ther loves me; Sis - ter loves me; Bro - ther loves me;
But Je - sus love me much, much more. Yes, Je - sus loves me much, much more.
© 1988 by Enid G. Thorson.
106
Jesus Loves the Children
George F. Root
Je - sus loves the lit - tle chil - dren, All the chil - dren of the world; Red and
Yel - low, Black and White, They are pre - cious in His sight— Je - sus loves the lit - tle chil - dren of the world.

Jesus Loves the Little Ones

107

Sidney E. Cox / Adapt. by Jean Harwood

Sidney E. Cox / Arr. by Harry Dixon Loes

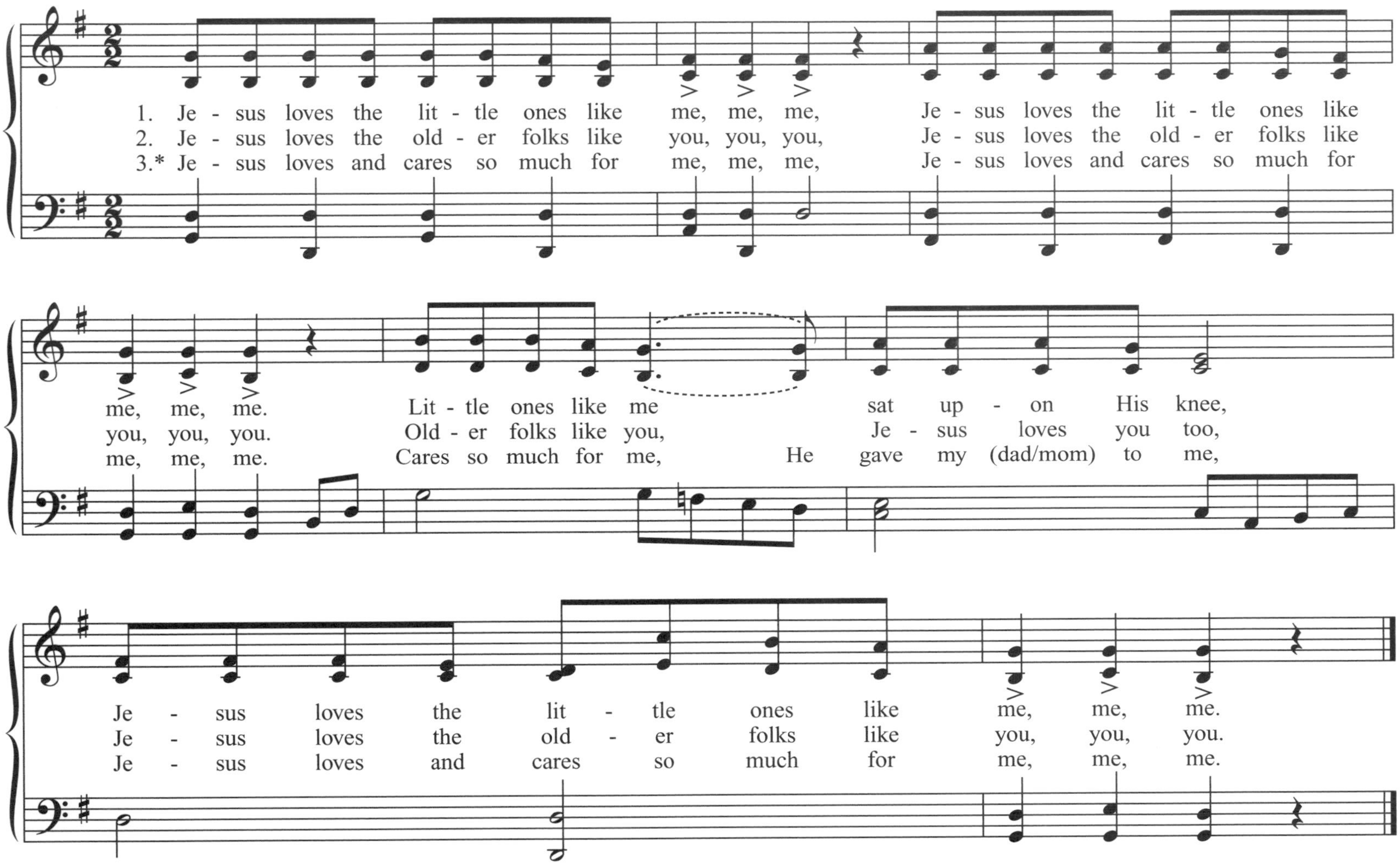

1. Je - sus loves the lit - tle ones like me, me, me, Je - sus loves the lit - tle ones like me, me, me. Lit - tle ones like me sat up - on His knee, Je - sus loves the lit - tle ones like me, me, me.

2. Je - sus loves the old - er folks like you, you, you, Je - sus loves the old - er folks like you, you, you. Old - er folks like you, Je - sus loves you too, Je - sus loves the old - er folks like you, you, you.

3.* Je - sus loves and cares so much for me, me, me, Je - sus loves and cares so much for me, me, me. Cares so much for me, He gave my (dad/mom) to me, Je - sus loves and cares so much for me, me, me.

*Verse 3 by Jean Harwood.

108
Jesus Never Fails
A. A. LUTHER
A. A. LUTHER
Je - sus nev - er fails, Je - sus nev - er fails;
Heav'n and earth may pass a - way, But Je - sus nev - er fails.
109
Jesus Sees Me
DOROTHY ROBISON
DOROTHY ROBISON / ARR. BY MARGARET EDGE
1. Je - sus sees me, yes, He sees me. Je - sus sees me night and day. Je - sus sees me, yes, He sees me, When I work and when I play.
2. Je - sus sees me, yes, He sees me. Je - sus sees when I o - bey. Je - sus sees me, yes, He sees me, Here in Sab - bath school to - day.

Jesus, Friend of Little Children 110

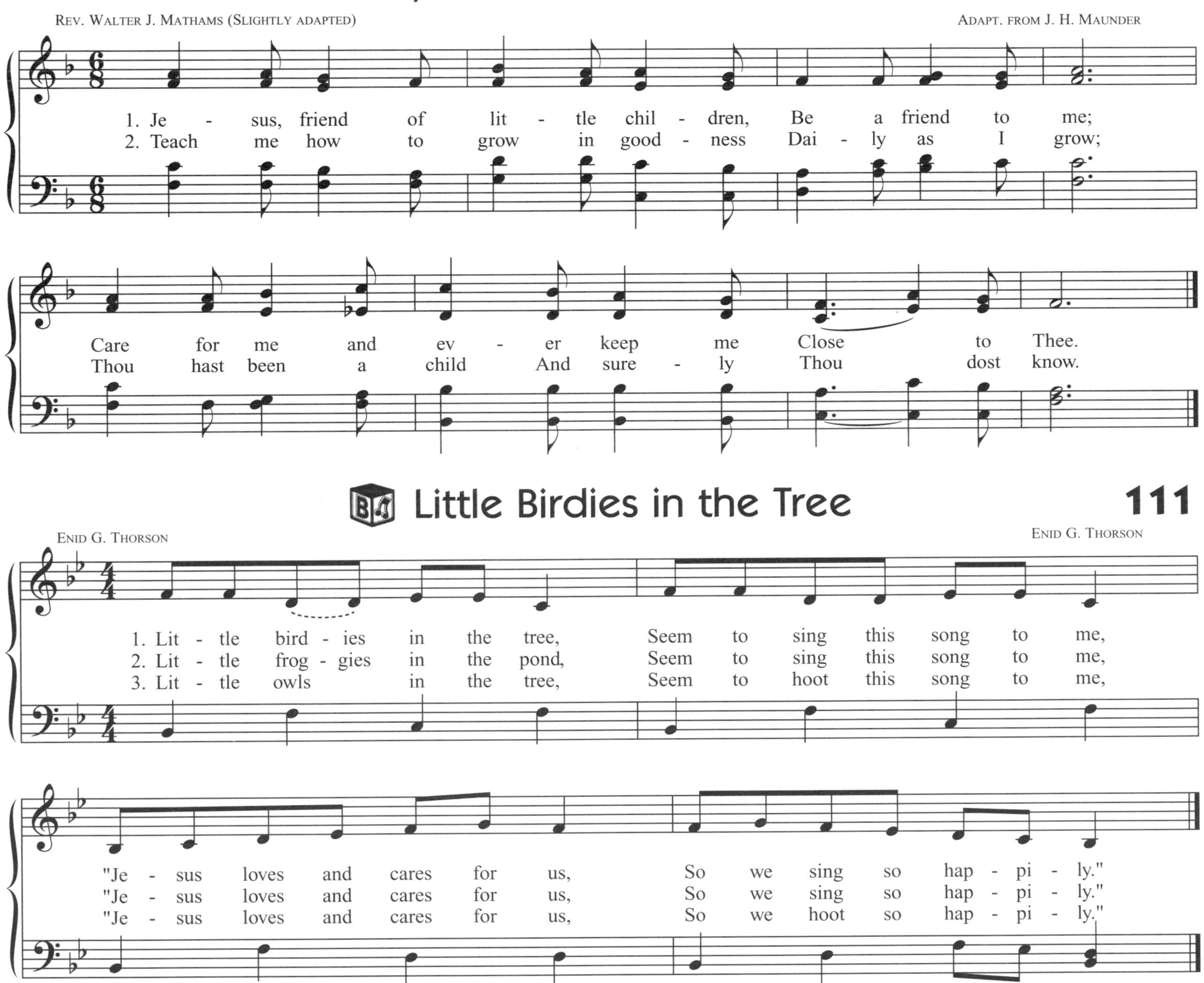
REV. WALTER J. MATHAMS (SLIGHTLY ADAPTED)
ADAPT. FROM J. H. MAUNDER
1. Je - sus, friend of lit - tle chil - dren, Be a friend to me;
2. Teach me how to grow in good - ness Dai - ly as I grow;
Care for me and ev - er keep me Close to Thee.
Thou hast been a child And sure - ly Thou dost know.
Little Birdies in the Tree 111
ENID G. THORSON
ENID G. THORSON
1. Lit - tle bird - ies in the tree, Seem to sing this song to me,
2. Lit - tle frog - gies in the pond, Seem to sing this song to me,
3. Lit - tle owls in the tree, Seem to hoot this song to me,
"Je - sus loves and cares for us, So we sing so hap - pi - ly."
"Je - sus loves and cares for us, So we sing so hap - pi - ly."
"Je - sus loves and cares for us, So we hoot so hap - pi - ly."

Use felt or plastic birds, trees, or other objects, varying the objects now and then.

112 My God Is So Great

UNKNOWN

ARR. BY LOIS C. HALL

My God is so great, so strong and so migh - ty, There's noth - ing my God can - not do! (clap, clap) My
God is so great, so strong and so migh - ty, There's noth - ing my God can - not do! (clap, clap) The
Stop here for beginners.
1 moun - tains are His, the 2 riv - ers are His, The 3 stars are His han - di - work too. My
God is so great, so strong and so migh - ty! There's noth - ing my God can - not do! For you! (spoken)

Actions:
1. Arms above head in shape of mountains.
2. Wiggle fingers and move side to side.
3. Hold hands up. Wiggle fingers and move them down.

The Big Blue Ocean

113

JANET SAGE — JANET SAGE

The big blue o - cean makes me think of Je - sus' love, The big blue o - cean, the big blue o - cean; The big blue o - cean makes me think of Je - sus' love; Let's learn of Je - sus at the o - cean!

114 The Shepherd Loves His Lambs

Enid G. Thorson

Enid G. Thorson

The Shep - herd loves His lambs, and Je - sus loves me. The
Shep - herd loves His lambs, and Je - sus loves me.

Use felt shepherd, sheep, and lambs. Children sing the song and put felt lambs beside the shepherd. Say "Jesus loves and takes care of us just as the Good Shepherd took care of the sheep and lambs." Put felt children beside a felt Jesus to emphasize His "loving care," not that they are lambs.

The Trees Are Gently Swaying (Motion Song) 115

MILDRED ADAIR | MILDRED ADAIR

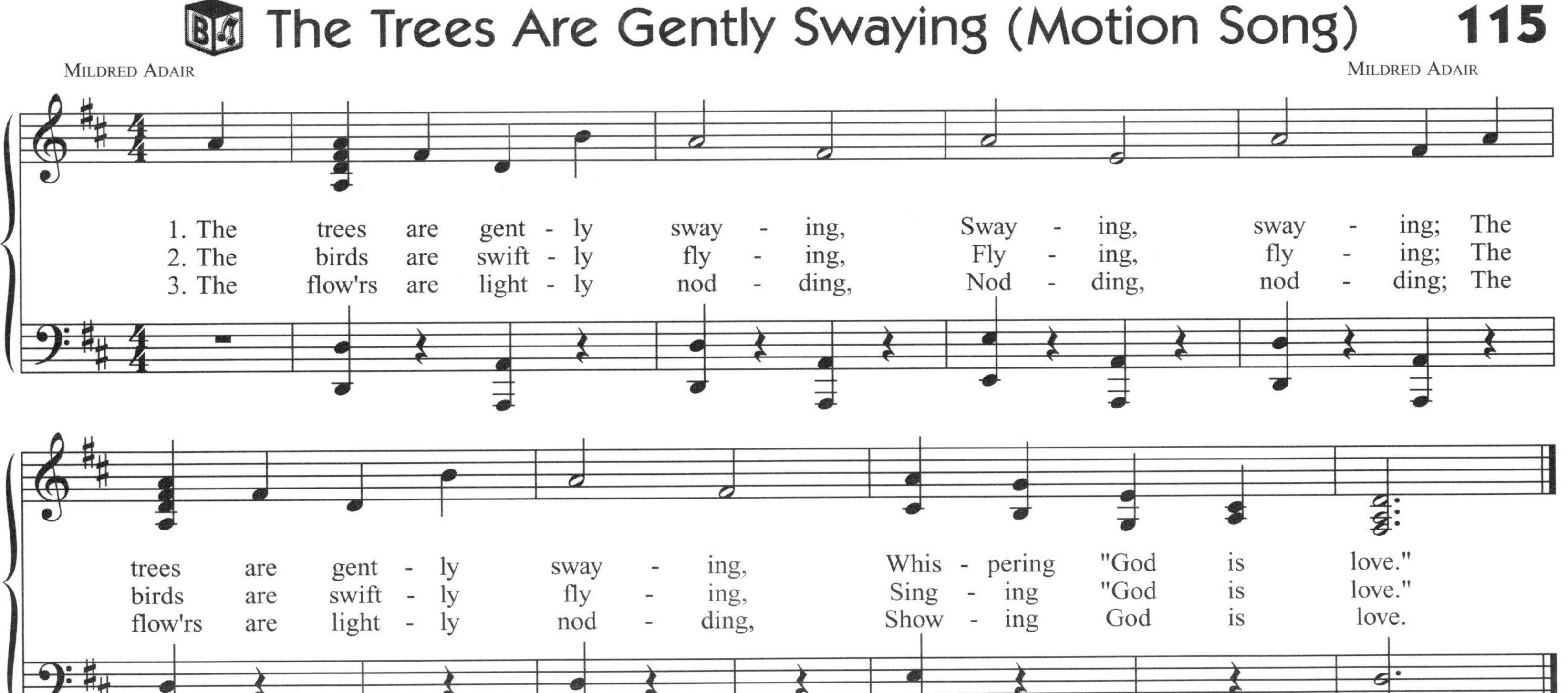
1. The trees are gent - ly sway - ing, Sway - ing, sway - ing; The
2. The birds are swift - ly fly - ing, Fly - ing, fly - ing; The
3. The flow'rs are light - ly nod - ding, Nod - ding, nod - ding; The
trees are gent - ly sway - ing, Whis - pering "God is love."
birds are swift - ly fly - ing, Sing - ing "God is love."
flow'rs are light - ly nod - ding, Show - ing God is love.

GRACE

GOD'S LOVE AND CARE

116 Then Jesus Came

General Conference Sabbath School Department

Kenneth D. Logan

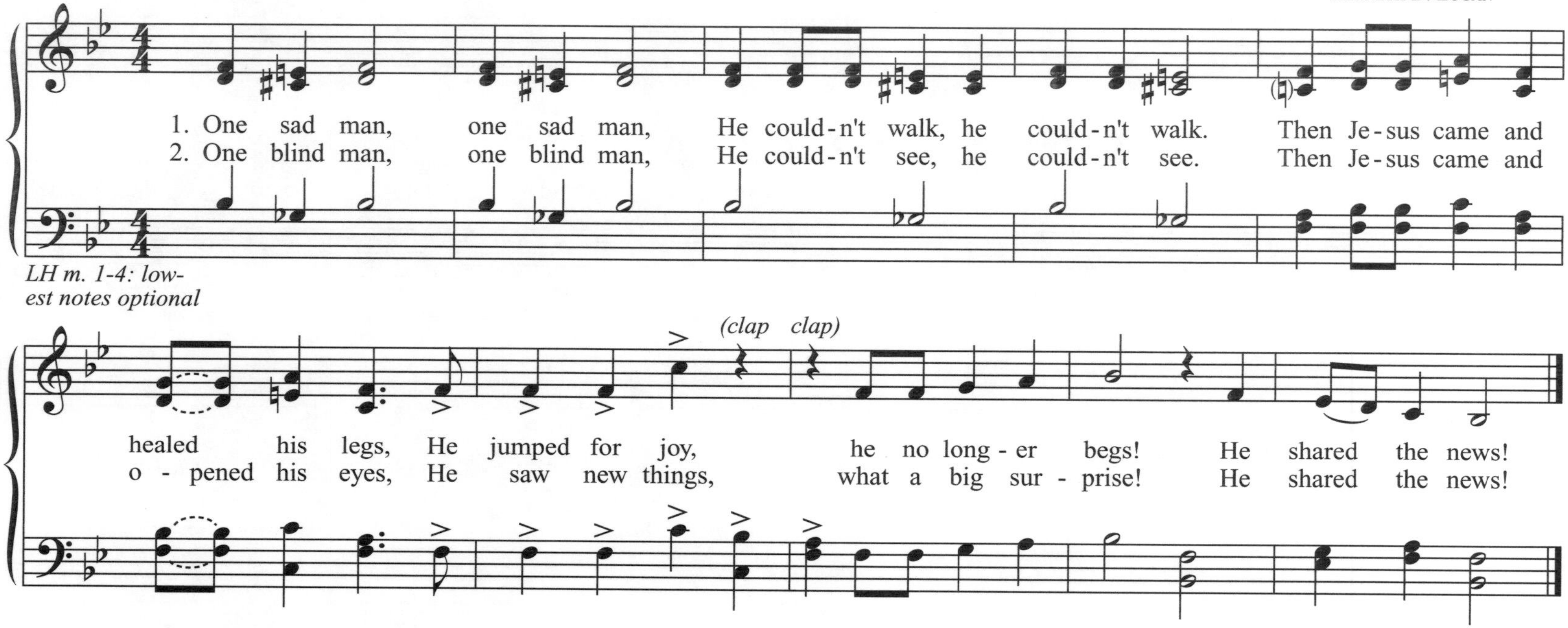

1. One sad man, one sad man, He could-n't walk, he could-n't walk. Then Je-sus came and healed his legs, He jumped for joy, (clap clap) he no long-er begs! He shared the news!
2. One blind man, one blind man, He could-n't see, he could-n't see. Then Je-sus came and o-pened his eyes, He saw new things, (clap clap) what a big sur-prise! He shared the news!

LH m. 1-4: lowest notes optional

Who Am I?

Janet Sage — Janet Sage

Who am I? Who am I? Some - one spe - cial to Je - sus;
I am ________, I am ________. I am spe-cial to Je - sus!

Pianist: Keep the accompaniment smooth and flowing, but not too fast.

Leader: One of the most important concepts children need to form is their own self-image. They need to be sure they're loved by someone who considers them a very special person. This song helps the children to sense their personal value to Jesus. Not all children's names will fit easily into the syllabic distribution called for in this rhythm, although most common names will work nicely. Rhythmic manipulation may be necessary to make some names fit, but it can be done.

GOD'S LOVE AND CARE

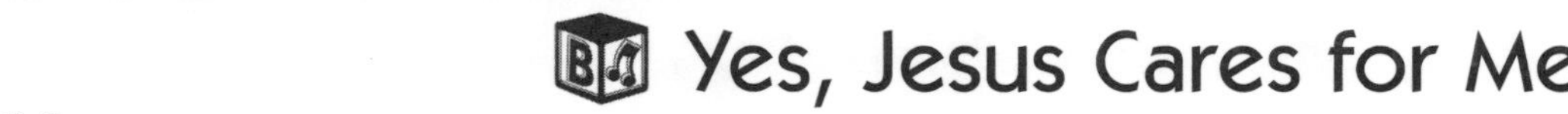

118 Yes, Jesus Cares for Me

ENID G. THORSON — ENID G. THORSON

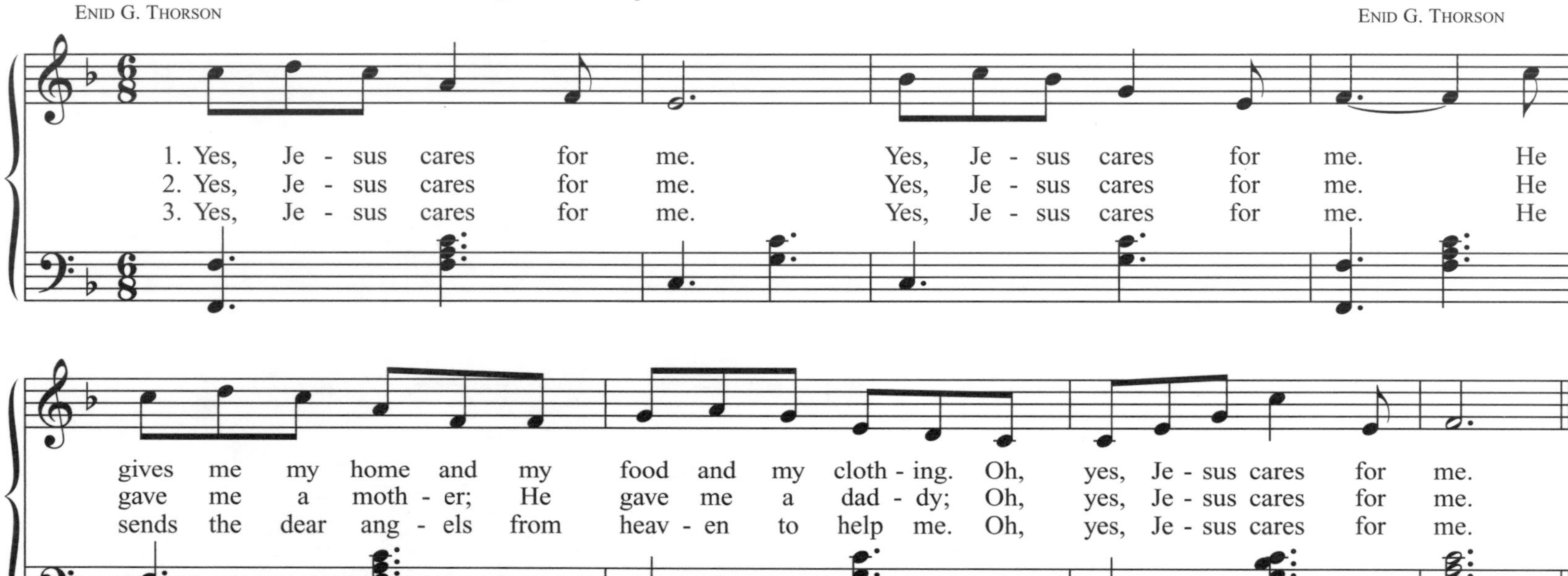
1. Yes, Je - sus cares for me. Yes, Je - sus cares for me. He gives me my home and my food and my cloth - ing. Oh, yes, Je - sus cares for me.
2. Yes, Je - sus cares for me. Yes, Je - sus cares for me. He gave me a moth - er; He gave me a dad - dy; Oh, yes, Je - sus cares for me.
3. Yes, Je - sus cares for me. Yes, Je - sus cares for me. He sends the dear ang - els from heav - en to help me. Oh, yes, Je - sus cares for me.

Leader: You can illustrate with real articles, persons, felts, or pictures. Jesus helps Mother and Daddy to get these things for us.

All Night, All Day

119

Arr. by Kenneth D. Logan

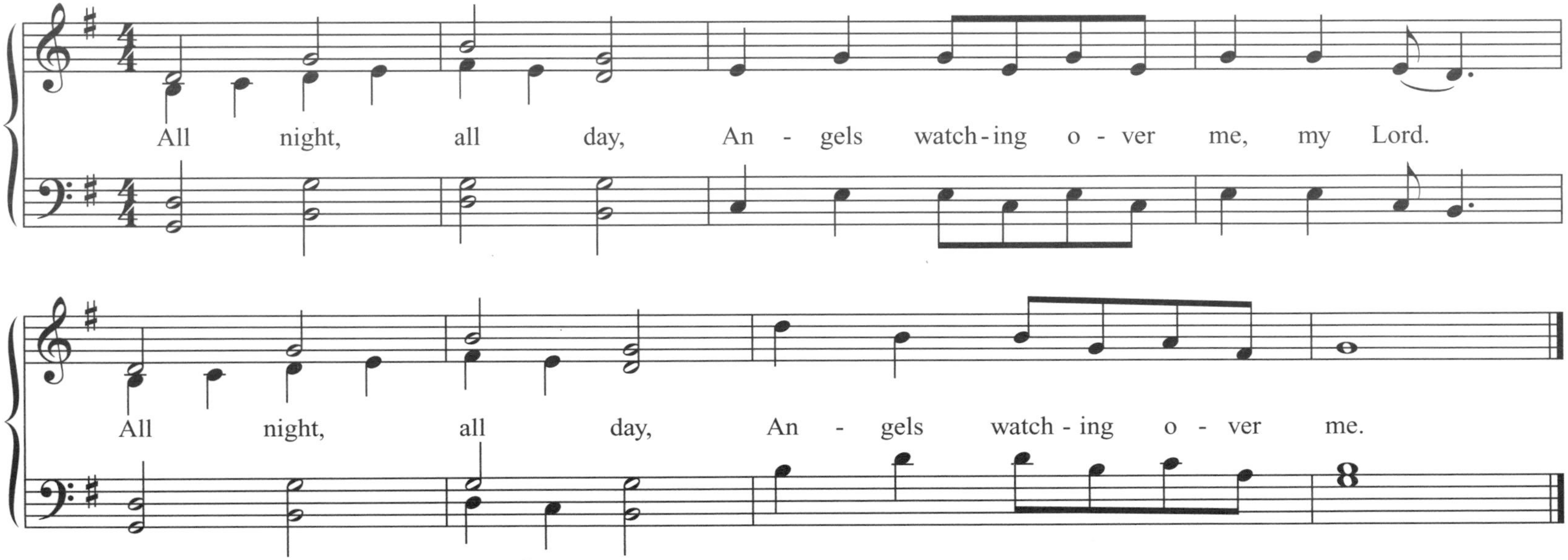

All night, all day, An - gels watch-ing o - ver me, my Lord.
All night, all day, An - gels watch - ing o - ver me.

An Angel Came Down

120

Janet Sage

Janet Sage

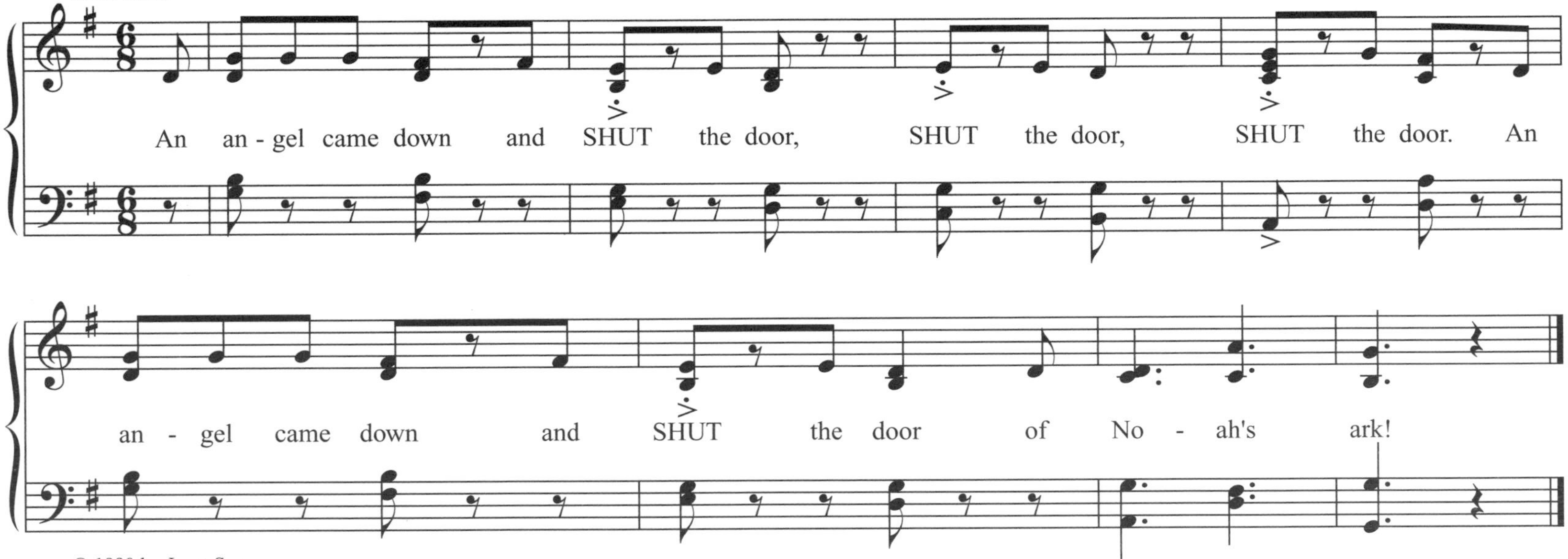

An an - gel came down and SHUT the door, SHUT the door, SHUT the door. An
an - gel came down and SHUT the door of No - ah's ark!

121 Angels

Doris Nielson — Doris Nielson

1. An - gels came to Ja - cob Down the lad - der steep;
2. An - gels cared for Dan - iel In the li - ons' den;
3. An - gels showed the shep - herds Where Baby Je - sus lay;
4. An - gels watched o'er Je - sus On the E - gypt flight;
An - gels come to us now If God's Word we keep.
An - gels care for us now Just as they did then.
An - gels now will help us If we ask and pray.
An - gels watch o'er us now Through the day and night.

At Sleep or at Play, God Sees

122

Mildred Adair
Mildred Adair
1. At sleep or at play, God sees, God sees, By night or by day, God sees, He sees.
2. When good and when true, God knows, God knows, His will try to do, God knows, He knows.
3. A soft whis-pered prayer, God hears, God hears, A song bright and fair, God hears, He hears.
Carol Greene
Johannes Brahms, adapted
Gently
1. The good shep-herd watch-es, So sheep may safe-ly feed. He keeps them from dan-ger And gives them all they need.
2. Lord Je-sus, our Shep-herd, Will watch us all our days. He'll keep us from dan-ger And lead us in God's ways.

The Good Shepherd

123

Leader: Pretend to be a shepherd and lead the children as your sheep. "Come over here, little sheep. Here's some really good grass to eat. Oh, oh! There's a bear! Get out of here, you bear!" Explain that Jesus lovingly protects us as His little lambs and gives us everything we need.

124 God's Angels Care for Me

Cora Landrum Pendleton

Cora Landrum Pendleton

God sends His an-gels to watch o-ver me, When I sleep, when I play.
God sends His an-gels to watch o-ver me, When it's dark, when it's day.
An-gels know all that I do and say. If I'm bad, they're sad! So sad!
An-gels know all that I do and say. If I'm good, they're glad! They're glad!

GRACE

God's Protection

He's Got the Whole World in His Hands

American Spiritual

Traditional

1. He's got the whole world in His hands, He's got the
2. He's got the wind and the rain in His hands, He's got the
3. He's got the ti - ny lit - tle ba - by in His hands, He's got the
4. He's got you and me, bro - ther, in His hands, He's got
whole wide world in His hands, He's got the whole world
sun and the moon in His hands, He's got the wind and the rain
ti - ny lit - tle ba - by in His hands, He's got the ti - ny lit - tle ba - by
you and me, sis - ter, in His hands, He's got you and me, bro - ther,
in His hands, He's got the whole world in His hands.
in His hands, He's got the whole world in His hands.
in His hands, He's got the whole world in His hands.
in His hands, He's got the whole world in His hands.

126 Jesus Is Near

Jackie Bishop

Traditional / Arr. by Kenneth D. Logan

Rock - a - bye ba - by, Je - sus is near,
While you are sleep - ing we will not fear.
Je - sus is watch - ing; He's al - ways here,
Rock - a - bye ba - by, rock - a - bye dear.
(with gently rocking motion)

Grace

God's Protection

A Real Little Bear to Play With

127

ROSALIE BLACKMORE

ROSALIE BLACKMORE

1. A real lit - tle bear to play with, A real lit - tle bear there'll be. A real lit - tle bear in the new earth, And the lit - tle bear won't hurt me! A
2. A real big li - on to play with, A real big li - on there'll be. A real big li - on in the new earth, And the big li - on won't hurt me! A
3. A real lit - tle squir - rel to play with, A real lit - tle squir - rel there'll be. A real lit - tle squir - rel in the new earth, And the lit - tle squir - rel won't hurt me! A
1.
2.
new earth, And he won't be a - fraid of me!
new earth, And it won't be a - fraid of me!
new earth, And it won't be a - fraid of me!

GRACE

HEAVEN

128 Alway

VIRGINIA CASON — VIRGINIA CASON / ARR. BY WAYNE HOOPER

I may not be ver - y tall, But I can love Je - sus best of all! And
when He comes on that hap - py day, Then I'll be with Him al - way!

129 On the Streets of Gold

THELMA H. WILSON / JEAN DILLOW PAYNE — THELMA H. WILSON / JEAN DILLOW PAYNE

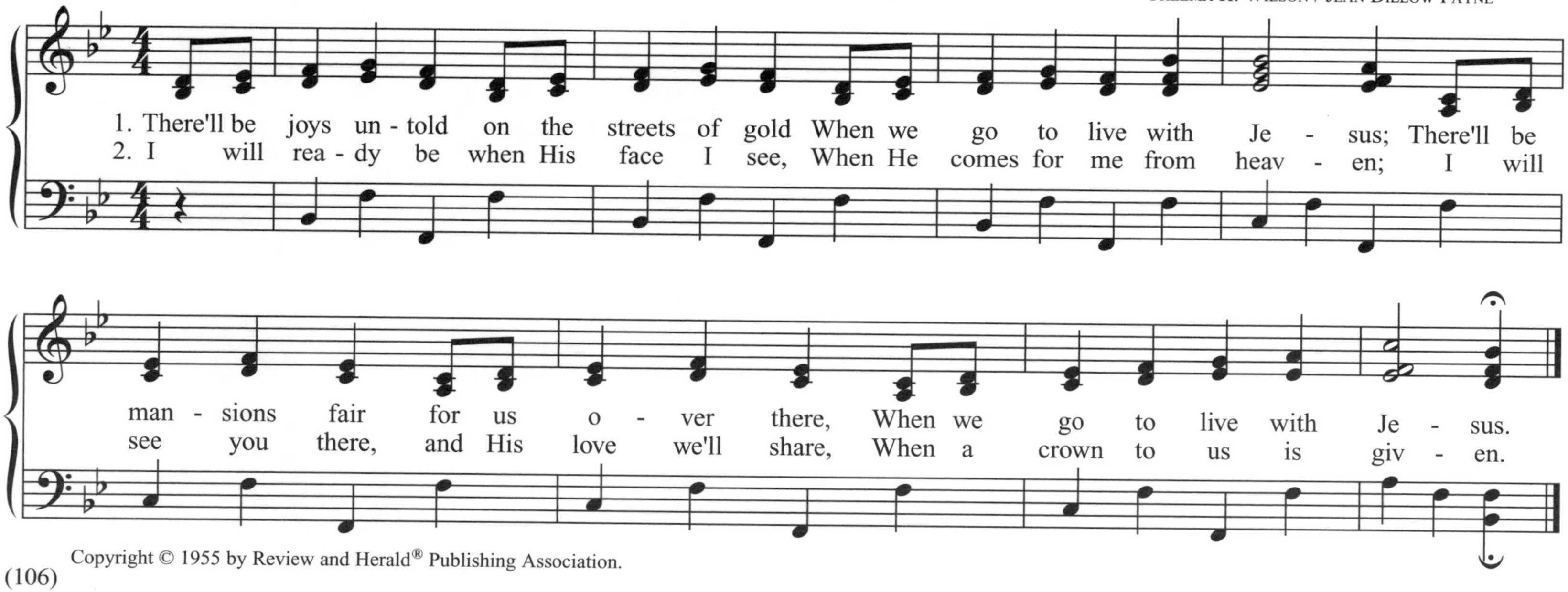

1. There'll be joys un - told on the streets of gold When we go to live with Je - sus; There'll be
man - sions fair for us o - ver there, When we go to live with Je - sus.

2. I will rea - dy be when His face I see, When He comes for me from heav - en; I will
see you there, and His love we'll share, When a crown to us is giv - en.

Animals in Heaven

UNKNOWN

UNKNOWN

1. There'll be li - ons there, and a big brown bear, and I'm sure there'll be a tall gi -
2. All the dogs bow - wow, and the cats me - ow, and the roo - sters cock - a - doo - dle -

raffe. There'll be bun - nies too, and a kang - a - roo, great big
doo. All the hens cluck - cluck, and the ducks quack - quack, and the

el - e - phants, lit - tle mon - keys, too. And we'll all be hap - py up in heav - en.
cows moo - moo, and the sheep baa - baa. And the tur - keys gob - ble, gob - ble, gob - ble.

131 Heaven Is a Happy Place

Ruby E. Dubois

Ruby E. Dubois
1. Heav - en is a hap - py place; Heav - en is a hap - py place;
2. Je - sus said there'll be no tears; Je - sus said there'll be no tears;
3. Je - sus said we'll not be sick; Je - sus said we'll not be sick;
4. Je - sus said we'll not get hurt; Je - sus said we'll not get hurt;
Heav - en is a hap - py place; O I want to be there.
Je - sus said there'll be no tears When we get to heav - en.
Je - sus said we'll not be sick When we get to heav - en.
Je - sus said we'll not get hurt When we get to heav - en.

5. Jesus said we'll play with lions;
Jesus said we'll play with lions;
Jesus said we'll play with lions
When we get to heaven.

Grace

Heaven

I Will Wear a Crown

A. T. Hardy
Music by A. T. Hardy / Based on old tune
1. I will wear a crown in my Fa - ther's house, In my Fa - ther's house,
2. I will wear a robe in my Fa - ther's house, In my Fa - ther's house,
3. I will play a harp in my Fa - ther's house, In my Fa - ther's house,
in my Fa-ther's house, I will wear a crown in my Fa-ther's house. There'll be JOY! JOY! JOY!
in my Fa-ther's house, I will wear a robe in my Fa-ther's house. There'll be JOY! JOY! JOY!
in my Fa-ther's house, I will play a harp in my Fa-ther's house. There'll be JOY! JOY! JOY!

133 I'll Meet You in Heaven

MARILYN SCHOLES
MARILYN SCHOLES
Be hap - py, be kind, be lov - ing, be true. I'll
meet you in heav - en, and live up there with you.

Have a large door behind which a child may stand. Have the children close their eyes while the leader touches a child on the head and asks him or her to go behind the door. Open the door as you say the following verse, written by the author of the song:

Whom will I see in heaven?
Who'll live in a mansion fair?
Let's open the door and look inside.
Why, ______________ is living there.

After saying the verse, sing the song. This may be done several times. Each time mention the name of the child who is standing behind the door.

Jesus Is Building Mansions

134

JEAN DILLOW PAYNE | JEAN DILLOW PAYNE

Je - sus is build - ing beau - ti - ful man - sions; He's build - ing man - sions for me o - ver there. Je - sus is com - ing to take us to heav - en, To dwell in those man - sions with Him ev - er - more.

135 Sabbath in Heaven

BILLE K. BURDICK
BILLE K. BURDICK
Some day we'll keep Sab-bath in heav - en. Some day we'll see Je - sus there. I
know we'll love ev-'ry-thing God has made. I know we'll be hap - py there.

GRACE

HEAVEN

Jesus Was a Little Child

JACQUELINE McDONALD — JACQUELINE McDONALD

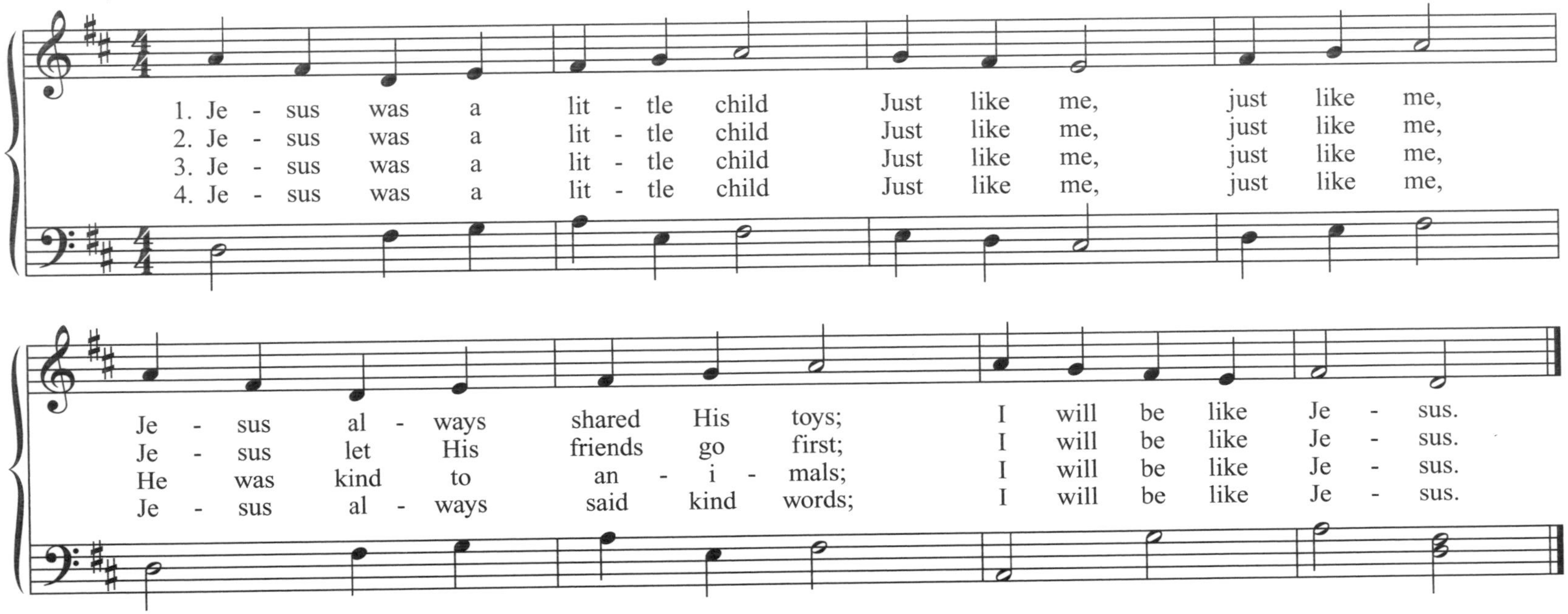

1. Jesus was a little child Just like me, just like me,
Jesus always shared His toys; I will be like Jesus.

2. Jesus was a little child Just like me, just like me,
Jesus let His friends go first; I will be like Jesus.

3. Jesus was a little child Just like me, just like me,
He was kind to animals; I will be like Jesus.

4. Jesus was a little child Just like me, just like me,
Jesus always said kind words; I will be like Jesus.

*or daddy

5. Jesus was a little child
Just like me, just like me,
Jesus helped His mommy* work;
I will be like Jesus.

6. Jesus was a little child
Just like me, just like me,
Jesus picked up all His toys;
I will be like Jesus.

137 Just a Little Donkey

NANCY J. STAGL-SCHIPPMANN

NANCY J. STAGL-SCHIPPMANN

1. Just a lit-tle don-key, ve-ry young was he; But the lov-ing Je-sus need-ed him, you see.
2. Just a lit-tle don-key Je-sus rode to town. Chil-dren sang, "Ho-san-na," cast-ing palm leaves down.

Felt board illustration of story needed.

138 The Sharing Song

GENERAL CONFERENCE SABBATH SCHOOL DEPARTMENT

TRADITIONAL / ARR. BY KENNETH D. LOGAN

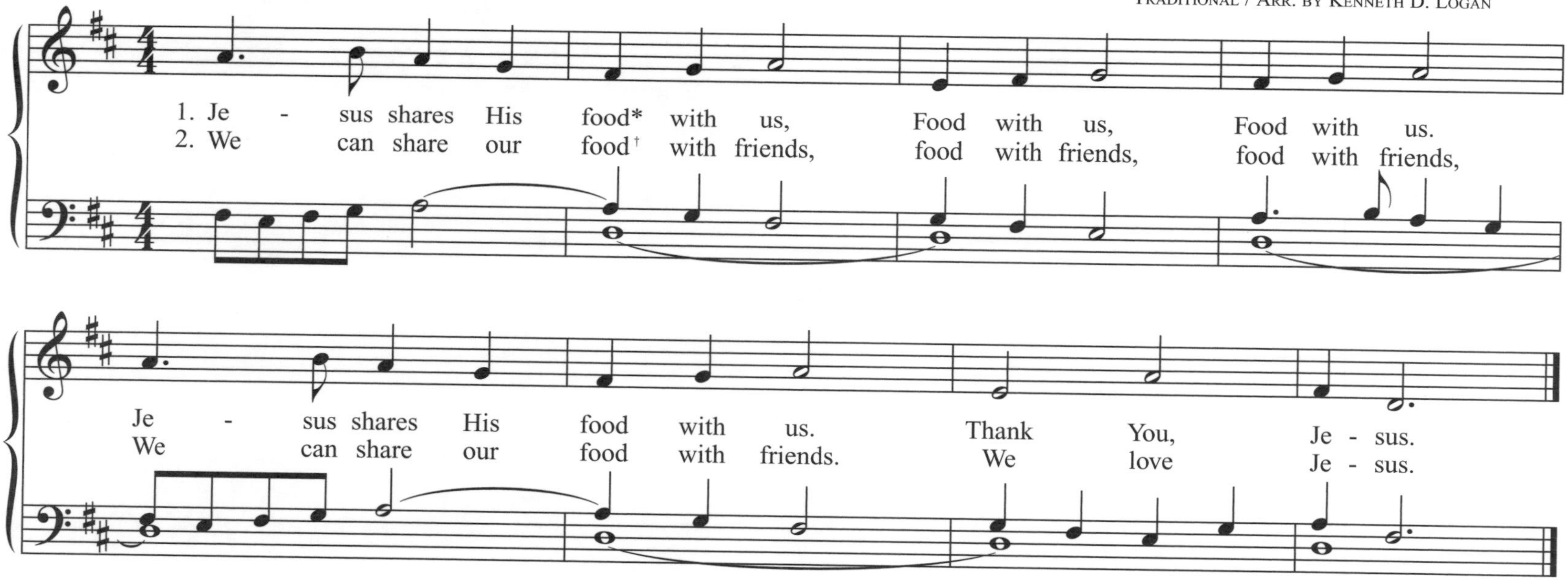

1. Je - sus shares His food* with us, Food with us, Food with us.
2. We can share our food† with friends, food with friends, food with friends,

Je - sus shares His food with us. Thank You, Je - sus.
We can share our food with friends. We love Je - sus.

*Substitute other words, such a "love."
† Substitute other words, such as "toys."

Things Jesus Liked When He Was a Child

139

Marilyn Scholes — Marilyn Scholes

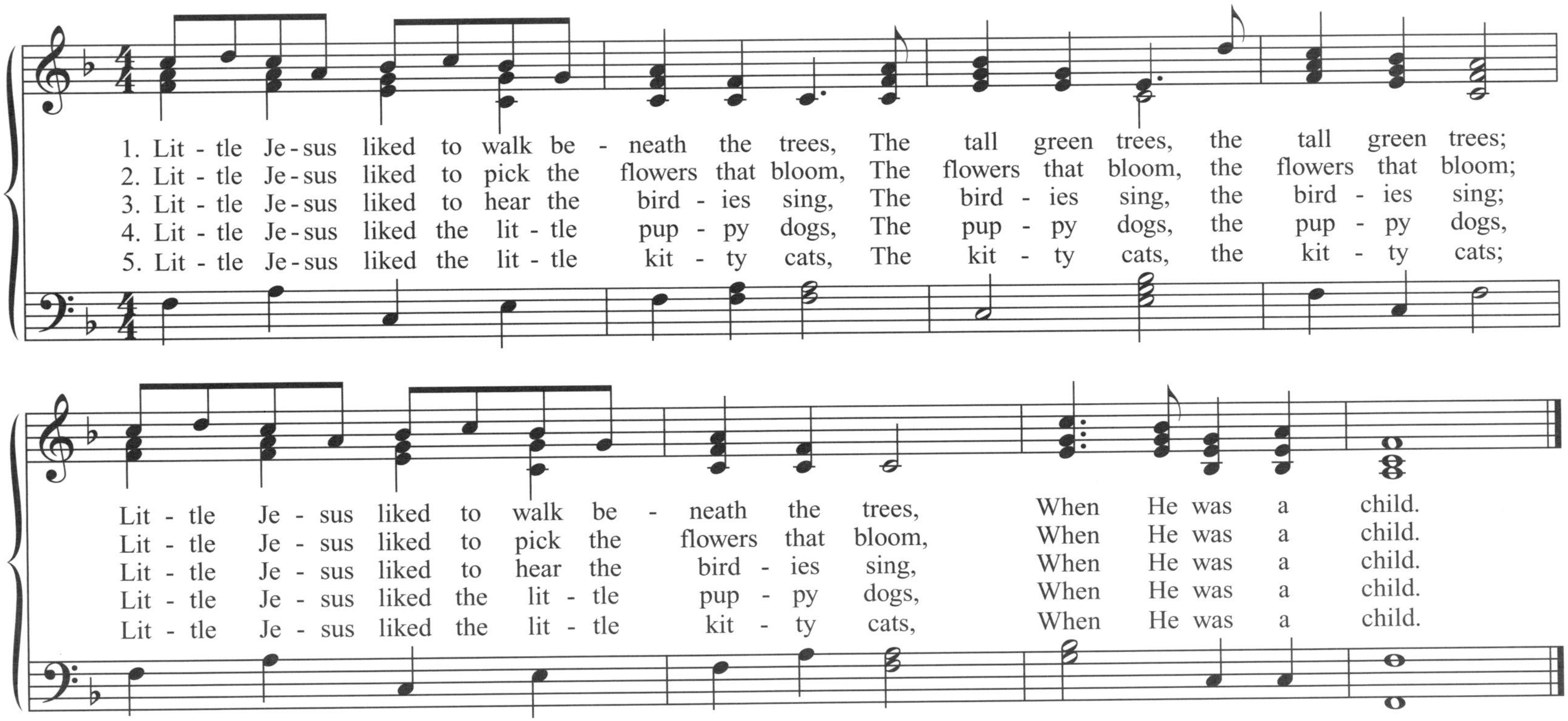

1. Little Jesus liked to walk beneath the trees, The tall green trees, the tall green trees;
Little Jesus liked to walk beneath the trees, When He was a child.

2. Little Jesus liked to pick the flowers that bloom, The flowers that bloom, the flowers that bloom;
Little Jesus liked to pick the flowers that bloom, When He was a child.

3. Little Jesus liked to hear the birdies sing, The birdies sing, the birdies sing;
Little Jesus liked to hear the birdies sing, When He was a child.

4. Little Jesus liked the little puppy dogs, The puppy dogs, the puppy dogs,
Little Jesus liked the little puppy dogs, When He was a child.

5. Little Jesus liked the little kitty cats, The kitty cats, the kitty cats;
Little Jesus liked the little kitty cats, When He was a child.

140 Angels Singing

Virginia Cason / Adapt. by General Conference Sabbath School Department

Virginia Cason / Arr. by Wayne Hooper

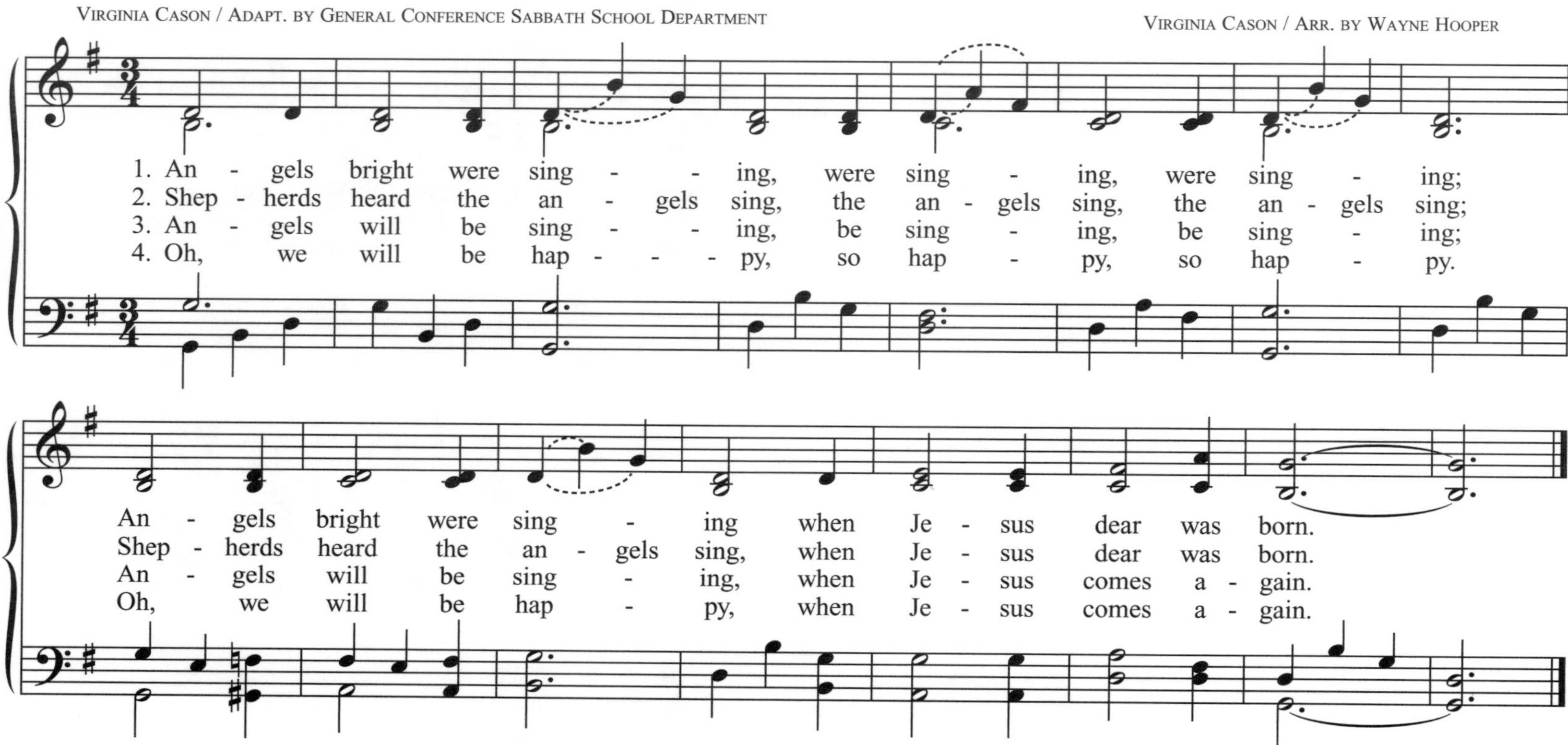
1. An - gels bright were sing - - ing, were sing - ing, were sing - ing;
2. Shep - herds heard the an - gels sing, the an - gels sing, the an - gels sing;
3. An - gels will be sing - - ing, be sing - ing, be sing - ing;
4. Oh, we will be hap - - - py, so hap - py, so hap - py.
An - gels bright were sing - ing when Je - sus dear was born.
Shep - herds heard the an - gels sing, when Je - sus dear was born.
An - gels will be sing - ing, when Je - sus comes a - gain.
Oh, we will be hap - py, when Je - sus comes a - gain.

5. Wise men came to seek Him,
to seek Him, to seek Him;
Wise men came to seek Him,
to bring Him gifts so fine.

Away in a Manger

MARTIN LUTHER
MARTIN LUTHER
1. A - way in a man - ger, No crib for a bed, The lit - tle Lord Je - sus Laid down His sweet head; The stars in the sky Looked down where He lay, The lit - tle Lord Je - sus, A - sleep on the hay.
2. The cat - tle are low - ing, The Ba - by a - wakes, But lit - tle Lord Je - sus, No cry - ing He makes; I love Thee, Lord Je - sus! Look down from the sky, And stay by my cra - dle, Till morn - ing is nigh.
3. Be near me, Lord Je - sus, I ask Thee to stay Close by me for - ev - er, And love me, I pray; Bless all the dear chil - dren In Thy ten - der care, Pre - pare us for heav - en, To live with Thee there.

GRACE

JESUS' BIRTH

142 Baby Jesus

JANET SAGE
JANET SAGE
Ba - by Je - sus, sweet Ba - by Je - sus, Ba - by Je - sus, I love you.

Pianist: Play the piece slowly and softly. The open chords in the left hand emphasize the song's sweet simplicity. Do not fill them in or add extra chords to the measures.

Leader: The pure minor mode has been used for this song. Do not be afraid to use it with beginning children. There is a lovely sweetness in this minor sound that the little ones accept readily. This lullaby follows the same basic style of the beloved Christmas carol "What Child Is This?" ("Greensleeves").

143 Christmas Star

JANET SAGE

JANET SAGE

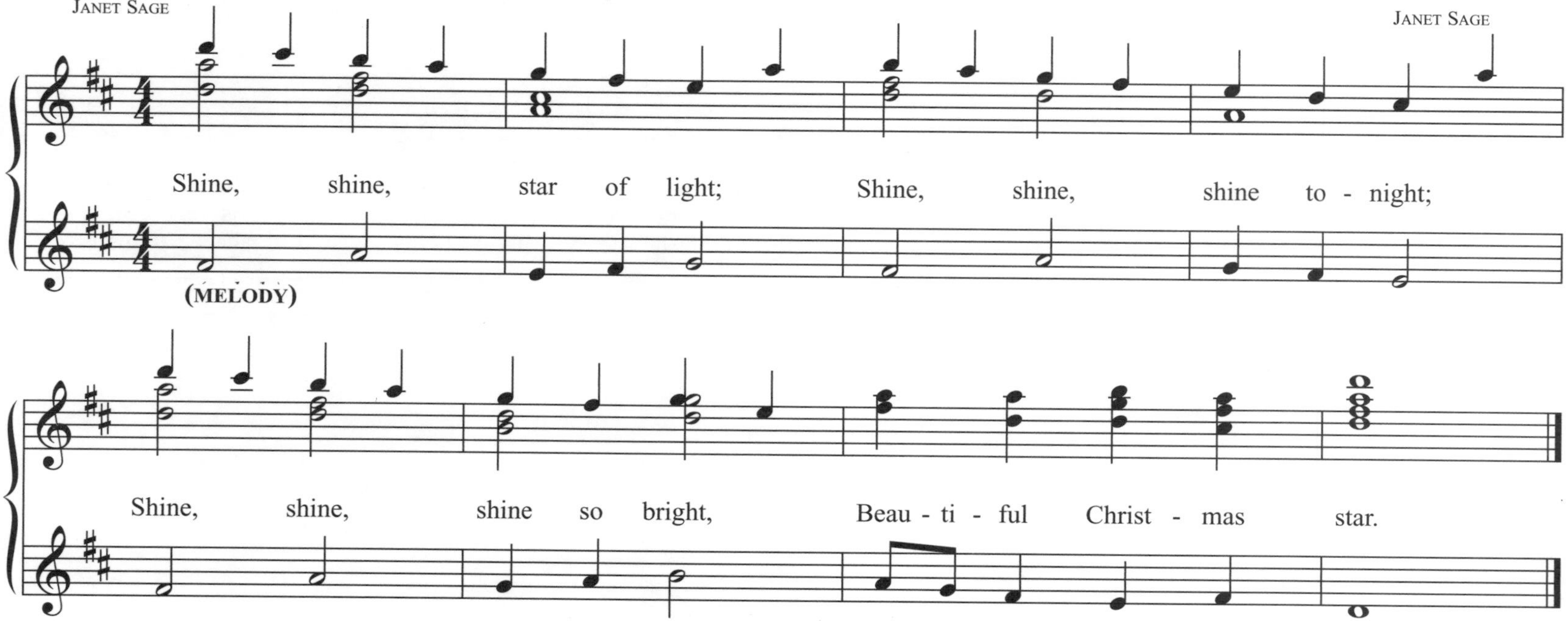

Shine, shine, star of light; Shine, shine, shine to - night;

(MELODY)

Shine, shine, shine so bright, Beau - ti - ful Christ - mas star.

Christmastime

Janet Sage

Janet Sage

Christ-mas-time, Christ-mas-time Tells of Je - sus' love; Christ-mas-time,

Christ-mas-time Tells of Je - sus' love; Mer-ry Christ - mas, Me - rry Christ - mas,

Sing the hap - py song! Christ-mas - time, Christ-mas - time Tells of Je - sus' love.

145 God's Best Gift

Lois L. Curley / Jeannae P. Lawler

Bortniansky

1. God's best gift to us is Je - sus, Born on earth at Christ - mas time.
2. In God's Word, the Ho - ly Bi - ble, We are told why Je - sus came.
Je - sus came from heav'n a - bove To be a friend of yours and mine.
God wants us to al - ways love Him And for - ev - er praise His name.
Mer - ry Christ - mas, Mer - ry Christ - mas, Je - sus Christ the Lord is born.
We will praise our God in heav - en, We will thank Him for His love.

 Here We Come to Bethlehem

EMMA F. BUSH EMMA F. BUSH

1. Here we come to Beth - le - hem, Here we come to Beth - le - hem,
Here we come to Beth - le - hem, To see the ba - by King.

2. Here we see the shep - herds kneel, Here we see the shep - herds kneel,
Here we see the shep - herds kneel, Be - fore the ba - by King.

3. Here the Wise Men bring their gifts, Here the Wise Men bring their gifts,
Here the Wise Men bring their gifts, To give the ba - by King.

147 I'll Share My Home

JANET SAGE

JANET SAGE

"I'll share my home with You, Ba - by Je - sus," Said the
spot - ted cow,* Said the spot - ted cow;* "I'll
share my home with You, Ba - by Je - sus," Said the
spot - ted cow* long a - go.

*woolly lamb, donkey gray, cooing dove

It Was a Happy Day
148
Janet Sage
Janet Sage
1. It was a hap - py day, hap - py day, hap - py day When lit - tle Ba - by Je - sus was born; It was a hap - py day, hap - py day, hap - py day When lit - tle Ba - by Je - sus was born.
2. The an - gels sang for joy, sang for joy, sang for joy When lit - tle Ba - by Je - sus was born. The an - gels sang for joy, sang for joy, sang for joy When lit - tle Ba - by Je - sus was born.
3. The shep - herds came to pray, came to pray, came to pray When lit - tle Ba - by Je - sus was born. The shep - herds came to pray, came to pray, came to pray When lit - tle Ba - by Je - sus was born.
4. The Wise Men brought their gifts, brought their gifts, brought their gifts, When lit - tle Ba - by Je - sus was born. The Wise Men brought their gifts, brought their gifts, brought their gifts, When lit - tle Ba - by Je - sus was born.

149 Little Baby in the Manger, I Love You

CARRIE B. ADAMS

CARRIE B. ADAMS

Lit - tle Ba - by in the man - ger, "I love you!" Ly - ing there, to earth a stran - ger, "I love you!"
Wise Men saw the star and an - swered, "I love you!" Shep - herds heard the an - gels sing - ing, "I love you!"

Mary Loved Baby Jesus

Mary E. Schwab

Mary E. Schwab

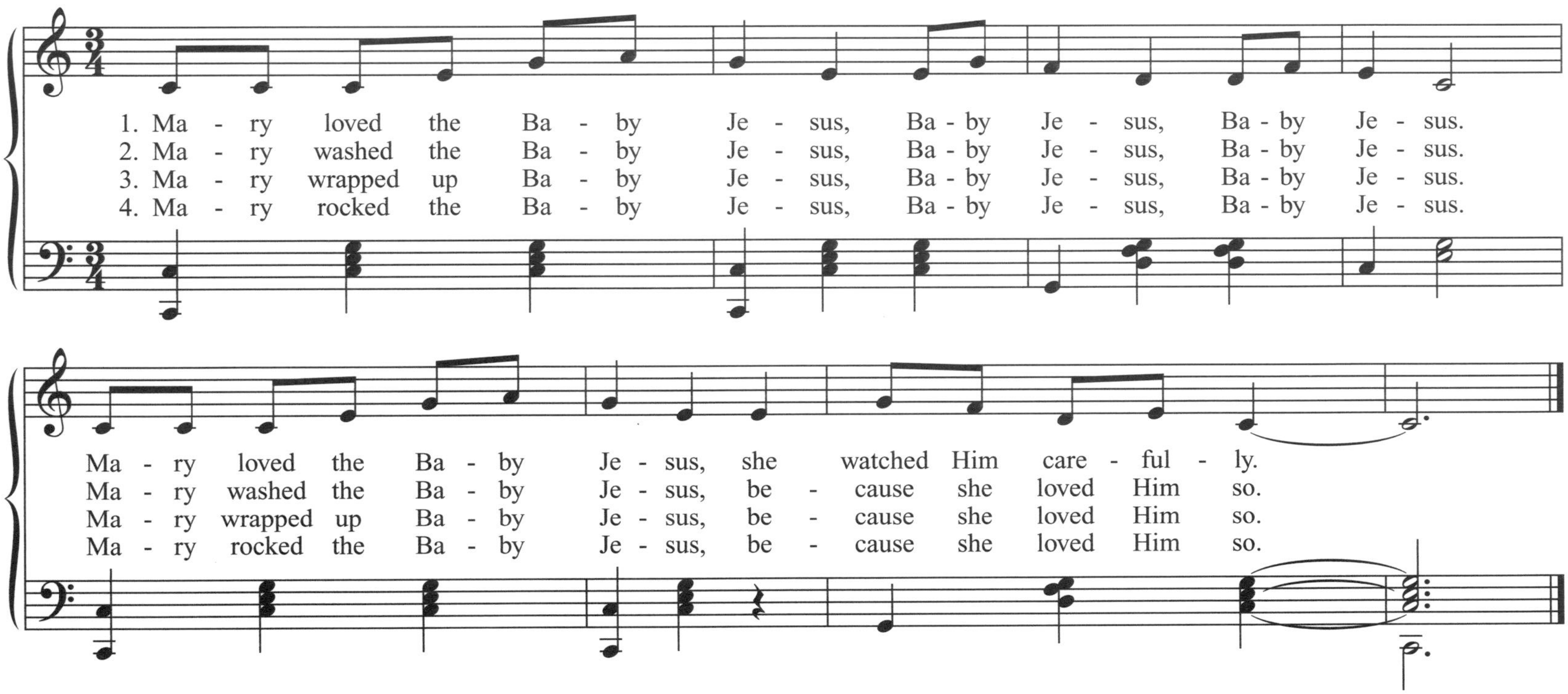

1. Ma - ry loved the Ba - by Je - sus, Ba - by Je - sus, Ba - by Je - sus.
Ma - ry loved the Ba - by Je - sus, she watched Him care - ful - ly.

2. Ma - ry washed the Ba - by Je - sus, Ba - by Je - sus, Ba - by Je - sus.
Ma - ry washed the Ba - by Je - sus, be - cause she loved Him so.

3. Ma - ry wrapped up Ba - by Je - sus, Ba - by Je - sus, Ba - by Je - sus.
Ma - ry wrapped up Ba - by Je - sus, be - cause she loved Him so.

4. Ma - ry rocked the Ba - by Je - sus, Ba - by Je - sus, Ba - by Je - sus.
Ma - ry rocked the Ba - by Je - sus, be - cause she loved Him so.

5. Mary sang to Baby Jesus,
Baby Jesus, Baby Jesus.
Mary sang to Baby Jesus,
because she loved Him so.

Actions: 1. Hand out dolls while singing the first stanza. 2. Talk about how Mary gave Baby Jesus a bath and made Him nice and clean. He smelled sweet like all babies do when they have just had a bath. Children pretend to wash their dolls as the second stanza is being sung. 3. Hand out small squares of flannel for blankets. Talk about how Mary wrapped Baby Jesus in His little blanket. Children may wrap their dolls as third stanza is sung. 4. Rock dolls back and forth as the fourth and fifth stanzas are sung.

151 Mary's Little Baby

Harvey R. Davies / Harvey R. Davies

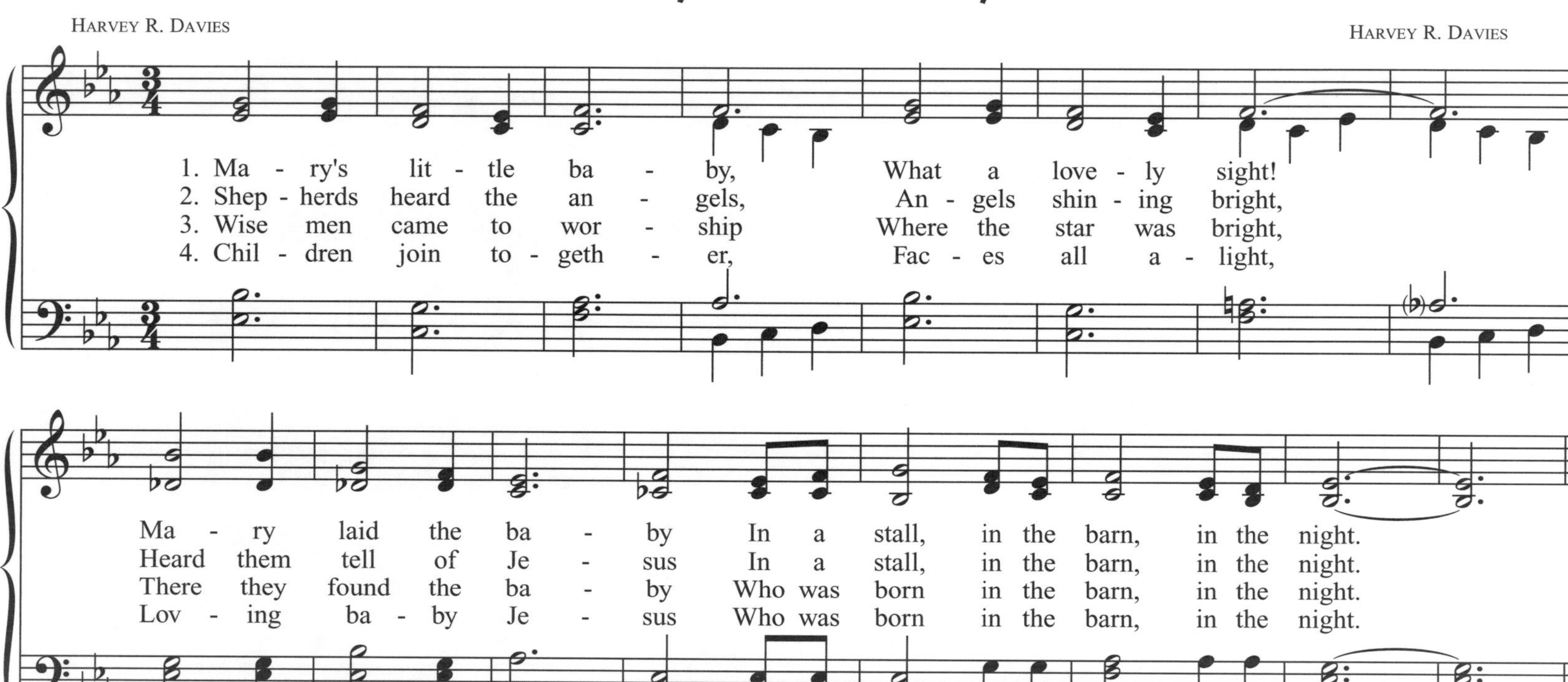
1. Ma - ry's lit - tle ba - by, What a love - ly sight!
2. Shep - herds heard the an - gels, An - gels shin - ing bright,
3. Wise men came to wor - ship Where the star was bright,
4. Chil - dren join to - geth - er, Fac - es all a - light,
Ma - ry laid the ba - by In a stall, in the barn, in the night.
Heard them tell of Je - sus In a stall, in the barn, in the night.
There they found the ba - by Who was born in the barn, in the night.
Lov - ing ba - by Je - sus Who was born in the barn, in the night.

GRACE
JESUS BIRTH

Riding on a Camel

JANET SAGE

JANET SAGE

Rid - ing on a cam - el, a cam - el, a cam - el; Fol - low - ing a star, Fol - low - ing a star; Rid - ing on a cam - el, a cam - el, a cam - el; See the Wise Man come from a - far.

(all black keys)

153 Ring the Bells

153
Ring the Bells
CAROL GREENE
CAROL GREENE
(bells)
(drum)
Marchlike
Ring the bells!
Beat the drum!
(clap)
1. (clap)
2. (clap)
Clap your hands! The Ba - by's come!
Sing twice, then repeat from beginning and take second ending.
What lit - tle Ba - by? Lit - tle Ba - by Je - sus! What lit - tle Ba - by? God's own Son!

Children will enjoy using rhythm instruments with this song. For a performance, you might want older children to play bells with you.

For Me

154

Virginia Cason — Virginia Cason / Arr. by Wayne Hooper

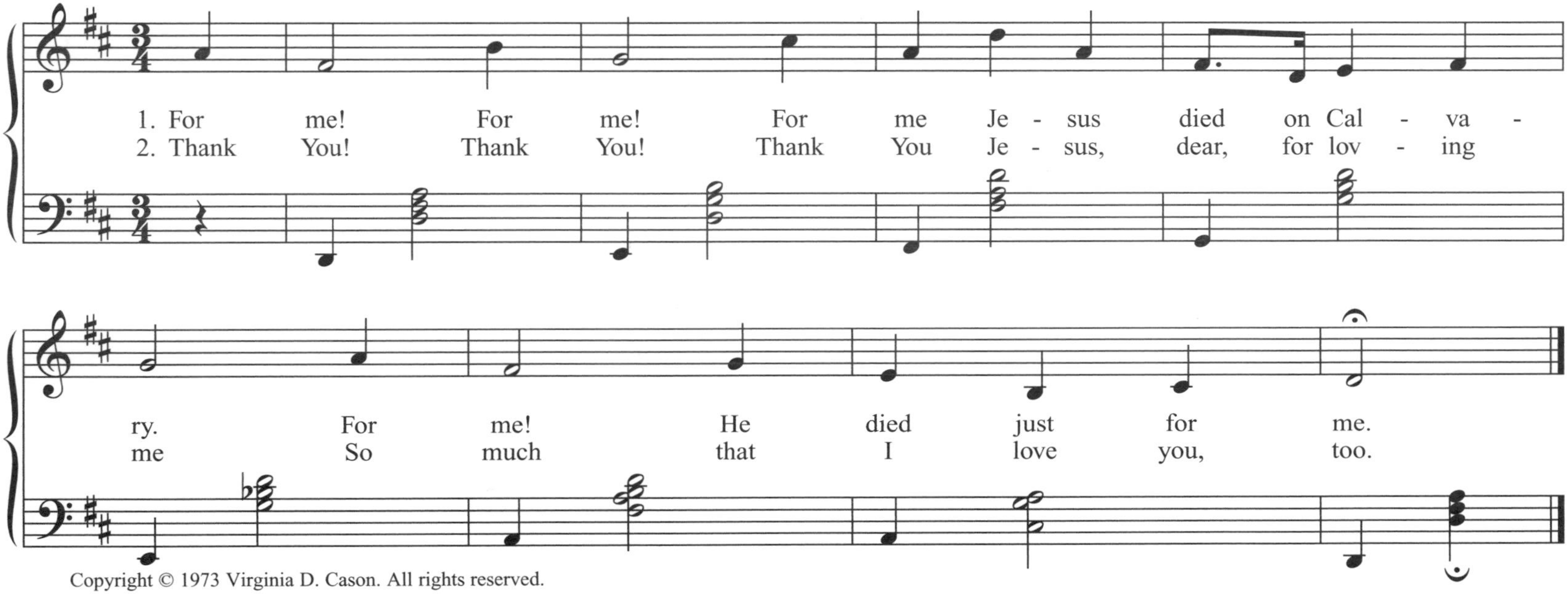

1. For me! For me! For me Jesus died on Calvary.
For me! He died just for me.

2. Thank You! Thank You! Thank You Jesus, dear, for loving me
So much that I love you, too.

Jesus Died Upon the Cross

155

Anita Reith Stohs — Kenneth D. Logan

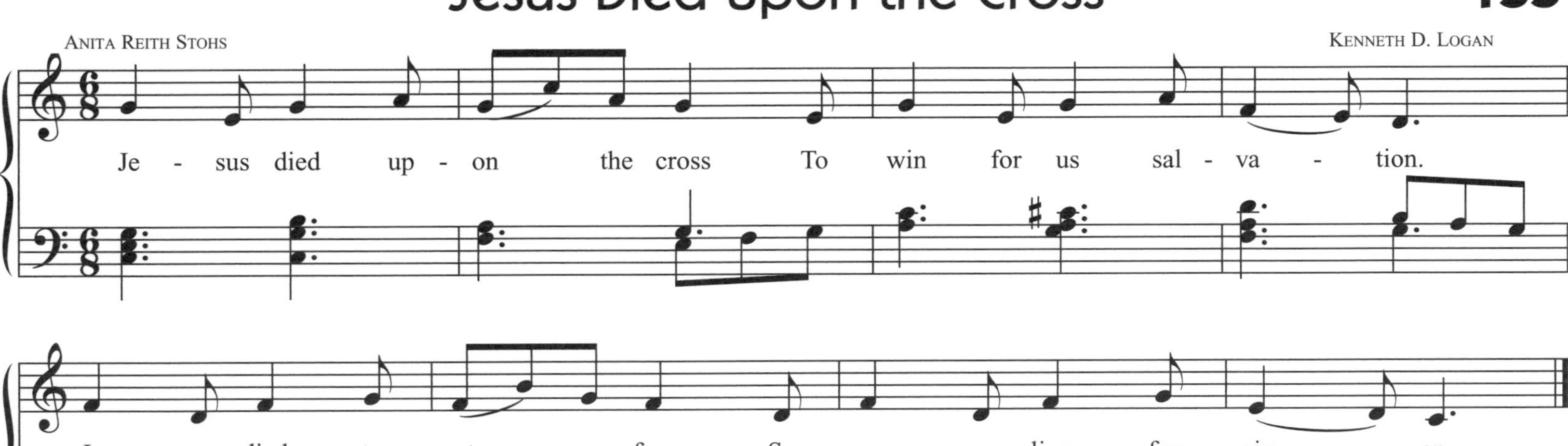
Je - sus died up - on the cross To win for us sal - va - tion.
Je - sus died to set us free So we can live for - giv - en.

Take time to explain the meaning of "salvation" if used with young children.

Jesus Is Risen

CAROL GREENE

CAROL GREENE

1. Je - sus is ris - en Out of death's pris - on.
2. Shout it and say it. Sing it and play it.
Tell all the world that the Lord is a - live.
Tell all the world that the Lord is a -
1.
2.
live. Oh, tell all the world that the Lord is a -
live. Oh, tell all the world that the Lord is a - live!

Show the children how to sing each "tell all the world" phrase in the second ending with more volume.

GRACE

JESUS' DEATH AND RESURRECTION

Bubbles

157

JANET SAGE

JANET SAGE

Bub - bles, bub - bles, I like to play with bub - bles;

Je - sus must like pret - ty things, be - cause He made the bub - bles!

Clip-clop

158

JANET SAGE

JANET SAGE

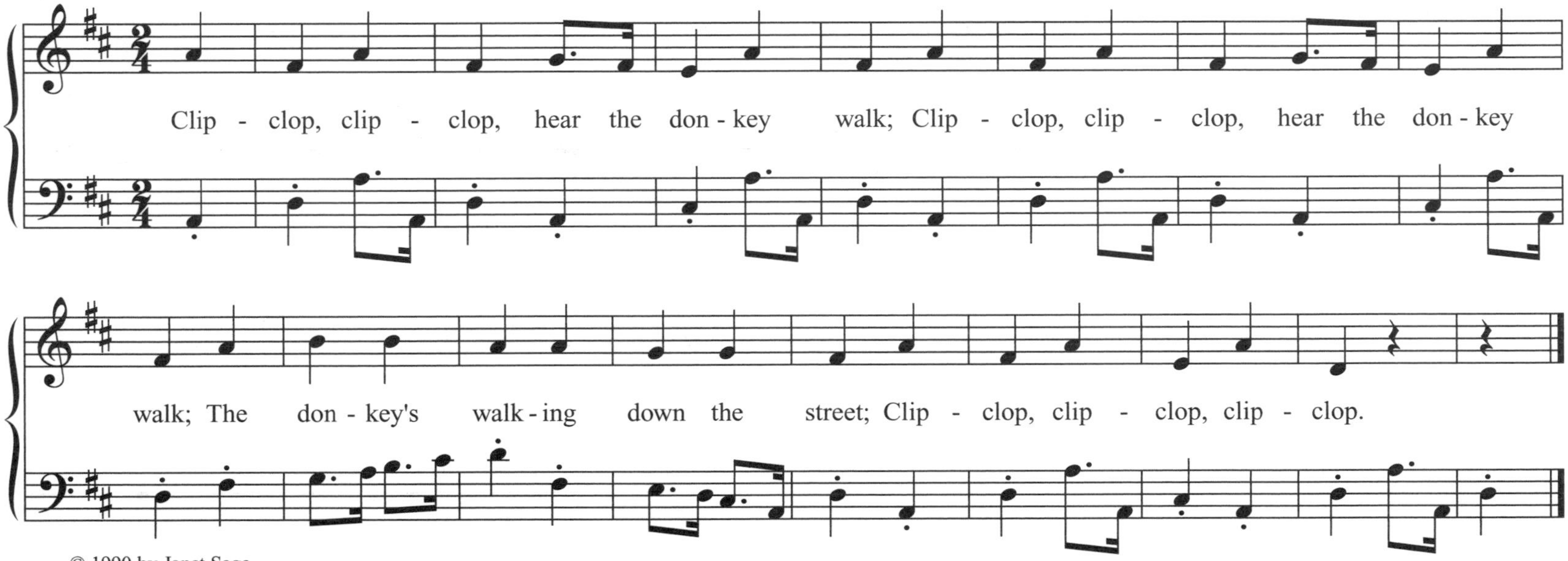

Clip - clop, clip - clop, hear the don - key walk; Clip - clop, clip - clop, hear the don - key

walk; The don - key's walk - ing down the street; Clip - clop, clip - clop, clip - clop.

159
Colors
JANET SAGE
JANET SAGE
*Col - ors, col - ors, pret - ty col - ors; Col - ors, col - ors, pret - ty col - ors;
Je - sus made the pret - ty col - ors just for you and me.
© 1990 by Janet Sage.
*Also: yellow, red, blue, etc.
160
Seashells
JANET SAGE
JANET SAGE
Sea - shells, sea - shells, Man - y pret - ty sea - shells, Rough and shin - y ones,
Big and tin - y ones; Je - sus made the sea - shells.
(132)
© 1990 by Janet Sage.

Fishy, Fishy

Janet Sage | Janet Sage

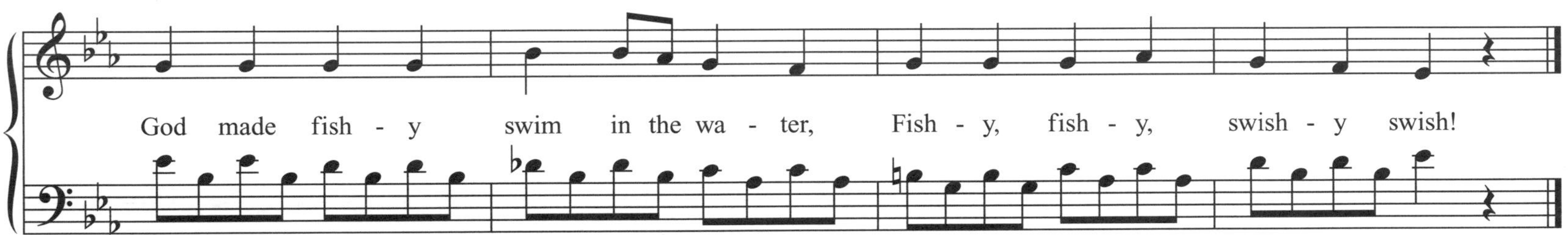
Fish - y, fish - y, swim in the wa - ter, Fish - y, fish - y, swish - y swish!
God made fish - y swim in the wa - ter, Fish - y, fish - y, swish - y swish!

Pianist: Keep the song moving quickly and play the left-hand eighth notes smoothly to give the effect of swishing water. If the second half of the song causes difficulty, repeat the first three and a half measures, finishing with the final measure as written (this isn't as good musically, however).

Leader: The accompaniment creates a swishing water impression, and the specific word combination of "fishy-swishy" helps the little ones in their learning of sounds and articulation. Please avoid substituting words or making the song serve some other purpose. Fish mitts for the children to wear would be nice with this song after it is well learned, or they might just wiggle their hands without mitts. Live or toy fish might be used effectively also.

162 God Made Everything

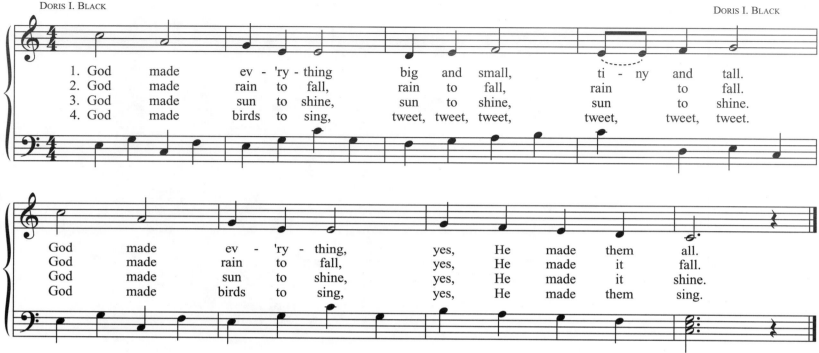

Doris I. Black Doris I. Black

1. God made ev - 'ry - thing big and small, ti - ny and tall.
2. God made rain to fall, rain to fall, rain to fall.
3. God made sun to shine, sun to shine, sun to shine.
4. God made birds to sing, tweet, tweet, tweet, tweet, tweet, tweet.
God made ev - 'ry - thing, yes, He made them all.
God made rain to fall, yes, He made it fall.
God made sun to shine, yes, He made it shine.
God made birds to sing, yes, He made them sing.

CHARLES M. FILLMORE CHARLES M. FILLMORE

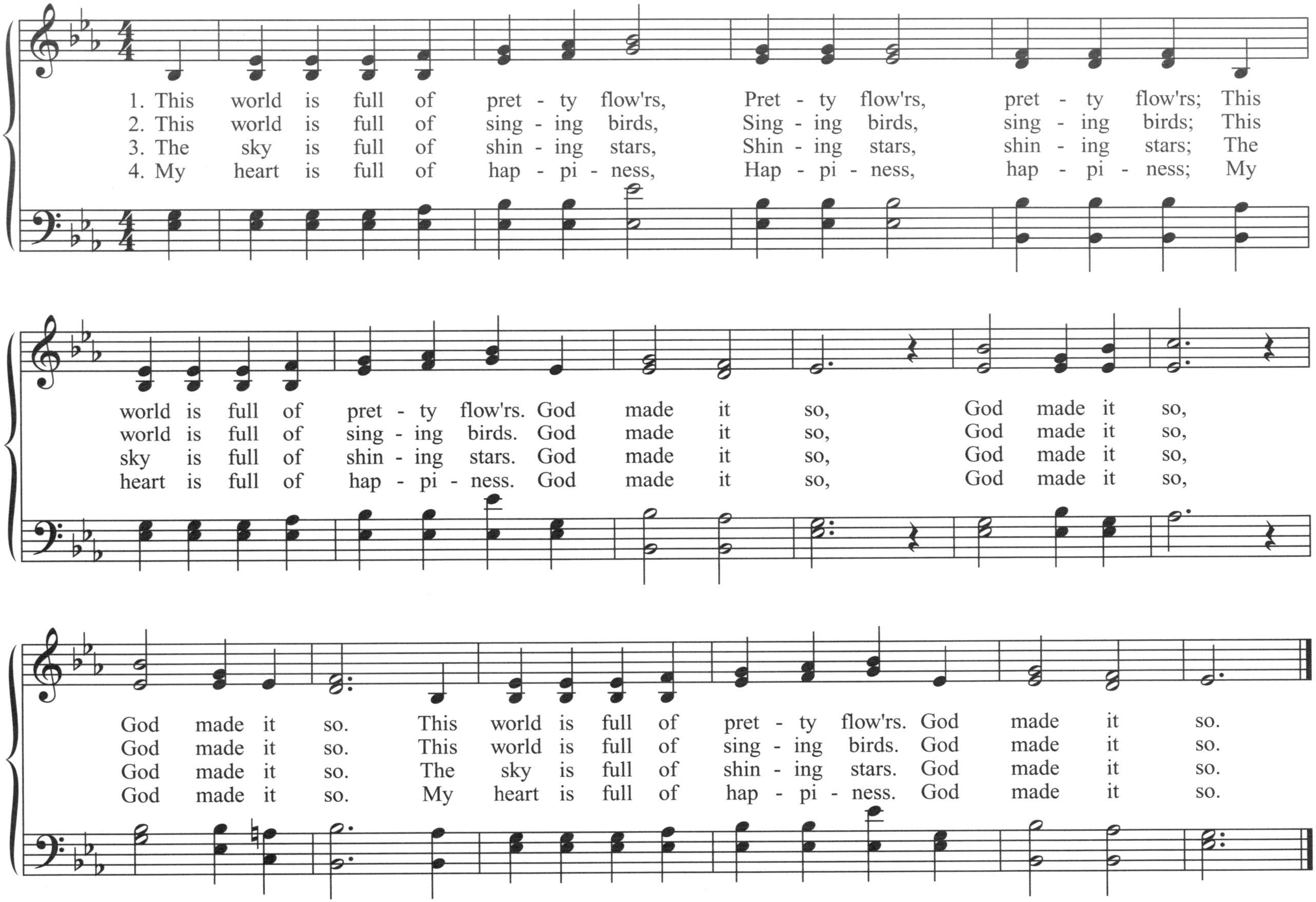

1. This world is full of pret - ty flow'rs, Pret - ty flow'rs, pret - ty flow'rs; This world is full of pret - ty flow'rs. God made it so, God made it so, God made it so. This world is full of pret - ty flow'rs. God made it so.
2. This world is full of sing - ing birds, Sing - ing birds, sing - ing birds; This world is full of sing - ing birds. God made it so, God made it so, God made it so. This world is full of sing - ing birds. God made it so.
3. The sky is full of shin - ing stars, Shin - ing stars, shin - ing stars; The sky is full of shin - ing stars. God made it so, God made it so, God made it so. The sky is full of shin - ing stars. God made it so.
4. My heart is full of hap - pi - ness, Hap - pi - ness, hap - pi - ness; My heart is full of hap - pi - ness. God made it so, God made it so, God made it so. My heart is full of hap - pi - ness. God made it so.

God Made Me

Clara M. Striplin

Clara M. Striplin

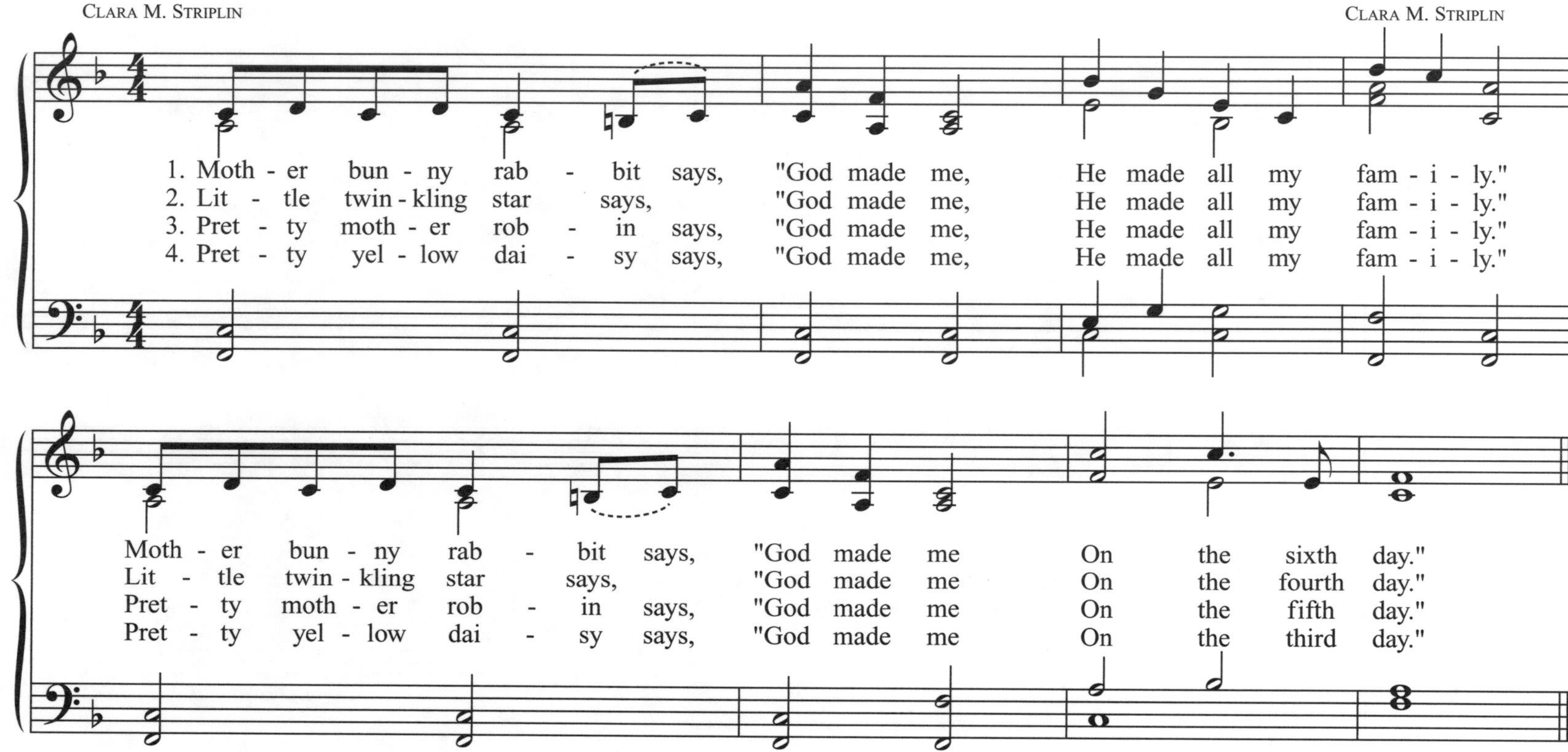
1. Moth - er bun - ny rab - bit says, "God made me, He made all my fam - i - ly."
2. Lit - tle twin - kling star says, "God made me, He made all my fam - i - ly."
3. Pret - ty moth - er rob - in says, "God made me, He made all my fam - i - ly."
4. Pret - ty yel - low dai - sy says, "God made me, He made all my fam - i - ly."
Moth - er bun - ny rab - bit says, "God made me On the sixth day."
Lit - tle twin - kling star says, "God made me On the fourth day."
Pret - ty moth - er rob - in says, "God made me On the fifth day."
Pret - ty yel - low dai - sy says, "God made me On the third day."

5. Lovely morning light says, "God made me,
All the colors you can see."
Lovely morning light says, "God made me
On the first day."

6. Fleecy little cloud says, "God made me,
High up in the air so free."
Fleecy little cloud says, "God made me
On the second day."

7. Blessed Sabbath day says, "God made me,
Best of all the week to be."
Blessed Sabbath day says, "God made me
On the seventh day."

GRACE

NATURE

God Made the Sun and Moon and Stars

REBECCA EDWARDS-LESSER

REBECCA EDWARDS-LESSER / ARR. BY KENNETH D. LOGAN

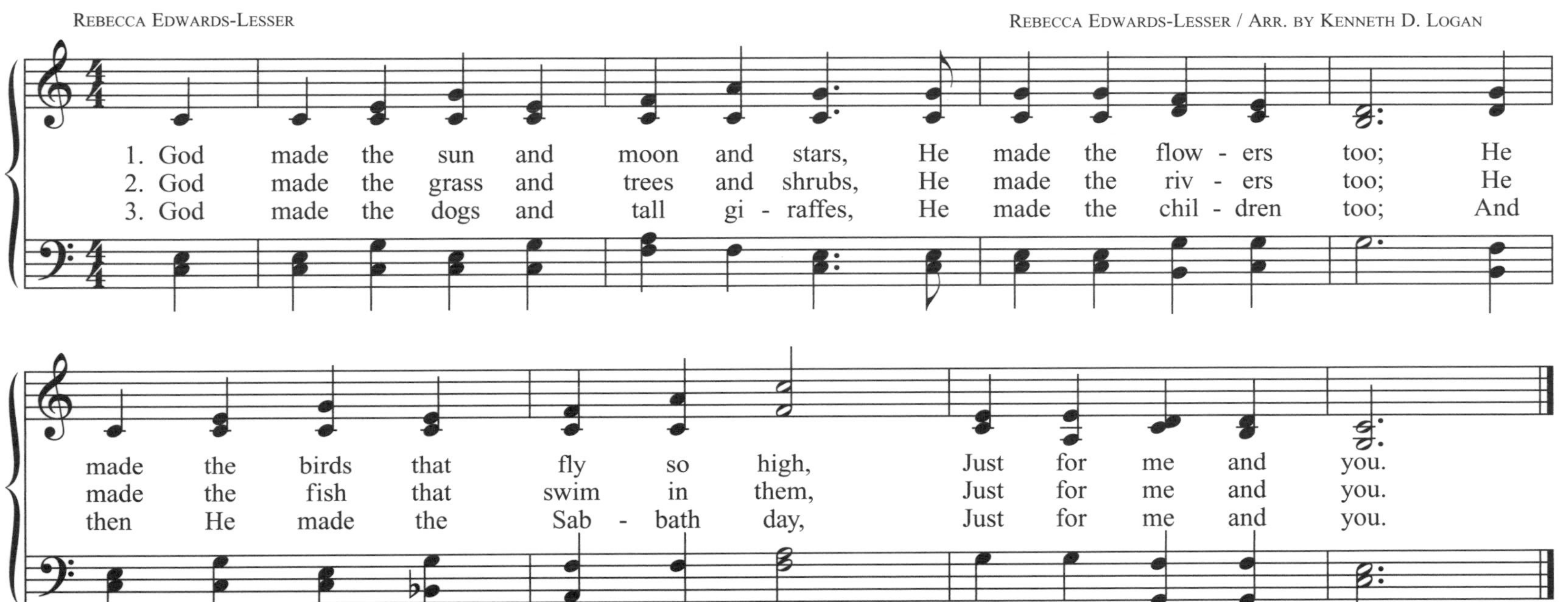
1. God made the sun and moon and stars, He made the flow - ers too; He made the birds that fly so high, Just for me and you.
2. God made the grass and trees and shrubs, He made the riv - ers too; He made the fish that swim in them, Just for me and you.
3. God made the dogs and tall gi - raffes, He made the chil - dren too; And then He made the Sab - bath day, Just for me and you.

166 God Makes Roses Grow in My Garden

Kathryn B. Myers — Kathryn B. Myers

1. God makes ros - es grow in my gar - den, He loves me.
   God makes ros - es grow in my gar - den, I love Him.
2. God makes pan - sies grow in my gar - den, He loves me.
   God makes pan - sies grow in my gar - den, I love Him.
3. God makes jon - quils grow in my gar - den, He loves me.
   God makes jon - quils grow in my gar - den, I love Him.
4. God makes tu - lips grow in my gar - den, He loves me.
   God makes tu - lips grow in my gar - den, I love Him.

5. God makes daisies grow in my garden,
   He loves me.
   God makes daisies grow in my garden,
   I love Him.

I Like to Eat an Apple

167

Joy Hicklin Stewart | Joy Hicklin Stewart

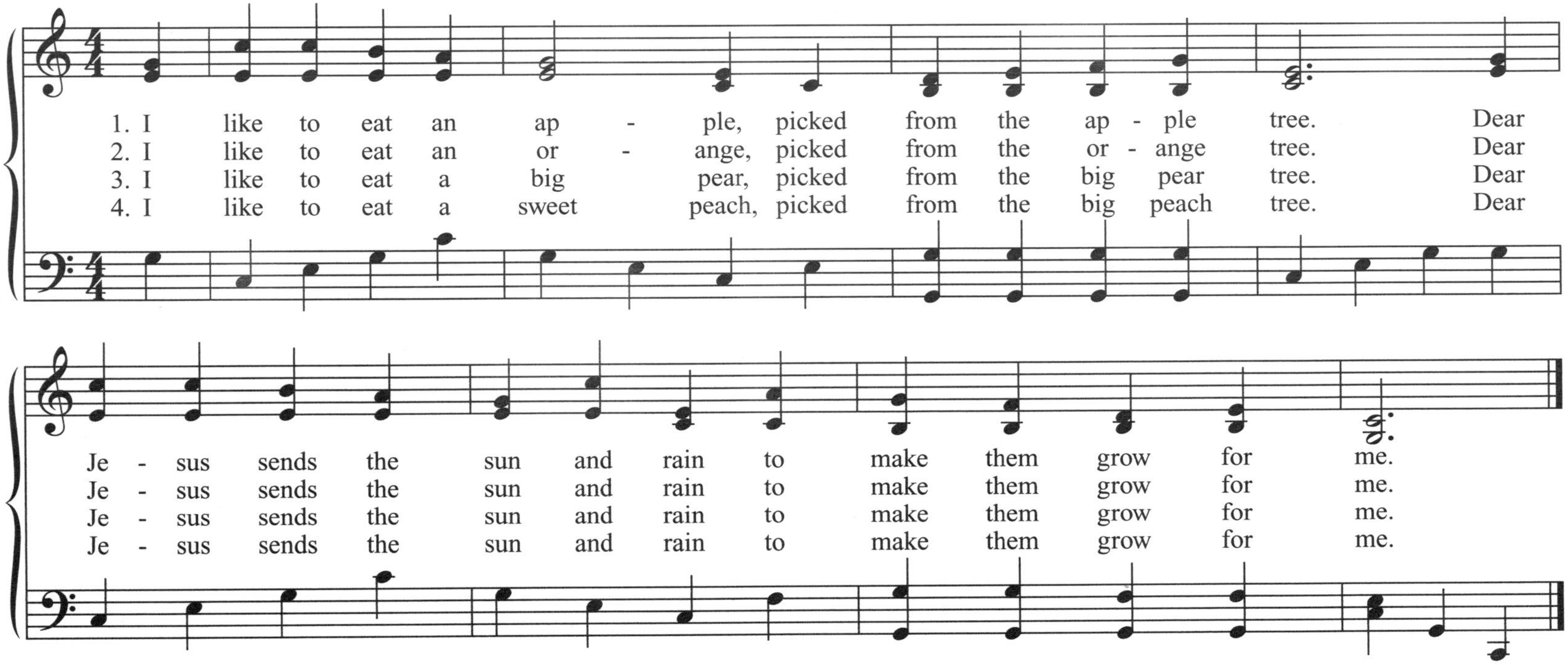

1. I like to eat an apple, picked from the apple tree. Dear Jesus sends the sun and rain to make them grow for me.
2. I like to eat an orange, picked from the orange tree. Dear Jesus sends the sun and rain to make them grow for me.
3. I like to eat a big pear, picked from the big pear tree. Dear Jesus sends the sun and rain to make them grow for me.
4. I like to eat a sweet peach, picked from the big peach tree. Dear Jesus sends the sun and rain to make them grow for me.

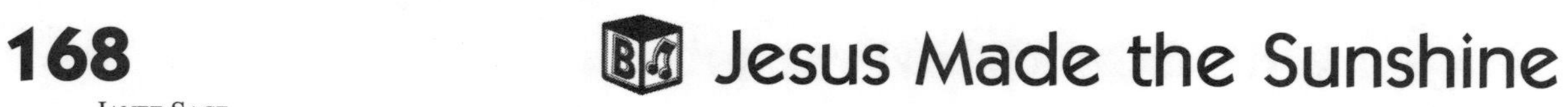

Jesus Made the Sunshine

Janet Sage

Janet Sage

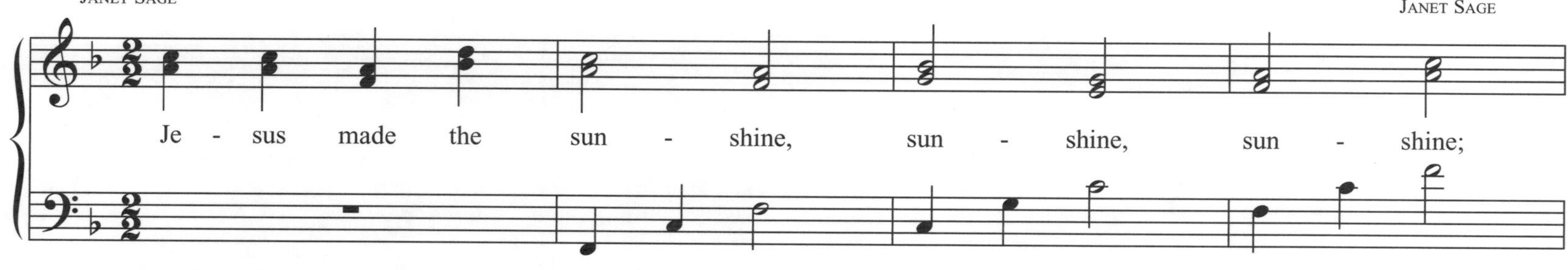
Je - sus made the sun - shine, sun - shine, sun - shine;

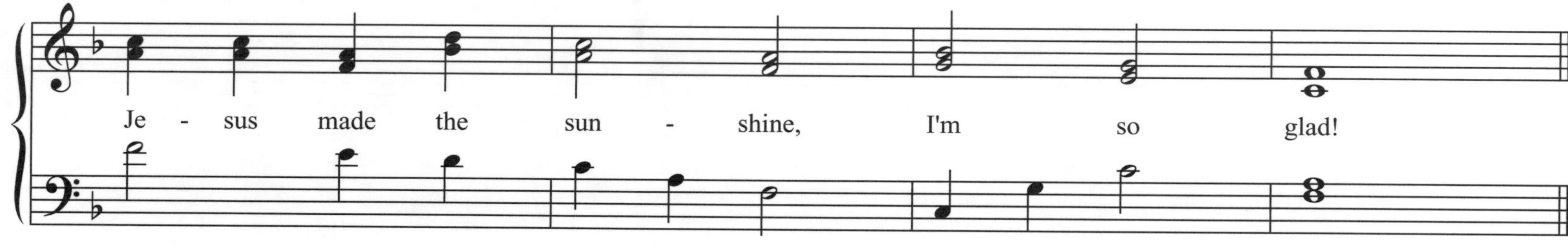
Je - sus made the sun - shine, I'm so glad!

Grace

Nature

Leader: Many words may be substituted for "sunshine" in this song. If using the piece with the story of Creation, you could use the following: (1) bright light; (2) fresh air; water; white clouds; rivers; soft breeze; (3) green grass; flowers; tall trees; mountains; big rocks; brown dirt; meadows; forest; white sand; good fruit; (4) moonlight; starlight (stars bright); (5) fishies (goldfish, starfish, seahorse, dolphin, big whale); birdies (bluebird, robin, sparrow, eagle, owl); froggies; turtles; long snakes; lizards; (6) animals (reindeer, lion, squirrel, bunny, doggy, kitty, camel, donkey); (7) insects (spiders, butterflies, buzzy bees, ladybugs); (8) people (mommies, daddies, children, babies).

Little Bird Song

169

KATE DOUGLAS WIGGIN

KATE DOUGLAS WIGGIN / ARR. BY KENNETH D. LOGAN

1. Up, up in the sky, the lit - tle birds fly; Down, down in the nest the lit - tle birds rest, With a wing on the left, and a wing on the right, We'll let the dear bird - ies rest all the long night.
2. The round sun comes up, the dew floats a - way; "Good morn - ing, bright sun - shine!" the lit - tle birds say. "How bright are the flow'rs, how green is the wood, Our heav - en - ly Fa - ther, how kind and how good!"

GRACE

NATURE

170 Someone Cares

R. Curtis Barger

1. There were three ti - ny eggs in a wee, wee, nest In the tree, In the tree. And the
2. There is Some - one who cares for the bird - ies wee; Je - sus does, Je - sus does! And I
dear moth - er bird kept them 'neath her breast, Blue eggs three, Blue eggs three. But now
know Je - sus takes care of you and me; Yes, He does, Yes, He does! He will
three lit - tle birds in the nest up so high Watch the dear moth - er bird as she
watch o - ver you and will watch o - ver me Like the dear moth - er bird o'er her

Grace

Nature

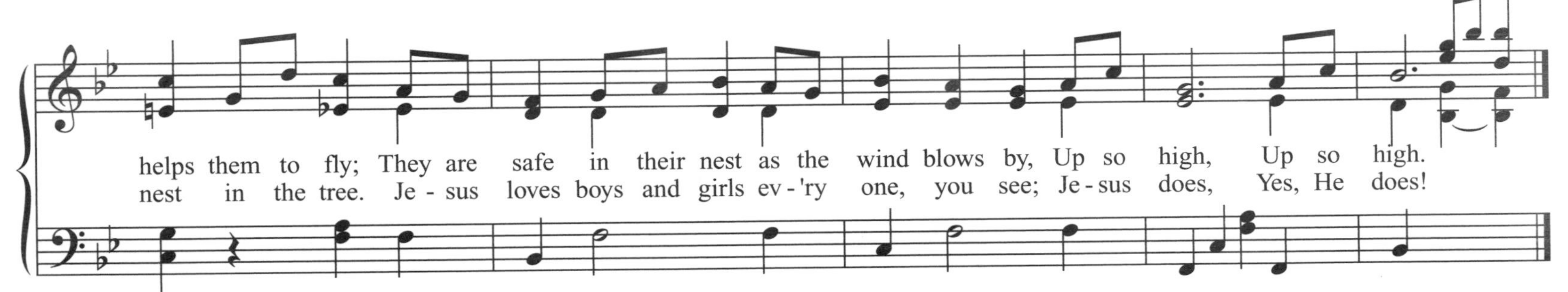
helps them to fly; They are safe in their nest as the wind blows by, Up so high, Up so high.
nest in the tree. Je - sus loves boys and girls ev - 'ry one, you see; Je - sus does, Yes, He does!

171 Woolly, Woolly Lamb

JANET SAGE

JANET SAGE

Wool - ly, wool - ly lamb, Wool - ly, wool - ly lamb, Je - sus made you soft and wool - ly;
Wool - ly, wool - ly lamb, Wool - ly, wool - ly lamb, Je - sus made you soft and wool - ly.

GRACE
NATURE
172
See the Boat
JANET SAGE
JANET SAGE
Rock, rock, rock, rock, See the boat on the wa - ter;
Rock, rock, rock, rock, See the boat on the wa - ter.
© 1990 by Janet Sage.
173
The Butterflies
DOROTHY ROBISON
DOROTHY ROBISON / ARR. BY MARGARET EDGE
I like to see the but - ter - flies,* Fly - ing high, Fly - ing low.
I like to see the but - ter - flies;* Je - sus made them, I know.
(144)
Copyright © 1960 by Review and Herald® Publishing Association.
*Alternate wording suggested by General Conference Sabbath School Department: "birdies fly."

The Hungry Cow 174

JANET SAGE JANET SAGE

Je - sus made the grass for the hun - gry cow; Let's feed the cow, Let's feed the cow;
Je - sus made the grass for the hun - gry cow; Let's feed the hun - gry cow.

Jesus made the nuts for the hungry squirrel . . .
Jesus made the hay for the hungry horse . . .
Jesus made the seeds for the hungry birds . . .

Twinkle, Twinkle, Little Star

Traditional / Arr. by Kenneth D. Logan

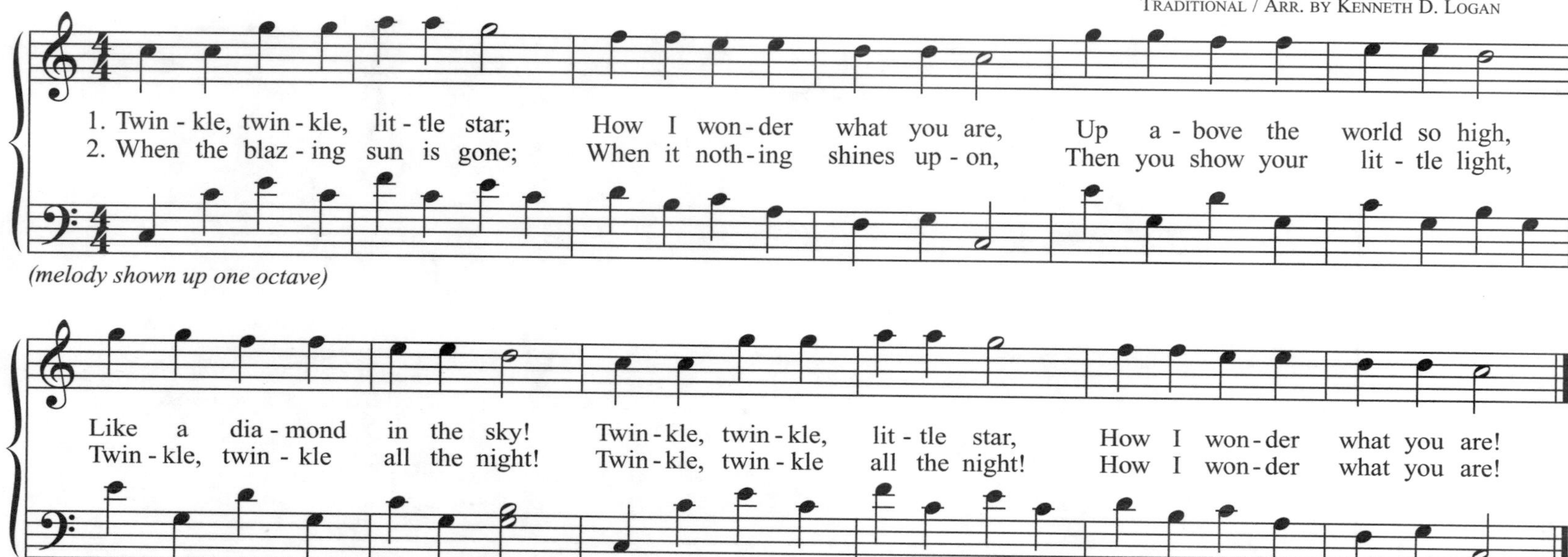
1. Twin - kle, twin - kle, lit - tle star; How I won - der what you are, Up a - bove the world so high,
2. When the blaz - ing sun is gone; When it noth - ing shines up - on, Then you show your lit - tle light,
(melody shown up one octave)
Like a dia - mond in the sky! Twin - kle, twin - kle, lit - tle star, How I won - der what you are!
Twin - kle, twin - kle all the night! Twin - kle, twin - kle all the night! How I won - der what you are!

Rejoice, I Have Found My Sheep

176

LUKE 15:6

JANET SAGE

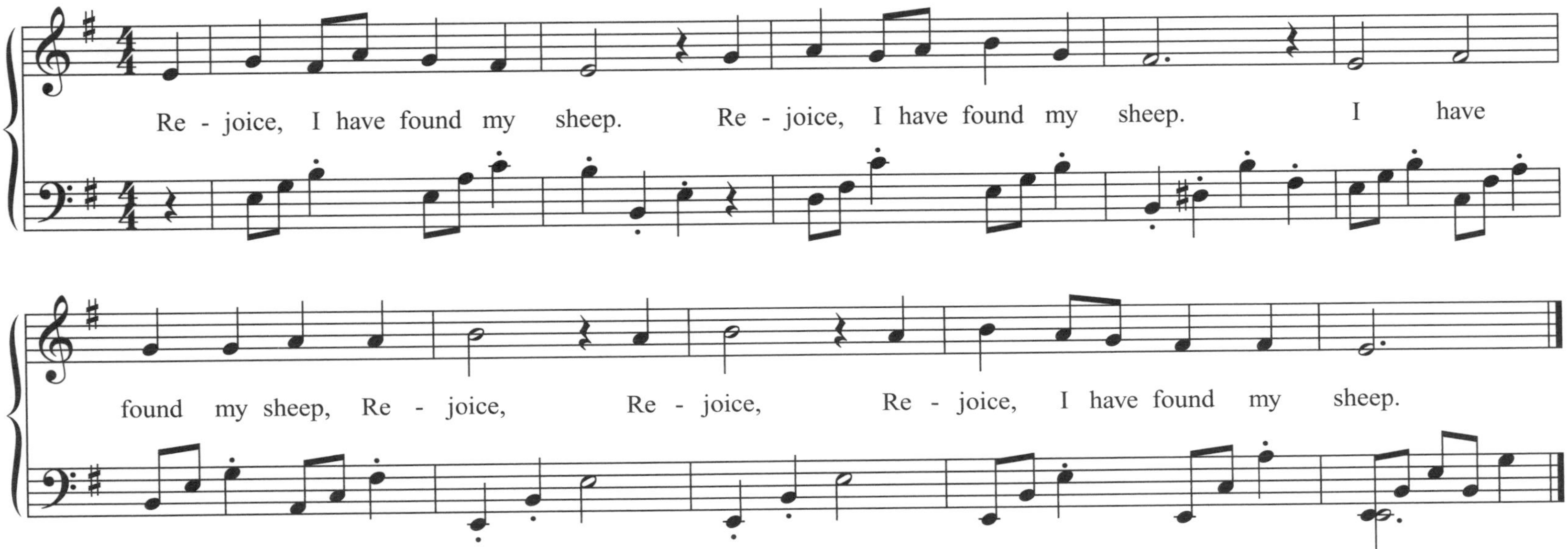

Re - joice, I have found my sheep. Re - joice, I have found my sheep. I have found my sheep, Re - joice, Re - joice, Re - joice, I have found my sheep.

Although this song is in a minor key, it is happy and bright. Let it bounce along.

A Child Like Me

177

VERNON OLIVER, SR.

VERNON OLIVER, SR.

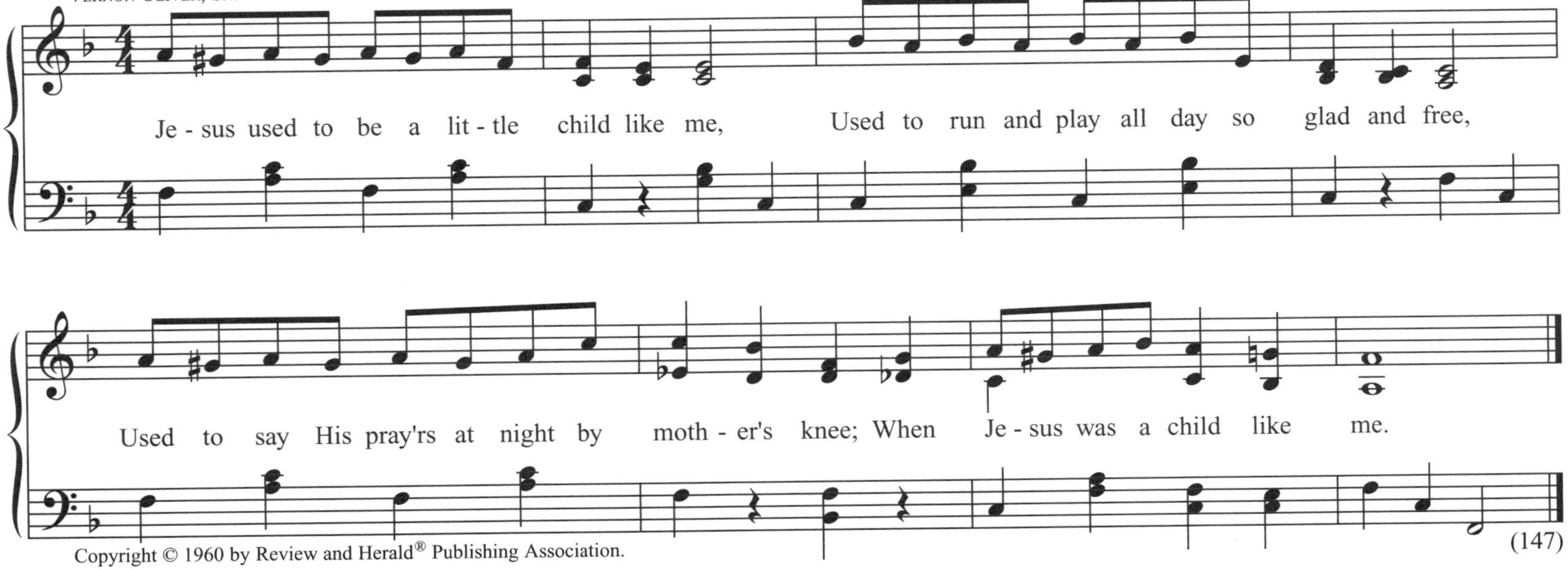

Je - sus used to be a lit - tle child like me, Used to run and play all day so glad and free, Used to say His pray'rs at night by moth - er's knee; When Je - sus was a child like me.

GRACE

PRAISE

178
All Children Need the Saviour

Marjorie A. Anderson
Ellen R. Thompson

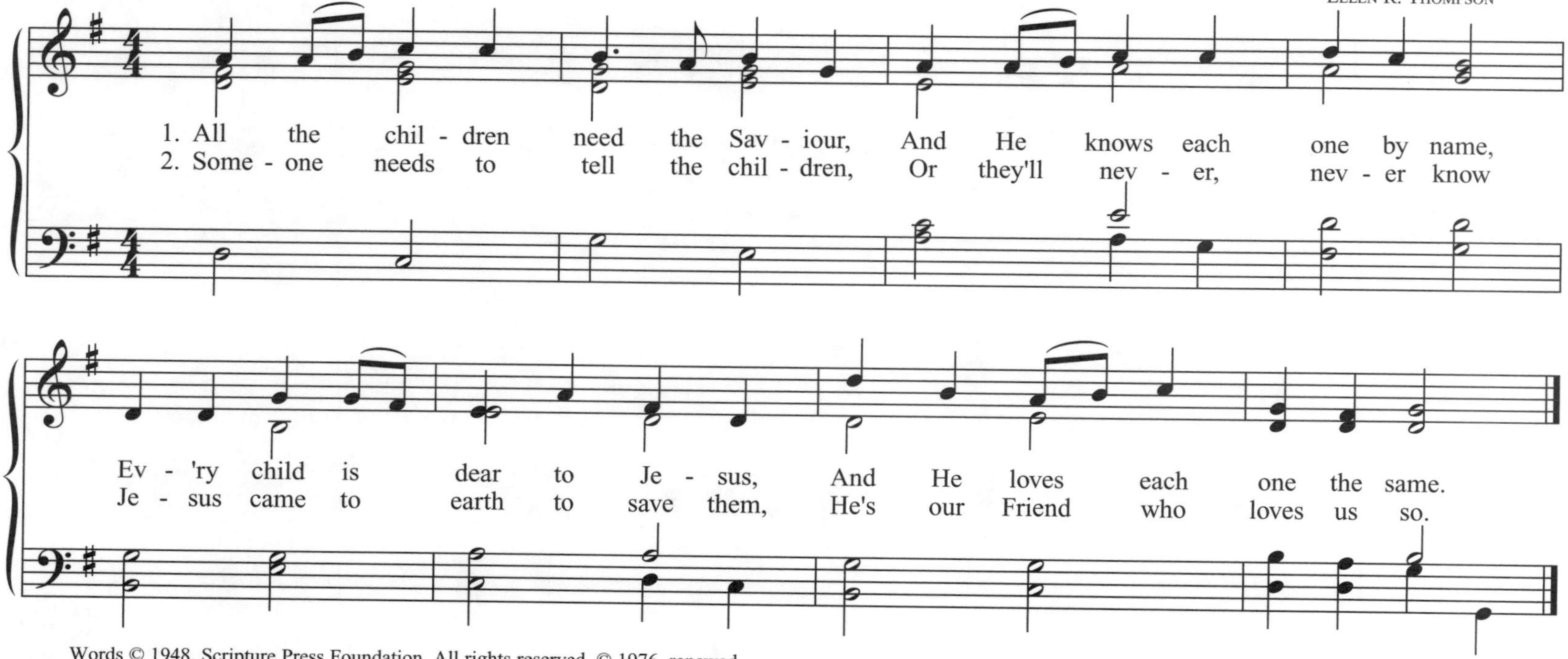

1. All the chil - dren need the Sav - iour, And He knows each one by name,
Ev - 'ry child is dear to Je - sus, And He loves each one the same.

2. Some - one needs to tell the chil - dren, Or they'll nev - er, nev - er know
Je - sus came to earth to save them, He's our Friend who loves us so.

Because I'm Happy 179

Virginia Cason — Virginia Cason / Arr. by Wayne Hooper

I sing because I'm hap - py For what Je - sus did for me. Now
Sa - tan can not have me, For Je - sus, my Help - er, set me free!

Who Is Jesus? 180

Anita Reith Stohs — Traditional / Arr. by Kenneth D. Logan

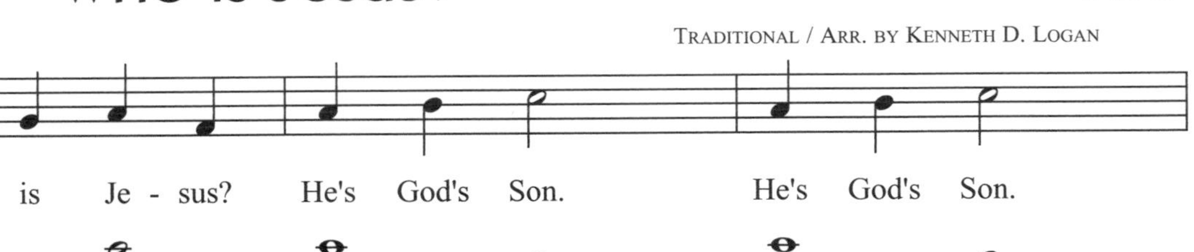

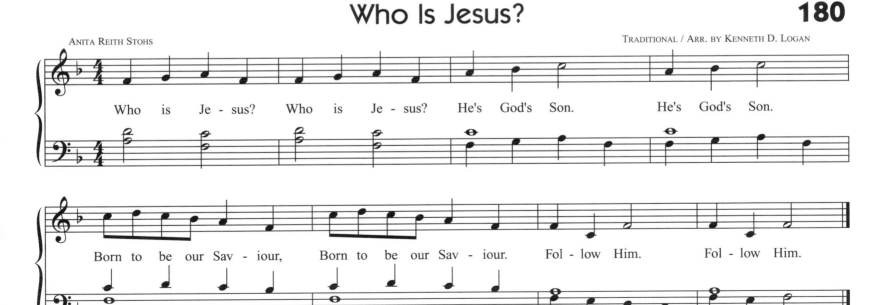

Who is Je - sus? Who is Je - sus? He's God's Son. He's God's Son.

Born to be our Sav - iour, Born to be our Sav - iour. Fol - low Him. Fol - low Him.

GRACE — SALVATION

181 God So Loved the World

Carol Greene
Carol Greene
1. God so loved the world. God so loved the world.
2. Je - sus loved the world. Je - sus loved the world.
3. That's why we sing praise. That's why we sing praise.
God so loved the world, He gave us His Son.
Je - sus loved the world. He gave us His life.
That's why we sing praise. God so loved the world.

Grace

Salvation

Jesus Is Coming

182

Dorothy Dart — Emelie Cope Albertson

1. Jesus is coming from heaven, He's coming for you and me, too. We'll live with Him there in heaven so fair. Oh, I want to be ready, don't you?
2. Angels are coming with Jesus, They're coming for you and me, too. We'll work and we'll pray, be helpful all day. Oh, I want to be ready, don't you?
3. Jesus will take us to heaven, And oh, what a wonderful place. We'll live with Him there in mansions so fair. Oh, I want to be ready, don't you?

183

Jesus Is Coming

Rebecca Edwards-Lesser

Rebecca Edwards-Lesser

1. Je - sus is com - ing for you and for me, He's com - ing, He's com - ing;
2. Je - sus is com - ing with an - gels so bright, He's com - ing, He's com - ing;
3. Je - sus is com - ing, and trum - pets will sound, He's com - ing, He's com - ing;
4. Je - sus is com - ing, the dead will a - wake, He's com - ing, He's com - ing;
Je - sus is com - ing for you and for me, He's com - ing, He's com-ing soon.
Je - sus is com - ing with an - gels so bright, He's com - ing, He's com-ing soon.
Je - sus is com - ing, and trum - pets will sound, He's com - ing, He's com-ing soon.
Je - sus is com - ing, the dead will a - wake, He's com - ing, He's com-ing soon.

5. Jesus is coming for all who love Him,
He's coming, He's coming;
Jesus is coming for all who love Him,
He's coming, He's coming soon.

Grace

Second Coming

Jesus Is Coming

JOY HICKLIN STEWART

JOY HICKLIN STEWART

1. Je - sus has said He is com - ing, Com - ing in clouds up a - bove. He's
2. Moth - ers and dad - dies and ba - bies, Broth - ers and sis - ters too. We
3. We must tell all of our play - mates, Je - sus loves all of you too. He's
4. We must be kind to our play - mates, We must be kind to pets too. We

com - ing with all of the an - gels, To take us to heav - en a - bove.
all must get read - y for Je - sus; He's com - ing for you and me too.
com - ing to take us to heav - en; He's com - ing for you and me too.
want to be read - y for Je - sus; He's com - ing for you and me too.

185
God's House
Stella B. Daleburn
Stella B. Daleburn
1. I like to come to God's house, Where ev - 'ry - bod - y prays. I like to come to God's house And learn a - bout His ways.
2. I'm big e - nough for God's house; I'm big e - nough to pray. I'm big e - nough for God's house; I'm learn - ing to o - bey.
3. I like to help in God's house; I'm help - ing when I sing. I like to help in God's house; My mon - ey, too, I bring.
Copyright © 1947 Stella B. Daleburn.
186
Here Is the Way We Walk to Church
Louise M. Oglevee
William G. Oglevee
Here is the way we walk to church, Walk to church, walk to church;
Here is the way we walk to church Ev - 'ry Sab - bath morn - ing.

I Go to Church 187

NANCY J. STAGL-SCHIPPMANN
NANCY J. STAGL-SCHIPPMANN
I go to church on Sab - bath to wor - ship God a - bove, To
sing and pray to Je - sus and learn a - bout His love.

Jesus' House 188

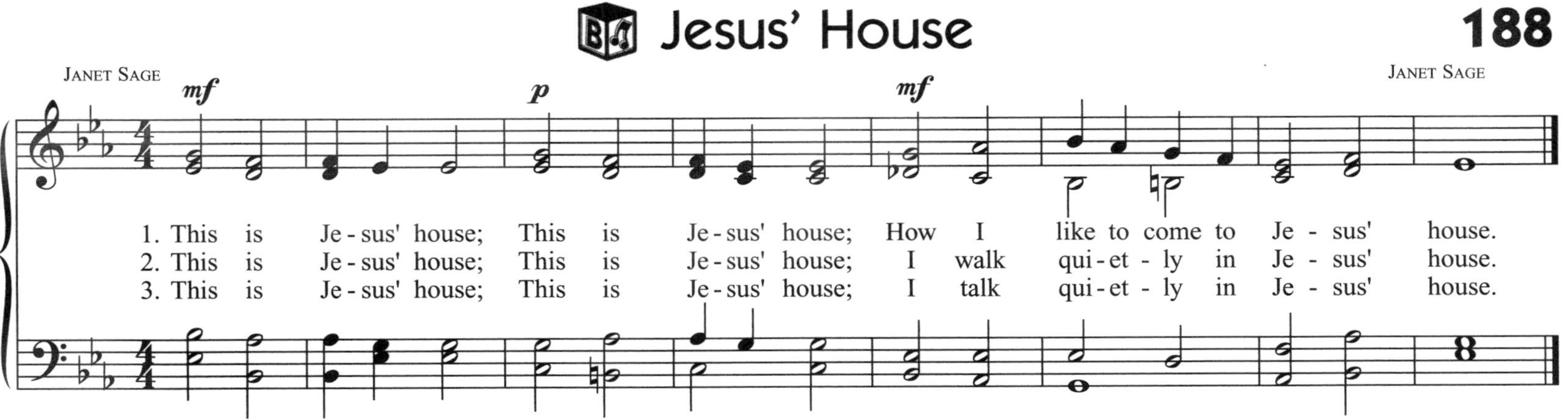
JANET SAGE
JANET SAGE
mf
p
mf
1. This is Je - sus' house; This is Je - sus' house; How I like to come to Je - sus' house.
2. This is Je - sus' house; This is Je - sus' house; I walk qui - et - ly in Je - sus' house.
3. This is Je - sus' house; This is Je - sus' house; I talk qui - et - ly in Je - sus' house.

Pianist: This is a hymn-like piece to play softly and reverently.

Leader: Small children can often become confused about the church being Jesus' house and heaven being where Jesus lives. Make a distinction between Jesus' home in heaven and Jesus' house here on earth where He comes to be with us each Sabbath.

WORSHIP

CHURCH

189 The Preacher Talks

JANET SAGE JANET SAGE

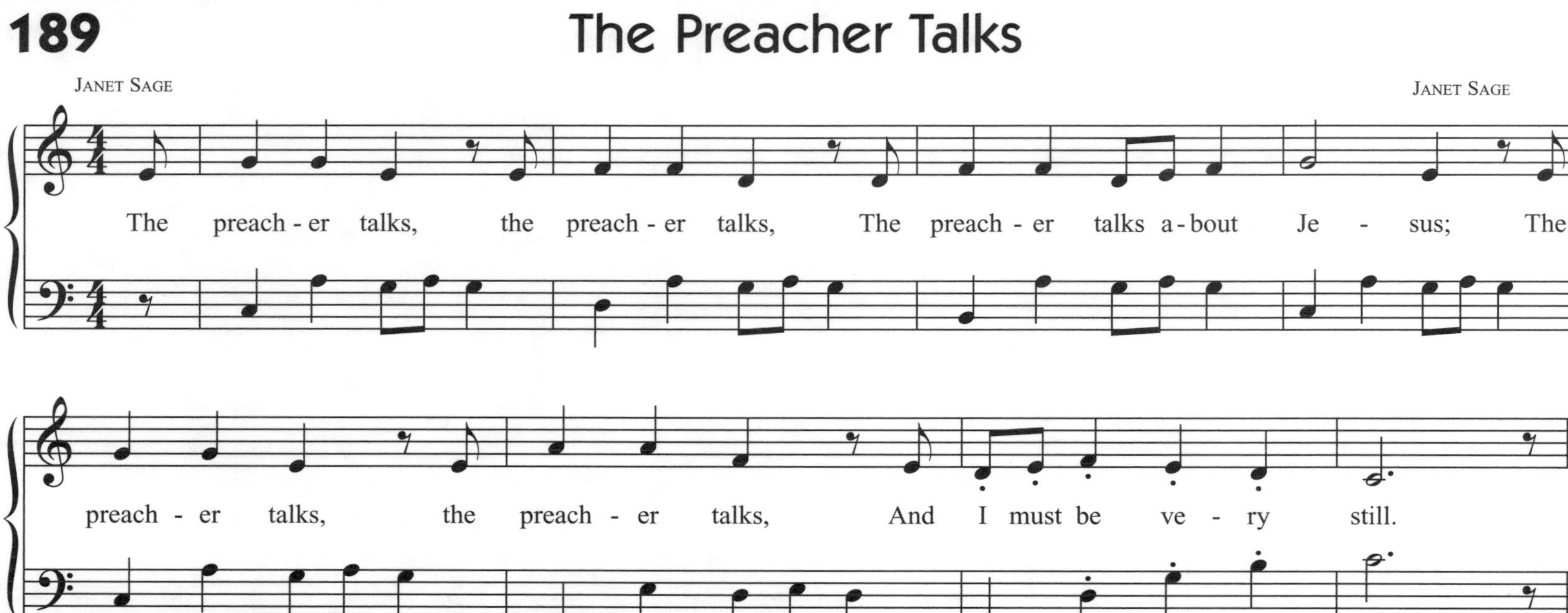
The preach - er talks, the preach - er talks, The preach - er talks a - bout Je - sus; The
preach - er talks, the preach - er talks, And I must be ve - ry still.

WORSHIP

CHURCH

Walking to Church

MARILYN SCHOLES MARILYN SCHOLES

Walk, walk, walk, walk, Walk, walk, walk; On our way to church to - day.
Walk, walk, walk, walk, Walk, walk, walk; There we learn to sing and pray.
Je - sus wants us to praise Him On His Sab - bath day, 'tis true.
I am go - ing up to church; Won't you come and praise Him too?

WORSHIP

CHURCH

191 Give Him Your Heart

Virginia Cason

Virginia Cason / Arr. by Wayne Hooper

If you will let Jesus have all of your heart, He'll fill it with happiness from the start, And you'll know that He loves you, though He's out of sight, Oh, give Him your heart tonight!

Worship

Commitment to Jesus

I Give Myself to Jesus

Joy Hicklin Stewart — Joy Hicklin Stewart

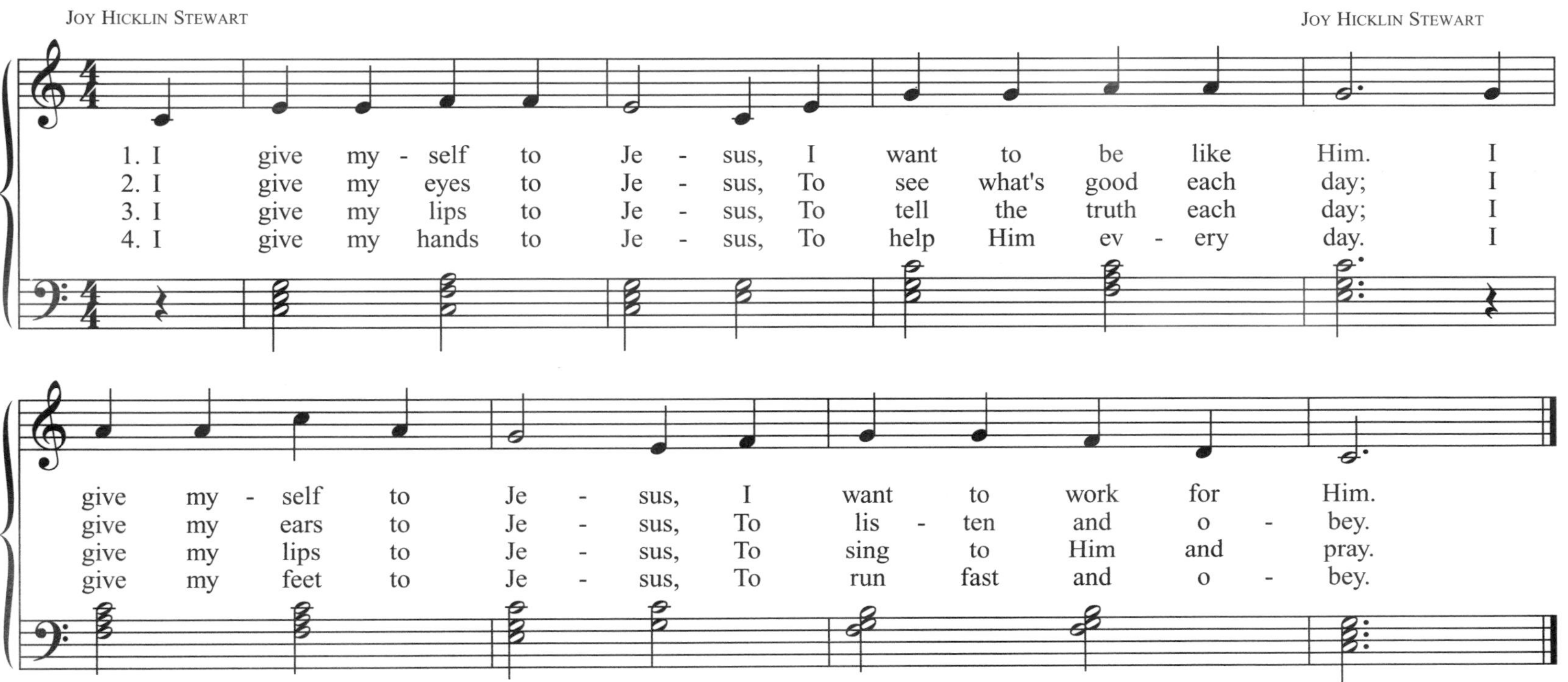
1. I give my - self to Je - sus, I want to be like Him. I
2. I give my eyes to Je - sus, To see what's good each day; I
3. I give my lips to Je - sus, To tell the truth each day; I
4. I give my hands to Je - sus, To help Him ev - ery day. I
give my - self to Je - sus, I want to work for Him.
give my ears to Je - sus, To lis - ten and o - bey.
give my lips to Je - sus, To sing to Him and pray.
give my feet to Je - sus, To run fast and o - bey.

5. I give myself to Jesus,
His helper I will be.
I give myself to Jesus,
His little child I'll be.

6. I give myself to Jesus,
I want to be like Him.
I give myself to Jesus,
I want to work for Him.

7. I want to be like Jesus,
God's rules I will obey.
I want to be like Jesus,
And love God every day.

The following lines may be substituted for the last line of verse 7:

And pray to God each day.
And say good words each day.
And keep the Sabbath day.
And love my parents dear.
And be kind every day.
And take just what is mine.
And tell the truth each day.
And want just what is mine.

193 I Have Decided to Follow Jesus

TRADITIONAL

1. I have de - cid - ed to fol - low Je - sus; I have de - cid - ed to fol - low Je - sus; I have de - cid - ed to fol - low Je - sus; No turn - ing back, no turn - ing back.
2. The world be - hind me, the cross be - fore me; The world be - hind me, the cross be - fore me; The world be - hind me, the cross be - fore me; No turn - ing back, no turn - ing back.
3. Though none go with me, still I will fol - low; Though none go with me, still I will fol - low; Though none go with me, still I will fol - low; No turn - ing back, no turn - ing back.
4. Will you de - cide now to fol - low Je - sus? Will you de - cide now to fol - low Je - sus? Will you de - cide now to fol - low Je - sus? No turn - ing back, no turn - ing back.

I Want to Be Like Jesus

MARLENE GILLEROTH

MARLENE GILLEROTH

I want to be like Je - sus, For Him I want to live. I want to be like Je - sus, My life to Him I give.

Into My Heart

195

HARRY D. CLARKE

HARRY D. CLARKE

In - to my heart, in - to my heart, Come in - to my heart, Lord Je - sus; Come in to - day, come in to stay, Come in - to my heart, Lord Je - sus.

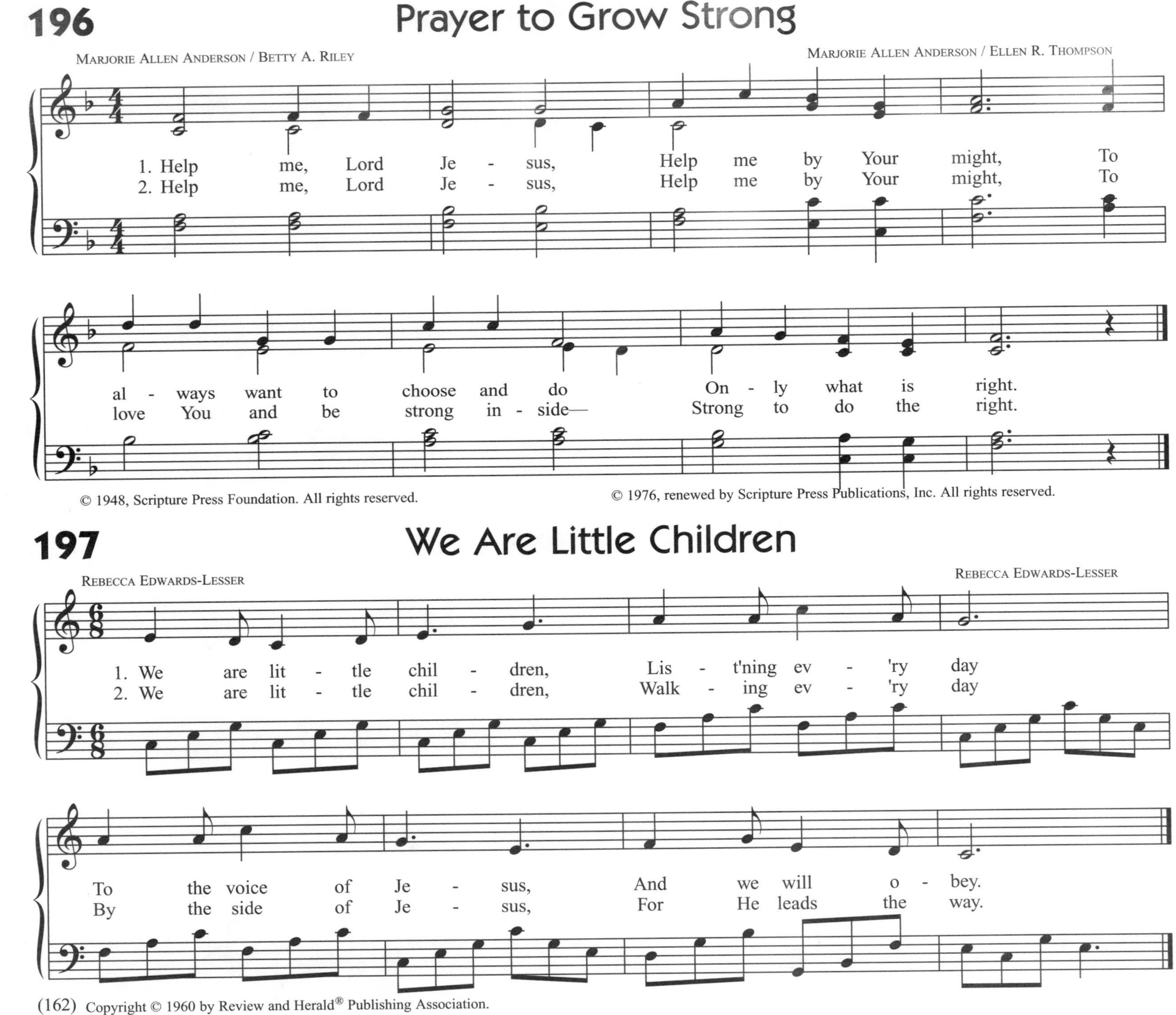
196
Prayer to Grow Strong
Marjorie Allen Anderson / Betty A. Riley
Marjorie Allen Anderson / Ellen R. Thompson
1. Help me, Lord Je - sus, Help me by Your might, To al - ways want to choose and do On - ly what is right.
2. Help me, Lord Je - sus, Help me by Your might, To love You and be strong in - side— Strong to do the right.
© 1948, Scripture Press Foundation. All rights reserved.
© 1976, renewed by Scripture Press Publications, Inc. All rights reserved.
197
We Are Little Children
Rebecca Edwards-Lesser
Rebecca Edwards-Lesser
1. We are lit - tle chil - dren, Lis - t'ning ev - 'ry day To the voice of Je - sus, And we will o - bey.
2. We are lit - tle chil - dren, Walk - ing ev - 'ry day By the side of Je - sus, For He leads the way.
Worship
Commitment to Jesus
(162) Copyright © 1960 by Review and Herald® Publishing Association.

Happy All the Time

ANON.
A. B. SIMPSON / ARR. BY MRS. HENRY GRUBS

[1]I'm [2]in - right, [3]out - right, [4]up - right, [5]down - right, [6]hap - py all the time; [1]I'm
[2]in - right, [3]out - right, [4]Up - right, [5]down - right, [6]hap - py all the time; [4]since Je - sus Christ came [7]in, I
[8]gave my heart to Him, [1]I'm [2]in - right, [3]out - right, [4]up - right, [5]down - right, [6]hap - py all the time!

Motions: 1. Point up to heaven. 2. To heart. 3. Out from body. 4. Up. 5. Down. 6. Clap hands with music. 7. With both hands point to self. 8. With both hands make a large heart in front of self.

199 I Am So Happy

Dorothy Dart

Emelie Cope Albertson

Oh, I am so hap - py, As hap - py as can be,
1. For I have a pup - py dog That Je - sus made for me.
2. For I have a kit - ty cat That Je - sus made for me.
3. For I have some love - ly flow'rs That Je - sus made for me.
4. For I have some ros - es red That Je - sus made for me.

5. For I have some violets blue
   That Jesus made for me.

6. For I have some pansies sweet
   That Jesus made for me.

7. For I have a big pink rose
   That Jesus made for me.

8. For I have a mother dear
   That Jesus gave to me.

9. For I have a father strong
   That Jesus gave to me.

10. For I have a Bible true
    That Jesus gave to me.

If You're Happy

200

ALFRED SMITH

TRADITIONAL / ARR. BY KENNETH D. LOGAN

(MELODY)

1. If you're hap - py and you know it, clap your hands.
If you're hap - py and you know it, clap your hands.
If you're hap - py and you know it, then your face will sure - ly show it.
If you're hap - py and you know it, clap your hands.

2. If you're sav'd and you know it, say "A - men!"
If you're sav'd and you know it, say "A - men!"
If you're sav'd and you know it, then your life will sure - ly show it.
If you're sav'd and you know it, say "A - men!"

201 I'll Be Happy

Kathryn B. Myers Kathryn B. Myers

I'll be hap-py all the day, If I live like Je - sus. I'll be kind in ev-'ry way, Then I'll be like Je - sus.

Worship

Happiness

Jesus Wants Me for a Sunbeam
202
Nellie Talbot
E. O. Excell
1. Je - sus wants me for a sun - beam, To shine for Him each day;
In ev - 'ry way try to please Him, At home, at school, at play.
2. Je - sus wants me to be lov - ing, And kind to all I see,
Show - ing how pleas - ant and hap - py His lit - tle one can be.
3. I will ask Je - sus to help me, To keep my heart from sin,
Ev - er re - flect - ing His good - ness And al - ways shine for Him.
4. I'll be a sun - beam for Je - sus, I can, if I but try,
Serv - ing Him mo - ment by mo - ment, Then live with Him on high.
REFRAIN
A sun - beam, a sun - beam, Je - sus wants me for a sun - beam; A
sun - beam, a sun - beam, I'll be a sun - beam for Him.
Worship
Happiness

203 Scrubbing

Cynthia Patterson Coston | Cynthia Patterson Coston

1. Scrub - bing, scrub - bing, Scru - ub - bing. Bath - time scrub - bing makes me clean.
2. First, my face, my hands, my hair. I am clean, yes, ev' - ry - where.

204 God, You Are So Great and Good

Noelene Johnsson | Traditional / Arr. by Lois C. Hall

God, You are so great and good, great and good, great and good.

God, You are so great and good! How much we love You.

I Love Jesus!

205

JANET SAGE
JANET SAGE
I love Je-sus! O I love Je-sus! O I love Je - sus and He loves me too!
I love Je - sus, O I love Je - sus, O I love Je - sus and He loves me too!

Pianist: This song needs to be played with a full tone, expressing a joyful freedom.

Leader: This is an excellent theme song for programs on Jesus' love, or it may be included in practically any program.

206 I Love the Dear Jesus

BERTHA D. MARTIN
DOROTHY P. BOGGS / HARMONIZED BY AUDRA L. WOOD
1. I love the dear Je - sus, He cares for me, Cares for me, cares for me; I
2. I love the dear Je - sus, He'll come for me, Come for me, come for me; I
love the dear Je - sus, He cares for me, Love me and cares for me.
love the dear Je - sus, He'll come for me, Soon He will come for me.
207
I Love the Lord
LUKE 4:8; PSALM 18:1
HAYDN / ARR. BY KENNETH D. LOGAN
I love the Lord. Yes, I love the Lord. And
I wor - ship Him* be - cause I love the Lord.

*Optional phrases: I will be kind, I want to share, I learn from God's Word, I will thank Him, etc.

I Love Thee, O Lord 208

PSALM 18:1, RSV

JANET SAGE

I love Thee, O Lord, I love Thee, O Lord, I love Thee, O Lord, I love Thee, O Lord, I love Thee, O Lord, I love Thee, O Lord.

Oh, How I Love Jesus 209

FREDERICK WHITFIELD

TRADITIONAL

Oh, how I love Je - sus, Oh, how I love Je - sus, Oh, how I love Je - sus, Be - cause He first loved me.

210 Oh, Friend, Do You Love Jesus?

Unknown Unknown

Oh, friend,* do you love Je - sus? Oh, yes, I love Je - sus. Are you
sure you love Je - sus? Yes, I'm sure I love Je - sus. Then why do you love
Je - sus? Here's why I love Je - sus: Be - cause He first loved me.

*boys, girls, teacher, father, mother

Divide into two groups: Group 1 stands when asking the questions. Group 2 stands when answering the questions. Groups sit when not singing.

Come Praise the Lord

211

STEPHEN ELKINS

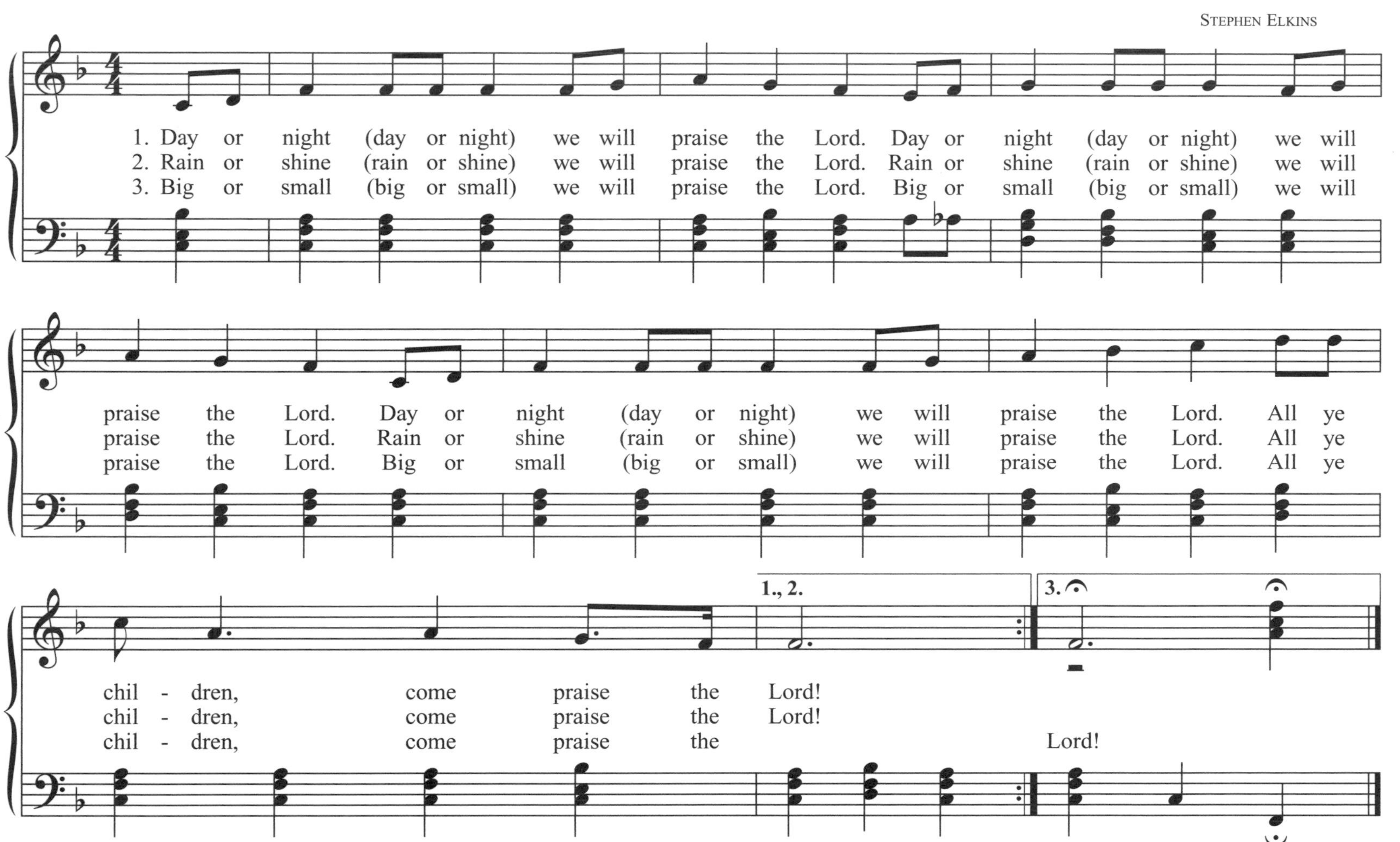
1. Day or night (day or night) we will praise the Lord. Day or night (day or night) we will
2. Rain or shine (rain or shine) we will praise the Lord. Rain or shine (rain or shine) we will
3. Big or small (big or small) we will praise the Lord. Big or small (big or small) we will
praise the Lord. Day or night (day or night) we will praise the Lord. All ye
praise the Lord. Rain or shine (rain or shine) we will praise the Lord. All ye
praise the Lord. Big or small (big or small) we will praise the Lord. All ye
1., 2.
3.
chil - dren, come praise the Lord!
chil - dren, come praise the Lord!
chil - dren, come praise the Lord!

212 Arky, Arky

UNKNOWN
1. The
Lord told No - ah, there's gon - na be a flood - y, flood - y,
Lord told No - ah to build him an ark - y, ark - y,
an - i - mals, the an - i - mals, they came in by two - sies, two - sies,
rain - ed and pour - ed for for - - - ty day - sies, day - sies,
Lord told No - ah, there's gon - na be a flood - y, flood - y.
Lord told No - ah to build him an ark - y, ark - y.
an - i - mals, the an - i - mals, they came in by two - sies, two - sies,
rain - ed and pour - ed for for - - - ty day - sies, day - sies,
Get those an - i - mals out of the mud - dy, mud - dy,
Build it out of go - pher bark - y, bark - y,
el - e - phants and kang - a - roos - ies, roos - ies,
al - most drove those an - i - mals craz - ies, craz - ies,

CHORUS
child - ren of the Lord. So rise and shine and
give God the glo - ry, glo - ry, rise and shine and give God the glo - ry, glo - ry.
Rise and shine and give God the glo - ry, glo - ry, child - ren
of the Lord.
1.-4.
2. The
3. The
4. It
5.

5. The sun came up and dried up the land-y, land-y,
it dried up the land-y, land-y,
[Spoken] (Look, - there's the sun!)
everything was fine and dand-y, dand-y,

Suggest that younger kids sing only the chorus.

WORSHIP

PRAISE

213 Hallelu, Hallelu

Arr. by Kenneth D. Logan

Hal - le - lu, hal - le - lu, hal - le - lu, hal - le - lu - jah! Praise ye the Lord! Hal - le -
lu, hal - le - lu, hal - le - lu, hal - le - lu - jah! Praise ye the Lord!
Praise ye the Lord, hal - le - lu - jah! Praise ye the Lord, hal - le - lu - jah!
Praise ye the Lord, hal - le - lu - jah! Praise ye the Lord!

Divide into two groups. Group 1 stands and sings on all the "Hallelus." Group 2 stands and sings on all the "Praise ye the Lords." Groups sit when not singing.

I Am Happy as Can Be! 214

JANET SAGE.
JANET SAGE
I am hap - py as can be! I am hap - py as can be For ev - 'ry - thing that Je - sus made for me!

Leader: This would be a good theme song for a program about the creation of God's gifts. Other words may be substituted for "ev'rything," such as "singing birds," "pretty flow'rs," "butterflies." With some further manipulation other items could be mentioned in the song. This is also a good clapping song. Once the children start to clap, however, they are not as likely to sing. Go over the song a time or two without the clapping.

I Have Hands That Clap 215

S. VANCE S. VANCE

1. I have hands that clap, clap, clap, I have hands that clap, clap, clap,
I have hands that clap, clap, clap. They were made for Je - sus.

2. I have fin - gers that wig - gle, wig - gle, wig - gle, I have fin - gers that wig - gle, wig - gle, wig - gle,
I have fin - gers that wig - gle, wig - gle, wig - gle. They were made by Je - sus.

3. I have feet that tip - py - tip - py toe, I have feet that tip - py - tip - py toe,
I have feet that tip - py - tip - py toe. They were made by Je - sus.

4. I have knees that bend by my chair, I have knees that bend by my chair,
I have hands that fold in prayer. Now I talk to Je - sus.

LVPH-23

216 I Have the Joy

ARR. BY HARRY DIXON LOES

1. I have the joy, joy, joy, joy, down in my heart, *Where?
2. I have the peace that pass - eth un - der - stand - ing down in my heart,
Down in my heart, *Where? down in my heart; I have the joy, joy, joy, joy,
Down in my heart, down in my heart; I have the peace that pass - eth un - der - stand - ing
down in my heart, *Where? Down in my heart to stay.
down in my heart, Down in my heart to stay.

3. I have the love of Jesus, love of Jesus, down in my heart,
Down in my heart, down in my heart;
I have the love of Jesus, love of Jesus, down in my heart,
Down in my heart to stay.

4. I have the good old Seventh-day Adventist message, down in my heart,
Down in my heart, down in my heart;
I have the good old Seventh-day Adventist message, down in my heart,
Down in my heart to stay.

* *Spoken:* "Where?"

WORSHIP

PRAISE

I Will Sing 217

Based on Psalm 89:1, ICB

René Alexenko Evans / Arr. by Kenneth D. Logan

I will sing a - bout the Lord's love, I will sing a - bout the Lord's love, I will
sing a - bout the Lord's love, His love to me.

My Best Friend Is Jesus 218

Mildred Adair Stagg

Mildred Adair Stagg

1. My best friend is Je - sus, Praise Him! Praise Him! My best friend is Je - sus, Praise Him!
2. My best friend is Je - sus, Thank Him! Thank Him! My best friend is Je - sus, Thank Him!
3. My best friend is Je - sus, Love Him! Love Him! My best friend is Je - sus, Love Him!
4. My best friend is Je - sus, Serve Him! Serve Him! My best friend is Je - sus, Serve Him!

219 Let's Give the Lord Our Praise

Anita Reith Stohs | Kenneth D. Logan

[1]Let's give the Lord our praise, [2]Let's give the Lord our prayers, [3]Let's give the
Lord our thanks [4]For all He does for us. [5]Let's thank Him for His love,
[6]Now, ev - ery girl and boy, [7]Wor - ship the Lord a - bove.

Motions: 1. Hold out hands. 2. Hold up hands. 3. Fold hands. 4. Clap hands. 5. Hold up hands. 6. Point around the group. 7. Clap hands.

WORSHIP

PRAISE

Making Music

Tommye Melendez

[1]Praise Him with the trum-pet, play it loud and clear,
[2]Then the drums and cym-bals, so ev-'ry-one can hear!
We're mak-ing [3]mu-sic for the Lord!
We're mak-ing mu-sic for the Lord!

Motions: 1. Play (imaginary) trumpets. 2. Play (imaginary) drums or cymbals. 3. Clap on the beat for remainder of song.

221 Praise Him, Praise Him

Anonymous / Adapt. by General Conference Sabbath School Department

Arr. by Hubert P. Main

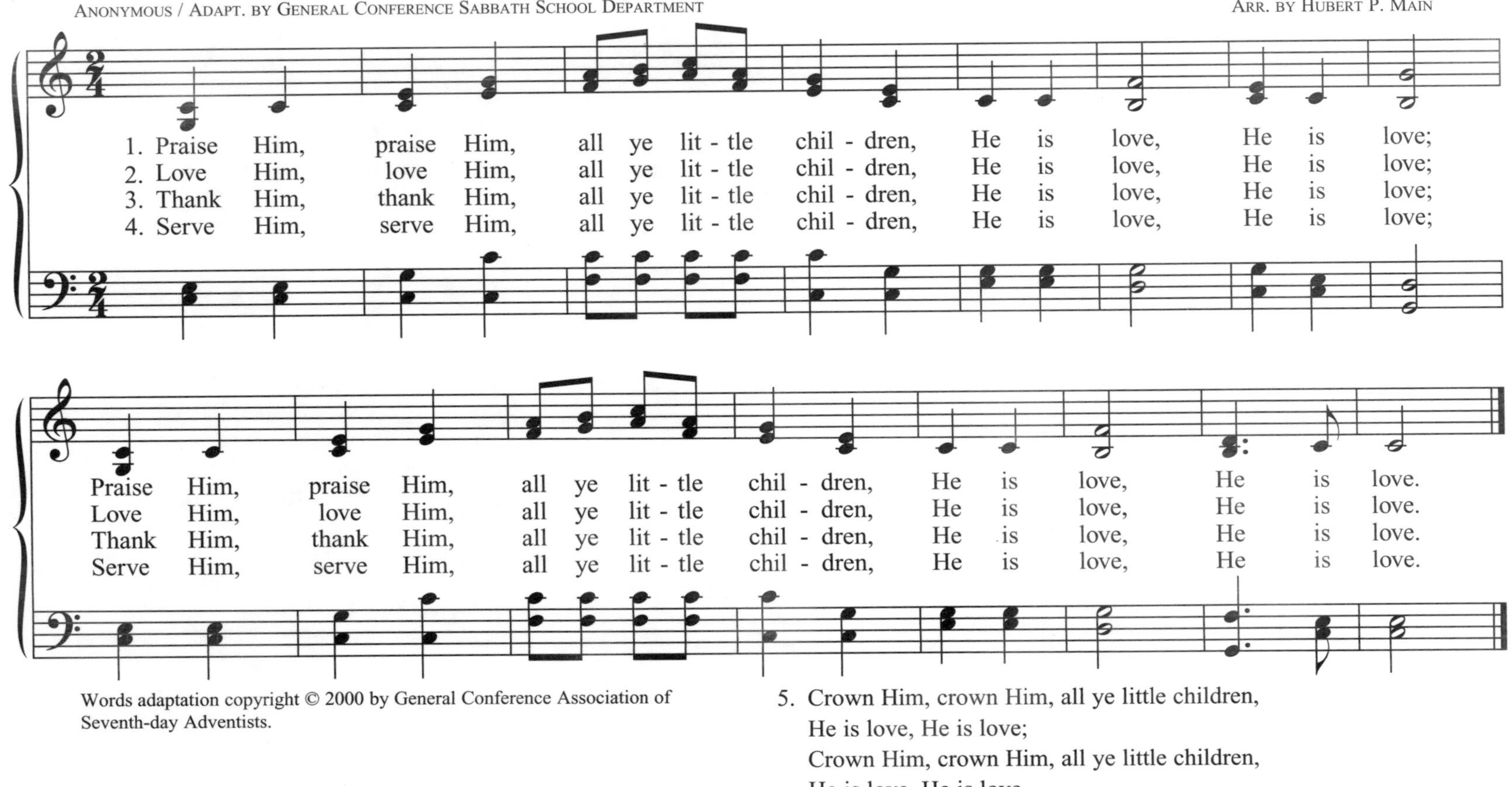

1. Praise Him, praise Him, all ye lit - tle chil - dren, He is love, He is love;
2. Love Him, love Him, all ye lit - tle chil - dren, He is love, He is love;
3. Thank Him, thank Him, all ye lit - tle chil - dren, He is love, He is love;
4. Serve Him, serve Him, all ye lit - tle chil - dren, He is love, He is love;
Praise Him, praise Him, all ye lit - tle chil - dren, He is love, He is love.
Love Him, love Him, all ye lit - tle chil - dren, He is love, He is love.
Thank Him, thank Him, all ye lit - tle chil - dren, He is love, He is love.
Serve Him, serve Him, all ye lit - tle chil - dren, He is love, He is love.

5. Crown Him, crown Him, all ye little children,
He is love, He is love;
Crown Him, crown Him, all ye little children,
He is love, He is love.

6. *Thank Him, thank Him, all you happy children,
Jesus came, Jesus came;
Thank Him, thank Him, all you happy children,
Jesus came, came to earth.

*Additional verse by General Conference Sabbath School Department.

Praise to Jesus* 222

Janet Sage

Adapt. by Janet Sage

Praise to Je-sus! Praise to Je-sus! We praise Him, We praise Him, We praise Him!

*Simplified "Hallelujah Chorus," from *Messiah,* G. F. Handel

What Can Baby Do? 223

Unknown

Unknown

1. What can ba - by do? When she's* in Sab - bath school? But pat - ty cake and pat - ty cake and play a peek - a - boo!
2. What can ba - by do? When she's* in Sab - bath school? But sing a song of Je - sus' love and play a peek - a - boo!

*he's

Worship

Praise

224 Praise Your God

Janine Max — Janine Max

Praise the God who made you. Shout with all your might. Praise
the One who changed the dark - ness in - to light.
Join in ce - le - bra - tion all of His cre - a - tion and praise, praise, praise Him!
Praise, praise, Him! Praise, praise, praise your God.

Worship

Praise

Rejoice in the Lord Always

Based on Philippians 4:4

Unknown

Re - joice in the Lord al - ways, and a - gain I say, re - joice! Re -
joice in the Lord al - ways, and a - gain I say, re - joice! Re -
joice, re - joice, and a - gain I say, re - joice! Re -
joice, re - joice, and a - gain I say, re - joice!

226 Wonderful, Wonderful

S. Jones

Arr. by Homer Hammontree

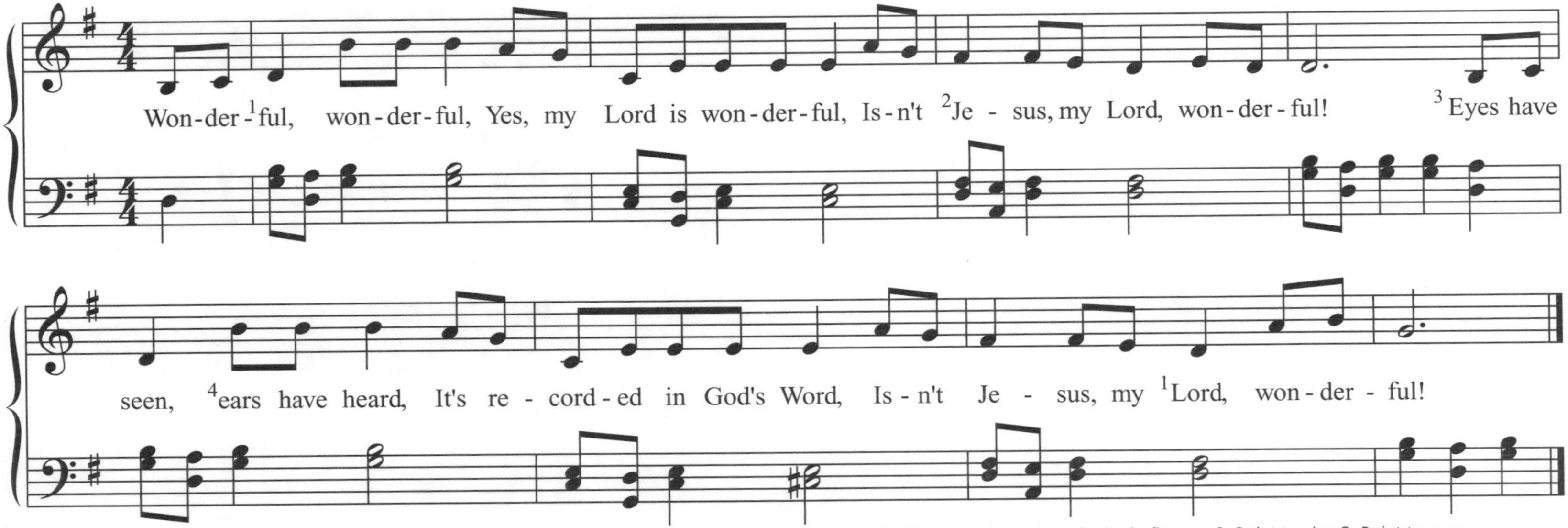

Won-der-[1]ful, won-der-ful, Yes, my Lord is won-der-ful, Is-n't [2]Je - sus, my Lord, won-der-ful! [3]Eyes have seen, [4]ears have heard, It's re - cord - ed in God's Word, Is - n't Je - sus, my [1]Lord, won - der - ful!

Motions: 1. Wave hands in air and wiggle fingers. 2. Point to sky. 3. Point to eyes. 4. Point to ears.

227 A Little Talk With Jesus

Anonymous

Arranged

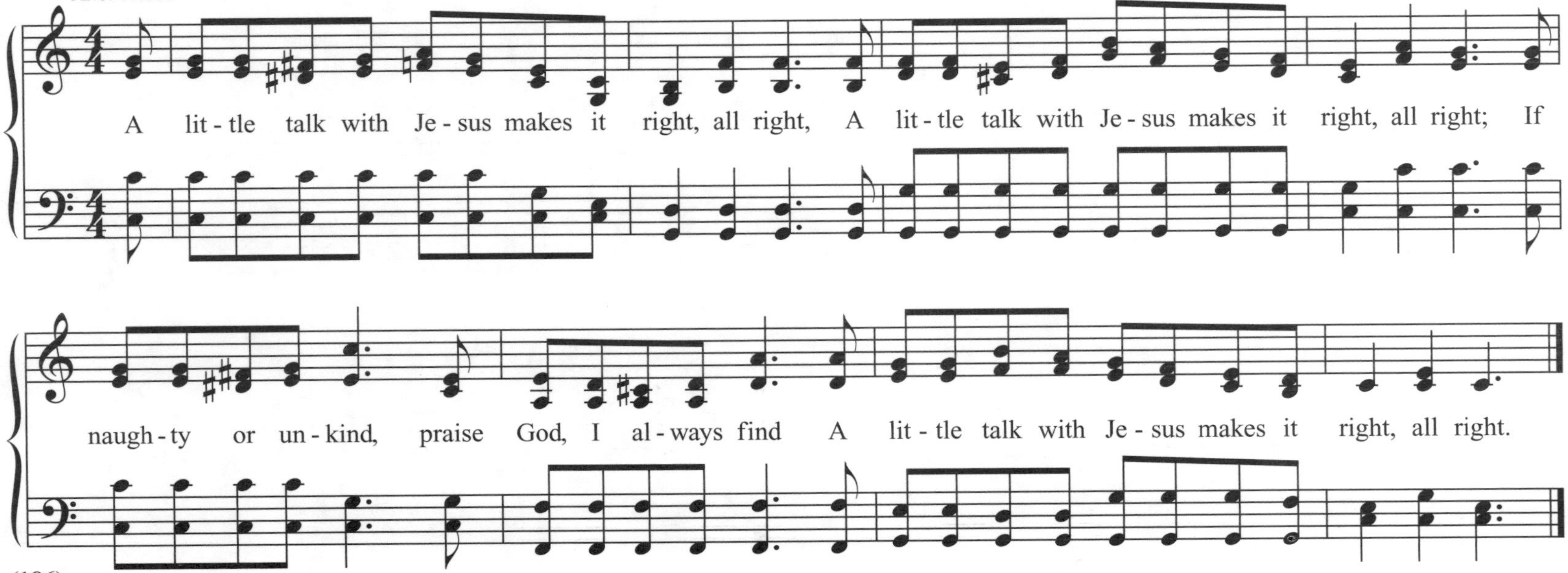

A lit - tle talk with Je - sus makes it right, all right, A lit - tle talk with Je - sus makes it right, all right; If naugh - ty or un - kind, praise God, I al - ways find A lit - tle talk with Je - sus makes it right, all right.

Worship

Praise

I Talk to Jesus

228

Jacqueline McDonald

Jacqueline McDonald

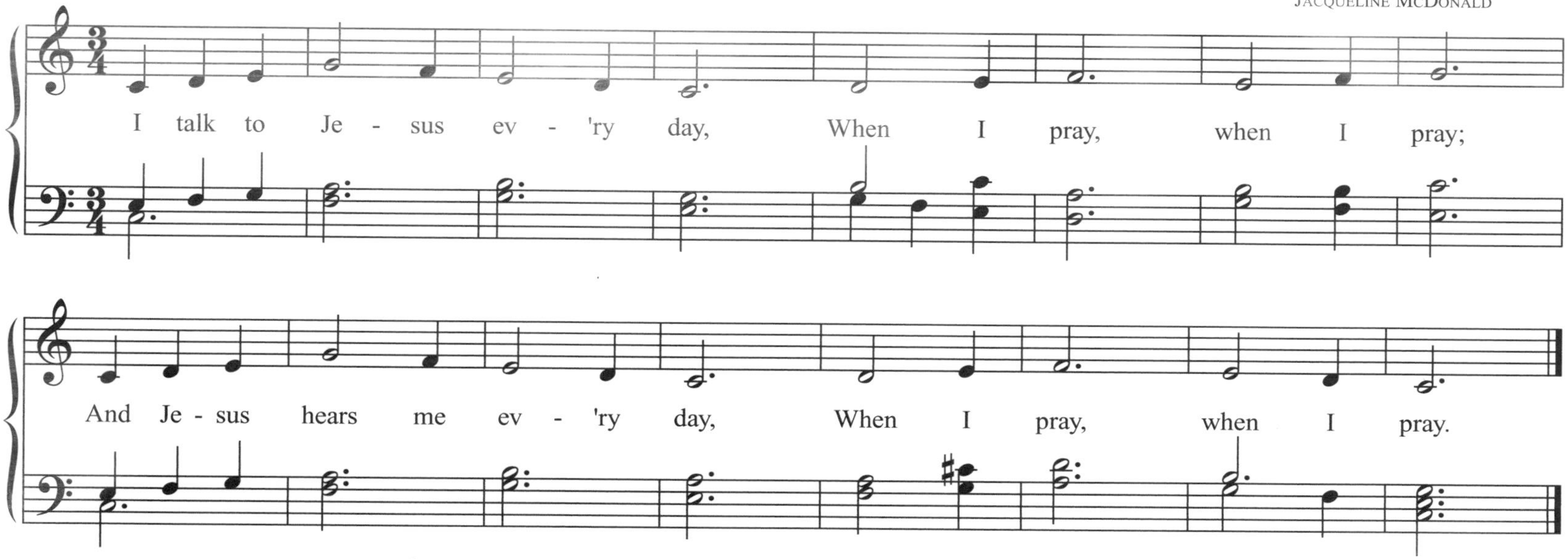

I talk to Je - sus ev - 'ry day, When I pray, when I pray;
And Je - sus hears me ev - 'ry day, When I pray, when I pray.

I Will Pray

229

Dorothy Robison

Dorothy Robison

1. I will pray to Je - sus, Morn - ing, noon, and night;
I will pray to Je - sus, Morn - ing, noon, and night.

2. I will thank dear Je - sus, Morn - ing, noon, and night;
I will thank dear Je - sus, Morn - ing, noon, and night.

Worship

Prayer

Jesus Is My Helper

Stella B. Daleburn

Stella B. Daleburn

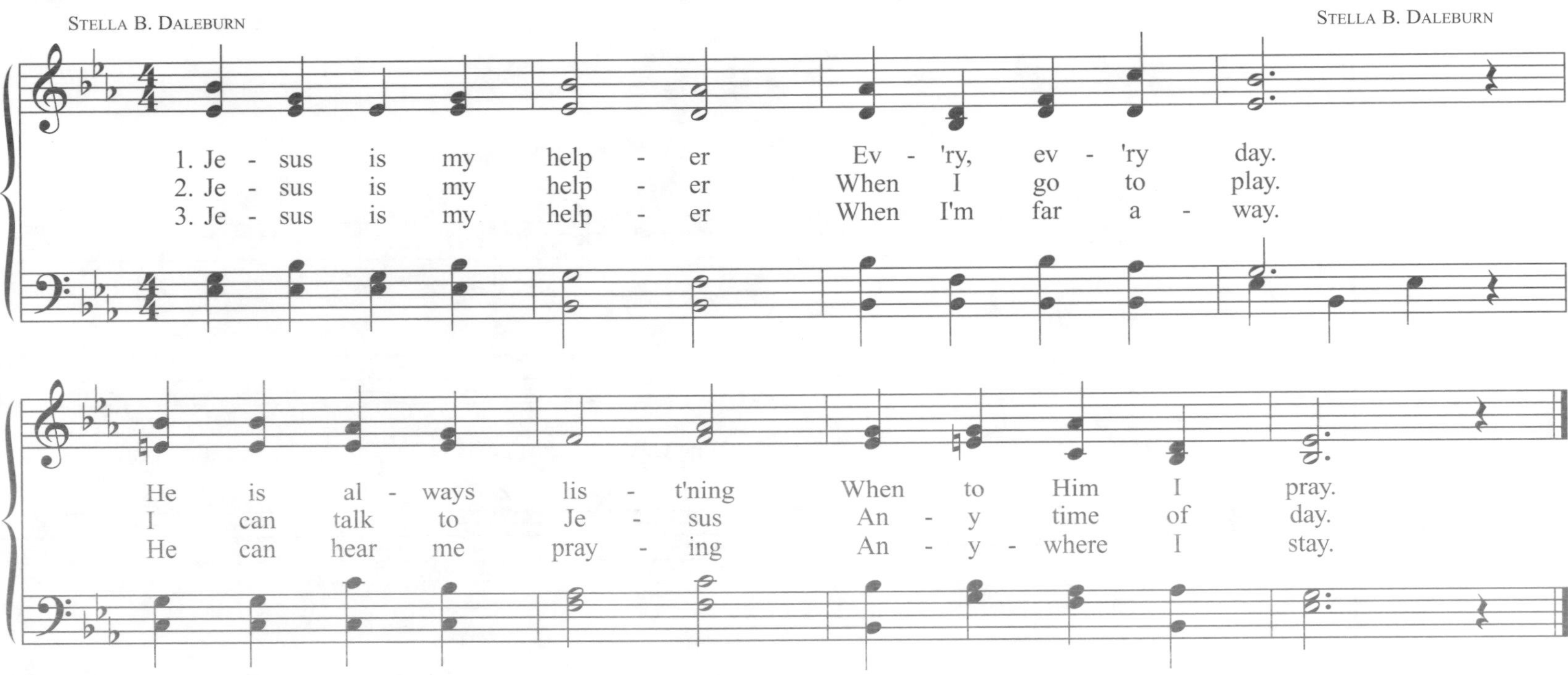
1. Je - sus is my help - er Ev - 'ry, ev - 'ry day.
2. Je - sus is my help - er When I go to play.
3. Je - sus is my help - er When I'm far a - way.
He is al - ways lis - t'ning When to Him I pray.
I can talk to Je - sus An - y time of day.
He can hear me pray - ing An - y - where I stay.

Worship

Prayer

Pray

231

Nancy J. Stagl-Schippmann

Nancy J. Stagl-Schippmann

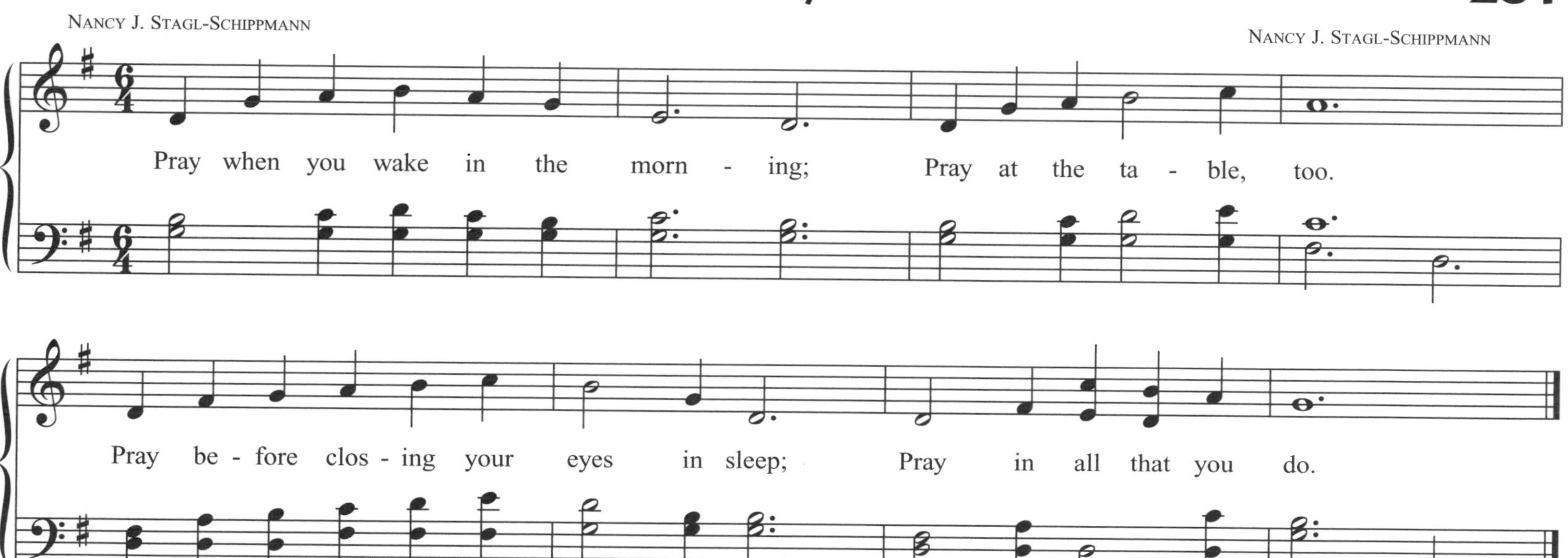
Pray when you wake in the morn - ing; Pray at the ta - ble, too.
Pray be - fore clos - ing your eyes in sleep; Pray in all that you do.

Praying Every Day

232

Vikki Montgomery

Vikki Montgomery

I can pray ev - 'ry day, an - y - time, an - y - where. I can pray ev - 'ry day, an - y - time, an - y - where.

233 Whisper a Prayer

UNKNOWN
UNKNOWN / ARR. BY KENNETH D. LOGAN
1. Whis - per a prayer in the morn - ing, Whis - per a prayer at noon,
Whis - per a prayer in the eve - ning To keep your heart in tune.
2. God an - swers prayer in the morn - ing, God an - swers prayer at noon,
God an - swers prayer in the eve - ning To keep your heart in tune.
3. Je - sus may come in the morn - ing, Je - sus may come at noon,
Je - sus may come in the eve - ning So keep your heart in tune.

Blessed Rest

Janine Max
Janine Max
When God had made the world and ev - 'ry - thing in it too He looked a - round and
said, "It's good! There's no more work to do!" The ve - ry next day, the sev - enth day, He de -
ci - ded to stop and rest. Then all cre - a - tion wor - shiped God, Who made the Sab - bath blessed.

235 Happy Sabbath

MARGARET KENNEDY (ADAPTED)

MARGARET KENNEDY

1. Sab - bath is a hap - py day, hap - py day, hap - py day,
2. First we go to Sab - bath school, Sab - bath school, Sab - bath school,
3. Then we like to stay for church, stay for church, stay for church,
4. Then we go see a sick friend, a sick friend, a sick friend,
Sab - bath is a hap - py day, I love ev - 'ry Sab - bath.
First we go to Sab - bath school, I love ev - 'ry Sab - bath.
Then we like to stay for church, I love ev - 'ry Sab - bath.
Then we go see a sick friend, I love ev - 'ry Sab - bath.

5. Then we like to take a walk,
take a walk, take a walk,
Then we like to take a walk,
I love ev'ry Sabbath.

WORSHIP

SABBATH

Listen to the Bells Ring

Florence P. Jorgensen — Florence P. Jorgensen

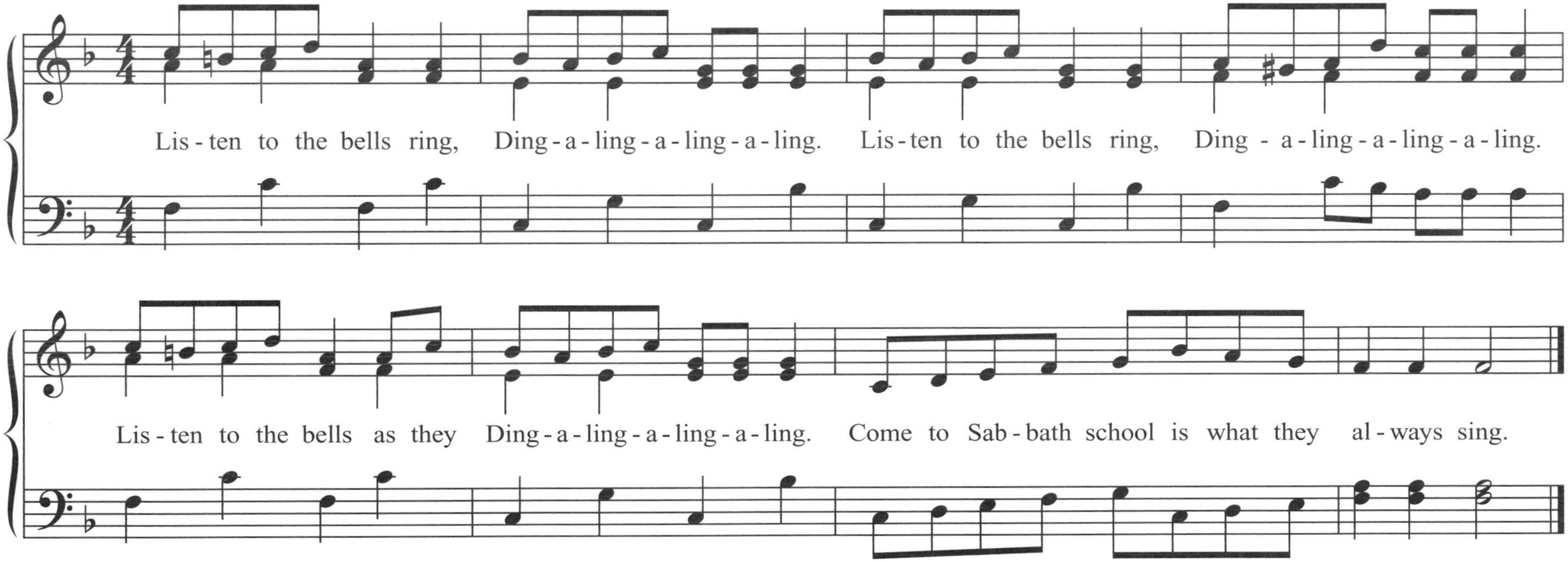

Lis - ten to the bells ring, Ding - a - ling - a - ling - a - ling. Lis - ten to the bells ring, Ding - a - ling - a - ling - a - ling.

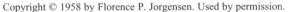

Lis - ten to the bells as they Ding - a - ling - a - ling - a - ling. Come to Sab - bath school is what they al - ways sing.

Sabbath Bells

Mildred Adair — Mildred Adair

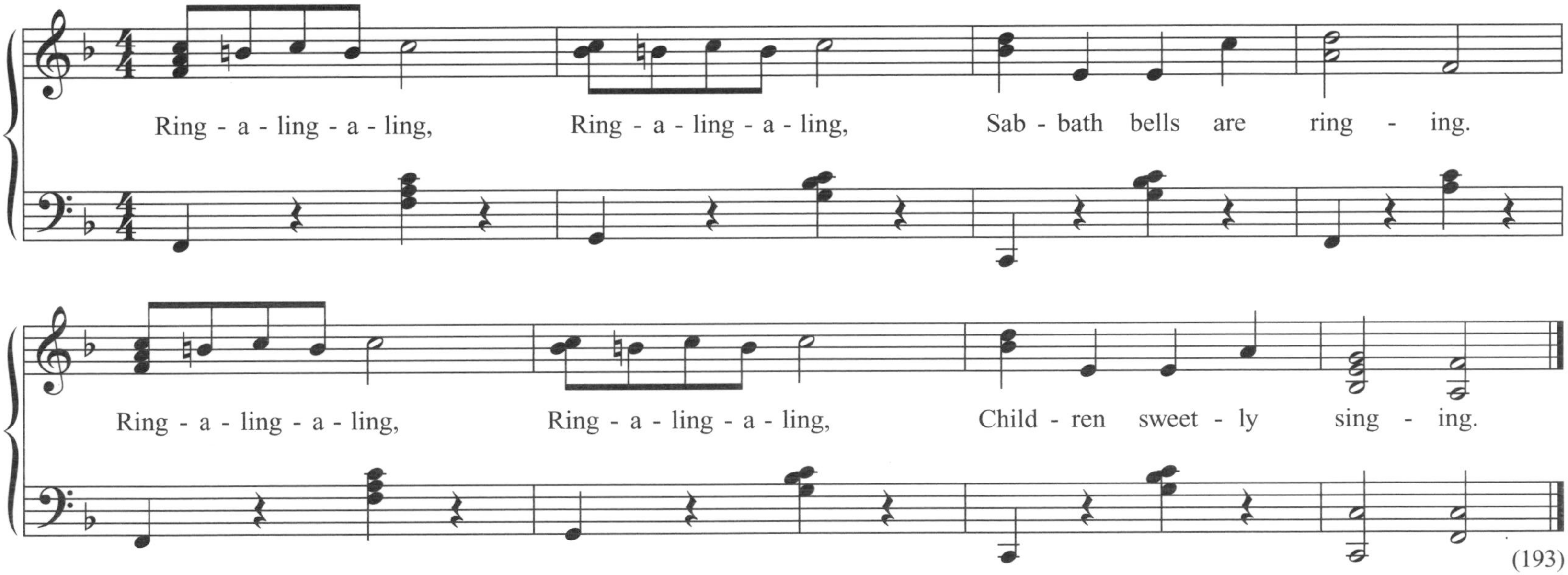

Ring - a - ling - a - ling, Ring - a - ling - a - ling, Sab - bath bells are ring - ing.

Ring - a - ling - a - ling, Ring - a - ling - a - ling, Child - ren sweet - ly sing - ing.

238 This Is the Day

Les Garrett / Based on Psalm 118:24

Les Garrett

This is the day, this is the day that the Lord has made, that the Lord has made.
We will re-joice, we will re-joice and be glad in it, and be glad in it.
This is the day that the Lord has made; we will re-joice and be glad in it.
This is the day, this is the day that the Lord has made.

Worship

Sabbath

All for Jesus

239

LOUISE M. OGLEVEE — MRS. MAUD KIPP SKAU

Two ears to hear of Je - sus; Two eyes al - ways to see
The love - ly world I live in, That He has giv - en me;
Two lips to pray to Je - sus And kind sweet words to say;
A heart to thank Him glad - ly For love and care each day.

WORSHIP

THANKFULNESS

240 O Give Thanks Unto the Lord

Based on Psalm 136:1

Janet Sage

O give thanks un - to the Lord, give thanks un-to the Lord. O give thanks un -
to the Lord, give thanks un - to the Lord. O give thanks, give
thanks un-to the Lord. O give thanks un - to the Lord, give thanks un-to the Lord.

Worship

Thankfulness

Our Thanksgiving Song

241

MRS. IVAR JOHNSON — MRS. IVAR JOHNSON

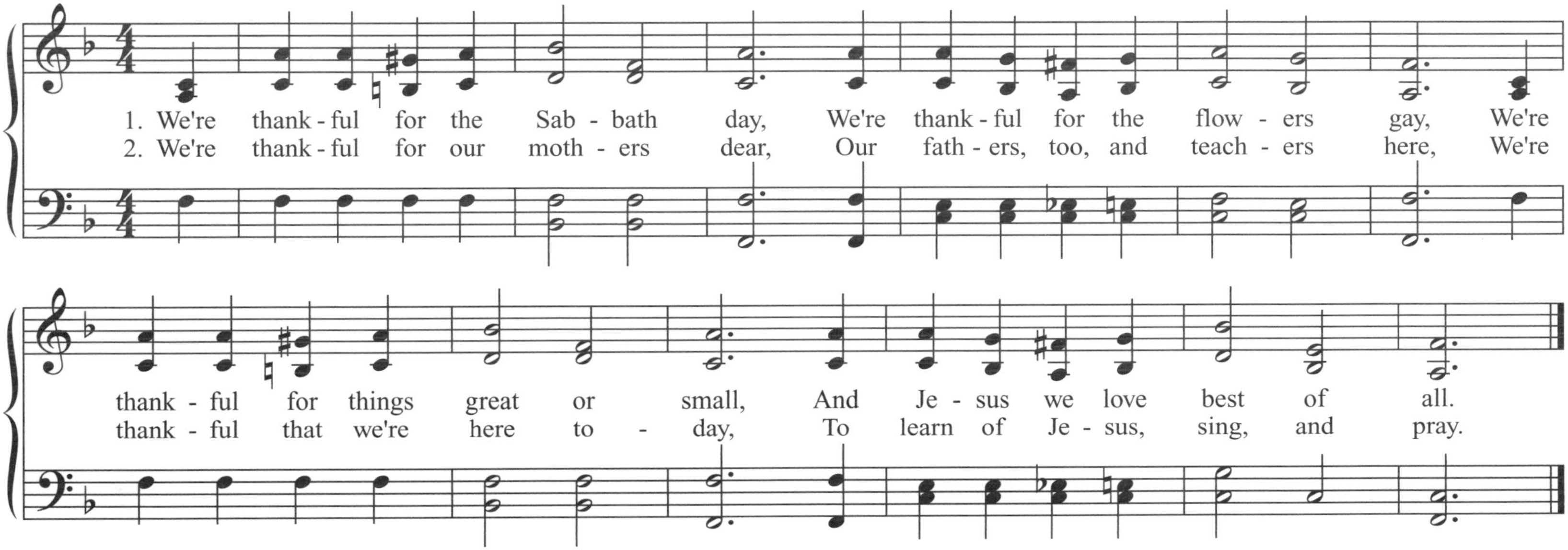

1. We're thank-ful for the Sab-bath day, We're thank-ful for the flow-ers gay, We're thank-ful for things great or small, And Je-sus we love best of all.
2. We're thank-ful for our moth-ers dear, Our fath-ers, too, and teach-ers here, We're thank-ful that we're here to-day, To learn of Je-sus, sing, and pray.

Teach Us to Share

242

EDITH CASSETT — EDITH CASSETT / ARR. BY MARY JEAN SMITH

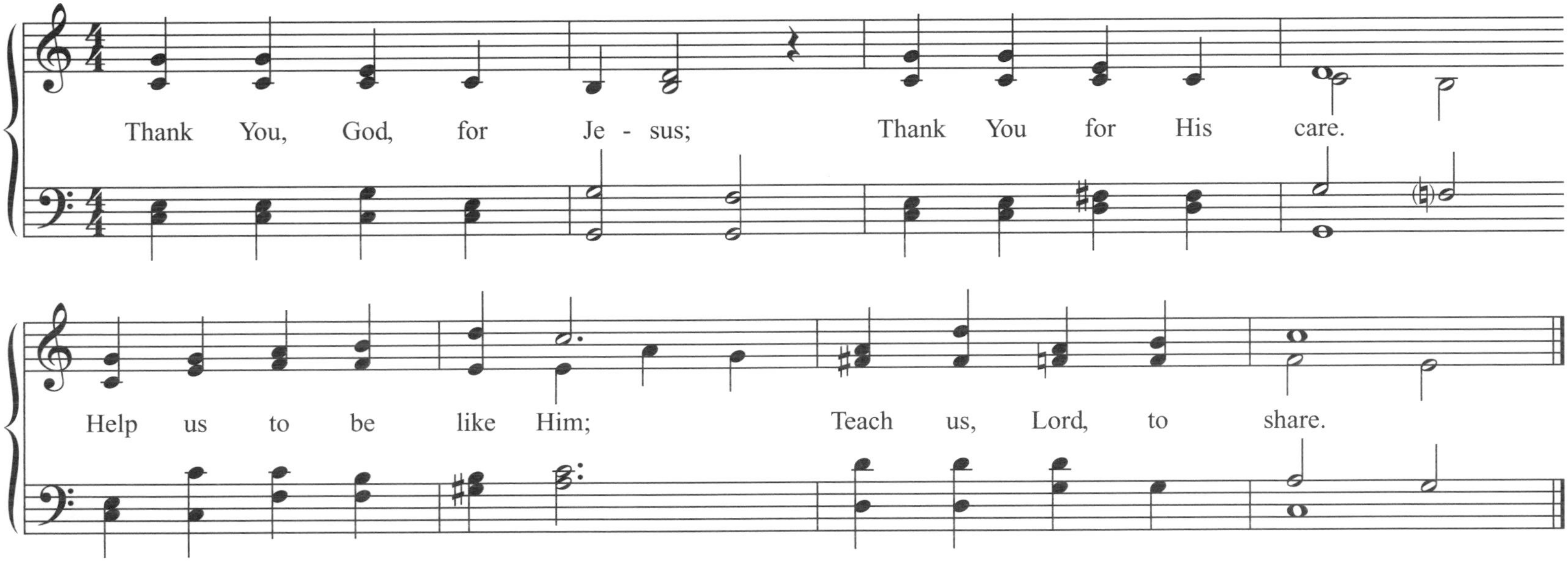

Thank You, God, for Je-sus; Thank You for His care.
Help us to be like Him; Teach us, Lord, to share.

WORSHIP

THANKFULNESS

243 Thank You, Jesus

RUTH G. HALLETT — JOHN C. HALLETT

1. Thank You, Jes - us, for all You've done, Thank You, Lord.
2. Thank You, Je - sus, for love like Thine, Thank You, Lord.
Thank You, Je - sus, for vic - t'ries won, Oh, thank You, Lord.
Thank You, Je - sus, for grace di - vine, Oh thank You, Lord.
For Your love and ten - der care, For Your Word and an - swered prayer,
For Your cross of Cal - va - ry, For Your blood that cleans - es me,

WORSHIP

THANKFULNESS

Thank You, Je - sus, for all You've done, Thank You, Lord.
Thank You, Je - sus, that You are mine, Thank You, Lord.

The Butterfly Song

Brian M. Howard
Brian M. Howard
Playfully
1. If I were a but - ter - fly, I'd thank You, Lord, for giv - ing me wings. And if I were a ro - bin in a tree, I'd thank You, Lord, that I could sing. And if I were a
2. If I were an el - e - phant, I'd thank You, Lord, by rais - ing my trunk. And if I were a kan - ga - roo, You know I'd hop right up to You. And if I were an
3. If I were a wig - gly worm, I'd thank You, Lord, that I could squirm. And if I were a croc - o - dile, I'd thank You, Lord, for my big smile. And if I were a

fish in the sea, I'd wig - gle my tail and I'd gig - gle with glee. But
oc - to - pus, I'd thank You, Lord, for my fine looks. But
fuz - zy - wuz - zy bear, I'd thank You, Lord, for my fuz - zy - wuz - zy hair. But
I just thank You, Fa - ther, for mak - ing me "me."
I just thank You, Fa - ther, for mak - ing me "me."
I just thank You, Fa - ther, for mak - ing me "me."
REFRAIN
For You gave me a heart and You gave me a smile. You gave me Je - sus and You
made me your child. And I just thank You, Fa - ther, for mak - ing me "me."

WORSHIP

THANKFULNESS

LVPH-26

245 Thank You Song

CAROL GREENE
CAROL GREENE
In 1
1. We thank You for sun - shine of yel - low and gold. We thank You for
2. We thank You for flow - ers of red, yel - low, blue. We thank You for
moon - light all sil - ver and cold, For crys - tal of star - light and
chil - dren of all col - ors too, For rain - bows that bright - en the
spar - kle of dew. You made them, dear Fa - ther, and so we thank You.
whole neigh - bor - hood. You made them, dear Fa - ther, and, oh, they are good!

Have the children name other things God has made that make them happy. They will enjoy waving colored streamers or scarves as they sing this song.

WORSHIP

THANKFULNESS

Don't Cry, Little Baby

JANET SAGE
JANET SAGE
Don't cry, little baby, don't cry, don't cry;
Jesus loves you, Jesus loves you; Don't
cry, little baby, don't cry, don't cry;
Jesus loves you, Jesus loves you.

Pianist: This lilting lullaby needs to flow along smoothly. Do not play it too slowly.

Leader: Once the children have learned the song, let them rock little dolls in their arms. The song is useful in illustrations of helpfulness, kindness, and family relations. It is a piece that the little ones can relate to easily, and it will bring out their own little parental instincts. Mothers will find it useful for many everyday circumstances.

247 Bye, Baby, Bye

Mildred Adair

Mildred Adair

B
________ has a new (sis - ter), Bye, ba - by, bye, We
(broth - er,)
pray that God will bless (her/him), Bye, ba - by, bye.

248 Plenty of Room in the Family

Gloria Gaither / William J. Gaither

William J. Gaither

Plen - ty of room in the fam - ily, Room for the young and the old.
Plen - ty of hap - pi - ness, plen - ty of love. Plen - ty of room in the fold.

Campfire

249

JANET SAGE
JANET SAGE
1. Camp - fire, camp - fire, Come to the camp - fire; We'll cook our sup - per at the camp - fire to - night; Camp - fire, camp - fire, Come to the camp - fire; Come to the camp - fire to - night.
2. Camp - fire, camp - fire, Come to the camp - fire; We'll hear a stor - y by the camp - fire to - night; Camp - fire, camp - fire, Come to the camp - fire; Come to the camp - fire to - night.
3. Camp - fire, camp - fire, Come to the camp - fire; We will keep co - zy by the camp - fire to - night; Camp - fire, camp - fire, Come to the camp - fire; Come to the camp - fire to - night.

FAMILY

COMMUNITY

250 I Love Mother

Noelene Johnsson

Traditional / Arr. by Kenneth D. Logan

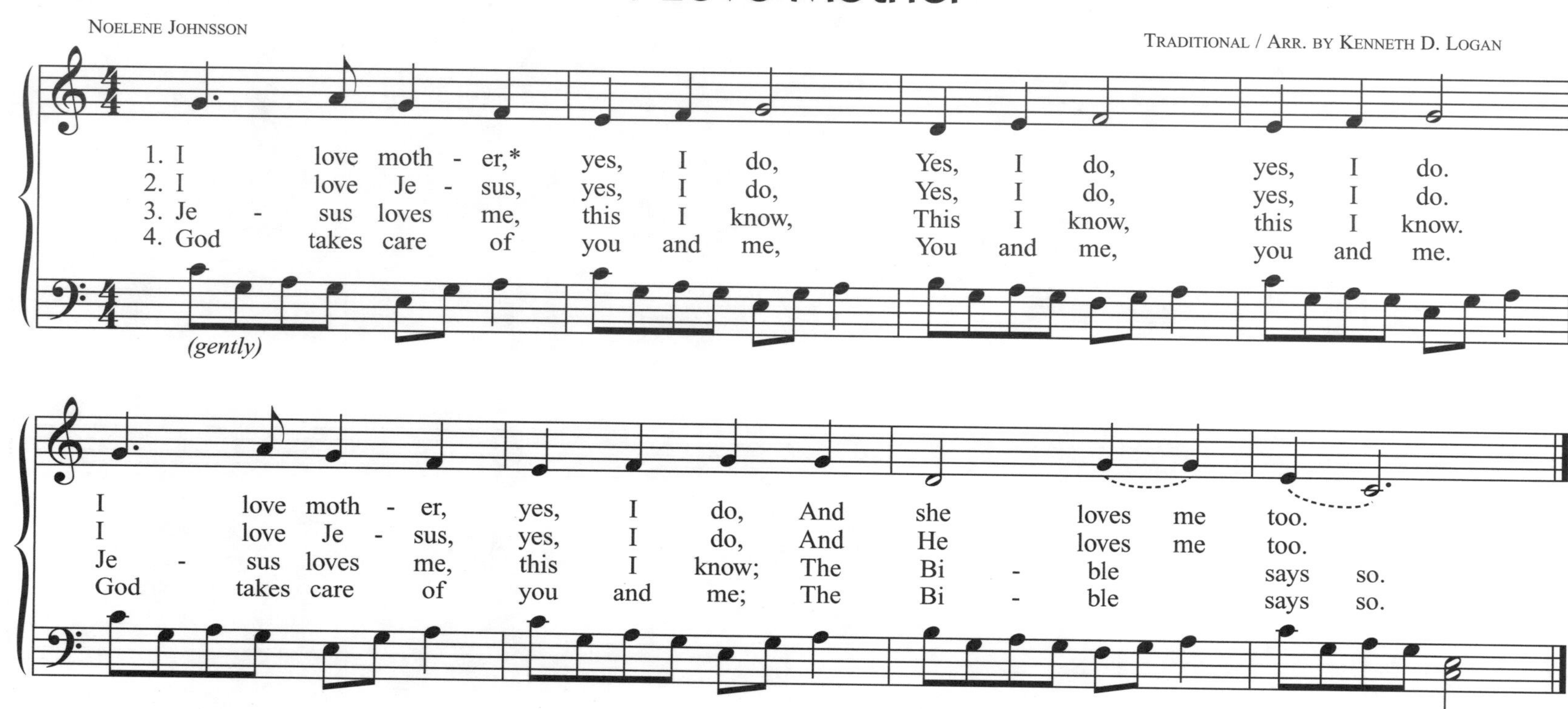
1. I love moth - er,* yes, I do, Yes, I do, yes, I do.
2. I love Je - sus, yes, I do, Yes, I do, yes, I do.
3. Je - sus loves me, this I know, This I know, this I know.
4. God takes care of you and me, You and me, you and me.
(gently)
I love moth - er, yes, I do, And she loves me too.
I love Je - sus, yes, I do, And He loves me too.
Je - sus loves me, this I know; The Bi - ble says so.
God takes care of you and me; The Bi - ble says so.

*father, brother, sister, grandma, grandpa, etc.

Family

Community

Jesus Gave Me a Mommy

Joy Hicklin Stewart

Joy Hicklin Stewart

1. Je - sus gave me a mom - my,* She says, "I love you."
2. Je - sus gave me a dad - dy, He says, "I love you."
3. I love Mom - my and Dad - dy, I love Je - sus, too.
4. I help Mom - my and Dad - dy, I help Je - sus, too.

Je - sus gave me a mom - my, She says, "I love you."
Je - sus gave me a dad - dy, He says, "I love you."
I love Mom - my and Dad - dy, I love Je - sus, too.
I help Mom - my and Dad - dy, I help Je - sus, too.

*For kindergarten: substitute "mother" for "mommy." Other verses: substitute "sister" for "mommy," "brother" for "daddy" in all verses. Substitute "grandma and grandpa" for "mommy and daddy."

252 My Family

General Conference Sabbath School Department
Edith Smith Casebeer
1. My fam - 'ly cooks good food for me, My fam - 'ly cooks good food for me, My fam - 'ly cooks good food for me, I love my fam - i - ly.
2. My fam - 'ly takes good care of me, My fam - 'ly takes good care of me, My fam - 'ly takes good care of me, I love my fam - i - ly.
3. I like to help my fam - i - ly, I like to help my fam - i - ly, I like to help my fam - i - ly, I love my fam - i - ly.

Family

Community

253

My Family

Jacqueline McDonald — Jacqueline McDonald

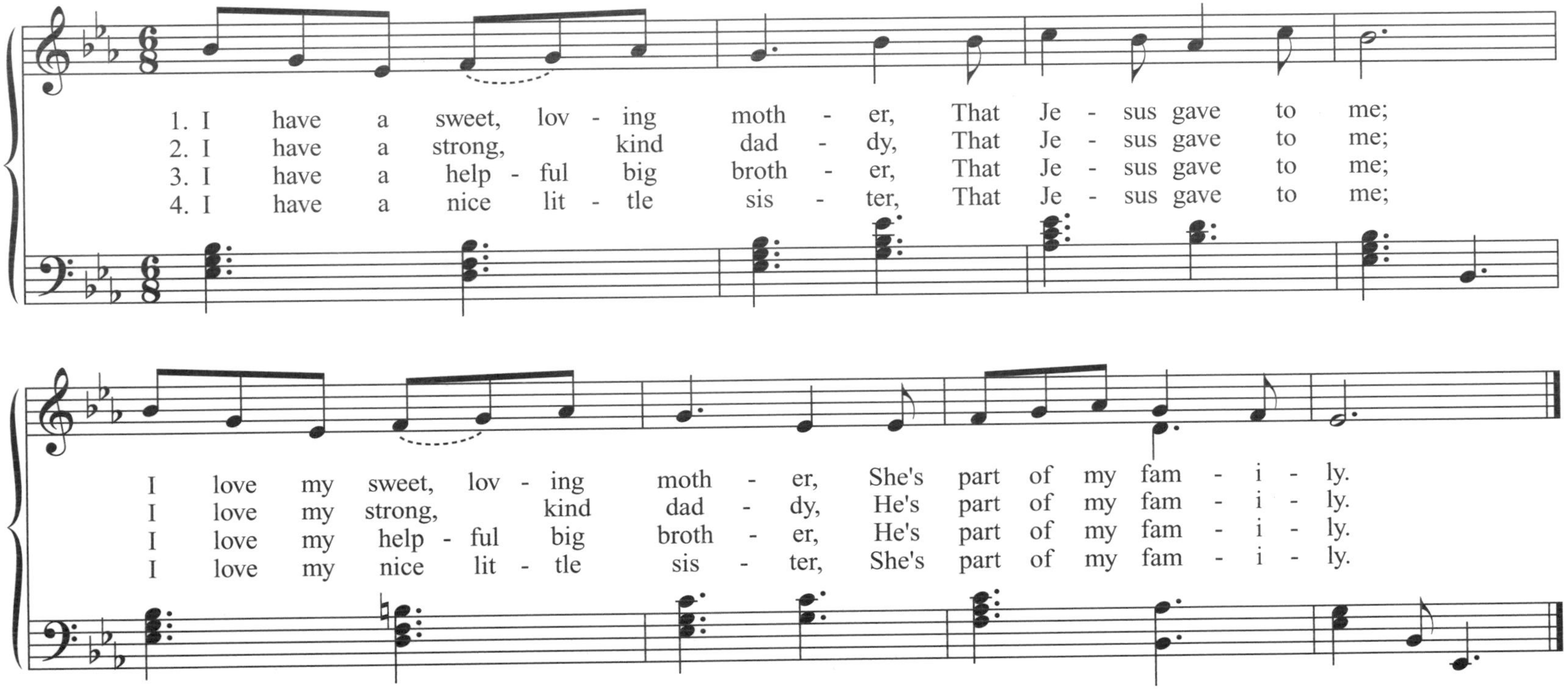

1. I have a sweet, lov-ing moth-er, That Je-sus gave to me;
I love my sweet, lov-ing moth-er, She's part of my fam-i-ly.

2. I have a strong, kind dad-dy, That Je-sus gave to me;
I love my strong, kind dad-dy, He's part of my fam-i-ly.

3. I have a help-ful big broth-er, That Je-sus gave to me;
I love my help-ful big broth-er, He's part of my fam-i-ly.

4. I have a nice lit-tle sis-ter, That Je-sus gave to me;
I love my nice lit-tle sis-ter, She's part of my fam-i-ly.

5. I have a new baby brother,
That Jesus gave to me;
I love my new baby brother,
He's part of my family.

254

A Friend of Jesus

RosAnne Tetz

RosAnne Tetz

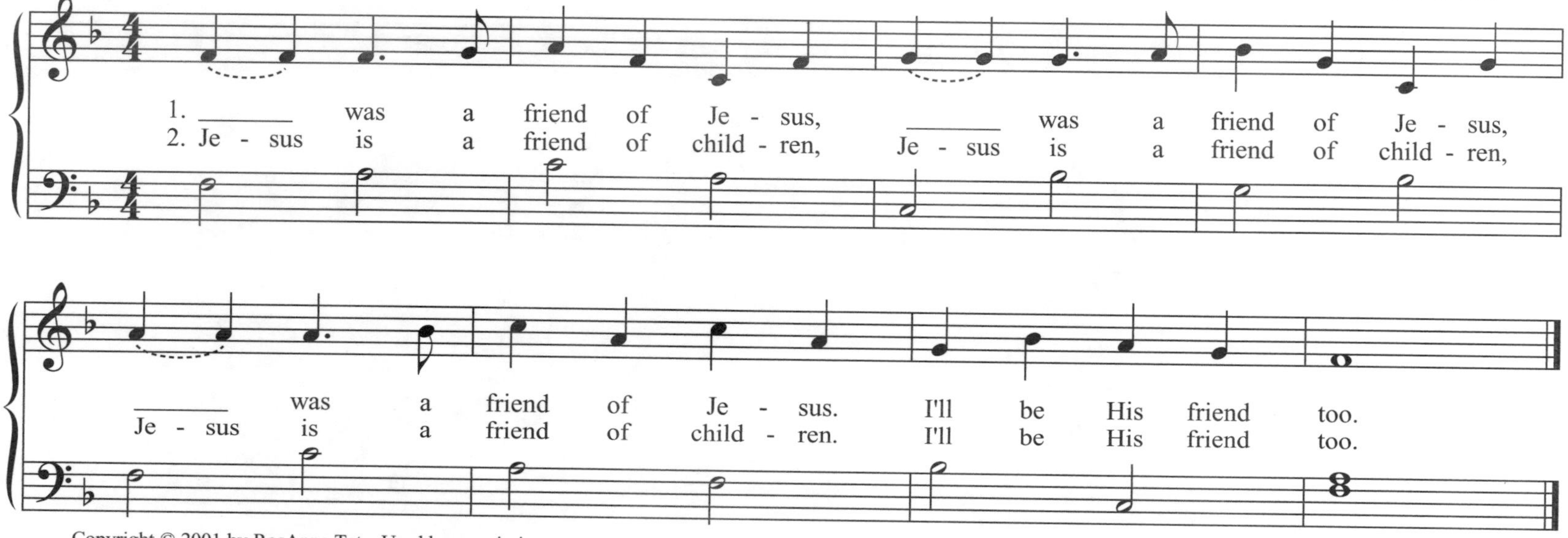

1. ______ was a friend of Je - sus, ______ was a friend of Je - sus,
2. Je - sus is a friend of child - ren, Je - sus is a friend of child - ren,

______ was a friend of Je - sus. I'll be His friend too.
Je - sus is a friend of child - ren. I'll be His friend too.

255

The Friendship Clap

Adapted

Traditional / Arr. by Lois C. Hall

1. Shake a hand and bend, Shake a hand and bend,
2. Friends to - geth - er clap, Friends to - geth - er clap,

Je - sus loves the both of us; Je - sus made us friends.
Friends to - geth - er right, left; Do a friend - ship clap.

Buddies

256

Susan E. Payne

Susan E. Payne / Ellen R. Thompson

Bud - dies, we're the best of bud - dies. We are friends 'cause
Je - sus helps us love each oth - er. We can play to - geth - er,
shar - ing just like (broth - ers) 'cause we're bud - dies— real good friends.
(sis - ters)

Friendship

Community

257 Our Church Is a Family

CAROL GREENE

FRANZ SCHUBERT, ADAPTED

Our church is a fam - i - ly, the fam - i - ly of God.
1. We're sis - ters and broth - ers in the fam - i - ly of God.
2. We love one an - oth - er in the fam - i - ly of God.
3. We wel - come all peo - ple in the fam - i - ly of God.

Teach children this old finger play as they learn this song.

Here is the church *(interlock fingers)*, and here is the steeple *(raise index fingers and touch tips to form steeple)*. Open the doors *(turn hands over to reveal interlocked fingers)* and see all the people.

Our Family

258

ROXY HOEHN / ADAPT. BY GENERAL CONFERENCE SABBATH SCHOOL DEPARTMENT

ROXY HOEHN

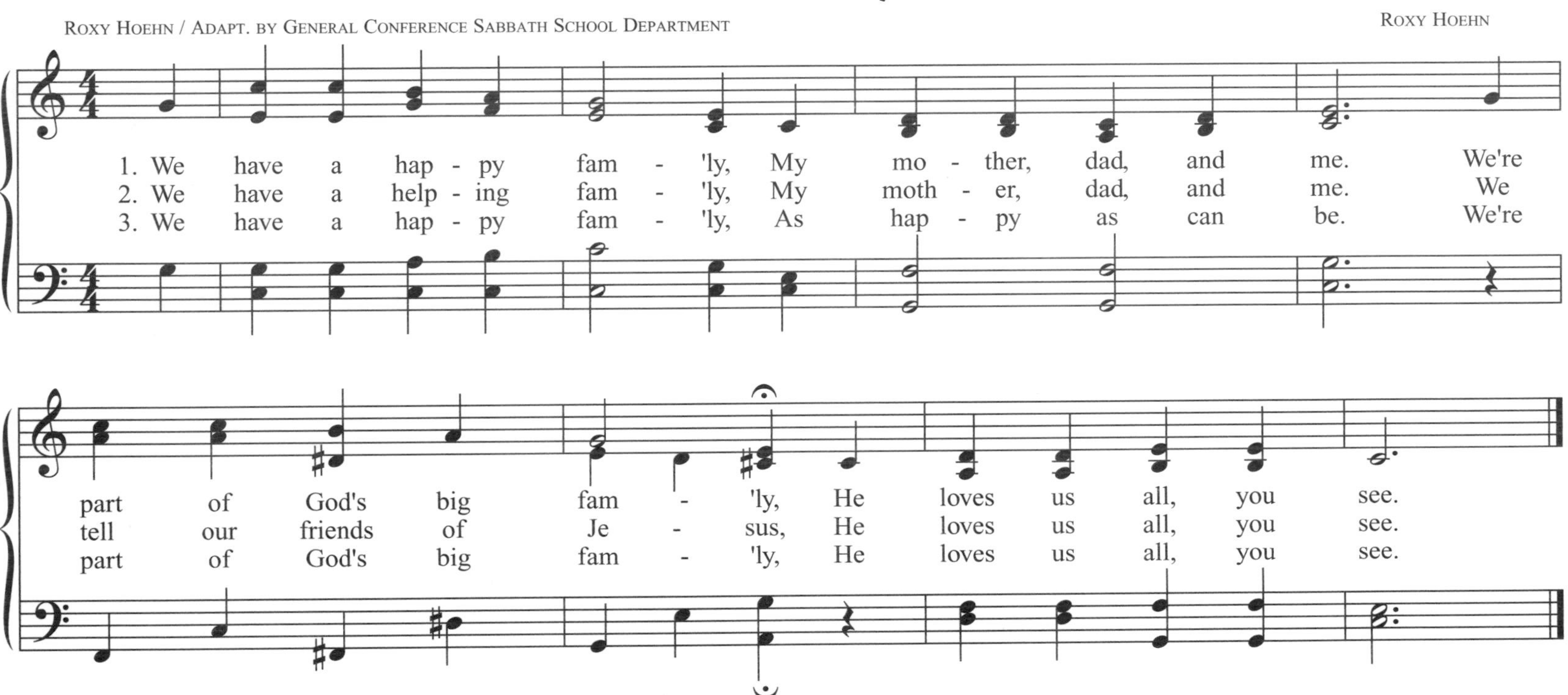

1. We have a hap - py fam - 'ly, My mo - ther, dad, and me. We're part of God's big fam - 'ly, He loves us all, you see.
2. We have a help - ing fam - 'ly, My moth - er, dad, and me. We tell our friends of Je - sus, He loves us all, you see.
3. We have a hap - py fam - 'ly, As hap - py as can be. We're part of God's big fam - 'ly, He loves us all, you see.

259

God's Ways

Mary LeBar

Ellen R. Thompson

1. I'll make my home* a hap - py home By fol - low - ing God's ways; If I am kind and lov - ing there, We shall have hap - py days.
2. I'll make my home a hap - py home By fol - low - ing God's ways; If I work well with oth - ers there, We shall have hap - py days.
3. I'll make my home a hap - py home By fol - low - ing God's ways; If I don't ev - er quar - rel there, We shall have hap - py days.

*The words "church" or "school" may be substituted for "home" in each stanza.

Be Kind to One Another

260

Based on Ephesians 4:32, RSV

Janet Sage

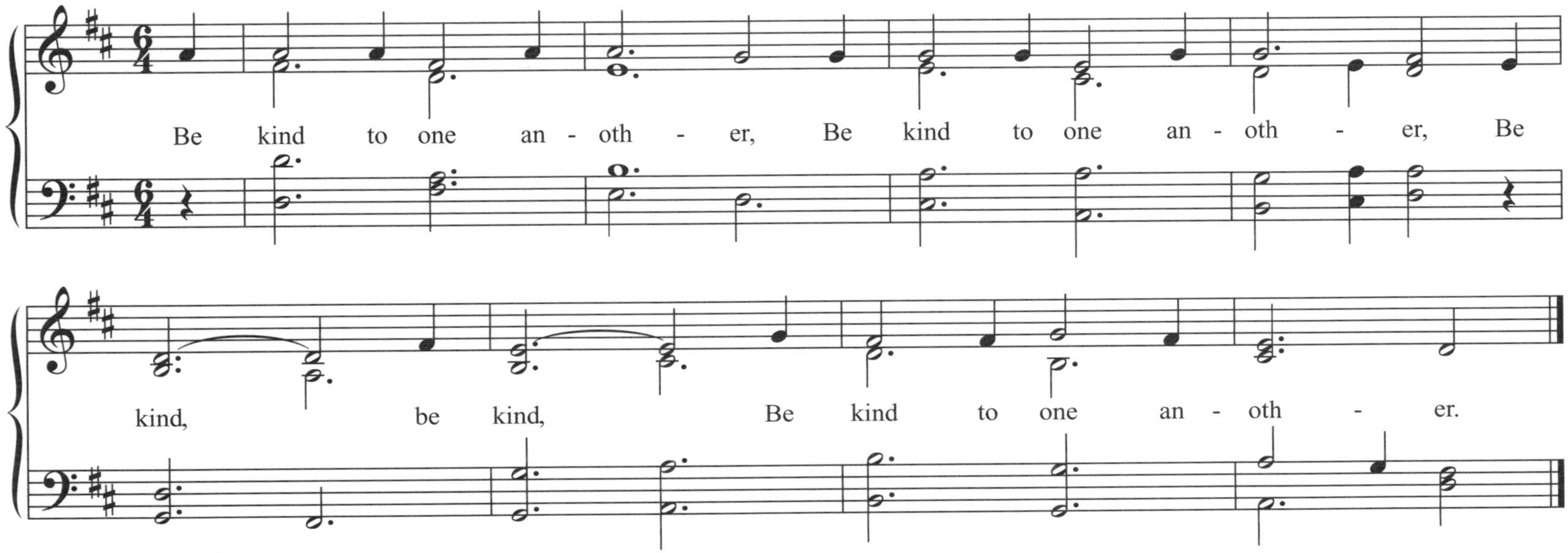

Be kind to one an - oth - er, Be kind to one an - oth - er, Be kind, be kind, Be kind to one an - oth - er.

Kindness

Community

261

Something Nice

CYNTHIA PATTERSON COSTON

CYNTHIA PATTERSON COSTON

I like to do some - thing nice for oth - ers ev - ery day.
Some - thing small or some - thing big, it's nice to be that way. I
like to do some - thing nice for oth - ers ev - ery day. With
Je - sus as my spe - cial friend, I'll al - ways find a way.

KINDNESS

COMMUNITY

Care for One Another

Betty A. Riley
Betty A. Riley
Care for one an - oth - er. Care for one an - oth - er. Care for the old,
care for the young. Care for the sick, and care for your friend. Care for one an - oth - er.
Care for one an - oth - er. For God's Word says, "Care for one an - oth - - - er."

You can teach 4-year-olds the last eight measures of this song first. Then let the song "grow" along with them, teaching them the remainder when they're 5.

263 Let Us Do Good

Ellis Anne Baar and Ellen R. Thompson

Ellen R. Thompson

1. Let us do good to ev - ery - one, Let us do good for Je - sus.
Say a kind word; Sing a glad song; Let us do good, Let us do good for Je - sus.

2. Let us do good to ev - ery - one, Let us do good for Je - sus.
Help with a smile; Tell of God's love; Let us do good, Let us do good for Je - sus.

264 Love One Another

John 15:12

Janet Sage

Love one an - oth - er, Love one an - oth - er, Love, love, love one an - oth - er.

Musical note: A feeling of richness, mellowness, and smoothness should be conveyed by the music.

Let Us Do Good to All Men

265

Based on Galatians 6:10, RSV

Janet Sage

Let us do good to all men, Let us do good, Let us do good,
Let us do good to all men, Let us do good.

266 Coming, Mother

Marilyn Scholes

Marilyn Scholes

Bob - by, Bob - by!* Please come here to me. Bob - by, Bob - by, wher -
ev - er you may be. Com - ing, Moth - er, as Je - sus wants me
to. Com - ing, Moth - er, I'm com - ing now to you.

*Insert child's name

Obedience

Community

I Obey

267

MARGARET M. SELF — TRADITIONAL

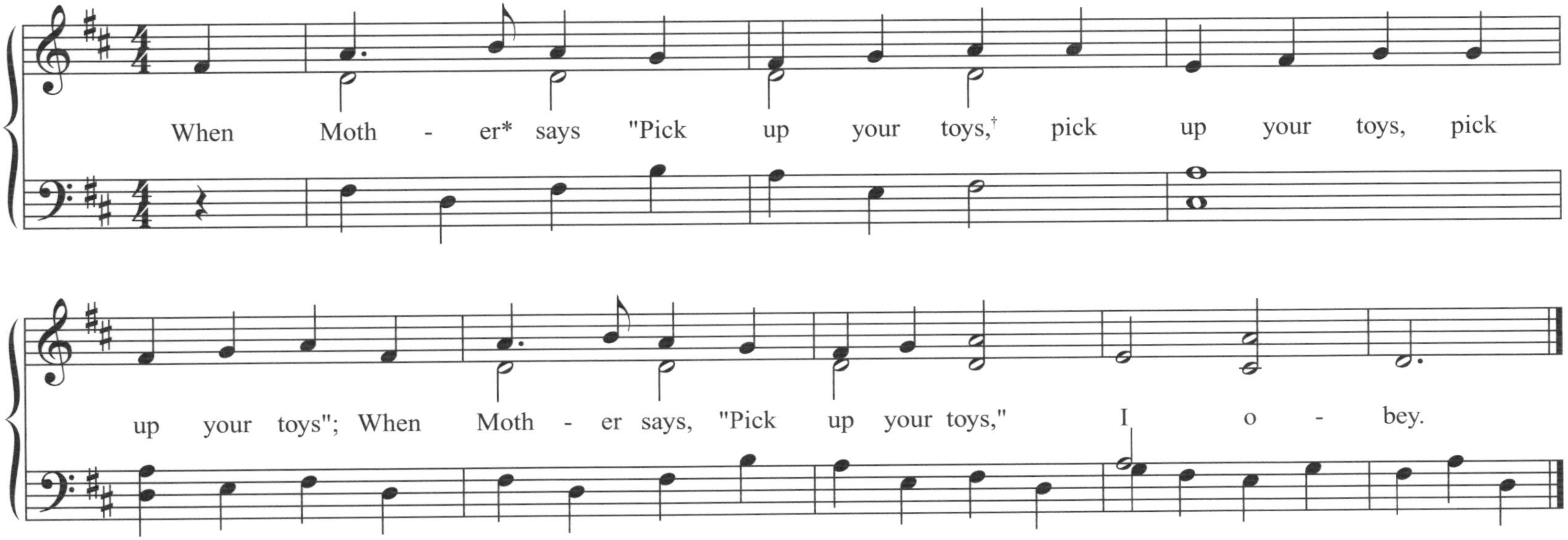

When Mother* says "Pick up your toys,† pick up your toys, pick up your toys"; When Mother says, "Pick up your toys," I obey.

* Substitute Daddy, teacher.
† Substitute "Put on your shoes"; "Hang up your coat"; "Please share your toys"; etc.

Jesus Is Happy

268

ROXY HOEHN — ROXY HOEHN

1. Je - sus is hap - py when I o - bey. I will go quick - ly when Mom - my calls to - day.
2. Je - sus is hap - py when I am kind. I'll share my dol - lies and Mom - my I will mind.
3. Je - sus is hap - py when I o - bey. He's sad when I'm bad, but He loves me an - y - way.

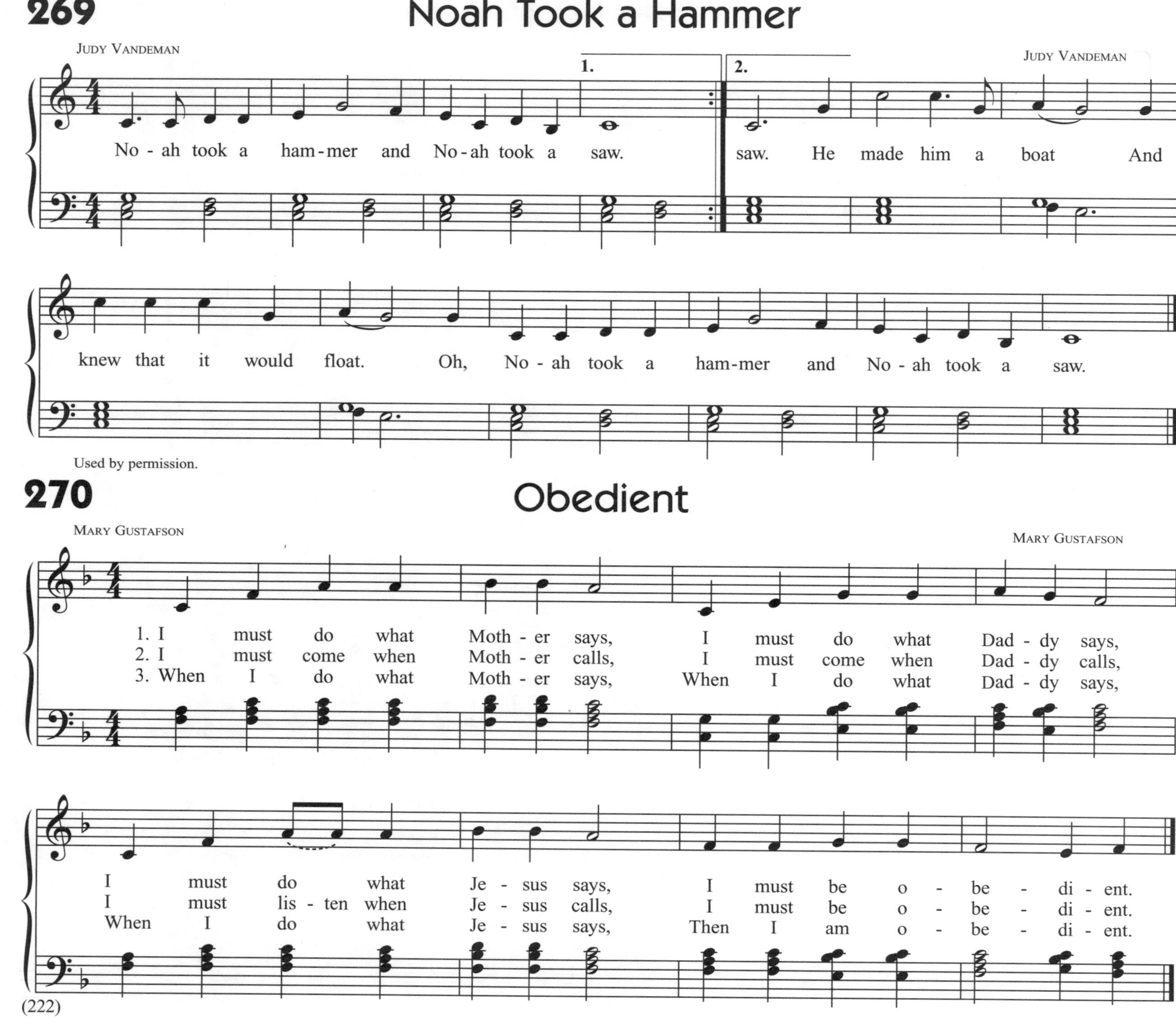
269
Noah Took a Hammer
Judy Vandeman
Judy Vandeman
1.
2.
No - ah took a ham-mer and No-ah took a saw.
saw. He made him a boat And
knew that it would float. Oh, No - ah took a ham-mer and No - ah took a saw.
Used by permission.
270
Obedient
Mary Gustafson
Mary Gustafson
1. I must do what Moth - er says, I must do what Dad - dy says,
2. I must come when Moth - er calls, I must come when Dad - dy calls,
3. When I do what Moth - er says, When I do what Dad - dy says,
I must do what Je - sus says, I must be o - be - di - ent.
I must lis - ten when Je - sus calls, I must be o - be - di - ent.
When I do what Je - sus says, Then I am o - be - di - ent.
Obedience
Community

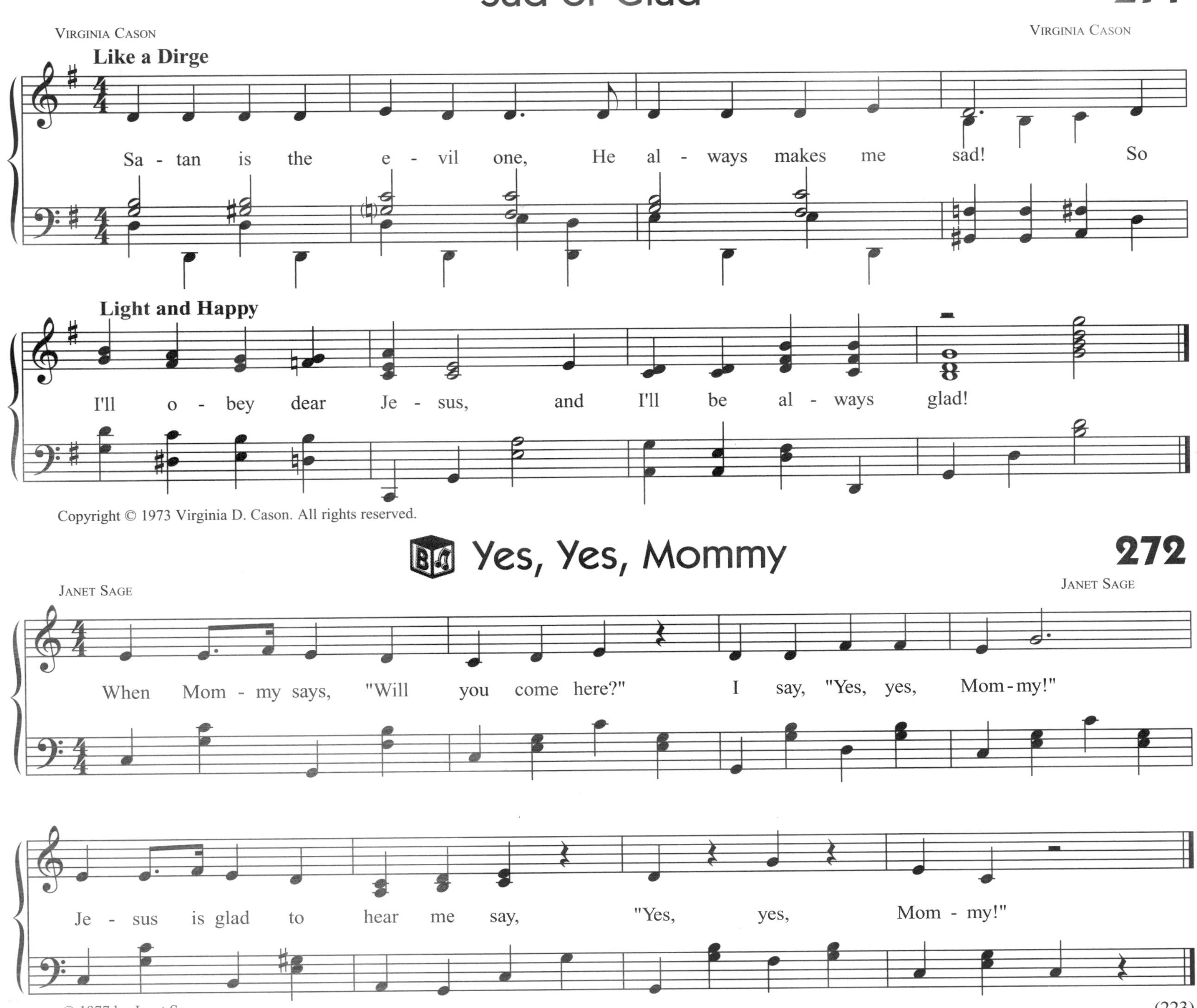
Sad or Glad
271
Virginia Cason
Virginia Cason
Like a Dirge
Sa - tan is the e - vil one, He al - ways makes me sad! So
Light and Happy
I'll o - bey dear Je - sus, and I'll be al - ways glad!
Copyright © 1973 Virginia D. Cason. All rights reserved.
Yes, Yes, Mommy
272
Janet Sage
Janet Sage
When Mom - my says, "Will you come here?" I say, "Yes, yes, Mom - my!"
Je - sus is glad to hear me say, "Yes, yes, Mom - my!"
© 1977 by Janet Sage.

273 With Jesus in the Family

ANONYMOUS

A. E. LIND

1. With Je - sus in the fam - i - ly, Hap - py, hap - py home, Hap - py, hap - py home,
2. With the Bi - ble in the fam - i - ly, Hap - py, hap - py home, Hap - py, hap - py home,
3. With Dad - dy in the fam - i - ly, Hap - py, hap - py home, Hap - py, hap - py home,
4. With Mom - my in the fam - i - ly, Hap - py, hap - py home, Hap - py, hap - py home,
Hap - py, hap - py home. With Je - sus in the fam - i - ly, Hap - py, hap - py home, Hap - py, hap - py home.
Hap - py, hap - py home. With the Bi - ble in the fam - i - ly, Hap - py, hap - py home, Hap - py, hap - py home.
Hap - py, hap - py home. With Dad - dy in the fam - i - ly, Hap - py, hap - py home, Hap - py, hap - py home.
Hap - py, hap - py home. With Mom - my in the fam - i - ly, Hap - py, hap - py home, Hap - py, hap - py home.

5. With (sister/brother) in the family,
Happy, happy home,
Happy, happy home,
Happy, happy home.
With (sister/brother) in the family,
Happy, happy home,
Happy, happy home.

6. With baby in the family,*
Happy, happy home,
Happy, happy home,
Happy, happy home.
With baby in the family,
Happy, happy home,
Happy, happy home.

*Verses 6-9: for "Baby Isaac" lesson.

7. When families feed their babies,
Happy, happy home,
Happy, happy home,
Happy, happy home.
When families feed their babies,
Happy, happy home,
Happy, happy home.

8. When families rock their babies,
Happy, happy home,
Happy, happy home,
Happy, happy home.
When families rock their babies,
Happy, happy home,
Happy, happy home.

9. When families play with babies,
Happy, happy home,
Happy, happy home,
Happy, happy home.
When families play with babies,
Happy, happy home,
Happy, happy home.

10. When we mind our daddies,
Happy, happy home,
Happy, happy home,
Happy, happy home.
When we mind our daddies,
Happy, happy home,
Happy, happy home.

11. When we mind our mothers,
Happy, happy home,
Happy, happy home,
Happy, happy home.
When we mind our mothers,
Happy, happy home,
Happy, happy home.

12. When we mind dear Jesus,
Happy, happy home,
Happy, happy home,
Happy, happy home.
When we mind dear Jesus,
Happy, happy home,
Happy, happy home.

When a Mother Calls

Kathryn B. Myers Kathryn B. Myers

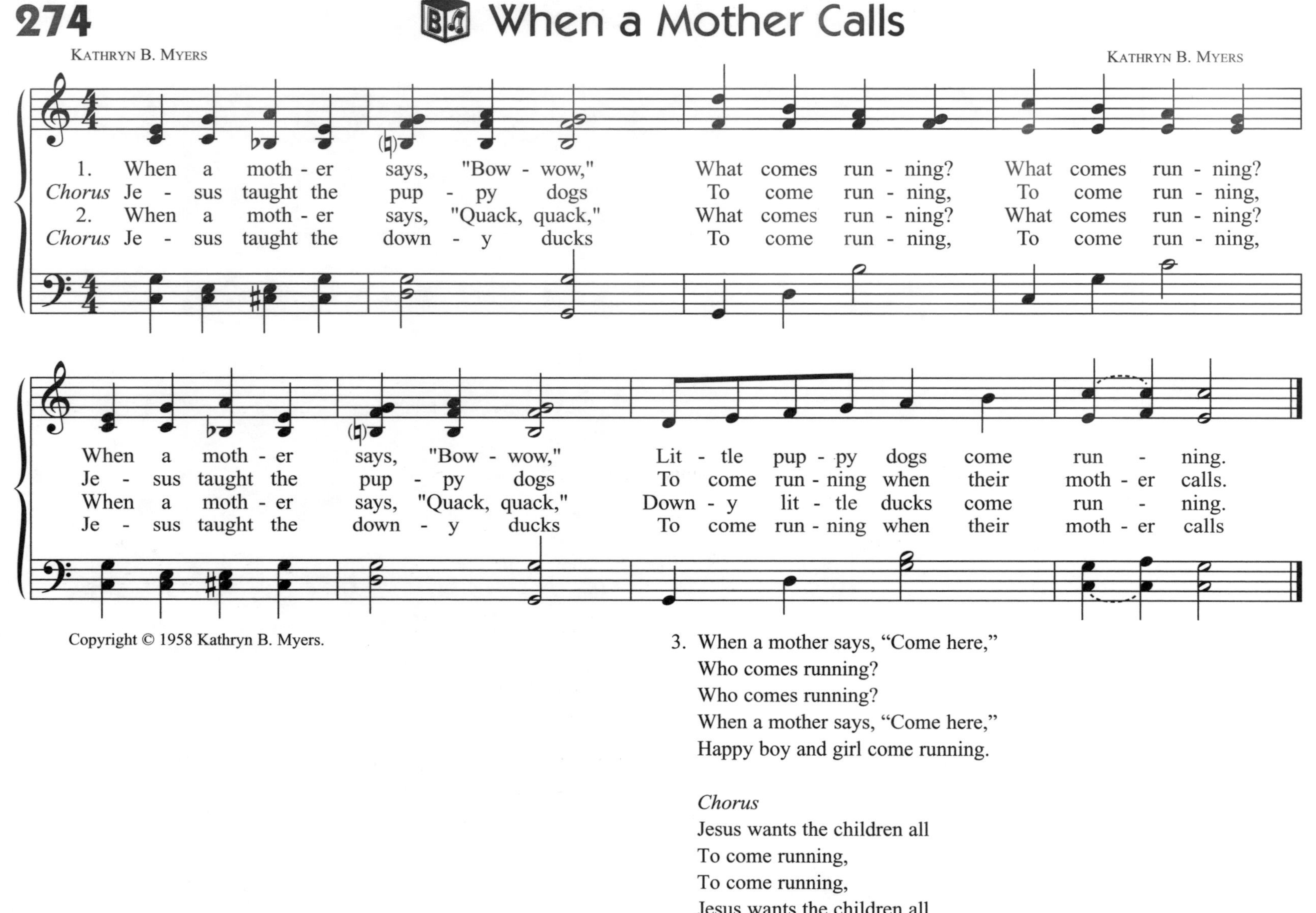
1. When a moth - er says, "Bow - wow," What comes run - ning? What comes run - ning?
Chorus Je - sus taught the pup - py dogs To come run - ning, To come run - ning,
2. When a moth - er says, "Quack, quack," What comes run - ning? What comes run - ning?
Chorus Je - sus taught the down - y ducks To come run - ning, To come run - ning,
When a moth - er says, "Bow - wow," Lit - tle pup - py dogs come run - ning.
Je - sus taught the pup - py dogs To come run - ning when their moth - er calls.
When a moth - er says, "Quack, quack," Down - y lit - tle ducks come run - ning.
Je - sus taught the down - y ducks To come run - ning when their moth - er calls

3. When a mother says, "Come here,"
Who comes running?
Who comes running?
When a mother says, "Come here,"
Happy boy and girl come running.

Chorus
Jesus wants the children all
To come running,
To come running,
Jesus wants the children all
To come running when their mothers call.

I'll Share My Only One

275

Rosalie Blackmore

Rosalie Blackmore / Arr. by Junerose McCulloch

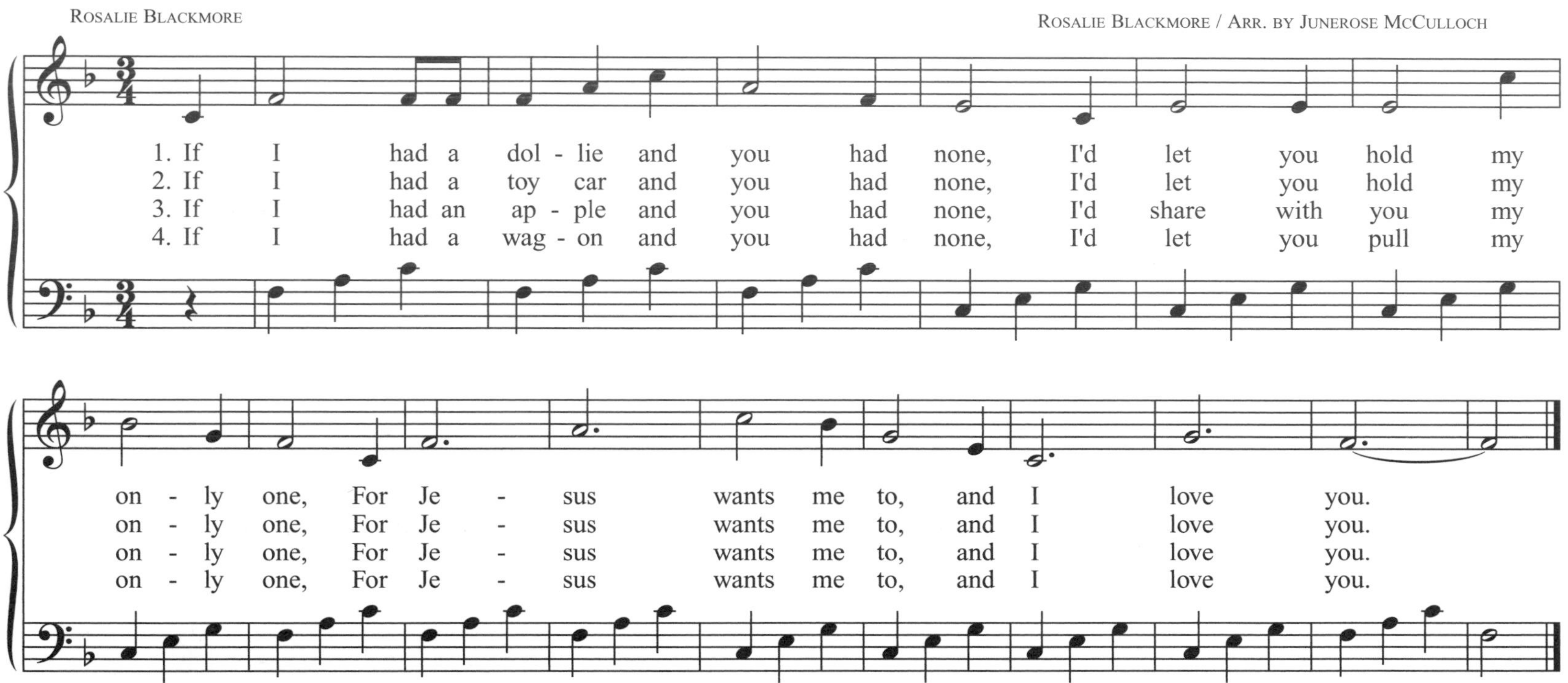
1. If I had a dol - lie and you had none, I'd let you hold my on - ly one, For Je - sus wants me to, and I love you.
2. If I had a toy car and you had none, I'd let you hold my on - ly one, For Je - sus wants me to, and I love you.
3. If I had an ap - ple and you had none, I'd share with you my on - ly one, For Je - sus wants me to, and I love you.
4. If I had a wag - on and you had none, I'd let you pull my on - ly one, For Je - sus wants me to, and I love you.

5. If I had a buggy and you had none,
I'd let you push my only one,
For Jesus wants me to,
and I love you.

6. If I had a Bible and you had none,
I'd share with you my only one,
For Jesus wants me to.
and I love you.

276 I'll Take Turns

JOY HICKLIN STEWART

JOY HICKLIN STEWART

1. I'll take turns when I'm swing - ing, I'll take turns with you.
2. I'll take turns with my air - plane, I'll take turns with you.
3. I'll take turns with my dol - ly, I'll take turns with you.
4. I'll take turns with my wag - on, I'll take turns with you.
I'll take turns when I'm slid - ing, For Je - sus wants me to.
I'll take turns with my tri - cy - cle, For Je - sus wants me to.
I'll take turns with my bug - gy, too, For Je - sus wants me to.
I'll take turns with my pic - ture book, For Je - sus wants me to.

SHARING

COMMUNITY

Share With You

277

CYNTHIA PATTERSON COSTON — CYNTHIA PATTERSON COSTON

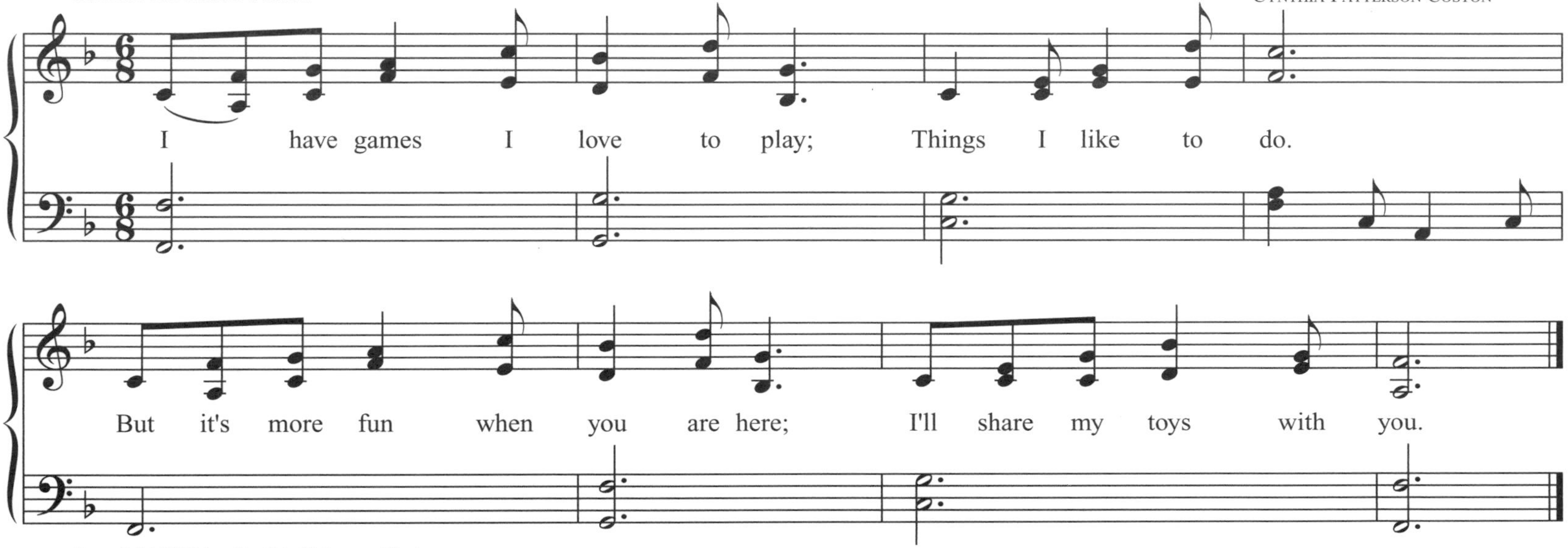

I have games I love to play; Things I like to do.
But it's more fun when you are here; I'll share my toys with you.

Sharing

278

JANET SAGE — JANET SAGE

Shar - ing, shar - ing, I have fun and so do you;
Shar - ing, shar - ing, It's a lov - ing thing to do.

Sharing Song

MYRTLE R. CREASMAN MYRTLE R. CREASMAN

1. I have two dol - lies and I am glad, You have no dol - ly and that's too bad. I'll
2. I have two Bi - bles and I am glad, You have no Bi - ble and that's too bad. I'll
3. I have two pa - pers and I am glad, You have no pa - pers and that's too bad. I'll
share my dol - lies, for I love you, And that's what Je - sus wants me to do.
share my Bi - bles, for I love you, And that's what Je - sus wants me to do.
share my pa - pers, for I love you, And that's what Je - sus wants me to do.

SHARING

COMMUNITY

We Are Sharing

280

ENID G. THORSON ENID G. THORSON

We are shar - ing, we are shar - ing; Je - sus wants me to share with you.
It was your turn; now it's my turn We are hap - py tak - ing turns.

Suggested uses: You can share real toys, food, or books. Give to another child when you sing, "It was our turn." Children will catch on to the sharing after a while.

SHARING

COMMUNITY

281 Tap, Tap, Tap

JANET SAGE JANET SAGE

Tap tap tap, Tap, tap, tap, That's how No - ah's ham - mer goes;
Dad - dy's
Tap, tap, tap, Tap, tap, tap, No - ah builds the ark.
Dad - dy shows his love.

Don't Mess It Up

CAROL GREENE

CAROL GREENE

Brightly
1. God made the world and it's ver - y, ver - y good.
2. Don't hurt the an - i - mals, don't hurt the trees.
Don't mess it up. Don't mess it up. God made the world and it's
Don't mess them up. Don't mess them up. Don't hurt the land and
ver - y, ver - y good. Don't mess up God's world. No, no, no!
don't hurt the seas. Don't mess up God's world. No, no, no!
(spoken)
Repeat st. 1 after st. 2.

Cut out magazine pictures to make a poster illustrating this song. Give each child a small paper sack and collect litter as you learn the song.

283 I Have a (Doggy/Kitty)

CYNTHIA PATTERSON COSTON
CYNTHIA PATTERSON COSTON
I have a dog - gy.* I have a dog - gy.* Je - sus gave her to me.
I must take care of her; feed, walk, and love her ev - 'ry day.

*kitty

CARE FOR ANIMALS

SERVICE

I Will Be Kind

284

FLORENCE P. JORGENSEN FLORENCE P. JORGENSEN

1. I will be kind to the kit - ties* each day, It makes Je - sus glad, it makes Je - sus glad; I will be kind to the kit - ties each day, For this makes dear Je - sus glad.
2. I will be kind to the dog - gies each day, It makes Je - sus glad, it makes Je - sus glad; I will be kind to the dog - gies each day, For this makes dear Je - sus glad.
3. I will be kind to the bird - ies each day, It makes Je - sus glad, it makes Je - sus glad; I will be kind to the bird - ies each day, For this makes dear Je - sus glad.
4. I will be kind to the wee lambs each day, It makes Je - sus glad, it makes Je - sus glad; I will be kind to the wee lambs each day, For this makes dear Je - sus glad.

*Could include "my brother," "my sister," "my mother," "my father."

285 Giving

Mary LeBar

A. Vivienne Blomquist / Arr. by Kenneth D. Logan

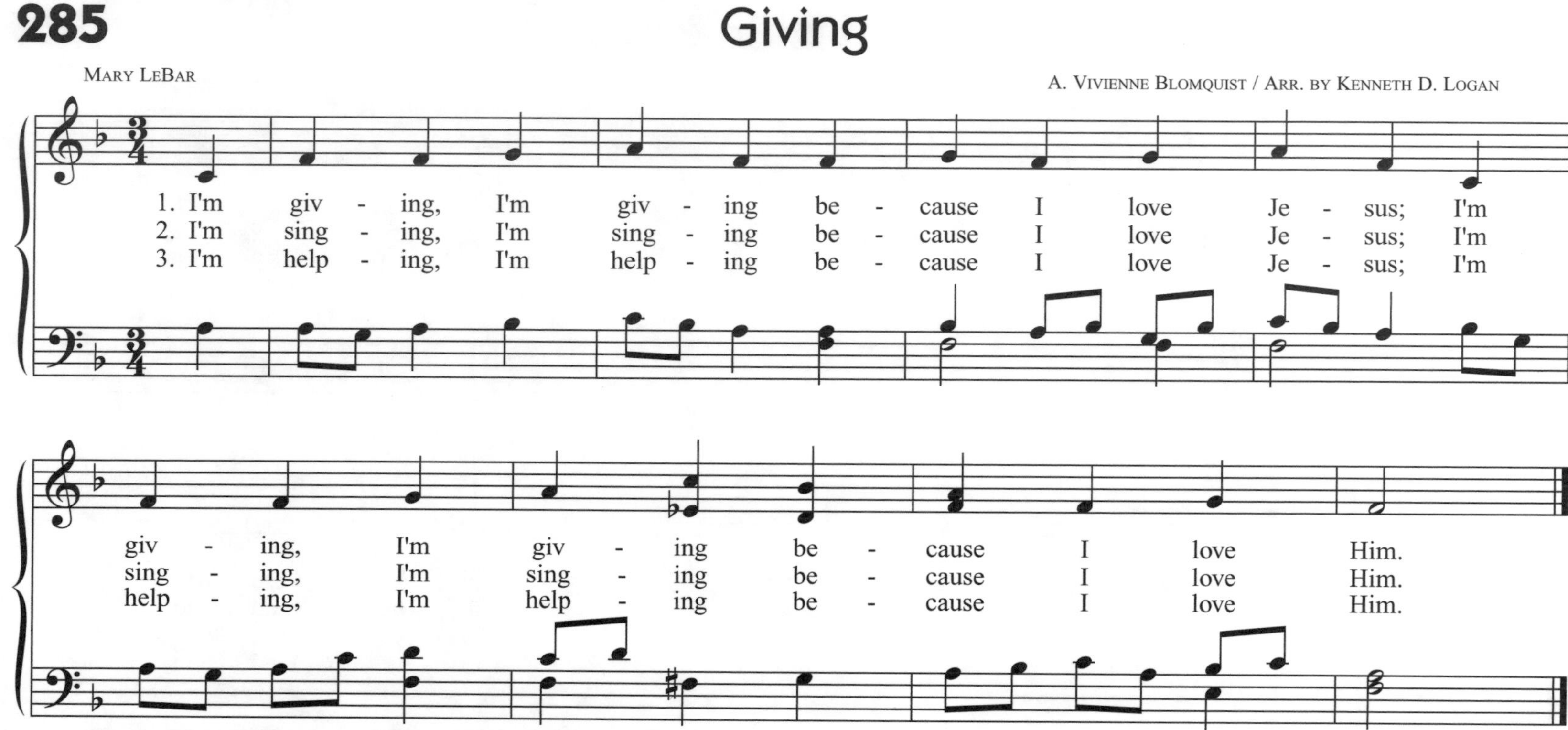
1. I'm giv - ing, I'm giv - ing be - cause I love Je - sus; I'm giv - ing, I'm giv - ing be - cause I love Him.
2. I'm sing - ing, I'm sing - ing be - cause I love Je - sus; I'm sing - ing, I'm sing - ing be - cause I love Him.
3. I'm help - ing, I'm help - ing be - cause I love Je - sus; I'm help - ing, I'm help - ing be - cause I love Him.

I Wonder Why

Virginia Cason
Virginia Cason / Arr. by Wayne Hooper
Light and airy
1. I won - der why Je - sus loves me so, loves me so, loves me so.
I won - der why Je - sus loves me so, loves me so.
2. It's just be - cause He's my dear - est friend, dear - est friend, dear - est friend,
It's just be - cause He's my dear - est friend, my dear - est friend.
3. Oh, how I love the dear Sab - bath day, hap - piest day as can be,
Je - sus has made it a spec - ial day, just for me!

287

God's Children Are Helpful

Dorothy Robison

Dorothy Robison / arr. by Margaret Edge

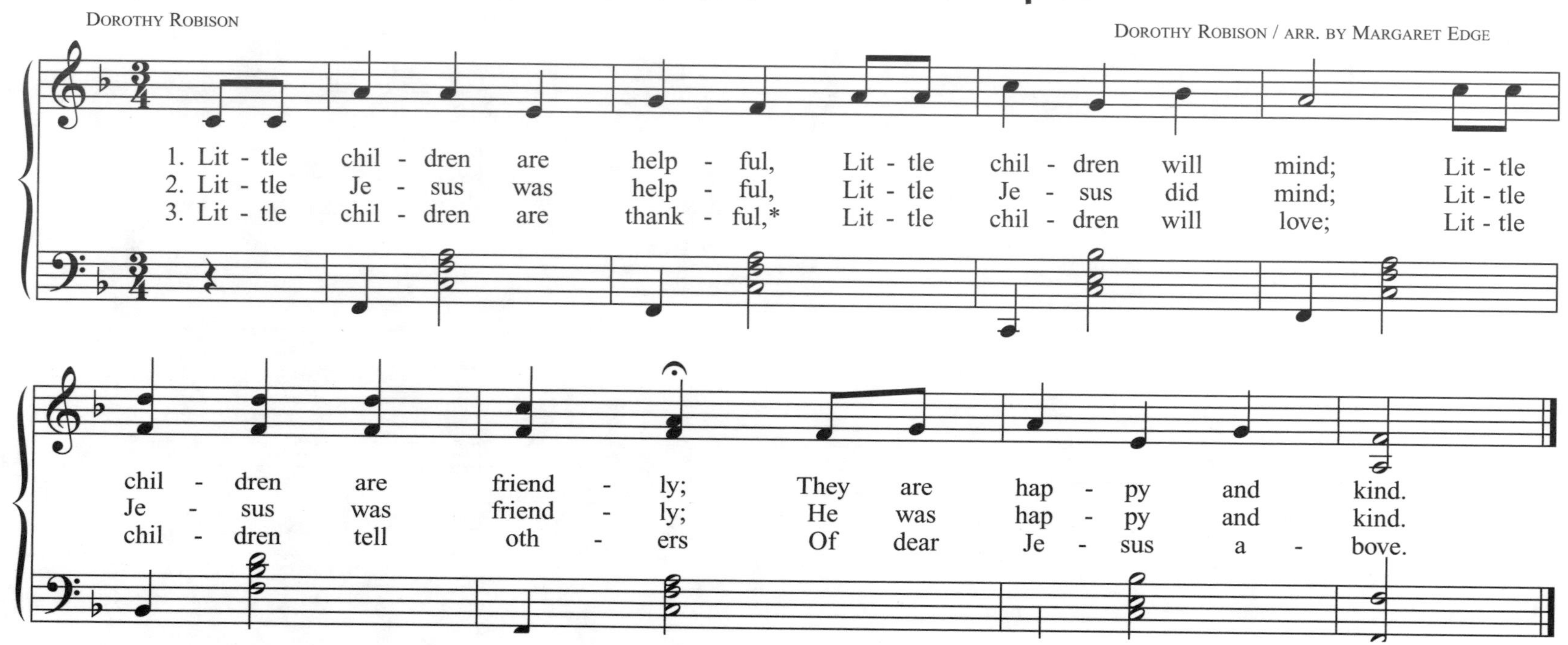
1. Lit - tle chil - dren are help - ful, Lit - tle chil - dren will mind; Lit - tle chil - dren are friend - ly; They are hap - py and kind.
2. Lit - tle Je - sus was help - ful, Lit - tle Je - sus did mind; Lit - tle Je - sus was friend - ly; He was hap - py and kind.
3. Lit - tle chil - dren are thank - ful,* Lit - tle chil - dren will love; Lit - tle chil - dren tell oth - ers Of dear Je - sus a - bove.

*quiet

Helping Song

288

Kathryn B. Myers

Kathryn B. Myers

1. Our lit - tle hands can be help - ing hands, When there's work to do.
2. Our lit - tle lips can be help - ing lips, When they smile at moth - er.
Our lit - tle feet can be help - ing feet, Run - ning er - rands too.
We can be help - ers for Je - sus dear, When we help each oth - er.

289 I Can Help

Susan E. Payne

Susan E. Payne / Ellen R. Thompson

Snappy
1.
I can help (I can help). I can help (I can help). Be - cause I love ('cause I love)

2.
Je - sus. (Je - sus). cause I love the Lord.

290 I Will Be a Helper

Marie Ingham

Marie Ingham

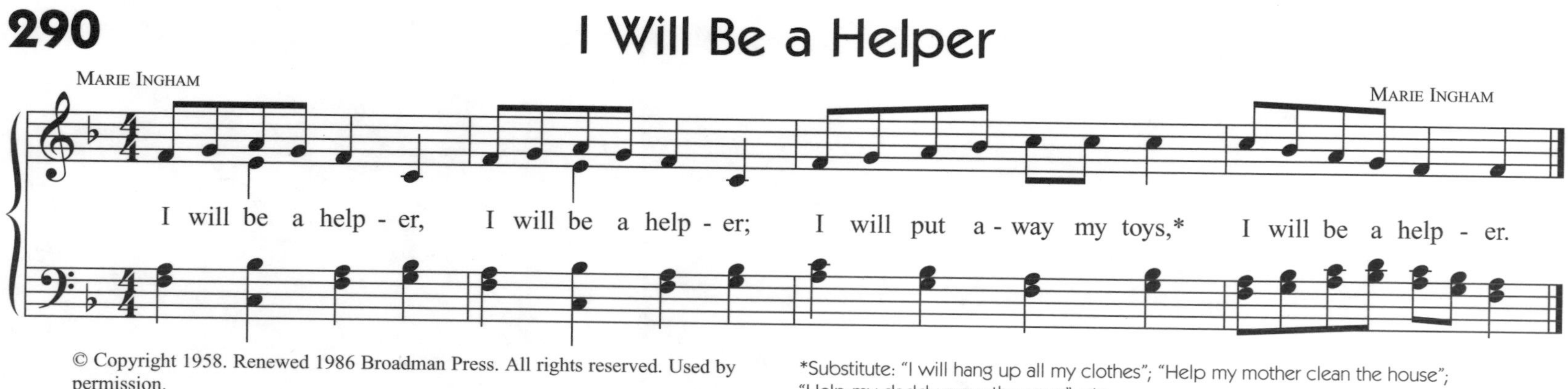

I will be a help - er, I will be a help - er; I will put a - way my toys,* I will be a help - er.

*Substitute: "I will hang up all my clothes"; "Help my mother clean the house"; "Help my daddy mow the grass"; etc.

I Like to Help My Mother

291

MARY E. SCHWAB — MARY E. SCHWAB

I like to help my moth - er,* Oh, yes, I real - ly do.
For when I help my moth - er Then I help Je - sus, too.

*father, brother, sister, teacher, pastor

I'll Pick Up My Toys

292

BILLE K. BURDICK — BILLE K. BURDICK

I'll pick up my toys and put them a - way. Pick up my toys, - put them a - way. I
make Je - sus hap - py and help Mom - mie too When I put my toys a - way.

293 I'm a Little Helper

JANET SAGE

JANET SAGE

I'm a lit - tle help - er, a help - er, a help - er, O
I'm a lit - tle help - er (for/like) Je - sus!

294 Let's Put All Our Toys Away

JANET SAGE

JANET SAGE

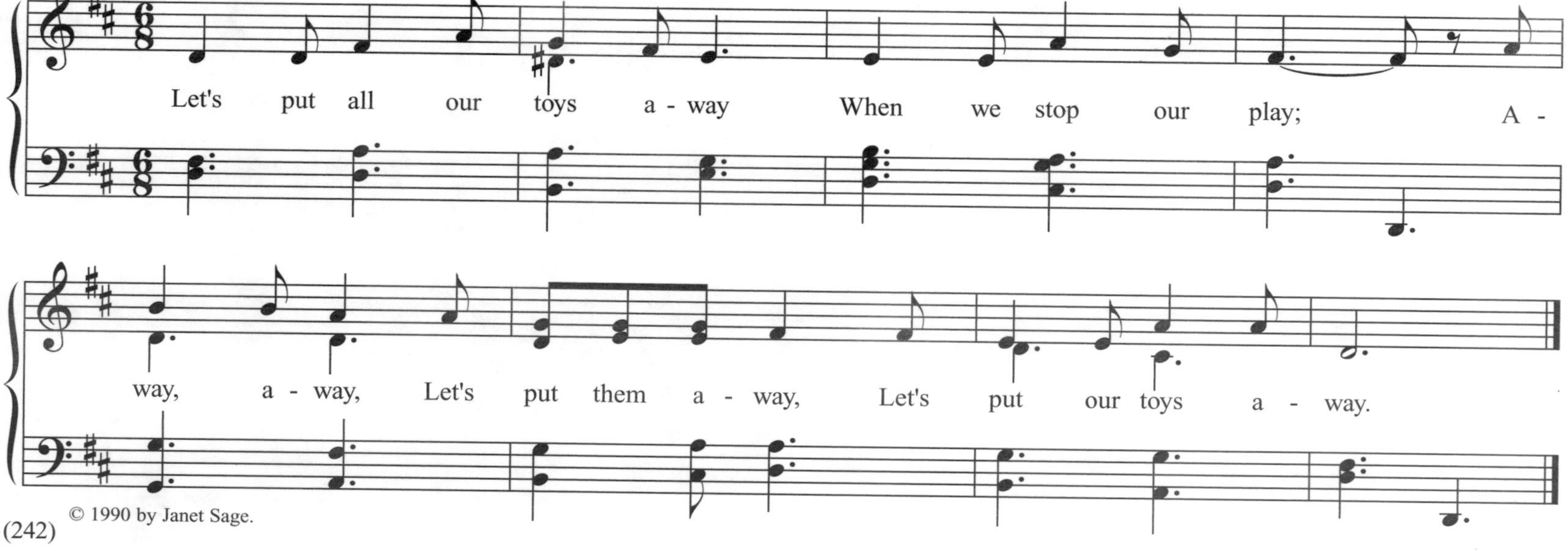

Let's put all our toys a - way When we stop our play; A -
way, a - way, Let's put them a - way, Let's put our toys a - way.

Jesus Was a Helper

295

LOIS L. CURLEY

LOIS L. CURLEY

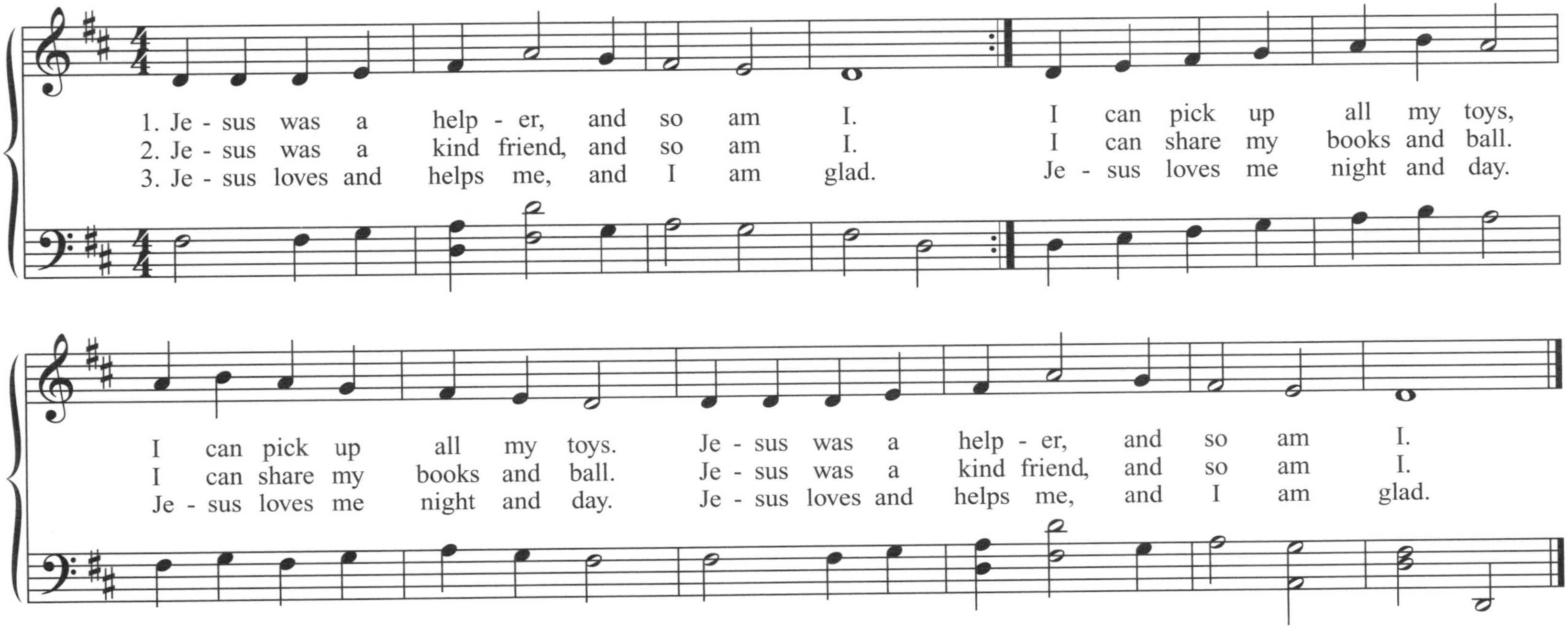

1. Je - sus was a help - er, and so am I. I can pick up all my toys,
2. Je - sus was a kind friend, and so am I. I can share my books and ball.
3. Je - sus loves and helps me, and I am glad. Je - sus loves me night and day.

I can pick up all my toys. Je - sus was a help - er, and so am I.
I can share my books and ball. Je - sus was a kind friend, and so am I.
Je - sus loves me night and day. Je - sus loves and helps me, and I am glad.

We Are Little Helpers

296

A. ADELE FLOWER

A. ADELE FLOWER

1. We are lit-tle help-ers, Help-ers, help-ers; We are lit-tle help - ers, Help-ing all the day.
2. We are lit-tle help-ers, Help-ers, help-ers; We are lit-tle help - ers, We please the Lord that way.

297 The Helping Song

MARTHA FELDBUSH | KENNETH D. LOGAN

Lively

I help you, you help me. We're a help - ing fam - i - ly. Help - ing, help - ing, help - ing, sing a help - ing song. Help - ing, help - ing all day long.

298 Who Is Jesus' Helper?

DOROTHY ROBISON | DOROTHY ROBISON

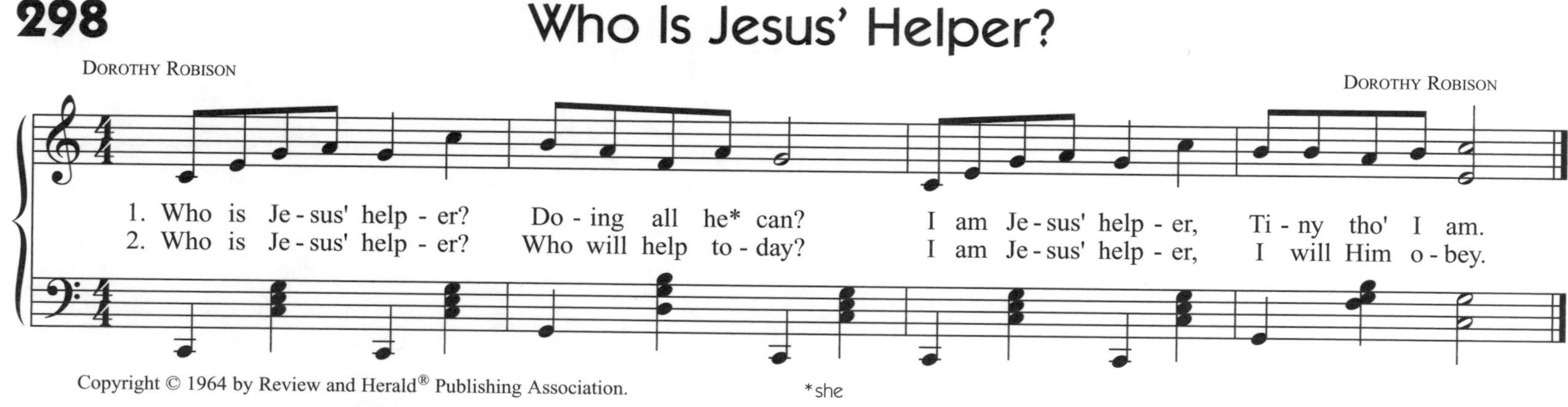
1. Who is Je - sus' help - er? Do - ing all he* can? I am Je - sus' help - er, Ti - ny tho' I am.
2. Who is Je - sus' help - er? Who will help to - day? I am Je - sus' help - er, I will Him o - bey.

*she

Things That I Can Do

Derrell Billingsley — Derrell Billingsley

1. There are man - y things that I can do; Doo - dle, doo - dle, doot, doot, doo. I can sing a song with notes so true: Doo - dle, doo - dle, doot, doot, doo.
2. There are man - y things that I can do; Doo - dle, doo - dle, doot, doot, doo. I can play a song with in - stru - ments: (Play instruments to the steady beat.)
3. There are man - y sounds that I can make; Doo - dle, doo - dle, doot, doot, doo. I can make a sound just like a cow:* Moo, moo, moo, moo, moo, moo, moo.

*Substitute: sheep . . . baa; duck . . . quack; etc.

300 Who's a Helper?

UNKNOWN
TRADITIONAL
3
3
Who's a help - er? _____'s* a help - er. Who's a help - er? _____'s* a help - er. Ev - ery day, ev - ery day.†

*Child's name, doctor, plumber, preacher, builder, etc.
† Or "Every day, every day."

301 Giving Jesus Me

VIRGINIA CASON

VIRGINIA CASON / ARR. BY WAYNE HOOPER

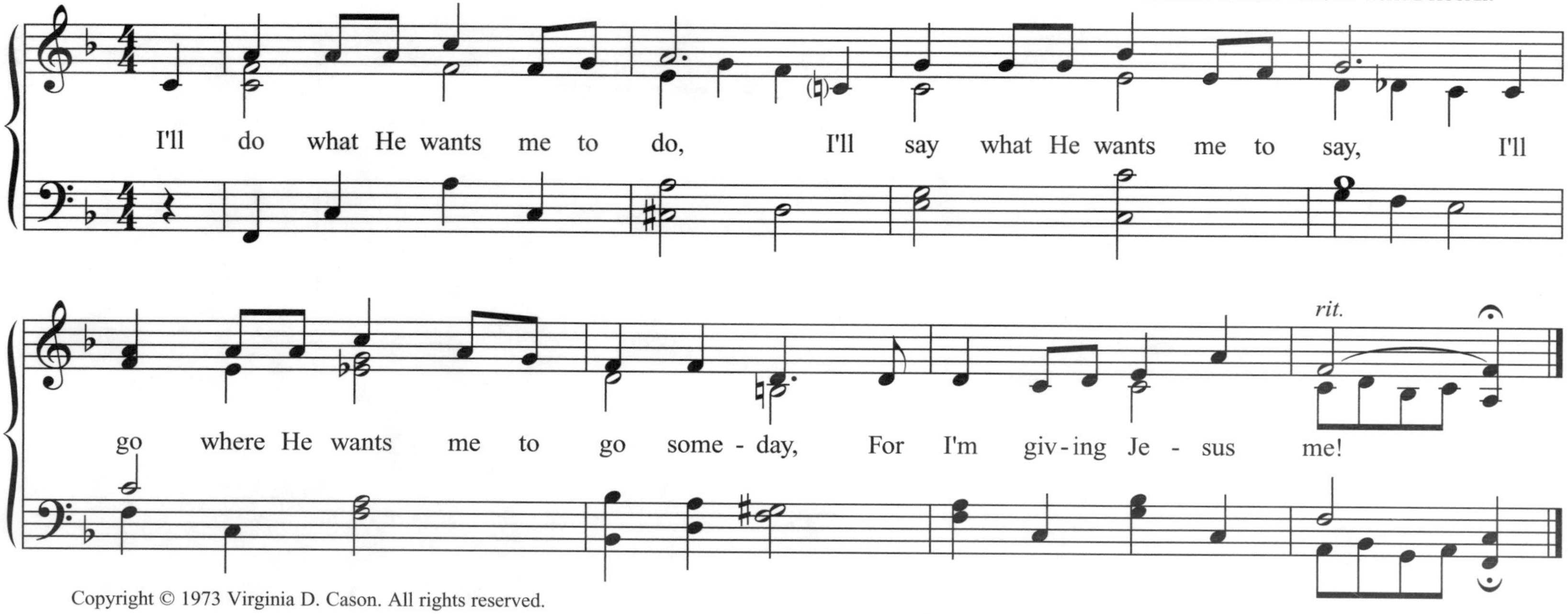

I'll do what He wants me to do, I'll say what He wants me to say, I'll go where He wants me to go some - day, For I'm giv - ing Je - sus me!

rit.

Blessings

Carol Greene | Carol Greene

Happily

1. I am a bless - ing. I am a bless - ing. God made me to be a bless - ing in the world. I am a bless - ing. I am a bless - ing. God made me to bless the whole wide world.

2. You are a bless - ing. You are a bless - ing. God made you to be a bless - ing in the world. You are a bless - ing. You are a bless - ing. God made you to bless the whole wide world.

Help the children think of ways in which they can share Jesus' love and be blessings. Have them point to themselves on the words "I" and "me" and to one another on the word "you."

Service

303 I Will Use My Hands for Him

ENID G. THORSON

ENID G. THORSON

Be - cause Je - sus loves me, I will use my hands* for Him. Be -
cause Je - sus loves me, I will use my hands for Him.

*Eyes, lips, feet, ears, arms, etc.

You can use a large felt girl or boy. Give the child a pointer or a stick that you use when singing. The child points to the parts of the body you are going to sing about. Other children can use motions, such as pointing heavenward when singing "because Jesus loves me," then to self. When singing "I will use my hands for Him," extend hands (palms up), to the front of their body.

Jesus Helps Me Choose

Roxy Hoehn Roxy Hoehn

1. Je - sus wants my words to be truth - ful ev - 'ry day.
2. Je - sus wants my act - ions to be lov - ing ev - 'ry day.
3. Je - sus wants my hands to do kind things ev - 'ry day.
4. I will ask dear Je - sus at the start of ev - 'ry day
He will help me choose what's best in all I do and say.
He will help me choose what's best in all I do and say.
He will help me choose what's best in all I do and say.
Please to help me choose what's best in all I do and say.

305
Little Eyes for Jesus
Mrs. John F. Underhill
Mrs. John F. Underhill
Lit - tle eyes for Je - sus Shin - ing ev - 'ry day, Lit - tle ears for Je - sus List - 'ning all the way.
Lit - tle lips for Je - sus Tell of Je - sus' love, Lit - tle feet to lead me To the home a - bove.
306
Two Little Eyes
Anonymous
S.V.R. Ford
1. Two lit - tle eyes to look to God, Two lit - tle ears to hear His Word;
2. One lit - tle tongue to speak His truth, One lit - tle heart for Him in youth;
Two lit - tle feet to walk His ways, Hands to serve Him all my days.
Take them, O Je - sus, let them be Al - ways will - ing, true to Thee.

Little Feet, Be Careful

Mrs. L.M.B. Bateman

J. H. Rosecrans

1. I washed my hands this morning, O very clean and bright,
And lent them both to Jesus To work for him till night.

2. I told my ears to listen Quite closely all day through,
For any act of kindness Such little hands can do.

3. My eyes are set to watch them About their work or play,
To keep them out of mischief For Jesus' sake all day.

CHORUS

Little feet, be careful, Where you take me to,
Anything for Jesus, Only let me do.

Five Little Missionaries

Harriet S. Jenks

1. Five little mis-sion-ar-ies Wish-ing there were more;
2. Four little mis-sion-ar-ies Hap-py as can be;
3. Three little mis-sion-ar-ies With God's work to do,
4. Two little mis-sion-ar-ies, Work-ing can be fun,
One went a-way and then there were four.
One went a-way and then there were three.
One went a-way and then there were two.
One went a-way and then there was one.
CHORUS
Mis-sion-ar-y, mis-sion-ar-y, good-bye. Mis-sion-ar-y, mis-sion-ar-y, good-bye.

5. One little missionary,
More work to be done,
He* went away and
then there was none.

*She

Missions

Service

Jesus Loves the Little Children

Unknown Unknown

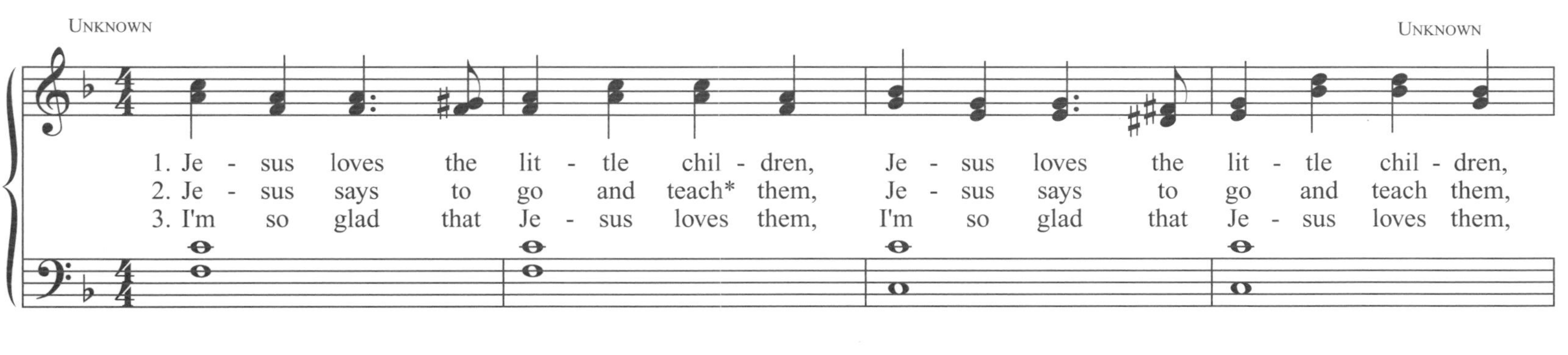
1. Je - sus loves the lit - tle chil - dren, Je - sus loves the lit - tle chil - dren,
2. Je - sus says to go and teach* them, Je - sus says to go and teach them,
3. I'm so glad that Je - sus loves them, I'm so glad that Je - sus loves them,

Je - sus loves the lit - tle chil - dren, The whole wide world a - round.
Je - sus says to go and teach them, The whole wide world a - round.
I'm so glad that Je - sus loves them, The Bi - ble tells me so.

*help, serve

Missions

Service

310 Kind Lips

Mary E. Schwab — Mary E. Schwab

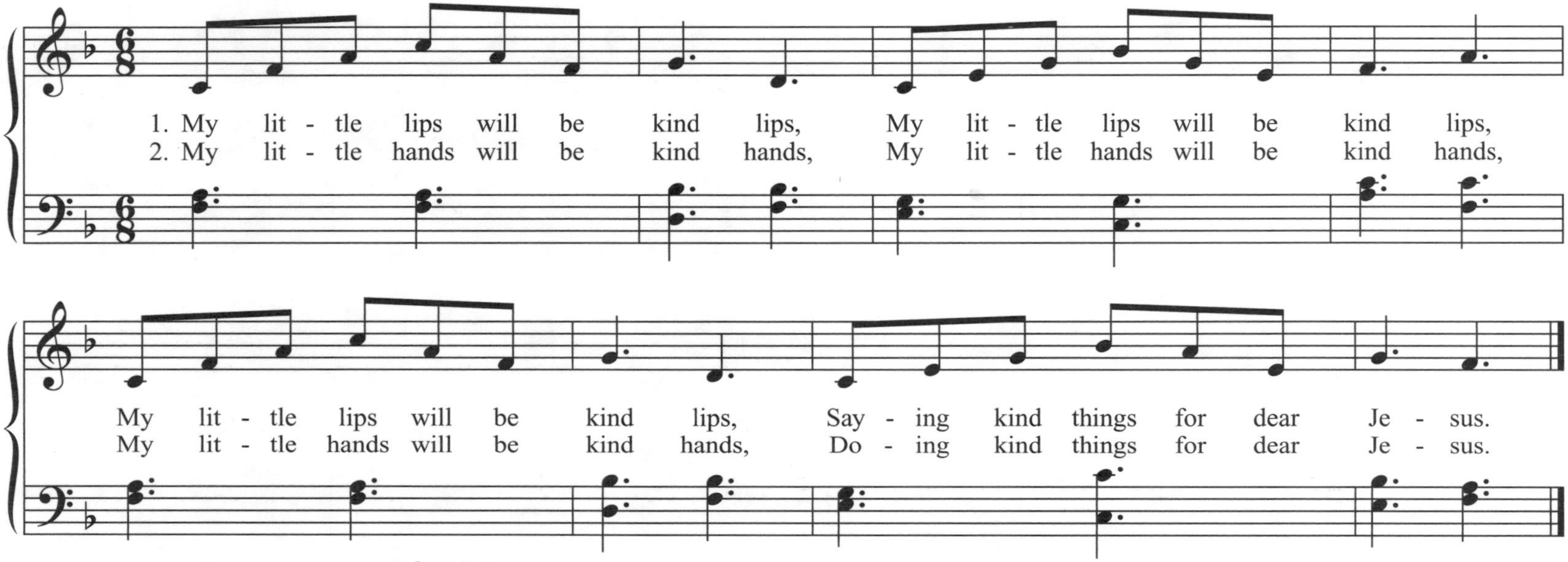

1. My lit - tle lips will be kind lips, My lit - tle lips will be kind lips,
My lit - tle lips will be kind lips, Say - ing kind things for dear Je - sus.

2. My lit - tle hands will be kind hands, My lit - tle hands will be kind hands,
My lit - tle hands will be kind hands, Do - ing kind things for dear Je - sus.

311 Oh, Where

Anita Reith Stohs — Traditional / Arr. by Kenneth D. Logan

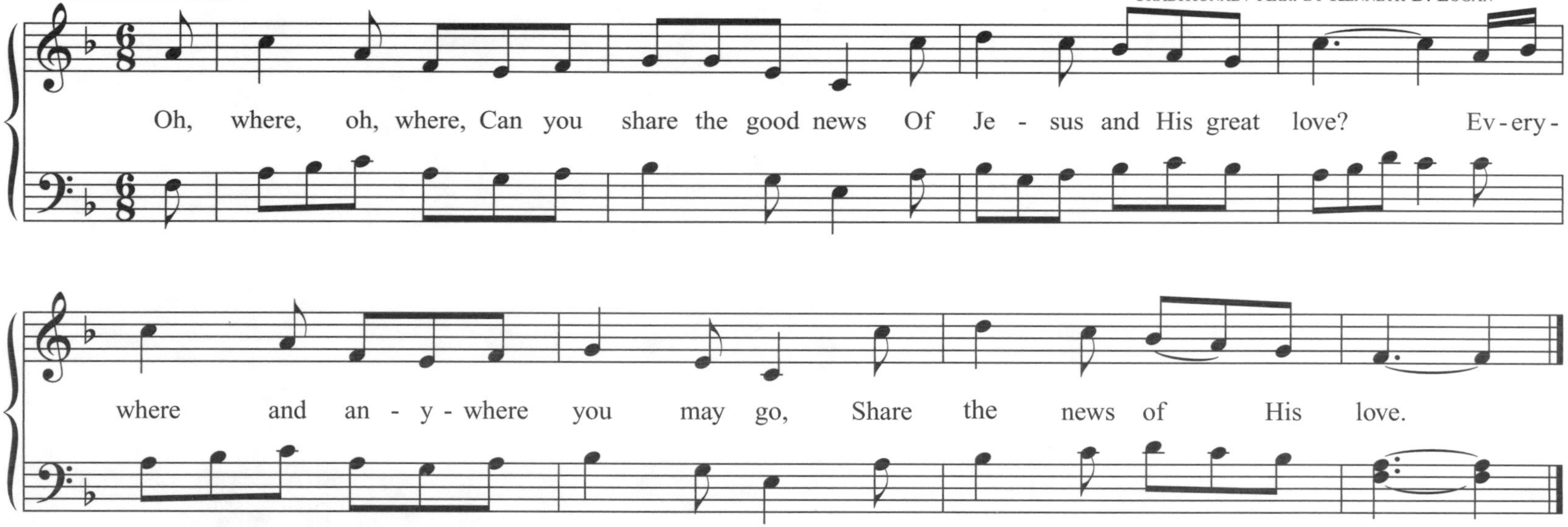

Oh, where, oh, where, Can you share the good news Of Je - sus and His great love? Ev - ery -

where and an - y - where you may go, Share the news of His love.

Share the Good News

Anita Reith Stohs

Traditional / Arr. by Kenneth D. Logan

Brightly

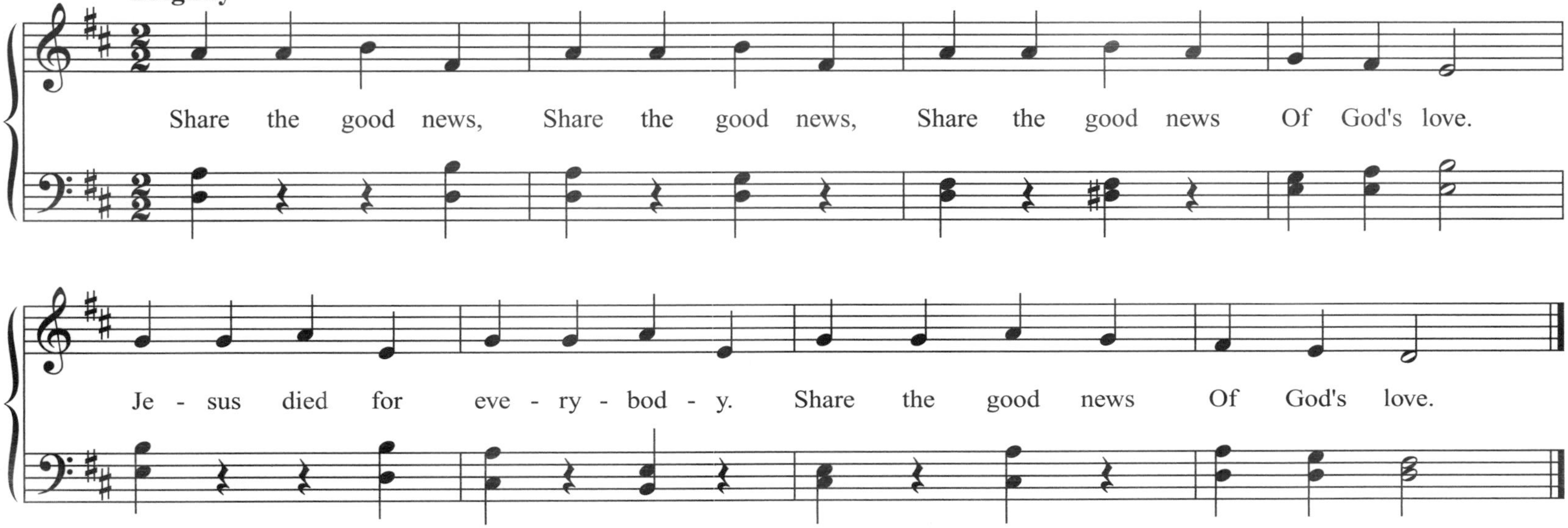

Share the good news, Share the good news, Share the good news Of God's love.

Je - sus died for eve - ry - bod - y. Share the good news Of God's love.

WITNESSING

SERVICE

313 This Little Light of Mine

Unknown

Unknown / Arr. by Kenneth D. Logan

1. This lit - tle light of mine, I'm gon-na let it shine.
2. Don't let Sa - tan blow it out. I'm gon-na let it shine.
3. Shine it round the neigh - bor - hood. I'm gon-na let it shine.
4. Hide it un - der a bush - el, NO! I'm gon-na let it shine.
This lit - tle light of mine, I'm gon-na let it shine, let it
Don't let Sa - tan blow it out. I'm gon-na let it shine, let it
Shine it round the neigh - bor - hood. I'm gon-na let it shine, let it
Hide it un - der a bush - el, NO! I'm gon-na let it shine, let it
shine, let it shine, let it shine!
shine, let it shine, let it shine!
shine, let it shine, let it shine!
shine, let it shine, let it shine!

5. Let it shine till Jesus comes.
I'm gonna let it shine.
Let it shine till Jesus comes.
I'm gonna let it shine, let it
shine, let it shine, let it shine!

We Are His Hands

Jeff Wood
Jeff Wood / Arr. by Kenneth D. Logan
1. We are His 1hands to touch the world a - round us.
2. We are His 4eyes to see the need in oth - ers.
We are His 2feet to go where He may lead.
We are His 5voice to tell of His re - turn.
CHORUS
And we are His 3love burn - ing in the dark - ness.
We are His 3love shin - ing in the night.
1.
night.
2.
night.

Actions: 1. Wave hands in air. 2. Stomp feet. 3. Hands make shape of heart. 4. Point to eyes. 5. Point to throat.

315 You've Got to Tell

Carol Greene
Carol Greene
Brightly
1. When you know Lord Je - sus and His love for you, There is just one thing you've sim - ply got to do.
2. Je - sus' love in - side you is - n't meant to stay. He's got more for you, so give that love a - way.
REFRAIN
You've got to tell, tell, tell, tell, tell. You've got to tell, tell, tell, tell, tell. In a whis - per, in a shout, Let it out, let it out! You've got to tell, tell, tell, tell, tell.

Ask the children to march in place during the song, then jump into the air at "Let it out! Let it out!"

Index of Titles and First Lines

A

A birthday 36
A boat goes sailing 35
A child like me 177
A friend of Jesus 254
A little talk with Jesus 227
A real little bear to play with 127
All children need the Saviour 178
All for Jesus 239
All night, all day 119
All our needs 85
Alway 128
An angel came down 120
And God said 66
Angels 121
Angels are watching over me 50
Angels bright were singing 140
Angels came to Jacob 121
Angels singing 140
Animals, animals 67
Animals in heaven 130
Arky, arky 212
At sleep or at play, God sees 122
Away in a manger 141

B

Baby Jesus 142
Be happy, be kind 133
Be kind to one another 260
Because I'm happy 179
Because Jesus loves me 303
Bible, Bible, Jesus talks to me 51
Blessed rest 234
Blessings 302
Bobby, Bobby! Please come here to me 266
Bubbles 157
Buddies 256
Busy little squirrel, playing in the trees 80
Bye, baby, bye 247

C

Campfire 249
Care for one another 262
Christmas star 143
Christmastime 144
Clip-clop 158
Close my eyes, kneel to pray 9
Colors 159
Come praise the Lord 211
Coming, mother 266
Count the birthday money 37
Creation 68

D

Daddy loves me; mother loves me 105
Day or night (day or night) we will praise the Lord 211

indicates Beginner-friendly

Dear Jesus 9
Dear Jesus, we thank Thee for Thy loving care 19
Dip, dip, dip in the river [BF] 56
Don't cry, little baby [BF] 246
Don't mess it up 282

E

Ev'ry thing that God makes is good 69
Everything He makes is good 69

F

Father God, I know You love me so 96
Fishy, fishy [BF] 161
Five little missionaries 308
For me 154
Forgiveness is a gift [BF] 75

G

Get ready to pray 8
Give Him your heart 191
Giving 285
Giving Jesus me 301
Go and wash 64
God cares for me [BF] *Shumate/Truss* 86
God cares for me *Doan* 87
God is so good [BF] 88
God loves a cheerful giver [BF] 29
God made everything 162
God made it so [BF] 163
God made me *Max* 70
God made me *Striplin* 164
God made our wonderful world 71
God made our world 71
God made the kangaroo 72
God made the moon that shines at night 73
God made the sun and moon and stars 165
God made the world and it's very, very good 282
God made us all 73
God makes roses grow in my garden [BF] 166
God sees me [BF] 89
God sees me when I am asleep [BF] 86
God sends His angels to watch over me 124
God sent His angels 47
God so loved the world [BF] 181
God takes care of me 90
God, You are so great and good 204
God's angels care for me 124
God's best gift 145
God's children are helpful 287
God's house [BF] 185
God's ways 259
Good morning [BF] 1
Good morning to you [BF] 3
Good-bye prayer [BF] 44
Good-bye to you 45
Greeting song [BF] 4

[BF] indicates Beginner-friendly

Guardian angel song 49

H

Hallelu, hallelu 213
Happy all the time 198
Happy birthday! *Lowden* 38
Happy birthday! *Sage* 39
Happy, happy home 273
Happy, happy, happy birthday 40
Happy Sabbath 235
He cares about you 91
Hear the money dropping 31
Heaven is a happy place 131
Help me, Lord Jesus 196
Helping song 288
Here is my money 32
Here is the way we walk to church 186
Here we come to Bethlehem 146
He's able 93
He's got the whole world in His hands 125

I

I am a blessing 302
I am happy as can be! 214
I am so glad that Jesus love me 101
I am so happy 199
I can feel things that are soft, soft, so soft 83
I can help 289
I can pray ev'ry day, anytime, anywhere 232
I did wrong, that's too bad 77
I give myself to Jesus 192
I go to church 187
I have a (doggy/kitty) 283
I have a sweet, loving mother 253
I have decided to follow Jesus 193
I have games I love to play 277
I have hands that clap 215
I have the joy 216
I have two dollies and I am glad 279
I help you, you help me 297
I know my mommy loves me 104
I know that Jesus loves me 95
I like to come to God's house 185
I like to do something nice for others every day 261
I like to eat an apple 167
I like to help my mother 291
I like to see the butterflies 173
I love Jesus! 205
I love mother 250
I love the dear Jesus 206
I love the Lord 207
I love Thee, O Lord 208
I may not be very tall 128
I must do what mother says 270
I obey 267
I open my Bible and read 26

indicates Beginner-friendly

I open my Bible book and read . . . 27
I open my Bible carefully . . . 28
I sing because I'm happy . . . 179
I talk to grandma on the phone . . . 10
I talk to Jesus *McDonald* . . . 228
I talk to Jesus *Robison* . . . 10
I want to be like Jesus . . . 194
I washed my hands this morning . . . 307
I will be a helper . . . 290
I will be kind . . . 284
I will bend my knees . . . 8
I will pray . . . 229
I will pray unto the Lord . . . 12
I will sing . . . 217
I will use my hands for Him . . . 303
I will wear a crown . . . 132
I wonder why . . . 286
I'll be happy . . . 201
I'll do what He wants me to do . . . 301
I'll make my home a happy home . . . 260
I'll meet you in heaven . . . 133
I'll pick up my toys . . . 292
I'll share my home . . . 147
I'll share my only one . . . 275
I'll take turns . . . 276
I'm a little helper . . . 293
I'm forgiven . . . 76
I'm giving, I'm giving . . . 285
I'm glad I came to Sabbath school . . . 5
I'm inright, outright . . . 198
I'm so small . . . 96
I'm special . . . 97
If I had a dollie and you had none . . . 275
If I were a butterfly . . . 244
If you will let Jesus have all of your heart . . . 191
If you're happy . . . 200
Into my heart . . . 195
It is time to say good-bye now . . . 44
It was a happy day . . . 148
It's about grace . . . 98

J

Jesus cares for all our needs . . . 85
Jesus cares for me . . . 100
Jesus cares for you . . . 91
Jesus died upon the cross . . . 155
Jesus, friend of little children . . . 110
Jesus gave me a mommy . . . 251
Jesus has said He is coming . . . 184
Jesus helps me choose . . . 304
Jesus' house . . . 188
Jesus is building mansions . . . 134
Jesus is coming *Dart/Albertson* . . . 182
Jesus is coming *Edwards-Lesser* . . . 183
Jesus is coming *Stewart* . . . 184
Jesus is happy . . . 268

indicates Beginner-friendly

Jesus is love BF ... 99
Jesus is my helper ... 230
Jesus is near BF ... 126
Jesus is risen ... 156
Jesus, listen now to me ... 13
Jesus loves even me ... 101
Jesus loves me *Warner/Bradbury* ... 102
Jesus loves me *GC SS Dept.* ... 103
Jesus loves me more ... 104
Jesus loves me much, much more BF ... 105
Jesus loves the children BF ... 106
Jesus loves the little children BF ... 106
Jesus loves the little children ... 309
Jesus loves the little ones BF ... 107
Jesus made my hands so they could clap for joy ... 84
Jesus made the grass for the hungry cow BF ... 174
Jesus made the sunshine BF ... 168
Jesus never fails ... 108
Jesus sees me BF ... 109
Jesus sends the angels BF ... 48
Jesus shares His food with us ... 138
Jesus smiles and forgives ... 77
Jesus talks to me BF ... 51
Jesus used to be a little child like me ... 177
Jesus wants me for a sunbeam ... 202
Jesus wants my words to be truthful ev'ry day ... 304
Jesus was a helper ... 295
Jesus was a little child BF ... 136
Just a little donkey ... 137
Just five years old today ... 38

K

Kangaroo, kangaroo ... 72
Kind lips ... 310

L

Let us do good ... 263
Let us do good to all men BF ... 265
Let's give the Lord our praise ... 219
Let's have a talk with Jesus BF ... 11
Let's put all our toys away ... 294
Let's walk together in our parade ... 41
Listen, little children ... 18
Listen to the bells ring BF ... 236
Little Baby in the manger, I love you ... 149
Little bird song ... 169
Little birdies in the tree BF ... 111
Little birds are singing ... 87
Little children are helpful ... 287
Little eyes for Jesus ... 305
Little feet, be careful ... 307
Little Jesus liked to walk beneath the trees BF ... 139
Look, look, look at the world BF ... 78
Love, Jesus is love BF ... 99
Love one another ... 264

BF indicates Beginner-friendly

M

Making music 220
Mary has a birthday, we're so glad 37
Mary loved Baby Jesus 150
Mary's little Baby 151
Mother bunny rabbit says, "God made me" 164
My best friend is Jesus 218
My family *GC SS Dept./Casebeer* 252
My family *McDonald* 253
My fam'ly cooks good food for me 252
My God is so great 112
My little lips are smiling 79
My little lips will be kind lips 310

N

Naaman has leprosy 65
Naaman was a man who had leprosy 64
Naaman's song 65
Noah built a great big boat 58
Noah took a hammer 269
Now we'll talk to God 14

O

O give thanks unto the Lord 240
O God, listen to my prayer 15
Obedient 270
Offering prayer song 33
Offering response 30
Oh, friend, do you love Jesus? 210
Oh, how I love Jesus 209
Oh, I am so happy 199
Oh, where 311
Oh, who can make a flower? 74
On the streets of gold 129
One little fish, two little fish 55
One sad man, one sad man 116
Our church is a family 257
Our family 258
Our Father made the sun 68
Our little hands can be helping hands 288
Our parade 41
Our Sabbath school is over 46
Our thanksgiving song 241

P

Peter and John just talked to God 16
Plenty of room in the family 248
Praise Him, praise Him 221
Praise Him with the trumpet 220
Praise the God who made you 224
Praise to Jesus 222
Praise your God 224
Pray 231

indicates Beginner-friendly

Pray when you wake in the morning ... 231
Prayer song *Bell* ... 18
Prayer song *Myers* ... 19
Prayer to grow strong ... 196
Praying every day ... 232
Presents ... 80
Promotion song ... 43

Q

Quietly, so quietly ... 42
Quietly tiptoe ... 42

R

Rejoice, I have found My sheep ... 176
Rejoice in the Lord always ... 225
Response ... 23
Riding on a camel ... 152
Ring the bells ... 153
Ring-a-ling-a-ling ... 237
Rock, rock, rock, rock ... 172
Rock-a-bye baby, Jesus is near ... 126
Roses bloom in my garden ... 81
Run to Jesus ... 57

S

Sabbath bells ... 237
Sabbath in heaven ... 135
Sabbath is a happy day ... 235
Sabbath school is over ... 46
Sad or glad ... 271
Satan is the evil one ... 271
Scrubbing ... 203
Seashells ... 160
See the boat ... 172
Shake a hand and bend ... 255
Shake a little hand ... 6
Shall we go for a walk today? ... 82
Share the good news ... 312
Share with you ... 277
Sharing ... 278
Sharing song ... 279
Shine, shine, star of light ... 143
Some day we'll keep Sabbath in heaven ... 135
Someone cares ... 170
Something nice ... 261

T

Talk to God ... 16
Tap, tap, tap ... 281
Teach us to share ... 242
Thank God for angels bright ... 50
Thank You, dear Jesus ... 22
Thank You for hearing our prayer ... 20
Thank You, God, for Jesus ... 242
Thank You, God, thank You, God ... 20
Thank You, Jesus ... 243

Thank You, Jesus, for ev'rything 21
Thank You, Jesus, for loving me 23
Thank You, Jesus, now we sing 30
Thank You song 245
The animals came a-walking 59
The Bible. 53
The Bible is God's Word to me 52
The big blue ocean 113
The blackbird song 54
The butterflies 173
The butterfly song. 244
The friendship clap 255
The Good Shepherd 123
The helping song 297
The hungry cow 174
The loaves and the fishes 55
The Lord told Noah, there's gonna be a floody, floody. . . 211
The preacher talks. 189
The raindrops fall 94
The sharing song. 138
The Shepherd loves His lambs 114
The tall green trees are swaying. 100
The trees are gently swaying. 115
The wise man and the foolish man. 62
The wise man built his house upon the rock 62
The world is full of pretty flow'rs 163
Then Jesus came 116
There are many things that I can do 299
There were three tiny eggs in a wee, wee nest. 170
There'll be joys untold on the streets of gold. 129
There'll be lions there, and a big brown bear. 130
Things Jesus liked when He was a child 139
Things that I can do 299
This is Jesus' house 188
This is the day. 238
This is what the clock says 2
This little light of mine. 313
This world is full of pretty flow'rs. 163
Tick-tock song 2
Tiny tot response 21
To God's house 34
Twinkle, twinkle, little star 175
Two ears to hear of Jesus 239
Two little eyes 306

U

Up, up in the sky, the little birds fly. 169

W

Walk, walk, walk, walk 190
Walking to church. 190
We are His hands 314
We are little children 197
We are little helpers 296
We are sharing 280
We have a happy fam'ly. 258

indicates Beginner-friendly

We have a visitor 24
We have bro't our off'ring on this Sabbath day 33
We thank You for sunshine of yellow and gold. 245
We welcome you 7
We'll fold our hands 14
We're glad you came to our Sabbath school 25
We're thankful for the Sabbath day 241
What can baby do? 223
When a mother calls 274
When a mother says, "bow-wow" 274
When Daniel was down in the dark lions' den 47
When God had made the world 234
When it's time to pray 17
When mommy says, "Will you come here?" 272
When mother says "Pick up your toys" 267
When mother tucks me in at night 49
When the children came to play 57
When you know Lord Jesus and His love for you 315
Where are you going? 54
Whisper a prayer. 233
Who am I? 117
Who can? 74
Who is Jesus? 180
Who is Jesus' helper? 298
Who made the beautiful rainbow? 60
Who made the rainbow? 60
Who's a helper? 300
Who's come to Sabbath school? 4
Who's in the ark? 61
With Jesus in the family 273
With Jesus in the family, happy, happy home 273
With the fingers Jesus gave me 83
Wonder song 74
Wonderful Jesus 84
Wonderful, wonderful. 226
Woolly, woolly lamb 171
Would you like to see the Bible? 53

Y

Yes, Jesus cares for me 118
Yes, yes, mommy 272
You're going to kindergarten on this Sabbath day 43
You've got to tell 315

Z

Zacchaeus 63

indicates Beginner-friendly

Topical Index

ANGELS

All Night, All Day 119
An Angel Came Down [B♫] *Sage* 120
God Sent His Angels *Schwab* 47
God's Angels Care for Me *Pendleton* 124
Guardian Angel Song *Myers* 49
Jesus Sends the Angels [B♫] *Jorgensen* 48
Thank God for Angels Bright [B♫] *Jarnes* 50

ANIMALS

Jesus Cares for Me *Schwab* 100

DONKEY
Clip-clop [B♫] *Sage* 158

FISH
Fishy, Fishy [B♫] *Sage* 161

LAMBS
Woolly, Woolly Lamb [B♫] *Sage* 171

RABBITS
God Made Me [B♫] *Striplin* 164

BIBLE

God's Best Gift *Curley, Lawler/Bortniansky* 145
I Am So Happy [B♫] *Dart/Albertson* 199
I Open My Bible and Read *Thomas* 26
I Open My Bible Book and Read [B♫] *Wood* 27
I Open My Bible Carefully [B♫] *Sage* 28
Jesus Talks to Me [B♫] *Davis* 51
Quietly Tiptoe *Stagl-Schippmann* 42
Sharing Song *Creasman* 279
The Bible *Casebeer* 53
The Bible Is God's Word to Me [B♫] *Thorson* 52
With Jesus in the Family [B♫] *Lind* 273
Wonderful, Wonderful *Jones* 226

BIBLE STORY

DANIEL
Angels *Nielson* 121
God Sent His Angels *Schwab* 47

DAVID
God Sent His Angels *Schwab* 47

ELIJAH
The Blackbird Song [B♫] *Sage* 54

HEALING THE BLIND MAN
Then Jesus Came [B♫] *GC SS Dept./Logan* 116

HEALING THE LAME MAN
Then Jesus Came [B♫] *GC SS Dept./Logan* 116

JACOB
Angels *Nielson* 121

JESUS
Angels *Nielson* 121
Run to Jesus *Max* 57

MOSES
God Sent His Angels *Schwab* 47

NAAMAN
Dip, Dip, Dip in the River [B♫] *Johnson/Traditional* . 56

[B♫] indicates Beginner-friendly

Go and Wash *Jacobs/Traditional* 64

Naaman's Song *Jacobs/Traditional* 65

NOAH/THE FLOOD
An Angel Came Down *Sage* 120

Arky, Arky 212

God Sent His Angels *Schwab* 47

Noah Built a Great Big Boat *Schwab* 58

Tap, Tap, Tap *Sage* 281

The Animals Came a-Walking *Cason* 59

Who Made the Rainbow? *McKinney* 60

Who's in the Ark? *Sage* 61

PETER AND JOHN (adaptable)
Talk to God *Feldbush* 16

THE GOOD SHEPHERD
The Good Shepherd *Greene/Brahms* 123

The Shepherd Loves His Lambs *Thorson* 114

THE LOAVES AND THE FISHES
The Loaves and the Fishes *Sage* 55

THE WISE MAN AND THE FOOLISH MAN
The Wise Man and the Foolish Man 62

TRIUMPHANT ENTRY
Just a Little Donkey *Stagl-Schippmann* 137

ZACCHAEUS
Zacchaeus 63

BIBLE STORIES WITH BOATS

See the Boat *Sage* 172

BIRDS

God Made Everything *Black* 162

God Made It So *Fillmore* 163

God Made Me *Striplin* 164

God Made Our World *Lawrence* 71

Jesus Cares for Me *Schwab* 100

Little Bird Song *Wiggin* 169

Little Birdies in the Tree *Thorson*. 111

Presents *Schwab* 80

Someone Cares *Barger* 170

The Blackbird Song *Sage* 54

BIRTHDAY

A Birthday *Adair* 36

Count the Birthday Money *Wood* 37

Happy Birthday! *Lowden* 38

Happy Birthday! *Sage* 39

Happy, Happy, Happy Birthday *Greene* 40

CARE

Jesus Wants Me for a Sunbeam *Talbot* 202

CARE FOR ANIMALS

Don't Mess It Up *Greene* 282

I Have a (Doggy/Kitty) *Coston* 283

I Will Be Kind *Jorgensen* 284

The Hungry Cow *Sage* 174

indicates Beginner-friendly

CHURCH

God's House *Daleburn* 185
Happy Sabbath *Kennedy* 235
Here Is the Way We Walk to Church *Oglevee/Oglevee* 186
I Go to Church *Stagl-Schippmann* 187
Jesus' House *Sage* 188
Our Church Is a Family *Greene/Schubert* 257
The Preacher Talks *Sage* 189
To God's House *Max* 34
Walking to Church *Scholes* 190

CLOSING

Good-bye Prayer *Maguire* 44
Good-bye to You *Vance* 45
Sabbath School Is Over 46

COMFORT

Don't Cry, Little Baby *Sage* 246
Happy Sabbath *Kennedy* 235

COMMITMENT TO JESUS

Give Him Your Heart *Cason* 191
Giving Jesus Me *Cason* 301
Happy All the Time *Simpson* 198
I Give Myself to Jesus *Stewart* 192
I Have Decided to Follow Jesus *Traditional* 193
I Want to Be Like Jesus *Gilleroth* 194
Into My Heart *Clarke* 195
Jesus Wants Me for a Sunbeam *Talbot* 202
Oh, Friend, Do You Love Jesus? 210
Prayer to Grow Strong *Anderson, Riley/Anderson, Thompson* 196
Two Little Eyes *Ford* 306
We Are Little Children *Edwards-Lesser* 197

COMMUNITY

A Birthday *Adair* 36
Count the Birthday Money *Wood* 37
God's Children Are Helpful *Robinson* 287
God's Ways *LeBar/Thompson* 260
Good Morning *Sage* 1
Good Morning to You *Adair* 3
Good-bye Prayer *Maguire* 44
Good-bye to You *Vance* 45
Greeting Song *McKinley* 4
Happy Birthday! *Lowden* 38
Happy Birthday! *Sage* 39
Happy, Happy, Happy Birthday *Greene* 40
Helping Song *Myers* 288
I Can Help *Payne/Thompson* 289
I Like to Help My Mother *Schwab* 291
I Obey *Self/Traditional* 267
I Talk to Jesus *Robison* 10
I Will Be a Helper *Ingham* 290
I'll Meet You in Heaven *Scholes* 133

indicates Beginner-friendly

I'll Pick Up My Toys *Burdick* 292
I'm a Little Helper [B] *Sage* 293
Jesus Helps Me Choose *Hoehn* 304
Jesus Is Coming *Stewart* 184
Jesus Is Happy *Hoehn* 268
Jesus Loves Me More *Sage* 104
Jesus Loves Me Much, Much More [B] *Thorson* . . 105
Jesus Wants Me for a Sunbeam *Talbot* 202
Jesus Was a Helper *Curley* 295
Jesus Was a Little Child [B] *McDonald* 136
Kind Lips *Schwab* 310
Let's Put All Our Toys Away *Sage* 294
My Family [B] *GC SS Dept./Casebeer* 252
My Family [B] *McDonald* 253
Obedient *Gustafson* 270
Our Church Is a Family [B] *Greene/Schubert* 257
Our Family *Hoehn* 258
Our Parade *Traditional* 41
Plenty of Room in the Family *Gaither/Gaither* 248
Promotion Song [B] *Stewart* 43
Quietly Tiptoe *Stagl-Schippmann* 42
Sabbath School Is Over [B] 46
Shake a Little Hand *Johnsson/Traditional* 6
Teach Us to Share *Cassett* 242
The Helping Song [B] *Feldbush/Logan* 297
The Sharing Song *GC SS Dept./Traditional* 138
This Little Light of Mine 313
We Are Little Helpers *Flower* 296
We Have a Visitor [B] *Sage* 24
We Welcome You *Adair* 7
We're Glad You Came to Our Sabbath School [B] . . 25
Who's a Helper? 300
With Jesus in the Family [B] *Lind* 273

COOPERATION

God's Ways *LeBar/Thompson* 259

CREATION

And God Said *Wood* 66
Animals, Animals *Sage* 67
Blessed Rest *Max* 234
Creation *Knox/Campbell* 68
Everything He Makes Is Good *Max* 69
God Made Everything *Black* 162
God Made It So [B] *Fillmore* 163
God Made Me *Max* 70
God Made Me *Striplin* 164
God Made Our World *Lawrence* 71
God Made the Kangaroo *Max* 72
God Made the Sun and
Moon and Stars *Edwards-Lesser* 165
God Made Us All *Martin/Boggs* 73
I Am Happy as Can Be! [B] *Sage* 214
I Have Hands That Clap [B] *Vance* 215
The Butterflies [B] *Robison* 173
Wonder Song (Who Can?) [B] *Owens/Parker* 74

[B] indicates Beginner-friendly

FAMILY

Bye, Baby, Bye *Adair* 247
Campfire *Sage* 249
I Am So Happy *Dart/Albertson* 199
I Know That Jesus Loves Me *Johnsson/Traditional* . . 95
I Love Mother *Johnsson/Traditional* 250
I Talk to Jesus *Robison* 10
Jesus Gave Me a Mommy *Stewart* 251
Jesus Loves Me More *Sage* 104
Jesus Loves Me Much, Much More *Thorson* . . 105
My Family *GC SS Dept./Casebeer* 252
My Family *McDonald* 253
Our Family *Hoehn* 258
Plenty of Room in the Family *Gaither/Gaither* 248
The Helping Song *Feldbush/Logan* 297
With Jesus in the Family *Lind* 273

FLOWERS

God Made It So *Fillmore* 163
God Made Me *Striplin* 164
God Makes Roses Grow in My Garden *Myers* . 166
Jesus Cares for Me *Schwab* 100

FORGIVENESS

Forgiveness Is a Gift *Stohs/Traditional* 75
I'm Forgiven *Stohs/Logan* 76
It's About Grace *Herrington* 98
Jesus Died Upon the Cross *Stohs/Logan* 155
Jesus Smiles and Forgives *Femopase* 77

FRIENDSHIP

A Friend of Jesus *Tetz* 254
Buddies *Payne/Payne, Thompson* 256
Share With You *Coston* 277
The Friendship Clap 255

GIVING

Giving *LeBar/Blomquist* 285

GOD'S FAMILY

Our Church Is a Family *Greene/Schubert* 257
Our Family *Hoehn* 258

GOD'S GIFTS

Don't Mess It Up *Greene* 282
I Am So Happy *Dart/Albertson* 199
Look, Look, Look at the World *Greene* 78
My Little Lips Are Smiling *Myers* 79
Presents *Schwab* 80
Roses Bloom in My Garden *Stagg* 81
Shall We Go for a Walk Today? *Shumate/Truss* . 82
The Bible *Casebeer* 53
The Bible Is God's Word to Me *Thorson* 52
The Butterflies *Robison* 173
The Butterfly Song *Howard* 244
Things Jesus Liked When He Was a Child *Scholes* 139

indicates Beginner-friendly

With Jesus in the Family *Lind* 273
With the Fingers Jesus Gave Me *Sage* 83
Wonderful Jesus *Myers* 84
Yes, Jesus Cares for Me *Thorson* 118

GOD'S LOVE AND CARE

All for Jesus *Oglevee/Skau* 239
All Our Needs *Berge/Traditional* 85
Don't Cry, Little Baby *Sage* 246
For Me *Cason* 154
God Cares for Me *Shumate/Truss* 86
God Cares for Me *Doan* 87
God Is So Good *African Christian Folk Song* . . . 88
God Makes Roses Grow in My Garden *Myers* . 166
God Sees Me *Edwards-Lesser* 86
God So Loved the World *Greene* 181
God Takes Care of Me *Edwards-Lesser* 90
He Cares About You *Sage* 92
He's Able *Paino* 93
I Have the Joy 216
I Know That Jesus Loves Me *Johnsson/Traditional* . . 95
I Love Jesus! *Sage* 205
I Love Mother *Johnsson/Traditional* 250
I Love the Dear Jesus *Martin/Boggs* 206
I Open My Bible Book and Read *Wood* 27
I Open My Bible Carefully *Sage* 28
I Will Sing *Ps. 89:1/Evans* 217
I Will Use My Hands for Him *Thorson* 303
I Wonder Why *Cason* 286
I'm So Small *Scott* 96
I'm Special *Neely* 97
It's About Grace *Herrington* 98
Jesus Cares for Me *Schwab* 100
Jesus Cares for You *1 Peter 5:7,*
ICB/Beginners Writers Group 91
Jesus, Friend of Little Children *Mathams/Mauder* . . 110
Jesus Is Happy *Hoehn* 268
Jesus Is Love *Davis* 99
Jesus Is My Helper *Daleburn* 230
Jesus Is Near *Bishop/Traditional* 126
Jesus Loves Even Me *Beall, Nipp* 101
Jesus Loves Me *GC SS Department/Traditional* . . . 103
Jesus Loves Me *Warner/Bradbury* 102
Jesus Loves Me More *Sage* 104
Jesus Loves Me Much, Much More *Thorson* . . 105
Jesus Loves the Children *Root* 106
Jesus Loves the Little Ones *Cox* 107
Jesus Never Fails *Luther* 108
Jesus Sees Me *Robison* 109
Jesus Smiles and Forgives *Femopase* 77
Little Birdies in the Tree *Thorson* 111
My God Is So Great 112
Noah Built a Great Big Boat *Schwab* 58
Oh, Friend, Do You Love Jesus? 210
Oh, How I Love Jesus *Whitfield/Traditional* 209
Our Thanksgiving Song *Johnson* 241

LVPH-35

indicates Beginner-friendly

Praise Him, Praise Him *GC SS Dept.* 221
Rejoice, I Have Found My Sheep *Sage* 176
Response *Schwab* 23
Run to Jesus *Max* 57
Someone Cares *Barger* 170
Thank You, Jesus *Hallett* 243
The Animals Came a-Walking *Cason* 59
The Bible Is God's Word to Me *Thorson* 52
The Big Blue Ocean *Sage* 113
The Blackbird Song *Sage* 54
The Butterfly Song *Howard* 244
The Good Shepherd *Greene/Brahms* 123
The Hungry Cow *Sage* 174
The Loaves and the Fishes *Sage* 55
The Raindrops Fall *Adair* 194
The Shepherd Loves His Lambs *Thorson* 114
The Trees Are Gently Swaying *Adair* 115
The Wise Man and the Foolish Man 62
Then Jesus Came *GC SS Department/Logan* . . 116
What Can Baby Do? 223
Whisper a Prayer 233
Who Am I? *Sage* 117
Yes, Jesus Cares for Me *Thorson* 118
Zacchaeus 63

GOD'S PROTECTION

All Night, All Day 119
An Angel Came Down *Sage* 120
Angels *Nielson* 121
At Sleep or at Play, God Sees *Adair* 122
God Cares for Me *Shumate/Truss* 86
God Sent His Angels *Schwab* 47
God's Angels Care for Me *Pendleton* 124
Guardian Angel Song *Myers* 49
He's Got the Whole World in His Hands. 125
Jesus Is Near *Bishop/Traditional* 126
Jesus Loves Me *GC SS Dept./Traditional* 103
Jesus Sends the Angels *Jorgensen* 48
My Little Lips Are Smiling *Myers* 79
Someone Cares *Barger* 170
Thank God for Angels Bright *Jarnes* 50
The Good Shepherd *Greene/Brahms* 123
Who's in the Ark? *Sage* 61

GRACE

A Friend of Jesus *Tetz* 254
A Little Talk With Jesus 227
All for Jesus *Oglevee/Skau* 239
Arky, Arky 212
Bye, Baby, Bye *Adair* 247
Campfire *Sage* 249
Don't Cry, Little Baby *Sage* 246
Don't Mess It Up *Greene* 282
God, You Are So Great and Good
Johnsson/Traditional 204
Happy Sabbath *Kennedy* 235

indicates Beginner-friendly

I Am Happy as Can Be! Sage 214
I Am So Happy Dart/Albertson 199
I Have a (Doggy/Kitty) Coston 283
I Have Hands That Clap Vance 215
I Have the Joy 216
I Love Jesus! Sage 205
I Love Mother Johnsson/Traditional 250
I Love the Dear Jesus Martin/Boggs 206
I Open My Bible and Read Thomas 26
I Open My Bible Book and Read Wood 27
I Open My Bible Carefully Sage 28
I Will Sing Ps. 89:1/Evans 217
It's About Grace Herrington 98
Jesus Is Happy Hoehn 268
Jesus Loves Even Me Beall, Nipp 101
My Best Friend Is Jesus Stagg 218
Noah Took a Hammer Vandeman 269
Oh, Friend, Do You Love Jesus? 210
Oh, How I Love Jesus Whitfield/Traditional 209
Oh, Where Stohs/Traditional 311
Our Thanksgiving Song Johnson 241
Praise Him, Praise Him GC SS Dept. 221
Response Schwab 23
Sabbath Bells Adair 237
Share the Good News Stohs/Logan 312
Talk to God Feldbush 16
Tap, Tap, Tap Sage 281
Teach Us to Share Cassett 242
Thank You Song Greene 245
Thank You, Jesus Hallett 243
The Butterfly Song Howard 244
Whisper a Prayer 233
With Jesus in the Family Lind 273
Wonderful, Wonderful Jones 226
You've Got to Tell Greene 315

HAPPINESS

Give Him Your Heart Cason 191
God's Ways LeBar/Thompson 259
Happy All the Time Simpson 198
I Am Happy as Can Be! Sage 214
I Am So Happy Dart/Albertson 199
I'll Be Happy Myers 201
If You're Happy Smith/Traditional 200
Jesus Wants Me for a Sunbeam Talbot/Excell 202
My Little Lips Are Smiling Myers 79

HEALTHY LIVING

Scrubbing Coston 203

HEAVEN

A Real Little Bear to Play With Blackmore 127
Alway Cason 128
Animals in Heaven 130
Heaven Is a Happy Place Dubois 131
I Will Wear a Crown Hardy 132
I'll Meet You in Heaven Scholes 133

BB indicates Beginner-friendly

Jesus Is Building Mansions *Payne* . . . 134
Jesus Is Coming *Dart/Albertson* . . . 182
Jesus Is Coming *Edwards-Lesser* . . . 183
Jesus Is Coming *Stewart* . . . 184
On the Streets of Gold *Wilson, Payne* . . . 129
Sabbath in Heaven *Burdick* . . . 135

HELPFULNESS

God's Children Are Helpful *Robison* . . . 287
God's House *Daleburn* . . . 185
Helping Song *Myers* . . . 288
I Can Help *Payne/Payne, Thompson* . . . 289
I Give Myself to Jesus *Stewart* . . . 192
I Like to Help My Mother *Schwab* . . . 291
I Obey *Self/Traditional* . . . 267
I Will Be a Helper *Ingham* . . . 290
I'll Pick Up My Toys *Burdick* . . . 292
I'm a Little Helper *Sage* . . . 293
Jesus Gave Me a Mommy *Stewart* . . . 251
Jesus Was a Helper *Curley* . . . 295
Let's Put All Our Toys Away *Sage* . . . 294
My Family *GC SS Dept./Casebeer* . . . 252
Our Family *Hoehn* . . . 258
Scrubbing *Coston* . . . 203
The Helping Song *Feldbush/Logan* . . . 297
Things That I Can Do *Billingsley* . . . 299
We Are Little Helpers *Flower* . . . 296
Who Is Jesus' Helper? *Robison* . . . 298
Who's a Helper? . . . 300

HELPING

Giving *LeBar/Blomquist* . . . 285

IMAGE OF GOD

God Made Me *Max* . . . 70

JESUS

A Friend of Jesus *Tetz* . . . 254
A Little Talk With Jesus. . . . 227
All Children Need the Saviour *Anderson/Thompson* 178
Angels *Nielson* . . . 121
God So Loved the World *Greene* . . . 181
Jesus Loves the Little Ones *Cox* . . . 107
Jesus Was a Helper *Curley* . . . 295
Jesus Was a Little Child *McDonald* . . . 136
Just a Little Donkey *Stagl-Schippmann* . . . 137
My Best Friend Is Jesus *Stagg* . . . 218
On the Streets of Gold *Wilson, Payne* . . . 129
Teach Us to Share *Cassett* . . . 242
Thank You, Jesus *Hallett* . . . 243
The Good Shepherd *Greene/Brahms* . . . 123
The Sharing Song *GC SS Department/Traditional* . . 138
Things Jesus Liked When He Was a Child *Scholes* . 139
Wonderful Jesus *Myers* . . . 84
Wonderful, Wonderful *Jones* . . . 226

indicates Beginner-friendly

JESUS' BIRTH

Angels Singing *Cason* 140
Away in a Manger *Luther* 141
Baby Jesus *Sage* 142
Christmas Star *Sage* 143
Christmastime *Sage* 144
God's Best Gift *Curley, Lawler/Bortniansky* 145
Here We Come to Bethlehem *Bush* 146
I'll Share My Home *Sage* 147
It Was a Happy Day *Sage* 148
Little Baby in the Manger, I Love You *Adams* 149
Mary Loved Baby Jesus *Schwab* 150
Mary's Little Baby *Davies* 151
Riding on a Camel *Sage* 152
Ring the Bells *Greene* 153

JESUS' DEATH AND RESURRECTION

For Me *Cason* 154
God Is So Good *African Christian Folk Song* . . . 88
Jesus Died Upon the Cross *Stohs/Logan* 155
Jesus Is Risen *Greene* 156
Thank You, Jesus *Hallett* 243

KINDNESS

Be Kind to One Another *Based on*
Eph. 4:32, RSV/Sage 260
Care for One Another *Riley* 262
Don't Cry, Little Baby *Sage* 246
God's Ways *LeBar/Thompson* 259
I'll Meet You in Heaven *Scholes* 133
Jesus Helps Me Choose *Hoehn* 304
Jesus Is Coming *Stewart* 184
Jesus Is Happy *Hoehn* 268
Jesus Wants Me for a Sunbeam *Talbot/Excell* 202
Jesus Was a Helper *Curley* 295
Jesus Was a Little Child *McDonald* 136
Kind Lips *Schwab* 310
Let Us Do Good *Baar, Thompson* 263
Something Nice *Coston* 261

LIVING FOR JESUS

All for Jesus *Oglevee/Skau* 239
Blessings *Greene* 302
Give Him Your Heart *Cason* 191
Giving Jesus Me *Cason* 301
I Give Myself to Jesus *Stewart* 192
I Have Decided to Follow Jesus *Traditional* 193
I Want to Be Like Jesus *Gilleroth* 194
I Will Use My Hands for Him *Thorson* 303
I'll Be Happy *Myers* 201
Jesus, Friend of Little Children *Mathams/Maunder* . 110
Jesus Helps Me Choose *Hoehn* 304
Jesus Wants Me for a Sunbeam *Talbot/Excell* 202
Little Eyes for Jesus *Underhill* 305
Little Feet, Be Careful *Bateman/Rosecrans* 307
My Little Lips Are Smiling *Myers* 79

indicates Beginner-friendly

Praise Him, Praise Him *GC SS Dept.* 221
Prayer to Grow Strong *Anderson, Riley, Thompson* . 196
Sabbath School Is Over [B♫] 46
Sharing Song *Creasman* 279
Teach Us to Share *Cassett* 242
This Little Light of Mine 313
Two Little Eyes *Ford* 306
We Are His Hands *Wood* 314
We Are Little Children *Edwards-Lesser* 197
Who Is Jesus' Helper? *Robison* 298
With Jesus in the Family [B♫] *Lind* 273
Yes, Yes, Mommy [B♫] *Sage* 272

LOVE AND CARE FOR OTHERS

Don't Cry, Little Baby [B♫] *Sage* 246

LOVE FOR GOD

I'm So Small *Scott* 96

LOVE FOR JESUS

Alway *Cason* 127
Baby Jesus [B♫] *Sage* 142
God Is So Good [B♫] *African Christian Folk Song* . . . 88
I Love Mother *Johnsson/Traditional* 250
Little Baby in the Manger, I Love You *Adams* 149
Mary's Little Baby *Davies* 151
My Best Friend Is Jesus *Stagg* 218
Our Thanksgiving Song *Johnson* 241
Praise Him, Praise Him *GC SS Dept.* 221
The Sharing Song *GC SS Dept./Traditional* 138
With Jesus in the Family [B♫] *Lind* 273

LOVING GOD

God, You Are So Great and Good
Johnsson/Traditional 204
I Love Jesus! [B♫] *Sage* 205
I Love the Dear Jesus *Martin/Boggs* 206
I Love the Lord *Luke 4:8; Ps. 18:1/Haydn* 207
I Love Thee, O Lord [B♫] *Ps. 18:1, RSV/Sage* 208
Oh, Friend, Do You Love Jesus? 210
Oh, How I Love Jesus *Whitfield/Traditional* 209

LOVING OTHERS

Care for One Another *Riley* 262
I Love Mother *Johnsson/Traditional* 250
Jesus Helps Me Choose *Hoehn* 304
Let Us Do Good *Baar, Thompson/Thompson* 263
Let Us Do Good to All Men [B♫] *Based on*
Gal. 6:20, RSV/Sage 265
Love One Another *John 15:12/Sage* 264
Our Church Is a Family [B♫] *Greene/Schubert* 257

MEMORY VERSE

I Open My Bible and Read *Thomas* 26
I Open My Bible Book and Read [B♫] *Wood* 27
I Open My Bible Carefully [B♫] *Sage* 28
I'm Glad I Came to Sabbath School [B♫] *Casebeer* . . . 5

[B♫] indicates Beginner-friendly

MISSIONS

A Boat Goes Sailing *Haas* 35
All Children Need the Saviour *Anderson/Thompson* 178
Five Little Missionaries *Jenks* 308
Jesus Loves the Little Children 309

NATURE

And God Said *Wood* 66
Animals, Animals *Sage* 67
Bubbles *Sage* 157
Campfire *Sage* 249
Clip-clop *Sage* 158
Colors *Sage* 159
Creation *Knox/Campbell* 68
Don't Mess It Up *Greene* 282
Everything He Makes Is Good *Max* 69
Fishy, Fishy *Sage* 161
God Cares for Me *Doan* 87
God Made Everything *Black* 162
God Made It So *Fillmore* 163
God Made Me *Striplin* 164
God Made Our World *Lawrence* 71
God Made The Kangaroo *Max* 72
God Made the Sun and Moon and Stars *Edwards-Lesser* 165
God Made Us All *Martin/Boggs* 73
God Makes Roses Grow in My Garden *Myers* . 166
He's Got the Whole World in His Hands. 125
I Am So Happy *Dart/Albertson* 199
I Have a (Doggy/Kitty) *Coston* 283
I Like to Eat an Apple *Stewart* 167
Jesus Cares for Me *Schwab* 100
Jesus Made the Sunshine *Sage* 168
Little Bird Song *Wiggin* 169
Little Birdies in the Tree *Thorson* 111
Look, Look, Look at the World *Greene* 78
My God Is So Great 112
Noah Built a Great Big Boat *Schwab* 58
Presents *Schwab* 80
Roses Bloom in My Garden *Stagg* 81
Seashells *Sage* 160
See the Boat *Sage* 172
Shall We Go for a Walk Today? *Shumate/Truss* . 82
Someone Cares *Barger* 170
Thank You Song *Greene* 245
The Animals Came a-Walking *Cason* 59
The Big Blue Ocean *Sage* 113
The Blackbird Song *Sage* 54
The Butterflies *Robison* 173
The Butterfly Song *Howard* 244
The Hungry Cow *Sage* 174
The Raindrops Fall *Adair* 94
The Trees Are Gently Swaying *Adair* 115
Things Jesus Liked When He Was a Child *Scholes* . 139
Twinkle, Twinkle, Little Star *Traditional* 175
Who Made the Rainbow? *McKinney* 60

indicates Beginner-friendly

With the Fingers Jesus Gave Me [B♫] *Sage* 83
Wonder Song (Who Can?) [B♫] *Owens/Parker* 74
Wonderful Jesus *Myers* 84
Woolly, Woolly Lamb [B♫] *Sage* 171

OBEDIENCE

Coming, Mother [B♫] *Scholes* 266
God's Angels Care for Me *Pendleton* 124
I Obey *Self/Traditional* 267
Jesus Helps Me Choose *Hoehn* 304
Jesus Is Happy *Hoehn* 268
Jesus Sees Me [B♫] *Robison* 109
Little Feet, Be Careful *Bateman/Rosecrans* 307
My Little Lips Are Smiling *Myers* 79
Noah Took a Hammer *Vandeman* 269
Obedient *Gustafson* 270
Sad or Glad *Cason* 271
Tap, Tap, Tap [B♫] *Sage* 281
When a Mother Calls [B♫] *Myers* 274
Who Is Jesus' Helper? *Robison* 298
With Jesus in the Family [B♫] *Lind* 273
Yes, Yes, Mommy [B♫] *Sage* 272

OFFERING

A Boat Goes Sailing [B♫] *Haas* 35
Count the Birthday Money [B♫] *Wood* 37
God Loves a Cheerful Giver [B♫] *2 Cor. 9:7, RSV/Sage* . 29
Hear the Money Dropping [B♫] *DeWitt/Kirkpatrick* . . 31
Here Is My Money [B♫] *Sage* 32
I'm Glad I Came to Sabbath School [B♫] *Casebeer* . . . 5
Offering Prayer Song *Bell* 33
Offering Response [B♫] *Stagl-Schippmann* 30
To God's House *Max* 34

PRAISE

Arky, Arky 212
Because I'm Happy *Cason* 179
Come Praise the Lord *Elkins* 211
Giving *LeBar/Blomquist* 285
God Sees Me [B♫] *Edwards-Lesser* 89
God So Loved the World [B♫] *Greene* 181
God, You Are So Great and Good
Johnsson/Traditional 204
God's Best Gift *Curley, Lawler/Bortniansky* 145
Hallelu, Hallelu 213
Happy All the Time *Simpson* 198
I Am Happy as Can Be! [B♫] *Sage* 214
I Have Hands That Clap [B♫] *Vance* 215
I Have the Joy 216
I Will Sing [B♫] *Based on Ps. 89:1, ICB/Evans* 217
If You're Happy *Smith/Traditional* 200
It's About Grace *Herrington* 98
Let's Give the Lord Our Praise *Stohs/Logan* 219
Making Music *Melendez* 220
My Best Friend Is Jesus *Stagg* 218
My God Is So Great 112

[B♫] indicates Beginner-friendly

Praise Him, Praise Him *GC SS Department* 221
Praise to Jesus *Sage* 222
Praise Your God *Max* 224
Rejoice, I Have Found My Sheep *Sage* 176
Rejoice in the Lord Always *Based on Phil. 4:4* 225
Ring the Bells *Greene* 153
What Can Baby Do? 223
Wonderful Jesus *Myers* 84
Wonderful, Wonderful *Jones* 226

PRAYER

A Child Like Me *Oliver* 177
A Little Talk With Jesus 227
At Sleep or at Play, God Sees *Adair* 122
Dear Jesus *Max* 9
Get Ready to Pray *Stagl-Schippmann* 8
God Sees Me *Edwards-Lesser* 86
Good-bye Prayer *Maguire* 44
I Have Hands That Clap *Vance* 215
I Talk to Jesus *McDonald* 228
I Talk to Jesus *Robison* 10
I Will Pray *Robison* 229
I Will Pray Unto the Lord 12
Into My Heart *Clarke* 195
Jesus Is My Helper *Daleburn* 230
Jesus, Listen Now to Me *Cason* 13
Let's Give the Lord Our Praise *Stohs/Logan* 219
Let's Have a Talk With Jesus *Maguire* 11
Now We'll Talk to God *Cachiaras* 14
O God, Listen to My Prayer *Sage* 15
Offering Prayer Song *Bell* 33
Offering Response *Stagl-Schippmann* 30
Pray *Stagl-Schippmann* 231
Prayer Song *Myers* 19
Prayer to Grow Strong *Anderson, Riley, Thompson* . 196
Praying Every Day *Montgomery* 232
Talk to God *Feldbush* 16
Thank You, Jesus *Hallett* 243
Tiny Tot Response *Stewart* 21
When It's Time to Pray *Sage* 17
Whisper a Prayer 233
Wonderful Jesus *Myers* 84

PRAYER AND PRAISE

Five Little Missionaries *Jenks* 308
I Go to Church *Stagl-Schippmann* 187
Into My Heart *Clarke* 195
Jesus Talks to Me *Davis* 51
Jesus' House *Sage* 188
Prayer to Grow Strong *Anderson, Riley, Thompson* . 196
Praying Every Day *Montgomery* 232
Sabbath Bells *Adair* 237
The Bible *Casebeer* 53
The Bible Is God's Word to Me *Thorson* 52
Walking to Church *Scholes* 190
What Can Baby Do? 223

LVPH-36

indicates Beginner-friendly

Whisper a Prayer 233

PRAYER RESPONSE

O God, Listen to My Prayer *Sage* 15
Prayer Song *Bell* 18
Prayer Song *Myers* 19
Response *Schwab* 23
Thank You, Dear Jesus *Sage* 22
Thank You for Hearing Our Prayer *Sage* 20
Tiny Tot Response *Steward* 21

PROMOTION

Promotion Song *Stewart* 43

RABBITS

God Made Me *Striplin* 164

SABBATH

And God Said *Wood* 66
Blessed Rest *Max* 234
God Made the Kangaroo *Max* 72
Good Morning to You *Adair* 3
Greeting Song *McKinley* 4
Happy Sabbath *Kennedy* 235
Here Is the Way We Walk to Church *Oglevee* . 186
I Go to Church *Stagl-Schippmann* 187
I'm Glad I Came to Sabbath School *Casebeer* . . . 5
Jesus Sees Me *Robison* 109
Listen to the Bells Ring *Jorgensen* 236
Our Thanksgiving Song *Johnson* 241
Sabbath Bells *Adair* 237
Sabbath in Heaven *Burdick* 135
Sabbath School Is Over 46
This Is the Day *Based on Ps. 118:24/Garrett* 238
Tick-tock Song *Parker* 2
Walking to Church *Scholes* 190

SABBATH SCHOOL

Happy Sabbath *Kennedy* 235
Tick-tock Song *Parker* 2

SALVATION

All Children Need the Saviour *Anderson/Thompson* . . 178
Because I'm Happy *Cason* 179
For Me *Cason* 154
God So Loved the World *Greene* 181
Jesus Died Upon the Cross *Stohs/Logan* 155
Who Is Jesus? *Stohs/Traditional* 180

SCRIPTURE SONGS

1 SAMUEL 7:5
I Will Pray Unto the Lord 12

PSALM 18:1
I Love Thee, O Lord *Sage* 208

PSALM 61:1
O God, Listen to My Prayer *Sage* 15

indicates Beginner-friendly

PSALM 89:1
I Will Sing *Evans* 217

PSALM 118:24
This Is the Day *Garrett* 238

PSALM 136:1
O Give Thanks Unto the Lord *Sage* 240

LUKE 15:6
Rejoice, I Have Found My Sheep *Sage* 176

JOHN 15:12
Love One Another *Sage* 264

2 CORINTHIANS 9:7
God Loves a Cheerful Giver *Sage* 29

GALATIANS 6:10
Let Us Do Good to All Men *Sage* 265

EPHESIANS 4:32
Be Kind to One Another *Sage* 259

1 PETER 5:7
He Cares About You *Sage* 92

SECOND COMING

Angels Singing *Cason* 140
God Is So Good *African Christian Folk Song* . . . 88
Good-bye to You *Vance* 45
I Love the Dear Jesus *Martin/Boggs* 206
Jesus Is Building Mansions *Payne* 134
Jesus Is Coming *Dart/Albertson* 182
Jesus Is Coming *Stewart* 184
Jesus Is Coming *Edwards-Lesser* 183
On the Streets of Gold *Wilson, Payne* 129
Whisper a Prayer 233

SERVICE

A Boat Goes Sailing *Haas* 35
All Children Need the Saviour *Anderson/Thompson* . . 178
Care for One Another *Riley* 262
Coming, Mother *Scholes* 266
Don't Cry, Little Baby *Sage* 246
God Loves a Cheerful Giver *2 Cor. 9:7/Sage* . . . 29
God's House *Daleburn* 185
God's Ways *LeBar/Thompson* 259
Happy Sabbath *Kennedy* 235
Hear the Money Dropping *DeWitt/Kirkpatrick* . . 31
Here Is My Money *Sage* 32
I Give Myself to Jesus *Stewart* 192
I Obey *Self/Traditional* 267
I Want to Be Like Jesus *Gilleroth* 194
I'll Share My Only One *Blackmore* 275
I'll Take Turns *Stewart* 276
I'm Glad I Came to Sabbath School *Casebeer* . . . 5
Jesus Gave Me a Mommy *Stewart* 251
Jesus Is Coming *Stewart* 184
Jesus Is Risen *Greene* 156
Jesus Loves the Little Children 309
Jesus Wants Me for a Sunbeam *Talbot/Excell* 202
Jesus Was a Little Child *McDonald* 136

indicates Beginner-friendly

Just a Little Donkey *Stagl-Schippmann* 137
Let Us Do Good *Baar, Thompson/Thompson* 263
Let Us Do Good to All Men *Gal. 6:10/Sage* ... 265
Little Eyes for Jesus *Underhill* 305
Little Feet, Be Careful *Bateman/Rosecrans* 307
My Best Friend Is Jesus *Stagg* 218
My Family *GC SS Dept./Casebeer* 252
Obedient *Gustafson* 270
Offering Prayer Song *Bell* 33
Offering Response *Stagl-Schippmann* 30
Our Church Is a Family *Greene/Schubert* 257
Our Family *Hoehn* 258
Praise Him, Praise Him *GC SS Dept.* 221
Scrubbing *Coston* 203
Share With You *Coston* 277
Sharing *Sage* 278
Sharing Song *Creasman* 279
Something Nice *Coston* 261
The Hungry Cow *Sage* 174
The Sharing Song *GC SS Dept./Traditional* 138
To God's House *Max* 34
We Are Little Children *Edwards-Lesser* 197
We Are Sharing *Thorson* 280
When a Mother Calls *Myers* 274
Who Is Jesus? *Stohs/Traditional* 180
With Jesus in the Family *Lind* 273
Yes, Yes, Mommy *Sage* 272

SHARING

Buddies *Payne, Thompson* 256
Care for One Another *Riley* 262
I'll Share My Home *Sage* 147
I'll Share My Only One *Blackmore* 275
I'll Take Turns *Stewart* 276
Jesus Was a Little Child *McDonald* 136
Share With You *Coston* 277
Sharing *Sage* 278
Sharing Song *Creasman* 279
Teach Us to Share *Cassett* 242
The Sharing Song *GC SS Dept./Traditional* 138
We Are Sharing *Thorson* 280

SUN, MOON, AND STARS

God Made Us All *Martin/Boggs* 73

THANKFULNESS

All for Jesus *Oglevee/Skau* 239
For Me *Cason* 154
God's Best Gift *Curley, Lawler/Bortniansky* 145
I Am So Happy *Dart/Albertson* 199
I Will Pray *Robison* 229
It's About Grace *Herrington* 98
Let's Give the Lord Our Praise *Stohs/Logan* 219
My Best Friend Is Jesus *Stagg* 218
O Give Thanks Unto the Lord *Based on Ps. 136:1/Sage* . 240
Our Thanksgiving Song *Johnson* 241

indicates Beginner-friendly

Praise Him, Praise Him *GC SS Dept.* 221
Response [B♫] *Schwab* 23
Teach Us to Share *Cassett* 242
Thank God for Angels Bright [B♫] *Jarnes* 50
Thank You, Dear Jesus [B♫] *Sage* 22
Thank You, Jesus *Hallett/Hallett* 243
Thank You Song *Greene* 245
The Butterfly Song *Howard* 244

THANKS

Thank You for Hearing Our Prayer [B♫] *Sage* 20

TRANSITIONS

Our Parade *Traditional* 41
Quietly Tiptoe *Stagl-Schippmann* 42

VISITOR

We Have a Visitor [B♫] *Sage* 24
We Welcome You *Adair* 7
We're Glad You Came to Our
Sabbath School [B♫] *Schwab* 25

WELCOME

Good Morning [B♫] *Sage* 1
Good Morning to You [B♫] *Adair* 3
Greeting Song [B♫] *McKinley* 4
I'm Glad I Came to Sabbath School [B♫] *Casebeer* . . . 5
Sabbath Bells [B♫] *Adair* 237
Shake a Little Hand *Johnsson/Traditional* 6
Tick-tock Song *Parker* 2
We Welcome You *Adair* 7
We're Glad You Came to Our Sabbath School [B♫] . . 25

WITNESSING

All Children Need the Saviour *Anderson/Thompson* 178
God's Children Are Helpful *Robison* 287
Jesus Is Coming *Stewart* 184
Jesus Is Risen *Greene* 156
Jesus Loves the Little Children 309
Kind Lips *Schwab* 310
Let Us Do Good *Baar, Thompson/Thompson* 263
Little Eyes for Jesus *Underhill* 305
Oh, Where *Stohs/Traditional* 311
Our Family *Hoehn* 258
Share the Good News [B♫] *Stohs/Logan* 312
This Little Light of Mine 313
We Are His Hands *Wood* 314
You've Got to Tell *Greene* 315

WORSHIP

Alway *Cason* 127
At Sleep or at Play, God Sees *Adair* 122
Baby Jesus [B♫] *Sage* 142
Because I'm Happy *Cason* 179
Blessings *Greene* 302
Come Praise the Lord *Elkins* 211
Coming, Mother [B♫] *Scholes* 266
Dear Jesus *Max* 9

[B♫] indicates Beginner-friendly

For Me *Cason* 154
Get Ready to Pray *Stagl-Schippmann* 8
Giving *LeBar/Blomquist* 285
Giving Jesus Me *Cason* 301
God Is So Good *African Christian Folk Song* . . . 88
God Loves a Cheerful Giver *2 Cor. 9:7/Sage* . . . 29
God Sees Me *Edwards-Lesser* 89
God So Loved the World *Greene* 181
God's Best Gift *Curley, Lawler/Bortniansky* 145
Hear the Money Dropping *DeWitt/Kirkpatrick* . . 31
Here Is My Money *Sage* 32
Here We Come to Bethlehem *Bush* 146
I Can Help *Payne, Thompson* 289
I Like to Help My Mother *Schwab* 291
I Love Mother *Johnsson/Traditional* 250
I Open My Bible and Read *Thomas* 26
I Open My Bible Book and Read *Wood* 27
I Open My Bible Carefully *Sage* 28
I Talk to Jesus *Robison* 10
I Will Pray Unto the Lord 12
I Will Use My Hands for Him *Thorson* 303
I'm Glad I Came to Sabbath School *Casebeer* . . . 5
I'm So Small *Scott* 96
Jesus, Friend of Little Children *Mathams/Maunder* . 110
Jesus Helps Me Choose *Hoehn* 304
Jesus Is Risen *Greene* 156
Jesus, Listen Now to Me *Cason* 13
Jesus Sees Me *Robison* 109
Jesus Talks to Me *Davis* 51
Just a Little Donkey *Stagl-Schippmann* 137
Kind Lips *Schwab* 310
Let Us Do Good *Baar, Thompson/Thompson* 263
Let Us Do Good to All Men *Gal. 6:10/Sage* . . . 265
Let's Have a Talk With Jesus *Maguire* 11
Listen to the Bells Ring *Jorgensen* 236
Little Baby in the Manger, I Love You *Adams* 149
Mary's Little Baby *Davies* 151
My God Is So Great 112
My Little Lips Are Smiling *Myers* 79
Now We'll Talk to God *Cachiaras* 14
O God, Listen to My Prayer *Sage* 15
Offering Prayer Song *Bell* 33
Offering Response *Stagl-Schippmann* 30
Oh, Where *Stohs/Traditional* 311
Prayer Song *Bell* 18
Prayer Song *Myers* 19
Response *Schwab* 23
Sabbath in Heaven *Burdick* 135
Share the Good News *Stohs/Logan* 312
Talk to God *Feldbush* 16
Thank You, Dear Jesus *Sage* 22
Thank You for Hearing Our Prayer *Sage* 20
The Bible *Casebeer* 53
The Bible Is God's Word to Me *Thorson* 52
Tiny Tot Response *Stewart* 21
To God's House *Max* 34

indicates Beginner-friendly

Two Little Eyes *Ford* 306
We Are His Hands *Wood* 314
We Are Little Helpers *Flower* 296
When It's Time to Pray *Sage* 17
Who Is Jesus? *Stohs/Traditional* 180
Who Is Jesus' Helper? *Robison* 298
With Jesus in the Family *Lind* 273
Wonderful Jesus *Myers* 84